I0776642

Also in the Orlell Chronicles

THE ORLELL CHRONICLES

Book 2

The Jewel of Power

Alice G. Bjornstedt

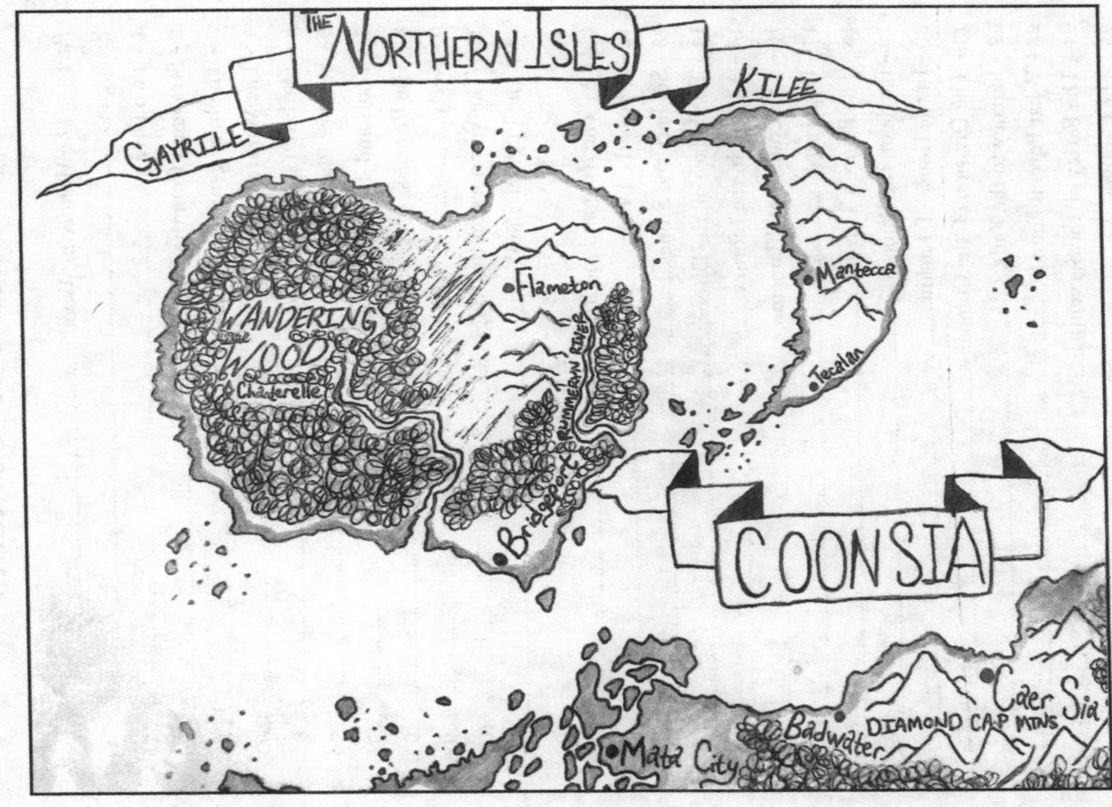
THE NORTHERN ISLES
GAYRILE
KILEE
WANDERING WOOD
Chanterelle
Flameton
RUMMERYN RIVER
Bridgeport
Mantecca
Tecalan
COONSIA
Mata City
Badwater
DIAMOND CAP MTNS
Caer Sia

Table of Contents

To the writers who fear failure, believe your work is never good enough, or doubt your own talent.

Your story is still being written.

This is for you.

PART 1

The Wandering Wood

Prologue

Lord Safacon, emperor of Gayrile, the feared sorcerer, stared out across the rugged wasteland of his kingdom and cursed softly.

His two aides behind him exchanged a worried glance. Their master was an intimidating person under regular circumstances—when he was angry, he was even more so.

In the last decade, disaster after disaster seemed to have rained upon his plans. First, that failed batch of immortal Serventiri—Safacon's artificial warriors, created by him to serve him. While terrifying creatures, they were still mortal. Safacon had unsuccessfully tried to solve that problem a few years ago, which had resulted in destroying the entire group. That was a disaster from the start. While he still had great numbers of powerful soldiers, they were still mortal.

And then there was his deputy Kado's failed conquest of Coonsia on the Mainland, with the Haze army. That had been almost seven years ago—seven long years waiting while hearing the laughter of his adversaries. It was infuriating. Kado had been a fool—an ambitious fool, but still a fool.

But the worst had happened years before, in the height of his power, when his greatest creation had been taken from him. When a band of insurgents, once known by some as the Guardians of Gayrile, had ruined everything, led by the one called Norrin.

Now, Safacon looked out over the courtyard, the craggy tips of the mountains barely visible through the fog that had enveloped the valley for weeks. The dreary weather did nothing to improve his mood.

There was only one thing he wanted now, one thing nagging away in his mind, as it had for years. The one hope of regaining control of this pathetic island—permanently.

He turned to the aides, his silk gray garments swooping around him, caught by the wind, and making him look like a wraith. Coupled with his dark eyes, set in a strikingly pale face, he was a chilling figure. "Bring me the hunters. I have need of them." His voice was low, calm.

The two aides moved to the door and motioned someone in. Two men, one tall and brawny, the other slim and sly, entered. Barret and Sariv, his hired daggers and bounty hunters.

"My hunters," Safacon said softly, studying them. They both bowed slightly. "You came from the eastern coasts, did you not? What news?"

"No word, my lord," the brawny man, Barret, growled. "Not a bloody thing. Squeezed a few town mayors till they squeaked—but they didn't have nothin' of interest."

"This clears the east coast hamlets from suspicion, if it makes any difference," Sariv said in his soft, leering voice, with the faintest accent of a desert dweller from the south.

Safacon smiled. The expression never reached his eyes—they were cold and hard as flint. "Indeed. Well then, forget the eastern coasts. We must look farther. We must look elsewhere."

Barret looked uncertain. "Where to? We're running out of places on Gayrile."

"Then search beyond Gayrile. I am sending you two to Mata City."

The two men exchanged puzzled glances. "Mata City?" Sariv said slowly.

"Those Cooper creatures can't know a thing," Barret protested. "Little better than dogs. Look like 'em too—all furry and walking on all fours. They can't be presumed to be wielding *it*."

Safacon took a breath to calm his rising temper. Of course, it had been years since they had searched Mata City. He had, admittedly, given up the thought of the stolen relic being there himself. But…

"There is a new development. After all, among those four-legged creatures, there is no shortage of wealth. Especially in Mata City."

The hunters looked interested. Safacon continued. "Find them. 'Squeeze them', as you put it. I will know by what way they gained such wealth."

Sariv studied his master carefully, slowly understanding what he meant. "You think… the wealthy Coopers—you think they've used the Jewel to create their riches?"

"Perhaps," Safacon mused. "They would have no knowledge of its true powers, if they had it. We will find out."

The two hunters started for the door, then Barret turned, remembering something. "My lord—what about our other target? The one called Norrin?"

Safacon took a breath, savoring the name like a bitter taste. *Norrin.* Almost as reviled a name as the Guardians of Gayrile were. Both of them out of history, both standing in the way.

Both needed to be erased, stamped out, for good.

"Find him. Bring him here." He turned to them, the faint light hiding the glint of his teeth as he smiled, this time at the thought of sweet revenge. "I'd like to slit his sorry throat myself."

1

Two Dreams

The young Cooper bounded along the canal edge, his paws skidding on the wet rock, running, chasing, laughing.

"I'm coming!" the voice called behind him; his mother's voice, light, teasing, cheerful—she was catching up.

The Cooper ducked behind a boulder, shaking with laughter and cold, his thick brown fur not quite enough to keep out the coastal breeze.

He felt paws grip him from behind, rolling him onto his back, and his mother was there, her blue eyes shining, her russet red fur sparkling with water droplets.

"I've got you, Jarus," she said, laughing as she held him. "I've got you."

Then darkness swallowed them both.

· · · · · ·

It was the fourth time Jarus had had that dream. Normally, in books or stories, if someone had the same dream multiple times, it bore some great importance. He wasn't sure how true that was, though it made little difference. If anything, it only offered a brief sweetness, an echo of an old memory, that became bitter with waking. Along with the harsh realization of the truth.

Jarus sat on the edge of one of the smaller canals near the home he shared with his father. It was a chill morning, but he was warm enough, his brown pelt of fur protecting him from the wind. The Coopers of Mata City, it was said, had been born from the sea itself, growing thick fur, webbed paws, and thick tails to allow them to swim at faster speeds and greater distances than any Two-Leg would be able to.

Jarus stood, stretching and arching his back like a cat, making the fur along his spine stand on end. His fur was dark brown, like his father's. But there was another color mixed in, a fiery auburn. A hue that echoed his mother's roots.

Thoughts of his mother swarmed his head again. Maybe it was the cold breeze, or the ending winter, or just the leftover memory of his dream that had brought her to his mind this morning. Memories of her laughing, cooking in the kitchen, or singing softly as she carved beads from whale bones.

Jarus shook his head sharply, as if to shake the thoughts from his mind. He had other things to do today, he reminded himself, and if he didn't get moving, someone else would take the job. Mata City was built right into the sea, with many canals interlocking the city so that its water-dwelling inhabitants could move about freely. Castle Mata, the dwelling place of Lord Roan, guarded the city from its position at the mouth of the bay. The canals also allowed the many boats and ships to unload their cargo where they needed. Fishing was Mata City's main industry, and the Coopers thrived on it. In fact, Jarus' father was probably out on the water now in his little boat.

The canals, though convenient and the envy of other coastal towns, had to be maintained. With the winter storms, the salt water would have eroded the rock heavily, and the current would have brought in a fair amount of debris. Cleaning the canals was cold, filthy work, but it had to be done, and it paid fairly well. Besides, in times like this, Jarus couldn't be picky about work.

Carus Puddlepaw, Jarus' father, was a tough old sea-dog of a Cooper, but he was getting on in years. He would fight till the end to provide Jarus with the best life he could, and Jarus was grateful for that. But Jarus was eighteen, old enough and strong enough to work. Canal cleaning might not be ideal, but it would at least pay enough to provide for another two weeks.

His family had never been wealthy. They, along with their neighbors, lived along the edge of the wealthy side of town, in a small strip known as the Gutter. This area of neighborhoods was sheltered into a low rock draw that ran down the length of Mata City. On the gentle sloping hills above the Gutter, the houses were large, extravagant even. Far more extravagant than the simple stone hut Jarus had lived in his whole life. He wasn't exactly complaining— his family had always had enough, and they had always been happy. At least, they had when his mother had been here.

His mother.

Five years, eleven months, twenty-two days. Had it only been that long? It felt like a lifetime ago. His mother, Ada, a strong, kind, and very beautiful Cooper had simply disappeared one night. There had been no warning. One minute she was there, singing her young son to sleep, pressed against her husband's fur in their small nest—then in the morning, she was gone.

The neighbors had suggested that she might have run off; they'd even implied it could have been with 'another Cooper,' but Jarus wouldn't—couldn't—believe that. Ada loved her husband Carus, and she loved her son, Jarus, who had been only twelve when it had happened. Somehow, Jarus knew she wouldn't leave for such a reason.

He shook his head. No…no matter how long it had been, no matter the doubt of their neighbors, he somehow felt that she was still alive, out in the wide world of Orlell, and one day she'd come back. She had to—they needed her.

Jarus surfaced, shaking the water out of his ears. A small line of Coopers, most of whom he knew, had formed to pick up their cleaning tools for the day. He slipped into line behind a younger Cooper with a twisted front leg. "Morning, Hal. How's your mam?"

The other Cooper grinned crookedly. "Oh, hiya, Jarus. She's feeling a lot better—thinks it was something she ate. She baked some bread earlier this morning, and told me to bring it over to your house later today."

"Well, thanks," Jarus said with a smile, edging forward in line.

"And she told me to tell you that you'd better tell your pop to take the bread. She says she thinks he's too stubborn for his own good." Hal shrugged with an apologetic grin.

"I think so too," Jarus said wearily, shaking his head. For once, he actually agreed with Hal's busy-body mother. His father, Carus, had made it quite clear to him on several occasions that he would never accept handouts, even the Poor Relief that Lord Roan, ruler of Mata City, had organized. "We'll work our way on our own," Carus had said, his eyes holding a spark of defiance, his pipe clutched between his teeth.

Hal took his tool satchel and sat to sling it over his body. Jarus took his satchel too and sat next to him to open the bag and examine the tools. "This pick is practically dull," he commented, holding the tool up.

"Can't be too bad, it'll still get the barnacles. Last week the one they gave me was so rusty it barely did anything." Hal shook his head and stretched his bad leg experimentally. "Achy today," he admitted. "Probably means there's a storm coming."

"Now you really sound like your mam," Jarus said with a teasing grin. "Which canals are you working today?"

"Near the southeast intersection, and then over in front of Raintail Manor," Hal told him. "They had a party last night, I think—my sister works as a maid over there, and she got home late."

Jarus nodded, following him back into the water. The Raintails were a wealthy family that lived a few houses down from the edge of the Gutter neighborhoods, where the Puddlepaws lived. It was bizarre to think that on one side of town, people could throw huge parties, while on the other side, their neighbors were struggling to provide enough for their tables.

"Did you hear about what's going on up north, in Gayrile?" Hal asked him, excited to share the gossip. "A couple big ships came down the Strait a few days ago, and my mam said she got the news from them. You remember all the excitement from that warlord a few years back… oh, what's his name… the one that tried to sack the Liznees?"

"Kado," Jarus filled in for him. That had been almost seven years ago—he didn't remember much about it. His own mother had heard the news in the market of a brief uprising in Caer Sia, the capital of Coonsia.

"Yep, him. Well, now people think Kado was working for some fancy fellow in Gayrile, some lord or the like." Hal chuckled. "That won't go well for him! If he gets exposed as being behind it all, it'd be quite a scandal."

"Mm," Jarus murmured in agreement. "You said the fishermen from Bridgeport brought that news in?" Bridgeport was Gayrile's main fishing port, and most of Mata City's news of the north came from there.

"Yeah, a few of them. And some Brownaes came too. Ever seen a Brownae? They're furry like us, but they walk on two legs like a human, maybe four feet tall, real wild-looking."

"I haven't," Jarus said, smiling.

"Mam says the Brownae tribes are at war with each other again, though I'm not sure how true that is," Hal mused.

They had reached the canal to be cleaned. It wasn't a main waterway, only twelve feet or so across, reserved for small skiffs or sailboats. Jarus dove beneath the surface to survey the mess. Mostly barnacles, attached to the very bottom. He knew those were harder for Hal to remove with his bad leg.

"You go clean closer to the intersection," he said, surfacing and turning to Hal. "I'll work my way towards you. Remember, watch out for the sharp parts."

Hal nodded gratefully and moved away. Jarus took a breath, then dove into the water to pick away the barnacles. While the barnacles weren't causing harm at the moment, if they built up on each other over time, they could be dangerous for sailors or swimmers. And they were easier to remove now.

As he worked, Jarus' thoughts slipped back to his and Hal's conversation. Unrest had plagued Gayrile for decades, he knew. His father had mentioned a "trouble-making politician" up north, and had been proven right after the drama with Kado's conquest.

But everything had seemed relatively quiet after that. In fact, the only news Mata City got from Gayrile nowadays was whatever the fishermen brought back. Those were strange stories, stories about a sorcerer named Safacon who had taken over Gayrile using spells and powerful magic. Jarus was pretty sure those were just rumors, though. Magic was practically extinct here now.

He chipped a few more barnacles off the stone, then surfaced to wipe the gritty sand out of his eyes.

"You're out early today."

Jarus looked up, wished in an instant that he wasn't as dirty, that his fur was less tousled, and that he could think of a reply. But he was tongue-tied, which tended to happen around *her*.

Sitting on the edge of the canal, tail neatly curled around her paws, was Maya Raintail, the girl who was in the eye of every young Cooper male in Mata City. Her family was also among the wealthiest Coopers in the city. Maya's father was a rich merchant, the owner of several large trading ships that sailed all throughout Orlell. Like Jarus, her mother was gone too—only her mother had died years ago.

Maya was, in a word, beautiful. Her fur was a gorgeous honey-blond, her face round with a pointed nose, high cheekbones, and highlighted by stunning sky blue eyes.

"Morning," Jarus said, because it was the only thing he could think to say.

Maya studied the tools Jarus held, then looked at him. "How are the canals today? Did we get much debris from that storm last week?"

"Yeah…yeah we did. I think I've—already got most of that, though," Jarus said slowly.

"Well, your pick seems kinda dull. If you want, my father could get you another—he always says how much he appreciates the canal cleaners."

"Well, that would be great," Jarus said with a smile. That was the best thing about Maya—not only was she pretty, she was smart and kind too, and she didn't seem to notice the effect she had on people.

Maya smiled and shrugged slightly, as if it was nothing. Her smile faded suddenly as a voice called from behind. "Maya? Where are you?"

They both looked up as a dark-furred Cooper approached. Hagar Groundrop was walking towards them—well, swaggering towards them. Jarus had never seen him walk without looking like a strutting rooster. Hagar had dark fur, groomed so that it glistened slightly, and dark eyes. He was handsome, admittedly, except those dark eyes blended so well with his fur that it gave him a permanently bored look.

He stopped beside Maya, a little too close to her, and let a slow smirk cross his face. "Thought you'd gone for a swim with the canal cleaners. Wouldn't want to have to take another bath, would you?"

"Hello, Hagar," Maya said, edging away slightly. "Where have you been? You weren't at dinner last night."

"Had some other business to do," Hagar sighed. "You know, had a few drinks with some couriers, that kind of thing. Don't worry," he nudged her lightly with another smirk, "none of them are as pretty as you."

Maya sighed. "You told my father you were going to be there to help us prepare—we needed your help."

"Ah, I'm sure you managed. That's what servants are for, right?" Hagar said coolly, winking at a group of Cooper girls that walked by, and making them all giggle. "Anyway, I'm having supper with your father and you tonight. I won't miss it, I promise."

"All right," Maya said quietly. Hagar nudged her again.

"Come on, you don't even have a smile for me? You need to come next Friday—I'm having another dinner party, the last of the season."

"Maybe," Maya replied. "Now, I need to go. I'll see you tonight."

"Excellent," Hagar said, turning away. He seemed to notice Jarus for the first time, and nodded shortly as he left. "Puddlepaw."

"Mister Groundrop," Jarus said with crisp formality. The Groundrops were one of those families that lived up to the stereotype of "rich, handsome, and stuck-up." Old Mr. Groundrop had died a few years back, leaving Hagar with a fortune that rivaled the Raintails'. Hagar himself had been courting Maya for months, which didn't improve Jarus' opinion of him.

"Have a good day," Maya murmured to him as she started down the lane again.

"Are you okay?" Jarus asked her, noticing the change in her mood.

Maya turned, bit her lip, then sighed. "It's Hagar. I overheard him and my father talking a few nights ago—he's offered my father one hundred shekals for...my hand in marriage."

Jarus looked at her in disbelief. He knew Mister Raintail was getting older, a little eccentric, a little featherbrained maybe—but he wouldn't have guessed this. "Oh," he said slowly, not sure how to respond. "Well...what are you going to do?"

Maya looked at him for a moment, and Jarus suddenly realized he'd said something dumb. "I'm not going to do anything, Jarus. In…our class…that's how things work. I just wish he'd chosen someone… someone else, that's all."

The underlying meaning hit Jarus in the chest. It wasn't like he'd ever guessed that he would be the one to end up with Maya Raintail, but he'd certainly daydreamed about it quite a bit. Now, all those daydreams dissolved in a flash. It wasn't a matter of love. It was a matter of wealth, of status, of who you knew—and in that case, Jarus was definitely out of his league. Maya's father—and Maya herself— would never think of him as anything more than a canal cleaner.

"Oh," he said again. "Well…maybe it'll turn out all right. With Hagar." *Yeah, right*, he thought inwardly. *And maybe next summer we'll have snow.* "Congratulations," he added lamely.

"Thanks," Maya said with a slight smile, and then padded away.

Jarus watched her go, trying in vain to dismiss the feelings he still felt. They were like a beast in his chest, stirring with hope and happiness every time Maya looked at him. Now slowly being crushed by the sickening sensation of loss. *She'll be with Hagar.*

He sighed, then dove back under water to finish cleaning the canal. The dull pick scraped uselessly against the barnacles, as though reminding him of the futility of his own hopes.

2

෨ ෨ ෨ ෨ ෨ ෨ ෨ ෨ ෨

Strangers from the North

It was the sound that woke him, the sound of uneasy voices in the middle of the night.

Jarus stirred in the fog of half-sleep, trying to get his bearings. He had arrived home just after his father. They had eaten a simple meal of fish and bread with plum jam, and then lay down in their respective nests and talked late into the night. Carus had news from town… Lord Roan was offering Poor Relief funds again, and Jarus knew his father really was struggling, because he had never been one to even consider financial assistance.

He blinked. There was lantern light coming from the other room—his father's nest was empty, and he could hear the faint sound of voices. It had to be just after midnight.

In the same way that his mind had foolishly concocted ideas about where his mother had gone, Jarus realized that any time something unusual happened, he immediately jumped to the hope that it had something to do with his mother. Maybe she was back. Maybe someone had found her—

He crept out of bed, the chilly air waking him fully with a rude slap. With it came reason, cold, cunning reason that smothered the

26

brief hope. Of course it wasn't his mother. If it was something about his mother, his father would have wakened him too, obviously, and they would all be sitting in the parlor together, drinking tea while his mother explained where she had been for the last five years, eleven months, and twenty-three days.

There were two voices—the familiar low purr of his father, his voice left slightly grating after years of captaining his fishing vessel; the other unfamiliar and rather loud.

He reached the front door, which was open and letting in drafts of cold air and ocean scents. Carus was seated beside the canal, smoking his pipe, his tail flicking the ground around him in agitation. The other speaker, a large gray Cooper Jarus recognized as the sheriff, sounded uncertain.

"I believe you, Carus, honestly I do—it's a bleak night and there's a storm coming in from the west. But aside from that, I don't know…"

"Something's up," Carus said, his voice low and level, gruff after years of shouting orders over the howling winds. "Maybe have your men circle the block again. Check up near Raintail Manor."

The sheriff shrugged slightly, still not convinced. "I'll do that for you, old friend, but I'm not sure there's any danger for those of us not at sea."

It was windy, and the slight tang in the air told Jarus that rain was coming. With this cold, it might hail, too. He looked at his father, not sure what was going on. "Pop…?"

Carus looked at his son, grinding his pipe between his teeth. He looked confused and slightly frustrated, which was unusual. Carus always seemed to know what to do, and seeing his father like this sent an uneasy chill through Jarus' core. "Something's wrong. Not just with the wind, though anyone on the sea at this moment will be in quite a fix. No, something's wrong here, in town. Can't you smell that?"

Jarus scented the billowing wind. He smelled the wet stones and fish and the smoke from his father's pipe, and…

His brow furrowed. There was another scent in the wind, one that he didn't recognize.

"I smell it too, Carus," the sheriff said, seeming torn between placating his old friend and still maintaining authority of the situation. Especially because there seemed to be no situation yet, Jarus reminded himself. Still… something felt amiss. He had sensed it too, back in bed.

There was a long, drawn-out silence. "I'll have my troops patrol the block one more time, just to check," the sheriff told them finally.

"I'm going to the harbor," Carus said, rising. "Whatever it is, they're not getting my ship."

He shuffled away before either of them could stop him.

"I'll keep an eye on him," Jarus told the sheriff, who looked grateful. He slipped briefly inside the house to grab his knife, which hung in its sheath, fastened to a belt of leather. Jarus had made both the sheath and the belt himself, from leather he managed to barter off of an old merchant last year. Leather was rare here—it came from cows and other such animals, and the rocky, coastal climate of Mata City didn't offer much for farming.

"Wait up, Pop," he called after his father, who was already halfway down the canal side. Swimming would be faster, but Carus still had his pipe and seemed happy to walk.

Jarus had almost caught up to him when a breeze brought a new wave of scents to his nose, and he paused. There was that strange smell they had noticed earlier, a foreign scent that he didn't have a name for. More scents were mixed in—human sweat, tar from a ship's deck…

The scents came from across the canal, towards the sweeping hills and rocky outcrops that guarded Raintail Manor, so he started up the incline, weaving his way through the small gravel sidewalks that marked separated properties. He thought of Maya, which briefly distracted in his exploration. Would Maya be asleep, or would she be awake too, laying in restless solitude, thinking of—

"If you take one more step, I'll skewer you, Cooper."

Jarus froze. The voices came from beyond the house, unfamiliar voices. The strange scent was stronger here, acrid, making his eyes water. His heart pounded, and it took him a few moments to realize the man who had spoken wasn't talking to him—there was no way he had seen Jarus, hiding in the rocks. Very cautiously, he peeked around the boulder outcrop.

A group of men stood in the flower beds in front of the Raintail's towering house. Four of them wore some kind of armor, which bore an emblem Jarus had never seen before. A blue star, framed in black. Two others were standing over something on the ground. One of them was pointing towards the canal on the other side of the house, away from Jarus…

"If you kill him, he's of no value to you."

Jarus started at the voice. It was fearful, without the usual sly, sneering tone—but the same nonetheless. Hagar Groundrop.

"We're not *going* to kill him," the man snapped back, sounding exasperated. His voice was loud and grating. "We just need him to come along, unless we drag him by his ears." He cracked the whip a few inches over the form on the ground, which moved slightly.

Jarus felt his stomach drop as he realized the ragged heap on the ground was the battered form of Mr. Raintail. The old Cooper gave a soft groan of pain and got to his feet stiffly. "I'll come… I'll come… just don't hurt the others…"

"We let your ratty servants go, if that's what you mean," Loud Voice snorted. His companion, shorter and slimmer than he was, very snake-like, looked up at the house and smiled.

"Actually, I think he means *her*."

"Stop!"

Maya's shaking, fearful voice broke the chill silence. She stood in the door of the house, her eyes darting from the men to Hagar to her father.

Hagar looked at her sharply, then back at the men. Fear crossed his face now, too. "She knows nothing. Let us go, and we won't tell anyone."

"Let him go," Maya stammered. "Please—let him go."

Two of the soldiers started forward, and Maya shrank back. Hagar took a step forward, standing between Maya and the soldiers. His eyes were still on the two men, who seemed to be in charge. His voice trembled slightly with fear. "This wasn't what you promised. You said I would turn him over and you wouldn't hurt him. You said your master could pay me much."

"So we did," said the other man, his voice sly and cold, sliding over the rocks like a snake. "And you've delivered, Groundrop. Safacon will greatly reward you."

"But you didn't say why," Hagar continued, his eyes darting around the group. "You keep taking people... Coopers... and you won't say why." The way Maya was looking at him, the horror and betrayal and hatred in her eyes—but Hagar didn't look at her.

There was a hiss of steel on leather. The snake-like man had drawn a lean knife, and was fingering it thoughtfully. "Curious little Groundrop, why do you wish to know?"

Hagar gulped, his voice fearful. "Because I have heard of your master. What he wishes, this Cooper cannot give you. None of us can. Perhaps...perhaps if you went to the Capital...to Caer Sia...maybe the Liznees could help you... they know more about this magic you speak of than we do. We're Coopers—we don't know—"

The big man struck him across the face with the whip, and Hagar crumpled with a cry. Maya flinched back, her whole body trembling.

"Gently, Barret," the snake-like man said coolly. "We need him alive too."

"I can pay you," Mister Raintail said weakly. "I can double your pay…I promise…please let us go…"

"Our *pay*?" the whip-man called Barret repeated with a sneer. He turned to his companion. "What say you to that, Sariv?"

The other man knelt down before the old Cooper on the ground, running his fingers over his knife delicately. "Our pay is nothing you can give us, Raintail. We seek the world." He smiled. "And Safacon rewards those who are faithful to him."

He stood up, nodding at the soldiers. "Bind them both. Back to the ship. Hurry or our master will have your heads."

The soldiers tied up Hagar and Mr. Raintail and dragged them down the road. One of them started toward Maya, who had frozen, too afraid to even tremble anymore. The big man seized her and dragged her forward, holding her up by the scruff of her neck. "We taking her, too?"

Jarus watched, wishing he was bigger and not such a wretched coward, that he could find the will to draw his knife and lunge forward. But he stood rooted to the spot, unable to move.

The snake-like man called Sariv moved forward, taking Maya's chin in his hand, peering into her face. He smiled. "No. We'll leave her here. I think she'd like that. And I think she's a smart little creature. She knows not to tell anyone about this, because she knows many dear friends near here with little children, doesn't she?" The way he said this, almost cheerfully, made Jarus feel sick. "And of course she knows by now that we have spies… spies everywhere."

He let go of Maya's chin, and the one called Barret dropped her into the flower beds. Jarus could see her shaking with silent, furious sobs.

"Let's go," Sariv said quietly, nodding in the direction of the harbor. "Any witnesses, take them also or kill them. Boss doesn't like witnesses."

In unison, the group vanished into the darkness. The wind blew for several minutes before their foreign scent had dispersed.

Jarus forced himself to take a breath. He realized he had, unconsciously, been holding it in during the moments when the intruders had spoken to Maya.

Maya…

He stumbled out of the shadows, not trusting himself to speak. He must have made some sound, though, because Maya looked up swiftly. Her fur was covered in dirt, and tears had formed bright lines on her face. Her eyes were hollow, wet, like sad shallow pools.

"What are you doing here?" she asked, too confused and scared to ask anything else.

"I… smelled them… and I heard them, so I came to see…" Jarus stammered, feeling bitter guilt fill him. He could have done something. Charged forward with his knife. Told the strange soldiers to leave. Something.

Maya clearly thought so too, but at least she didn't say it. "Hagar was working with them," she said finally, her voice dull, as if she could not believe it. "Hagar sold Father to them. They would have paid him for it, too, but they changed their minds. He asked too many questions."

"I saw," Jarus said. The thought of Hagar made his chest feel hot with rage. Hagar, that greedy and slime-filled idiot, who had betrayed them. He had regretted it though, Jarus reminded himself guiltily. He had tried to save Maya. Of course he had, he was engaged to her. Or something like that.

Rain was falling. The two of them walked inside without a word, both still in shock. Jarus had never been inside the Raintail's house, which was a real house, not a traditional stone hut. It was lavishly furnished and would have looked better if the furniture and trinkets hadn't been scattered across the room, many of them broken in pieces.

"They… didn't take any of your money?" he guessed, noticing a rather large wallet on the table.

"They didn't take anything," Maya said faintly. "Just smashed through it all and broke a lot of it. They didn't steal anything. They were looking for something."

Jarus frowned. This hadn't been a simple robbery—that much he knew. These men had been looking for something specific… and when they learned the Raintails didn't have it, they had taken the witnesses who would cause trouble and scared Maya into silence. What was it that man had said? *"We have spies everywhere."* That thought was enough to make both of them think twice before reporting this to the town guard. If those men came back…

"Where did they take them?" Jarus asked.

"I don't know. They said something about Safacon—I've heard a little about him. He's a lord from the Northern Isles, from Gayrile. They're looking for some sort of weapon… and someone called Norrin."

Voices outside caught their attention suddenly. It was a town guardsman and the sheriff, returning from the harbor.

"Boss, the ship's gone. And there's no sign of old man Puddlepaw."

Jarus looked up in horror, listening.

"What? Where did he go?" the sheriff demanded.

"Don't know," the town guardsman said. "We saw him go out towards the harbor about ten minutes ago, to check on his boat— now the strange ship's gone and so is he!"

The words slowly sank in. His father… his kind, caring, strong-willed father, had gone to protect that little boat—and they'd seen him. He was gone.

Jarus took a shaking breath. Maya looked at him in dismay. "Jarus…I'm so sorry…I didn't know…"

The men were gone, along with Mr. Raintail, Hagar Groundrop, and Carus Puddlepaw. They had taken them to Safacon, who was somewhere in Gayrile. And whatever he had planned couldn't be good—whatever they were looking for was important enough to Safacon that he'd kidnap Coopers to get it. They were looking for something, and they were desperate enough to hurt people to find it.

Jarus waited a moment, then made a decision.

"I'm going after those men," he announced.

Maya looked up at him, blinking in confusion. "You're…what?"

"Our fathers are captured. Those men are only going to come back and do this same thing to more people until they find whatever they're looking for. And we can't tell anyone, or they'll come back and start killing," Jarus said.

"I gathered that already," Maya said slowly. A little life was coming back to her eyes.

"Well, I'm going after them," Jarus declared. "You can come if you want," he told her.

Maya still didn't look sure. "How are we going after them?"

"Well…we can swim to Gayrile, we're Coopers, right?" Jarus said, knowing that was a terrible idea. Coopers are made for water—but the idea of swimming the entire way to Gayrile was laughable.

"Or… we could take your father's ship," Maya suggested slowly, a faint smile crossing her face.

Jarus looked at her gratefully. "Oh, right—that'll work. Um… what do you think we'll need?"

Maya finally smiled, which made her look more like her usual self. "I'll get some supplies."

Jarus nodded, glad to see the determination back in her eyes. "What will we do when we get to Gayrile?"

Maya shrugged. "Ask around. The locals are probably our best bet.

Maybe we can find someone to help us."

Jarus nodded and slipped back outside. He could feel the fear fading, replaced by excitement. They were going to Gayrile—Maya Raintail had smiled at him—

Then he remembered the look on the men's faces, the cruel satisfaction as they watched Mr. Raintail struggle, and the way the man Sariv had spoken of murder in such a calm, comfortable tone.

In a flash, the fear was back.

3

The Insurgents

It took the better part of the night before they left Mata City behind them. Carus' ship was docked in one of the smaller harbors only a half mile or so from the house. It was a small skiff, with a triangle shaped sail at the very front of the prow, looking like the half-extended wing of some kind of seabird. Made in the traditional design of Cooper sails, Carus had owned this boat for the better part of his life. He loved talking about his boat—explaining when he'd got it, how it had been made, how the triangle sail and light hull allowed her to slip through the water with very little wind.

If only I had stayed with him… Jarus' throat tightened. But the thought was a futile one.

They loaded up the few supplies Maya had wisely remembered to pack (after all, there was no telling how long the journey would really be) and Jarus navigated the boat through the canals that led out to open water. The network of canals would have been dizzying to unfamiliar eyes, but Jarus had lived here his whole life, and had spent most of that time in or around the water. The houses they passed were dark, quiet. Everyone was still asleep. In a little while, Jarus knew, the fishermen would be up, preparing to begin a day's work on the water. The faint light of dawn shone in the east.

By the time they reached the bay, the sky blushed pink with the coming dawn. The crescent moon shape of the cliffs encircled them, like a protective barrier between the city and the thundering sea. Jarus could see the distant towers of Castle Mata, overlooking the sea like a watchman.

Maya sat near the rail, watching the water. She was very quiet, and Jarus knew there was an additional pain for her to bear. He wasn't sure what to say, or if there was anything he could say to help at all. There were no words to heal the pain of Hagar's betrayal. He felt a brief hope surface as he realized that Maya Raintail was no longer engaged. Immediately, he felt guilty for feeling that. That was a selfish thing to think, considering that while Maya had been upset about her arranged marriage, she had still accepted it.

He shook the thoughts away. "We're almost out of the bay," he commented, unnecessarily—anyone could see the line of white foam that marked the edge of the reef and the gateway to the open ocean. "Hang on—this might be a little bumpy."

Maya nodded and edged away from the rail as Jarus adjusted the sail slightly. "Did your father teach you to sail?" she asked.

"Yes, I guess. I… actually haven't ever done this by myself," Jarus admitted. He'd sailed before, yes, a hundred times. But that had always been with his father or some other fishermen. He realized that wasn't a very reassuring thing to say, especially when Maya was counting on him to get them to Gayrile. "I mean—I know how to do it. I've done it before. Just not alone," he stammered quickly.

Maya smiled faintly. "Well, thanks for being honest. You know more than I do." She sounded a little disappointed in herself.

"Didn't your father ever let you sail?" Jarus asked, a little surprised. Mr. Raintail had a number of elegant little sailboats—it seemed he might have let his only daughter have one.

But Maya shook her head with another smile. "No way. It's not very 'proper.'" She mimicked a snooty, simpering voice as she said this, and both of them laughed.

They crested over the reef with a grinding bump that made Maya wince and look at him in alarm. "Did it break the hull?"

"No, we just bumped over the rocks. The grinding was the rocks, not us," Jarus said. He adjusted the sail again. There was a strong easterly breeze that caught them almost immediately. That would carry them towards the Northern Isles.

"I've read about sailing," Maya said. "I like knowing how things are made. The Cooper design of ships is actually a better design than a lot of others. The triangle sail helps move you… into the wind, right? What do you call that?"

"Tacking," Jarus said. "And it doesn't really let you sail straight into the wind. You move in a diagonal pattern instead of a straight line."

"The Coopers came up with that idea first. The only other species that uses that kind of design is the Jenna tribes in the east," Maya said.

Jarus looked at her, surprised. "Really? I didn't know that."

Maya looked a little embarrassed. "I—well, like I said, I like learning how things are built, and who made them. I know it's strange."

"Not really," Jarus said quickly. He was surprised though. Maya didn't strike him as… well, as a bookworm.

The next few hours passed in silence. As they continued sailing north, Jarus could see the landmass of Gayrile slowly becoming more distinct. The spiked ridge of the mountains, on the southeast part of the island, stood out against the gray sky. As they sailed into the harbor, Jarus could see the buildings of the city coming into focus through the haze of fog.

"No more canals," Maya murmured, half to herself.

Bridgeport, capital of Gayrile, was built quite different than the city Jarus had grown up in. The buildings were made of brick or slabs of stone, with flat roofs and slightly crooked chimneys. Smoke hung in a haze over the town, mixing with the mist from the sea. A strong scent filled the air, much stronger than the briny smell of the coast.

"Oil," Jarus guessed, seeing dense black smoke rising in dark columns from the shops nearest to the harbor. "Bridgeport is a whaling town. They hunt whales out in the water and bring in the oil."

"Seems cruel," Maya said, frowning slightly.

"They have to keep warm somehow," Jarus pointed out, shrugging slightly. He knew the winters in this part of the world were some of the harshest. Towards the center of the island, the climate was warm and dry, with the rain and storms blocked by the mountains.

He guided the ship into the harbor. The harbormaster stood there, a burly man with a pipe gripped between his teeth. He squinted up at them as the ship glided to a stop beside the pier.

Jarus nodded to Maya, and they climbed out. The harbormaster stopped them, glancing back at the ship. "Hold up there, you. Three pennies to dock here, and I'll need to know where you're from and why you're here." His voice was rough, the accent coarse as he addressed them in the Coonslan tongue.

Jarus looked up at him blankly. "We… we'll just be here for a little while. There's a lot of available places in the harbor to dock…"

"Isn't about open spots, Mainlander, it's policy." The man sounded annoyed.

Maya slipped back aboard their boat, returned with the packs, and produced the required fee. "Here you are, then. We don't want to cause any trouble."

The man took the coins, then looked at the Coopers. "And your whereabouts?"

"We're from Mata City," Jarus told him. "We're just here on a visit." That was technically true, although tracking down a kidnapper could hardly be considered a pleasant visit.

The harbormaster grunted, writing a few things down in a little book, then nodded to them. "Very well. Off you go, then."

"I didn't know they made us pay to dock," Jarus couldn't resist grumbling as they walked towards town.

"It's different here," Maya said, glancing around. "This isn't like

Mata City. And the people here will probably be a bit rougher, too, so we probably shouldn't start out by complaining about their policies." She said the last part with a smile, and Jarus nodded, knowing she was right.

They approached the town. Crowds moved through the muddy streets. A few filthy children chased a ball. The sights, smells, and noise overwhelmed Jarus for a moment.

"What now?" Maya asked, looking uncertain.

Jarus thought for a moment. Most likely, the men that had taken the Coopers would have come through this way. Maybe someone had seen where they had gone. "We'll ask around, I guess," he said out loud. "Maybe someone knows where they could have seen them."

They followed a group of fishermen across the street, then stopped in front of the market. The buzz of conversation around them was a mixture of the various tribal tongues of the people of Gayrile. But the vendors set up by booths and tables along the road advertised their wares in Coonsian, their voices rising over the crowd with the familiar language. Jarus stopped in front of a jewelry booth. A short woman with tanned skin and turquoise bangles noticed them and moved over. "Hello—can I help you find anything?"

"No thank you, we're just looking around," Jarus said with a smile. "We're looking for someone here—have you been here long?"

The woman grinned and nodded. "I've been here all morning—

seen all sorts of interesting characters come through. Who are you looking for?"

"A group of men—soldiers—and three Coopers with them," Jarus said, wishing he could provide a more accurate description. There weren't many Coopers here, though, so maybe that would be enough.

The woman thought for a moment, then shook her head. "I'm afraid not. The cobbler's been here longer than me, though—maybe ask him." She nodded across the road to another tent.

"Thanks," Maya said as Jarus turned away. She jogged up to him. "Jarus, there's a lot of people here. Are you sure someone would have seen them?"

Jarus hesitated, glancing back at the woman. "I don't know. If they came this way, someone would have noticed, though." He approached the cobbler, an old man who was completely bald and smoking a pipe as he stitched two slips of leather. "Excuse us, sir— we're looking for some… friends of ours."

The cobbler looked up blearily. Jarus continued. "Have you seen a group of soldiers, with three Coopers with them? The Coopers are from Mata City." That was probably an unnecessary detail, but the more information he could provide, the better.

The old man's eyes were distant, half-closed, and Jarus wasn't sure if he had been heard. "Excuse us, sir," he started again, louder.

"We're looking for someone called Safacon," Maya said, with the same volume. "We think he kidnapped our fathers."

It was as though someone had flipped a switch. The noise of the market was silenced, and Jarus felt all eyes on them. He looked up at the old cobbler in confusion—the old man was looking at something behind them, fear filling his eyes.

"Jarus—" Maya whispered; Jarus turned and bumped into the legs of a very tall man in armor.

"Is there a problem here, cobbler?" the soldier barked at the old man, not even looking at the Coopers.

"No sir, no sir," the cobbler wheezed, hunkering back into his tent.

"Good," the soldier said. Four other soldiers stood behind him, smirking, enjoying the cobbler's fear. Jarus looked at them in confusion. His eyes rested on the symbol on the armor—a bright blue star, rimmed in black—

It was the same as the emblem the soldiers who had taken his father had worn.

The soldier looked down at them, pretending to notice them for the first time. "Oy, Cooper. Is there a problem here?"

"No, sir," Jarus replied. The fur along his spine prickled in uneasiness.

"What were you just saying, then?" the soldier pressed, squatting down so that they were eye-to-eye. Jarus didn't like what he saw in the man's eyes. They were cold and cruel, and glittered with the satisfaction of frightening others.

"We were just shopping," Maya said quickly. "We just got here."

"Really?" the soldier asked sarcastically. "Well, welcome to Bridgeport. The lovely smoke-pit of Safacon's great empire." He gripped Maya's neck so fast she didn't even have time to flinch, holding her there with a cold smile. "You told an interesting story, pretty thing," he purred.

"Let her go!" Jarus shouted, bounding forward—another soldier grabbed his tail and hauled him back.

"A very interesting story," the lead soldier continued, still smiling wickedly at Maya—Maya's face was drawn with both fear and anger. "Something about our great Lord Safacon… what was it, kidnapping people? Maybe you ask too many questions. I'm afraid we don't tolerate liars here. No matter how interesting they are."

"Don't call me a liar," Maya said, but her voice trembled.

"Let her go!" Jarus shouted again, squirming in the second soldier's grip.

Boots pounded on the cobblestones behind him—he heard someone shouting up the road. "Captain! Hostiles in the next shop over—they're coming this way!"

The captain looked up sharply, letting go of Maya. "The insurgents?"

"Ten or so of them, Captain," the messenger continued, as Jarus squirmed to see, "they're burning the oil!"

He was cut off—there was a sudden, whooshing noise, and a plume of fire burst through the window of the building behind him. Jarus was dropped to the ground—he looked up in disbelief at the roiling flames. The soldiers were completely caught off guard. The captain bellowed orders at them, swearing profusely at his startled and panicked men. "After them, now—they can't go far—"

Jarus got to his feet, watching as the soldiers disappeared down the road toward the source of the commotion. Maya grabbed his arm, drawing him back into reality. "Are you all right?"

"Yes, I'm fine—are you?"

Maya nodded and looked back at the burning building. Vendors nearest to it were quickly packing up their wares and tents and fleeing the fire. But no tents had been set up directly in front of the building, in the path of the fire. In fact, aside from four or five vendors who had set up near the jewelry seller, that side of the square was vacant.

This had been planned.

A group of raggedly dressed men appeared from the opposite end of the road. Jarus recognized them as the fishermen they had followed earlier. As they passed, he caught the distinctive smell of burnt whale blubber on their clothes.

"Hey—wait," Jarus called after them, intrigued. None of the fishermen stopped—instead they moved straight to the tailor's booth, removed their ash-stained cloaks, and replaced them with new ones. Jarus watched as the tailor hid the dirty cloaks in a trunk.

"Do you think they…" Maya trailed off, leaving the question hanging unanswered in the air. Jarus stared at the group for a few moments, hesitating. These insurgents, as the captain had called them, didn't seem to be a danger to the market folk. But if they had started the fire, why?

Curiosity got the better of him, and he moved forward.

"Come on," he whispered to Maya, and they approached the fire starters. Several of them were already gone, fading into the crowd.

One stood outside the tailor's booth, silently scrubbing at a black streak on his arm.

He had removed his hood, allowing the light to shine on his face. He looked to be not quite twenty, Jarus guessed, with blue eyes like the sea on a summer day. His hair was dark, tousled, and messily cut, as if he had done it himself. The hair around his lips and chin was sparse, like he was still trying to grow it out.

He looked up as the Coopers approached, glancing between the two of them innocently. "Hello—can I help you? I don't work here, you'll have to ask the tailor if he has anything that will fit you."

"We're—we're not looking for clothes," Jarus stammered quickly.

"Who are you?" Maya asked at the same time, her voice lowered. "We saw what just happened. Are you one of the insurgents?"

"Huh—maybe the captain was right. Maybe you *do* ask too many questions," the stranger mused, without looking at them.

"Right, well, last I checked, nearly all of Bridgeport's income comes from the whalers, so why burn the oil? Seems like a simple question," Maya returned.

A very slow smile spread over the stranger's face. "Keep your voice down," he said absently, pulling his coat sleeve down over the ash stain on his arm. He slipped inside the tailor's booth, out of sight of the road. "You just arrived here, I'm guessing? Your accents are Mainlander."

"We're from Mata City," Jarus said, hesitating slightly. "We're looking for this Lord Safacon, or whatever you call him."

"Well, *I'd* call him a tyrant. But don't tell anyone I said that. Except for Lammar maybe, but you can tell him anything." He grinned. "Why are you after Safacon?"

"Let's say he took something we want back. Do you know who and where he is?" Jarus asked.

"Please," Maya added softly.

The stranger stood and stretched. "I know where he is, but you won't be able to get there alone. Definitely not by yourselves. I might know someone who can help you get there, though."

"You do?" Jarus said, feeling a surge of hope.

"I said I might. Follow me." He paused and looked back. "Sorry—never answered your first question, did I? My name is Rygal."

"I'm Maya Raintail, and this is Jarus Puddlepaw," Maya said, nodding to Jarus.

"Why *did* you burn the oil?" Jarus asked curiously, going back to the previous question.

Rygal's eyes scanned the marketplace for a moment before he ventured out on the road, confident there were no soldiers watching. Then he turned to look at them. "Come with me. Some things aren't safe to discuss out in the open."

4

The Wizard

Rygal led them through Bridgeport, slipping through back roads and alleyways on his way out of town. It was clear he knew how to get around without being seen. Although, considering he had just assisted in the destruction of a large profit of oil, Jarus wasn't too surprised.

He was fascinated by the way the day had unfolded. This young man seemed willing to help them find their fathers. Maybe he'd be willing to help get them back, too.

They left the town behind them and headed up a hill, through a scant, shabby forest full of trees weathered by the coastal wind. The road dwindled into a thin gravel path wound steadily up. The trees cleared out. A small cabin sat overlooking the cliff, sheltered by the trees. Smoke rose from the chimney.

Jarus stopped, suddenly unsure. It didn't matter if Rygal wasn't with Safacon, he was still a stranger and thus potentially dangerous. Rygal noticed their hesitation. "It's all right. You'll be safe here," he reassured them, and opened the door.

Inside, the scent of wood smoke and old books greeted them. The warmth was welcoming after the cold and rain, and despite his uncertainty, Jarus hurried inside and shut the door. The two of them stood uncertainly behind Rygal, looking around the small house.

An older man appeared through a door on the other side of the room. His hair and beard were roughly cut, and his clothes were slightly damp and carried the scent of the sea. He shook his head at Rygal, not noticing the Coopers.

"A fire in the marketplace, that is what Mr. Kellis told me just a little while ago, Rygal. Burning the oil will only make our enemies angrier, and it will make life harder for many people here."

"Burning the whaler's oil?" Rygal stammered, trying, too late, to look innocent. Unfortunately, he had already taken off his wet coat. The other man had seen the black ash on his arm, and arched an eyebrow sardonically.

"Forgive me. I suppose the oil just spontaneously ignited, then." He smiled wryly as Rygal sighed and shook his head in defeat, then noticed the Coopers and raised both eyebrows in surprise. "I see you brought company."

"Yes—they're from Mata City. Jarus and Maya, meet Norrin, my mentor," Rygal said.

The old man smiled and greeted the Coopers in turn. Norrin, Jarus judged, looked to be in his mid-sixties, although it was hard to tell with the twinkling smile in his brown eyes as he greeted them. His hair and beard were still peppered with dark brown, although much of the color had faded to gray. His face was lined and tanned from years of work at sea. There was something familiar about his name, but Jarus couldn't place it.

"Good to meet you both," Norrin said. "And what brings you to Bridgeport?"

"Well… it's a long story," Maya said, looking at Jarus. He could see the hesitation in her eyes, hesitation to trust these men. But Jarus knew they had to take the chance. He could tell, somehow, that Norrin and Rygal could answer the many questions in his mind.

"Both of our fathers were taken from Mata City last night," Jarus explained. "And Maya's…fiancé." Thinking of Hagar brought that hot, angry feeling back to his chest, and he quickly left the topic behind. "We think they were taken to Gayrile. The soldiers that took them had the same insignia as the ones here in the market."

"We think they were taken to someone called Safacon," Maya said.

A look crossed Norrin's face that Jarus didn't understand. Uncertainty, sorrow, and a strange resolve. "Safacon," he said finally, almost to himself. "So he's finally turned his sights south again. I suppose he's finally searched for it in all of Gayrile."

"Searched for what?" Maya asked, her brow furrowed. "The men—the men that took my father—they said something about searching for an object, too. And when my father didn't have it, they took him anyway."

"But what does this Safacon want with Coopers?" Jarus asked, studying Norrin's face. Now the old man looked at him, his expression thoughtful. His eyes held the same emotion Jarus had seen earlier, the uncertainty, the resolve. There was something in that look that somehow chilled him. Out of everyone else here, he knew Norrin knew exactly what Safacon had in mind. This man had seen things that none of them could even imagine.

"They were taken by Safacon?" Norrin asked finally, for confirmation.

"Well…that's what we figured," Jarus stammered. "They didn't steal anything at all. They were looking for something, something they thought Maya's father had. Then they took him, so they wouldn't have any witnesses."

Rygal looked at Norrin. "Do you think… do you think he's looking for…" he trailed off uncertainly.

"I would assume as much," Norrin said, straightening and moving to the fire.

"Then—this is the perfect time, Norrin. We have to fight," Rygal said. "We can't let them do it on their own. You know what Safacon is capable of…"

"Yes, I do," Norrin said quietly. "Quite better than any of you here." He put a log of wood to the fire, then turned back to the Coopers. "Very well. Come, sit, and I will tell you what is going on. Would anyone like tea?"

Jarus hadn't eaten all afternoon. He and Maya gratefully accepted some bread and two mugs of tea and sat on the sofa. The mugs were bigger than the ones Jarus was used to, made for human hands. But the tea was warm and soothing after the excitement of the past eighteen hours.

Norrin sat in the chair by the fire, and Rygal sat across from him. There was a moment of silence as everyone settled down. Jarus was trying to remember where he had heard Norrin's name before, but he couldn't place it. Then Maya spoke quietly.

"They were looking for you, too," she said. Her voice was very soft, fearful, as she looked at Norrin. "The men who took my father. They wanted information about someone called Norrin."

To Jarus' surprise, a faint smile appeared on the old man's face. "Did they? That's not too surprising. They've been looking for me for years." He chuckled and took a sip of tea.

"They… have?" Maya said, confused.

"Why?" Jarus asked.

Norrin set down his mug. "Well, that's a bit of a long story. To understand it all, we must start at the very beginning. With the Guardians of Gayrile."

The fire crackled. The room grew tense with anticipation of the story.

"Almost twenty years ago now," Norrin began, "after the fall of the cruel queen Kircadash and her war, both Coonsia and Gayrile were struggling. Coonsia, naturally, had the Liznees to help. The Isle of Gayrile was smaller, distant. And so the Guardians of Gayrile were established. Our mission was to help the commonwealth and keep peace and order. Over the next few years, we helped the people of Gayrile to prosper and grow, and protected them from danger. And that is when Safacon made his move.

"Safacon, you must understand, had been in Gayrile before any of this began. He grew up here, and when the Guardians of Gayrile were established, he joined us for a little while. I knew him, briefly, when he was young and learning the study of the ancient arts. He was ambitious, cunning, and smart." Norrin looked at the fire. "I even trained him in a few things, in strategy and battle-play."

"You *knew* Safacon?" Jarus repeated, stunned. This man, he was beginning to realize, was no mere fisherman.

"I did," Norrin said with a slight smile. "He was a popular public figure with the people. He was an alchemist, a diplomat, a friendly face. He was the type of person you would trust and follow without question. And that is exactly what people did here." His smile had faded. "Safacon promised security, prosperity, wealth—everything the common folk wanted in those days. Eventually, he took over as the ruling voice in Gayrile, even surpassing the king of the Diren people in power. He disbanded the Guardians of Gayrile the moment he could—and when we resisted, he used force."

"So he's… a lord now?" Maya asked slowly. "But if he was able to take control, then why doesn't the High King Jan do anything about it? Gayrile is under Coonsia's leadership, right?"

"Yes, but Safacon is no mere politician. And here we get to the dark part of the story," Norrin said. "To all outward appearances, Safacon is now the ruling lord of Gayrile. His soldiers enforce his laws, and his citizens follow his commands. But Safacon is more than that. I mentioned his love for alchemy and the magic arts before. That is the heart of his power.

"In the years before the Guardians of Gayrile, Safacon studied in the ancient arts of sorcery. At the height of his strength, Safacon created a weapon of great power. A Jewel. Forged from the core source of a fallen star. Safacon also made two sister objects from the Jewel—a Ring and a Knife. With the Knife of Destruction, one would become the greatest warrior in the world, and eliminate your enemies with a single word. With the Ring of Light, one could control light and day, and in a sense, the very flow of time itself." He paused.

"And… the Jewel?" Jarus asked slowly. The room had grown very quiet.

"It is the most powerful of the three," Norrin said. "The Jewel controls the other two and gives them their powers. Safacon learned much about its powers while building his kingdom. And he used it against the Guardians of Gayrile when we resisted his rule." His face was gray.

Jarus looked at him, sensing the gravity of the subject. He had heard a little about Safacon, but most of it had been rumors only, or facts with no explanation behind them. But he had never even heard of the dark magic Norrin spoke of now.

"What happened next?" Maya asked softly.

Norrin looked up at her. "When Safacon took control of the commonwealth of Gayrile, the Guardians resisted. He defeated us in open battle, with the power of the Objects. Many Guardians were lost, and Safacon placed great bounties on the heads of the survivors. Especially mine."

"Norrin led the resistance for a while," Rygal jumped in, excitement in his eyes as he spoke. "My father, Maran, fought too. They devised a plan to stop Safacon once and for all."

"You did?" Jarus said, impressed.

Norrin nodded slowly. "The Jewel, the Knife, and the Ring—they were our targets. Without them, Safacon would fall. He needed them to complete his conquest of the world. So we devised a plan to steal them."

"There are a few breeds of dragons that still live in the mountains near Safacon's fortress," Rygal told them. "Some of them have been domesticated by Safacon. My father managed to steal three of them, so that the group could fly right over the guards without them suspecting anything."

"Yes, he did," Norrin said, smiling fondly at the memory of his friend. "Well, our group got past the guards without any trouble. Maran, myself, and a young prince of the Brownae people. The Brownae, Deathcap—he guided us to Safacon's palace. What we did not know was that desire for the Jewel and the power it brought had already filled Deathcap's heart. The moment we were inside, he betrayed us."

"Did he get the Jewel?" Maya asked, wide-eyed.

"No—Maran prevented that, thank the Light. Deathcap did manage to steal the Knife, though its destructive powers pale in comparison to the Jewel's. Maran took the Jewel, and I the Ring. It was not easy. Safacon's guards had been alerted, and they pursued us, their archers firing after us. We managed to reach the dragons and took to the sky." He paused before continuing. "Maran... was struck by an arrow as we escaped. He fell with the Jewel into the wilderness."

Jarus glanced up at Rygal; his face was gray. "I'm sorry," Jarus said softly.

Rygal shrugged very slightly, as if trying to shake off the pain of the loss. "He died fighting against Safacon. I don't remember him much."

Maya looked at Norrin. "So… the Jewel was lost, and the Knife was stolen… what about the Ring?"

"The Ring, yes—and that brings us back to Deathcap," Norrin said, nodding. "Though he had the Knife, he was desperate to get the other Objects as well—the Jewel in particular. I meant to deliver the Ring to King Makana of the Direns, as he alone may have some idea of how to defeat Safacon. But Deathcap intercepted me on my way, near the Whitewash River. We fought, and the Ring was lost into the river. The last I saw of Deathcap, he had retreated to his fortress in the Wandering Wood, where he no doubt still plots my demise."

There was a brief pause. Jarus looked at Norrin. "Then… how does this explain why Safacon took our fathers?" he asked slowly. "Why kidnap Coopers?"

"Safacon has been searching for the Jewel for nearly two decades," Norrin said. "In fact, that was part of the conquest of Kado, almost seven years ago. Kado was sent to the Mainland, along with an army of immortal warriors, to undermine the Liznees' authority. That led to his defeat, as I am sure you have heard." He shared a brief smile with Rygal before continuing. "By now, Safacon must have concluded that the Jewel is not on Gayrile. Thus, he has turned his sights south. He has actually taken Mainlanders many times before, but he does it carefully and quietly, to avoid any outcry."

"Safacon's going after any wealthy civilians," Rygal explained. "From what you've told me, Maya, your family is quite well-off. Safacon may suspect that your father used the Jewel to make himself rich."

"But wouldn't Safacon know that the Jewel is on Gayrile?" Maya said slowly, still confused. "Norrin—you said Maran fell with the Jewel into the wilderness of Gayrile. Couldn't Safacon simply track where he fell?"

"He has already tried, as have I," Norrin said wearily. "But it is nearly impossible to guess where exactly the Jewel fell. The Wandering Wood is a vast expanse of forest that covers nearly half the island. Beyond that, the Jewel itself is a devious and peculiar thing. Whether it has an intelligence of its own I have yet to learn, but I do assume that if it chose to remain hidden, even from its former ally, it could and would do so."

The thought was baffling to Jarus, so he moved on for now, returning to his more pressing question. "Okay, so he kidnapped Mr. Raintail because he thought he had the Jewel, he took Hagar because Hagar knew too much, and he took my father so there wouldn't be any witnesses… well, how will we get them back?"

"That is the question, but I'm not quite sure I have an answer yet," Norrin said hesitantly.

Rygal looked at him, the light rekindling in his eyes. "Norrin— you mentioned before that Safacon could be stopped. That we could fight him. If we rallied the Guardians of Gayrile again, stirred up the resistance…"

"As proud as I am of you and your resistance efforts, Rygal, you know as well as I that Safacon's army would stop them," Norrin said gently. "And the Guardians are all in hiding. I could try to contact them, but we would still be outnumbered by the Serventiri."

"We're better fighters than the Serventiri, no matter the numbers," Rygal said confidently, folding his arms over his chest.

"Serventiri?" Jarus repeated, glancing at Norrin. "What are the Serventiri?"

Norrin turned to him. "The Jewel of Power can do many things, Jarus. Safacon created his fortress, his empire, and much of his strength with the Jewel. It's a temporary power, all of it, and will die when the Jewel is destroyed, but it is quite effective. The Serventiri are a host of created soldiers, brought into being by Safacon. They obey his bidding without question and are difficult to kill."

"Not impossible," Rygal said, then admitted, "but difficult. And Safacon has tons of 'em. He can't create any more of them now, not without the Jewel, but they are still a force to be reckoned with, and they search for the Jewel even now."

A sorcerer with great power, protected by an army of artificial beings, in a strong fortress… and he had their fathers. Jarus was beginning to feel overwhelmed. Even the Guardians of Gayrile, who had been the best warriors in the north, had been no match for Safacon.

"What if we found the Jewel?" Maya asked slowly. "If we found the Jewel, the Ring, and the Knife—we could trade them for our fathers' freedom."

"But then Safacon would win," Rygal said immediately.

"But we could fight him," Maya said, though she sounded doubtful.

"No, you don't understand," Rygal said, shaking his head. "If Safacon had the Objects again—especially the Jewel—all he'd have to do is say the words, and we'd all drop dead before we ever had a chance. Present threats, future threats, he could see them all. He'd kill us all, us and anyone else who might challenge his rule."

"We cannot give the Objects back," Norrin agreed. "They must be destroyed, broken upon the Golden Tablet that they were created on. Only then will Safacon be defeated." He paused. Firelight played over his features, and Jarus could almost see the thoughts turning in his head.

"You think we could find the Objects and destroy them before Safacon does," Jarus guessed finally.

They were all looking at Norrin now.

The old man nodded slowly. "It is the only way. The resistance can fight as much as they want, burn as much oil as they want, but ultimately it will only fuel the fire of Safacon's anger. The only way we can truly stop him is to find the Jewel."

"And then we fight," Rygal said, his eyes fierce and eager. "We'll free their fathers and all of Gayrile with them."

The words lit a spark of hope and excitement in Jarus. They would fight. They would defeat Safacon and save Gayrile from his tyrannical rule once and for all.

"How?" Maya asked softly, looking uncertain. "I mean—I know that's what has to be done. After everything you've told us, I understand that now. But we can't fight all of the Serventiri."

"Ideally we won't have to, alone," Norrin said. But a smile crossed his face as a thought occurred to him. "All the same, I know of another who will gladly join us."

5

The Siren's Song

Rain fell through the night, pattering against the windows in a rhythm that lulled Jarus asleep. Norrin had offered the spare bedroom to the Coopers. The human bed was too tall and soft for comfort, so Jarus gladly accepted the bedroll and blanket instead, allowing Maya to have the room to herself. The story Norrin had told them formed strange dreams in his mind, but he slept fitfully. He woke to someone shaking him awake.

"Morning, Jarus. It's time to go." Rygal's voice came dimly from above him.

Jarus opened his eyes, squinting at the light. "Huh?" he mumbled, mind foggy with sleep. "What time is it?"

"Time to get on the trail," said Rygal. He was grinning and looked wide awake. "More rain's coming again today—there's a big storm to the south. We leave too late, and we'll get soaked."

Jarus sat up slowly and began grooming through his fur. Rygal moved to the other side of the room to wake up Maya. The embers of last night's fire still smoldered, and the warmth made Jarus feel sleepy again. He shook his head to clear it.

Norrin stood by the door, packing supplies into leather packs. He smiled as he saw Jarus. "Good morning—roll up that mat and blanket as tight as you can, and put it in the bag. Rygal can help you."

"Here," Rygal said, as Jarus glanced uncertainly at the mat. He rolled it up tightly, slid the roll into a small bag, and helped Jarus situate it over his shoulder blades. "You'll carry your own gear. We have the food and water in the other packs, though."

"You've done this before," Jarus remarked with a slight grin.

Rygal shrugged as he helped Maya with her bedroll. "Trail packing. Pack as light as you can, but pack what you need."

It was drizzling rain as the four of them walked the streets of Bridgeport, towards the dark mass of wilderness on the other side of town. Norrin led the way, avoiding the main roads. Jarus noticed several soldiers patrolling the streets, and guessed that with the excitement of the fire yesterday, more troops would likely be out keeping watch.

"Are those Serventiri?" he asked Rygal softly as they passed a group of soldiers. One of them eyed them carefully, but thankfully didn't recognize Norrin or Rygal with their cloaks and simple clothes.

"No," Rygal replied in the same lowered tone. "Those are living people—men who joined Safacon. Whether they joined by choice or were forced too, I'm not sure. But there's a large number of them, unfortunately."

It was hard to picture people willingly joining Safacon, Jarus thought, but he knew it happened. He frowned as they passed the harbor, remembering something. "Oh, crud... the boat. My father's boat, it's the one we brought here. What should I do with it now?"

Rygal looked at the harbor, looking unconcerned. "It'll be there when we get back. They won't charge you anything for keeping it there longer."

Jarus looked at him, dumbfounded—the idea of leaving his father's boat unattended was absurd in his Cooper mind. This must be another thing he had to learn about human ways. "You're telling me I can just leave it there? Pops will kill me," he muttered as an afterthought.

"As a fellow fisherman, Jarus," Norrin said, "I trust the harbormaster. Your father's boat will be kept safe for as long as we take to return."

It was very looked down on in Mata City for someone to leave their boat unattended for that long… but there wasn't much Jarus could do about it. Apparently it was normal here.

"Where are we going?" Maya asked as they left the township behind.

"West," Norrin replied. "Towards the swamps. "

"I should warn you—" Rygal stopped abruptly.

"Warn us of what?" Jarus asked.

"Well…our friend, the one we're going to see…he's a little eccentric, that's all," Rygal said, looking slightly abashed. "Just don't be…alarmed."

It was midmorning before they left civilization behind, and reached the place Norrin had mentioned. The pine groves that had made up much of the coastal forest were replaced by drooping willows and large clumps of sage. The ground grew more and more soggy, until the gravel road was replaced by a wood boardwalk, the planks of which were covered in moss. The mangroves grew denser in around them, until the terrain became a universal green-gray. Below the boardwalk, the slow flowing river was thick and soupy. Jarus debated swimming at first, but could now see that most of the river was mud. Branches stuck out of it at odd angles, giving the area a spindly and starved look.

Rygal sidestepped a rotten board and continued walking. "The path is in much better condition than the last time I was here, at any rate," he commented. "We're nearly there."

"Do you trust this person, Norrin?" Maya asked as they followed Rygal.

"Indeed I do," Norrin said. "He is, as Rygal said, a little…peculiar. But I would trust him with my life, and I have faith that he will join our cause against Safacon."

"Here we are," Rygal said from up ahead, and Jarus' attention was drawn back to their surroundings.

The east bank of the river sloped up slightly. A thatch roof hut crouched in the mangroves, the walls made mostly of mud. If Rygal hadn't pointed it out, Jarus guessed he would have walked right by it. Large round windows were set high in the walls, giving it the appearance of a large frog.

Rygal stepped carefully from the boardwalk to the bank, his foot sliding back into the mud before he had his balance. "Come on, then."

The two Coopers followed. There was no door, only a tattered curtain that covered the entrance. Since the whole swamp was hot and muggy, Jarus guessed there was no need for a door; a curtain would allow more air flow.

Inside, the house looked like a honeycomb, with many small alcoves and shelves in the walls. Strange things were set in the shelves, antlers from exotic animals, small skulls and beads. Jarus couldn't even identify some. Maya looked around, curious but still uncertain.

"Knock, knock," Rygal called into the house, sidestepping a shelf.

A cloud of green mist swirled from the alcove directly above and in front of them, swirling into indistinct shapes. Whispering voices came from within it, voices from far away. Jarus realized his companions had stopped, but he moved on, suddenly no longer in control of his own body. The mist filled his head, clouding it with longing and softness from the faint melody coming from nowhere.

Rygal put a hand on his shoulder, stopping him. "Wait," he said simply. "He likes his tricks." He looked up. "The mist is a nice touch, Lammar. Did you change the melody of the song, too?"

The mist swirled and blew away, as though it had been bottled up. The voice that answered was new, with a lilting accent, and came from the alcove above. "I thought so. And the song needed some spicing up, like a good stew. The Cooper was quick to succumb, at any rate."

Padding down the stairs was a creature about the same size as

Jarus, but not a Cooper. His shape was almost like that of a lizard, with short back legs and a long body. His tail was thick, like a salamander's. The face was oval shaped, with yellow eyes and a pronounced jaw. As he spoke, Jarus could see rows of sharp teeth, tinted a faint blue. His skin was the same mottled green-gray as the swamp. A darker patch ran up his face across his eyes like a mask, giving him a roguish and mischievous look. A green frill ran around his chin, then down the back and length of the tail.

"What *are* you?" Jarus asked, before he could stop himself.

The newcomer turned and studied him critically. "I," he said, "am a Siren. Though I doubt you'd have seen one of us before, Cooper."

"A… what?" Jarus asked, still confused. The species was unfamiliar.

Maya shook her head. "A Siren, Jarus. A shape-shifter."

A Siren. Suddenly, the hypnotic fog and the distant song that had captured him moments before made sense. "Oh—so that was you?" he asked, motioning vaguely at the alcove. "With the… mist and everything?"

"Indeed it was," the Siren said, looking pleased. "Though next time you might try not to fall for it as quickly as you did just now."

Norrin had approached from behind. "Jarus, Maya, meet Lammar Skytooth, one of my oldest friends."

"Getting older," Lammar commented with a wry smile, and he and Norrin chuckled.

"Then—were you one of the Guardians of Gayrile too?" Jarus asked.

"A Guardian? Please. No, I never served with them. Supported them, spied for them, a little." The Siren's green eyes glinted with the past memories. "That's a story for another time, though. I'm guessing you didn't come here for my stories."

"How'd you figure that?" Jarus asked, startled.

Lammar gestured at them all with a webbed paw. "You're packed for a venture. Most likely a dangerous one, too, or you wouldn't be carrying weapons." He looked at Rygal, a little suspiciously. "Don't tell me you've a mind to go after Safacon himself?"

"I might tell you that," Rygal said slowly.

"Good," Lammar said briskly. "I'm quite interested to hear what you have in mind. And I'd like to know how you finally convinced old Norrin here to challenge Safacon again." He threw a good-natured grin at Norrin, who shook his head.

"Let's just say it only took Rygal's picking fights with Safacon's soldiers about a hundred times to convince me. The real story, though, is what they have to say." Norrin nodded to the Coopers.

"Well, tell it, then," Lammar said, leading them to the table. "I've just finished preparing lunch, and I'm very curious to hear your story."

6

∽ ∽ ∽ ∽ ∽ ∽ ∽ ∽ ∽

Further Plans

The companions sat around Lammar's round dining table. It was a little cramped, but they were all able to see the map Norrin had laid out on the table while they ate.

Lammar had prepared a spicy stew with wild rice. After a long day of walking, Jarus was starving, and devoured the meal appreciatively. "I'd want you along just to have you cook for us on the quest," he commented to Lammar as he accepted a second bowl of stew.

The Siren smiled. "I've a love for all things of the culinary nature. Unfortunately, adventures like yours aren't known for having the best meal plans." His smile faded at that.

Norrin explained the Coopers' story to Lammar, who listened without interruption. When he had finished, Lammar glanced between the four of them. "You're all bent on taking down Safacon, then?"

"Yes," Maya said. "We have to rescue my father and Mr. Puddlepaw."

"Indeed," Lammar said, nodding. "Well, what's your plan now?"

"Find the Objects," Maya said, then added doubtfully, "except we don't know how we'll do that. Other groups have been looking for them for years."

"They have, but they didn't have Norrin helping them," Lammar said with a grin. He looked at the wizard. "I'm guessing you have a

70

plan of some kind, to get this far."

Norrin nodded. "Maya is right, finding the Objects will be no easy quest. Especially the Jewel. Our best course of action now, I think, will be to look where the Jewel was last seen. That means searching the Wandering Wood."

"Lovely," Rygal mumbled sarcastically into his bowl.

"What's in the Wandering Wood?" Jarus asked, looking at Rygal.

"What's *not?*" Rygal asked wryly.

"We'll get to that," Norrin said. He turned back to Lammar. "Once we have the Objects, we will go to Flameton, and rally the Direns and King Makana. Then we will make our way south, to Safacon's fortress."

"Mm," Lammar murmured, looking thoughtful. "Well, that's a good plan, but we'll need more help than just the five of us. The Direns will probably join our cause without too much persuasion—King Makana has been working for years to stop Safacon. But there will likely be plenty of obstacles in our way before we reach Flameton, and I'd like more backup."

"What about Neely?" Rygal suggested suddenly. "Those are her people—she might help."

"Who's Neely?" Jarus asked.

"A young Diren, and my apprentice," Lammar said. "I was her mentor for a while after her parents were killed by Safacon. Yes, Rygal, that's a good idea, but Neely's in the east wood right now on an assignment, so I won't be able to reach her."

"Well, I will think about who else could help. Before we reach the desert, we must first go through the Wandering Wood," Norrin pointed out. "Even if the Jewel is no longer in the Wood, where Maran fell, it is still the fastest way to Flameton, to avoid the land of the rebel Direns."

Lammar frowned slightly. "Well, from what you've told me, it sounds like Safacon is no longer looking for the Jewel in the Wood. Not that it makes the Wood any safer, but with any luck we'll avoid the Serventiri."

"Hopefully," Norrin said, "but I won't count on it."

"We'll fight them if we have to," Rygal said confidently.

Lammar smiled grimly. "Maybe, but you haven't seen Safacon's latest toys he's provided for his army. Rumor is he's hired smugglers to steal and deliver weapons from the Liznees in Caer Sia."

Norrin set down his plate, startled. "Caer Sia? He wants… firearms?"

"I wouldn't put it past him. Even if those firearms are still an experimental invention, Safacon will want them for his warriors." Lammar looked at him. "That's the latest rumor, at any rate. If it's true, there could definitely be problems."

"Firearms?" Jarus repeated slowly. The word was vaguely familiar—he thought he had heard his father talking about it once.

"Weapons," Lammar said. "The type of weapons that can shoot tiny missiles with the power of three crossbows. Very new weapons—the Liznees only began using them a few years ago, after the whole Kado issue. But very destructive."

"Well, if the Serventiri are in the Wandering Wood, we can at least hope that the Jewel is, too," Norrin said. "The Serventiri were created by the Jewel, and can sense its presence. So can Safacon."

"So we get to go through the Wandering Wood," Lammar sighed. "Lovely."

"What's in the Wandering Wood?" Maya asked uncertainly.

Norrin frowned, seeming to decide how to explain. "Deathcap is," he said finally, "but compared to the Wood itself, Deathcap is a minor danger. The Brownae people have lived there for centuries, but it is far more dangerous to an outsider. It's not called the Wandering Wood for nothing, you know. The paths in there—you can't trust them. They wind all over the place. Yet I fear that is the fastest route to Flameton, the city of the Direns."

"Deathcap isn't the only concern, though," Lammar said. "The Brownae tribes—they're always warring over one thing or another."

"Brownaes?" Jarus repeated. He remembered Hal mentioning them back in Mata City, but he didn't know much about them.

"They're fierce warriors," Lammar told him. "They stand maybe four or five feet tall, and are covered with fur. Don't underestimate them because of their size, though. They can be very dangerous if provoked."

"Yes," Norrin said. "One of the largest tribes is the Chanterelle. The word is that Deathcap has bribed their chieftain with riches, robes, an assortment of weapons, anything, if the chief would give him the Jewel. But now, he's resorted to threats."

Lammar nodded. "Deathcap's out of his mind to get the Jewel before Safacon does. Rumor is that only a few months ago, he attacked the tribe, killed the chief's wife, and captured his beloved children, and is holding them hostage until Chief Cedar gives him the Jewel."

"But *does* Chief Cedar have the Jewel?" Jarus asked.

Lammar shrugged. "No one knows. Deathcap might be only seeking an excuse to go to war with the Chanterelle again. Then again, he may know something we don't."

"So would Deathcap know when the Jewel is near?" Maya asked.

"More than that, he could *feel* when it is near," Norrin said. "Like a prickling down his spine. He feels it strongest for the Knife of Destruction, because that is what he stole, like I can feel when the Ring is near, and likewise Rygal's father for the Jewel. But the Jewel has a darkness that anyone could feel, if you were close enough."

"How do you know all this, Norrin?" Jarus asked curiously. He knew Norrin had once been a Guardian, but he seemed to know a lot about Safacon's weapons.

Norrin smiled slightly. "When the Objects were created, the Guardians made it our priority to learn as much as we could about them, and how we could destroy them. But not many other species know the Jewel-lore, so I am not sure if the Brownaes would identify it if it were found."

"Not like the Jewel is especially inconspicuous, though," Lammar pointed out with a crooked grin. "It's a blue diamond, as big as a hen's egg. You think a Brownae would miss it?" He paused, thinking. "On second thought, you might be right. The Brownaes don't pay much attention to the Old Stories. Even if they did find it, they would probably grind it up and sprinkle it over mushrooms as seasoning." Lammar wrinkled his nose. "Very acquired taste, mushrooms. Personally, I would rather eat—"

Norrin cut him off quickly; Lammar could go on about food for hours. "Returning to battle plans, Jarus, I think most of them shall be discussed at Flameton. All we need to worry about for now is getting the Objects together, and then we can destroy them."

"How will we do that?" Jarus asked.

"All three Objects must be broken at the exact same moment upon the Golden Tablet," Norrin said. "That is the only way. And it must be done quickly. Safacon will hear of this venture soon enough, and once he does, we are all a threat to him."

big as her fist. You think? He was right.

7

∾ ∾ ∾ ∾ ∾ ∾ ∾ ∾ ∾

Trails and Tribes

They spent the night in Lammar's house. Jarus set up his mat beside the fireplace and watched the flames dwindle down as he dozed off. The smell of baking bread, and the sound of voices, woke him. Lammar crouched beside the fire, carefully removing a freshly baked loaf from over the coals.

"Morning," he said as Jarus stirred. "Pack your mat up and we can eat a little before we get on the trail."

"We're getting out early again?" Jarus asked groggily, stretching as he sat up. He noticed the other three bedrolls in the room were empty. His companions must already be up.

"There's only so much daylight," Lammar said with a shrug, and wrapped the loaf in a cloth.

Jarus yawned as Maya came into the room, along with Norrin. "No more rain," Maya reported cheerfully, moving to the warm fire. "There's a heavy fog over the swamp, but it's not as cold as yesterday."

"That's good," Jarus said, stifling another yawn as he rolled up the mat. He glanced over to the table. Norrin and Lammar were speaking in lowered tones, and Rygal was sharpening the blade of his sword. "Can you believe we're really doing this?" he asked Maya, grinning in spite of his weariness.

Maya glanced over at their companions and smiled. "I know. Finding our fathers doesn't seem quite as impossible anymore. Maybe we'll really do it."

"Hope so," Jarus murmured, trying to roll his mat up tighter. It still didn't fit in the stuff sack. He'd have to ask Rygal for help again.

They ate a quick meal, then headed outside. A thick fog hovered over the murky water, penetrated only by the rays of the rising sun. The calls of strange birds echoed eerily through the air as they walked down the wood plank path.

The sun had risen by the time they left the boardwalk behind and reached the edge of the swamp. A dirt path wound steadily into the dark woods ahead.

"Welcome to the Wandering Wood," Lammar said, nodding ahead. "This path is the main road through the forest, and we'll want to keep to it as best we can."

Jarus followed as they started into the wood, looking around in awe. Growing up on the rocky coast of Mata City, he had never seen a forest like this. The morning light afforded little sight in the woods, bathing everything in hazy gray. The trees towered above them, growing in dense ranks. The woods seemed to grow darker and denser as they went on, with ferns and briers forming a thick underbrush. The weather had become muggy and warm.

"Norrin," Jarus asked as they moved on, "how do we know which way to go? You said last night that the paths can't be trusted."

Norrin nodded. "Lammar has explored most of this part of the

Wood," he said. "After that, we will rely heavily on direction from the stars and sun. I'll teach you sometime." He smiled and moved on ahead.

A while later they stopped at a crossroads. The trail diverged into four paths, each winding away into the shadowed wood.

Lammar looked up at Norrin. "Which way?"

"Northeast," Norrin told him. "Toward the desert."

Lammar looked uncertain. "You're aware that most of this road is unmapped. Might just be a dead end. It would be better to head straight north, out of the wood, and take the east road to reach Flameton."

"Yes," Norrin admitted, "but we would lose a lot of time. King Makana must be made aware of what we are doing, so we must reach Flameton as soon as we can."

They continued on, following Norrin. Lammar looked wary, scenting the breeze, searching the smells that only his nose could catch. Jarus could smell things, too—but they were all unfamiliar, and he couldn't tell if any of them were dangerous or not.

Maya looked worried, and padded forward to catch up to Lammar. "What do you think is down this road, if it's unmapped?"

Lammar looked unsure. "Maybe nothing. Maybe Deathcap. These paths are tricky to judge. You can explore them for years and still not be sure."

Jarus glanced up, feeling a prickle of unease. "Deathcap? What would Deathcap do to us?"

Norrin overheard the question and answered. "It's difficult to guess the mind of Deathcap, he is so crazed with power. I highly doubt my presence, at least, would be welcome. The last time I saw Deathcap, he had sworn to kill me. And he might assume that I am trying to steal the Knife of Destruction from him."

"But we need the Knife, don't we?" Maya asked with a frown.

"We do, but Deathcap won't hand it over willingly, and it will be very difficult to take it from him by force. I am still determining what will be done to get the Knife," Norrin said.

Night fell early in the shadowy woods. They set up camp a little ways off the trail, and Rygal took the first watch. Jarus laid out his mat near Lammar. He felt safer near the Siren in these strange woods.

"You can turn into anything, then?" he asked curiously as they all settled down.

"Well, yes," Lammar said, looking pleased. "I have to see it first. And powers don't transfer over, unfortunately, or else I would have turned into some sort of indestructible creature and defeated Safacon long ago."

Jarus raised his eyebrows, guessing he was only half-joking.

Slowly, everyone else fell asleep, while Jarus lay awake, alone except Norrin who sat on the other side of camp. Jarus' mind felt too full to sleep. It had been only four days since they'd left home, he realized. Four days since everything had changed. His thoughts strayed to his father, taken by Safacon. *Was he still alive?* The unwelcome question crossed his mind, and he shuddered and pushed it away, unable to bear the possible answer.

. . . . . .

Rygal woke them the following morning, a little while after sunrise. Jarus could tell by the uneasiness in his eyes that something was wrong.

"Norrin, we might have a problem," Rygal reported as soon as he had awakened the wizard. "On watch a few hours ago—right before dawn—I heard something. I went to check it out, and found this." He held up a small, black-feathered dart with a razor sharp point.

"Where was it?" Norrin asked.

Rygal jerked his head toward the brush to the right. "Back there, maybe ten or twelve yards back. There's a lot of deer trails crisscrossing the main road, so I thought it might be an animal. But there's a lot of Brownae tracks too."

"Brownaes?" Maya repeated.

"Let me see that," Lammar said, motioning to the dart. Rygal held it out to him. Lammar sniffed the tip carefully for a moment, then nodded. "Poison. The Brownaes use it on their darts."

"You're sure?" Rygal asked.

"I'd say better safe than sorry for this," Lammar said, looking at Norrin. "Unless you plan to risk a confrontation."

"No," Norrin agreed. He sighed. "It was my fault—we should not have come this way. We'll need to go back to the crossroads and take the other road."

"We…have to?" Jarus said, not at all liking the thought of back-tracking.

"We have neither the strength nor the desire to clash with a Brownae war party," Norrin said. "No…this is what we need to do."

The day was even muggier than the day before, if that was possible. A dreary haze was falling, and the warmth made it unbearably humid. When the misty rain stopped at last, it was replaced by swarms of tiny gnats buzzing around them and stinging any part of exposed skin. Jarus inhaled two, and while he coughed them out to the others' sympathetic amusement, the rest of the insects swarmed around him, biting him behind his ears, on the back of his neck, between his shoulder blades—anywhere he couldn't swat them.

"Lovely place, isn't it?" Lammar commented dryly.

"We've got to be close to the crossroads," Rygal grumbled. "How far did—"

Then he stopped suddenly, listening. Jarus looked around, catching a strange scent in the air. Norrin and Lammar were both silent, listening intently. He felt a prickle go up his spine. Something was there…eyes were watching from the brush. Rygal drew his sword.

Then Maya gave a scream, and Jarus whirled around. A net had sprung out of the path, so well hidden by the leaves that Maya had stepped back right on top of it. Now she hung, high above, squirming desperately.

"Maya!" he shouted in alarm. He turned swiftly to Rygal, but froze, realizing there was a much larger problem to address.

A high-pitched whistling came from the trees, wild and chilling, and suddenly the woods came alive. Brownaes sprang from their hiding places, brandishing knives and slings. Four feet tall, their fur bristling, clad in tattered leather armor, their ears flicked back like angry wildcats, they attacked.

Norrin sent a shower of sparks from his staff, making many of them step back. "We have no quarrel with you, warriors," he said slowly, his voice calm. "May we speak to your leader before you fight us?"

Either the Brownaes didn't understand him, or just didn't care—they loosed a volley of darts and stones from their slings that rained down on the group. Norrin blocked the blows with his staff, the ends of which now crackled with yellow sparks.

Lammar joined him, his shape flickering as he transformed into a hissing snake. The snake made several more Brownaes scatter, but more and more kept coming. Rygal lunged forward, swinging his sword, but a rock from a sling struck him in the jaw, and he collapsed. Maya screamed again, squirming, helpless as she watched.

"Maya!" Jarus shouted again, reaching up for her, but she was too high—

He felt paws grasp him from behind, the claws digging into his shoulder blades—a Brownae hauled him back, slipping a noose around his neck. Jarus squirmed, lashing out, but then the Brownae pulled a ragged sack over his head, concealing the last light of the outside world.

He felt himself being hauled upright, and could hear Norrin's voice as he tried to reason with the Brownaes. Maya's voice came in the other direction, the words muffled and unrecognizable. At least they were all together.

He realized, dimly, that they were moving into the woods again. Only this time, they were captives.

· · · · · ·

Two hours, maybe, of stumbling blindly through the wood had passed before Jarus became aware that the terrain had changed. Sharp rocks jabbed at his paws, and judging from the light breeze, they were in an open area. He was pulled forward, into darkness, and forced down an echoing hall. He seemed to be inside a structure of some sort. The cobblestone was cold under his paws.

He was shoved forward abruptly, and the Brownae pulled off the sack. Jarus sat in a stone cell, alone and shivering. The Brownae locked the door and left without a word.

Taking shaking breaths, he settled down again, forcing himself to think. He didn't seem to be in the forest anymore—at least not directly. The floor beneath him was hard stone, cold and unyielding. There would be no digging out. He was in a stone cell. A door, made of interlocking steel bars, offered a limited view of the hall beyond. He could see more cells, but couldn't see if anyone was inside.

There was a rope around his neck and his wrists, which was tied to a post in the center of the room. He tugged on his bonds briefly to no avail, and panic filled him—the tight quarters of the cell made it feel like he couldn't breathe.

"Hey!" he shouted, staggering on three legs as he ran around the post like a leashed dog. Maddened for an instant, he gasped with fear for a few panicked seconds, mind swirling with thoughts. Where were his companions? Were they all dead? Was he the only one left?

"No," he said out loud, regaining control of himself. No—if the Brownaes were going to kill them, they would have done it in the woods, and not gone to all the work of capturing them alive. Which meant his companions were probably somewhere else in this stone fortress.

A clank made him jump, and a door at the far end of the line of cells opened, letting in a blaze of daylight. A party of three entered, two tough-looking men with tattoos on their bulging arms, and one Brownae. There was a cold and commanding presence about him. His fur was dark, groomed magnificently so that it shone, and there was a chain of bone and turquoise beads around his neck. His armor was also made of leather, but in better shape than the armor his warriors wore. A scar streaked his face, half hidden by fur. One of his eyes was green, the other was yellow, giving him a wild and utterly evil look.

"Leave us," the Brownae said to a small figure huddled by the door to Jarus' cell. It was another Brownae, younger, wearing a tattered tunic.

The young Brownae raised his head and answered softly in his native language. His eyes were frightened and sad, and Jarus guessed he would only be around fourteen in human years.

Whatever he had responded with made the dark one glare at him. "Are you deaf now, as well as stupid? Out," he ordered sharply, jerking his head at the door. The young slave got up and slunk down the hall and outside. As the door closed behind him, Jarus caught a glimpse of a wide courtyard, mottled with age and moss. It seemed he was in some sort of ruin, now inhabited by these Brownaes.

The door to his cell opened as the dark Brownae walked in. Jarus watched him warily.

"So," the Brownae purred finally, his voice soft. "A Cooper. In the Wandering Wood. In my lands."

"I…I didn't know they were your lands…sir," Jarus said hesitantly. That was true, at least.

"Did you not," murmured the Brownae, still calm. "And…your friends, did they know? Did your pretty Cooper girl know? We did not think so, and it was not…easy…to get her to talk." One of the ruffians gave a dark chuckle.

Maya. Fear for her safety filled Jarus, followed by a hot fire of rage. Before he realized what he was doing, he lunged forward, reaching to shake this smirking Brownae. His bonds stopped him abruptly, a few inches from the Brownae.

"If you hurt her—if you've even touched her—" he sputtered.

The Brownae looked at him, unfazed. "You'll what?" He reached out so fast Jarus barely saw the paws close around him. The Brownae gripped his neck and hauled him closer, making the rope tighten around Jarus' throat. "You have no power here, Cooper," the Brownae snarled, no longer calm. "I am Deathcap, lord of the Wandering Wood, and you will tell me what I wish to know."

He shoved Jarus back, and Jarus fell, gasping for air, his heart pounding. "Now tell me," Deathcap said, his voice lowering to a hiss, "why are you here?"

"I… we're…passing through," Jarus stammered. "We're trying to get to…the desert."

"The desert?" Deathcap asked. "Not… to Flameton?"

"No, no, of course not," Jarus said shakily. He was so terrified he could barely form words.

"*Really*?" Deathcap snarled, voice rising again. He stepped closer, his eyes full of a maddened fire. "Then please explain…why travel with that rat of a wizard Norrin?"

Jarus stared at him, unable to think of an answer. Deathcap struck him hard across the face, and he fell again, tasting blood in his mouth.

"You're after the Jewel!" Deathcap shouted, his voice echoing through the fortress.

"No—no, sir, I swear—"

"Don't lie to me, Cooper!" Deathcap snarled, seizing a handful of Jarus' fur and hauling him upright again. "We already know… that sweet little girl was quite talkative, after some persuasion, as I mentioned."

"No…" Jarus' fear for himself was swiftly replaced by fear for Maya. Innocent, brave, young Maya—she wouldn't know what to do—she would have been defenseless in the hands of these monsters.

At that moment a thunderous explosion shook the hall. Several large rocks dislodged from the ceiling, crashing to the ground. Deathcap let go of Jarus and whirled around, his face showing confusion and fury. "What—"

A guard appeared at the far end of the hall. "Sir—the gunpowder, the barrels the smugglers brought in—it's—it's gone sir, been exploded!"

"Exploded?" Deathcap snarled incredulously. "How the devil has it done that?"

"We don't know, sir," stammered the unfortunate guard. "It seems…a lantern…the fuse fell…took out five of our men—"

Deathcap unleashed a stream of profanities in the Brownae language, which Jarus was rather glad he couldn't understand, and stormed out the door with the guards. The door had barely closed when a slight figure slipped through the door, moving nimbly towards Jarus. Jarus stared in confusion as he recognized the young Brownae.

The slave unlocked the cell and entered. "Hurry," he said as he undid Jarus' bonds. "Get to the courtyard—watch out for the guards. Your friends are already there."

"What…how…" Jarus stammered, totally confused.

"You don't have much time—we bought you as much time as

we could," the Brownae interrupted him, his eyes wide with both excitement and fear.

"We?"

"The Siren—the one in your party. He turned into some sort of beetle and crawled out of his bonds—escaped—"

"Lammar escaped?" Hope started to fill him again.

The little Brownae nodded rapidly. "It's going to be total chaos out there in a moment, but you should be able to find your friends. All of us slaves are escaping in the confusion." His eyes had lit up. "Your leader—the one they call Norrin—he's one of the Guardians of Gayrile? You're going to stop Safacon?"

"Yes… yes, we were going to try," Jarus said slowly, following him out of the cell.

Thankfully his rescuer didn't ask any more questions—they reached the outer door, which hung by one rusted hinge. The young Brownae opened the door and peeked out. "The Siren said to have you meet in the courtyard, just outside the gate. Good luck," he added, then turned and trotted away down the hall.

Jarus stared after him, then turned the other way and bounded up a flight of stairs. The front door had been blown off, and outside he could see the chaos of the courtyard. Guards ran in all directions, some trying to put out the fire in the trees, others dodging large chunks of debris.

A large statue of Deathcap stood in the center of the courtyard, missing an arm. Jarus moved towards it carefully—the guards seemed to be distracted, but he wasn't taking any chances.

"Watch it," came a familiar voice from behind a large rock. Jarus turned to see Lammar, who was watching the confused and panicked guards in amusement.

Jarus ducked down beside him. "What's going on? Where are the others?"

"They're okay—that young Brownae kid got them out. Smart boy," Lammar said approvingly. "They're near the edge of the wood—I came back to find you."

"Is Maya..."

"She's fine," Lammar said. "She was worried for you—apparently the guards questioned her. She didn't talk though—good for Maya!"

"They did the same with me," Jarus said, relieved to hear that she was all right. He paused as a thought occurred to him. "Lammar... hang on. This is Deathcap's palace, right? So...does that mean he still has the Brownae princess... the one he captured from the Chanterelle tribe?"

Lammar thought a moment. "Got a good point there—if we rescued her, we could have the Chanterelle on our side."

"Then what if we rescued her?" Jarus suggested.

The Siren's eyes scanned the courtyard. "Well, I suppose we could try. How will we find her though?"

"I thought I told you to run," came a voice, and they both turned to see the young Brownae slave.

"We're working on a plan," Jarus started.

Lammar interrupted him, getting straight to the point. "Ah, just the Brownae we want to see. I suppose you know where they're holding the Princess Morel?"

The Brownae looked startled. "Well, I—yes, yes I do. Are you going to rescue her?"

"Planning to, yes. And we'd be delighted to have you join us, mister…?" Lammar looked inquiringly at him.

The Brownae bowed slightly. "Porcini Inmana. I can lead you to the princess' cell."

"Inmana?" Lammar repeated. He frowned. "As in…Cedar Inmana, the chieftain of the Chanterelle?"

"Yes…he's my father," the Brownae said shyly.

"Then you're a prince!" Jarus said, startled—the youth hadn't struck him as a princely type.

"Well, yes," Porcini said, looking bashful. "But I'd rather just be Porcini."

"Well, then," Lammar said, starting back toward the fortress entrance, "can you lead us to your sister?"

Porcini nodded, and they wove their way through the wreckage into the halls.

8

❧ ❧ ❧ ❧ ❧ ❧ ❧ ❧ ❧

The Princess

"So…can I ask you a question?" Porcini asked hesitantly as he led Lammar and Jarus down the halls. Most of Deathcap's guards were out in the courtyard trying to round up the escaping slaves, but twice Porcini's quick ears had saved them from being discovered. Now, below ground yet again, it was eerily quiet.

"Just one," Lammar said with a half grin.

"Well, I figured Deathcap might just be uptight about people being in his territory," Porcini said. "He's been in a bad mood since the rain started up again. But he doesn't normally interrogate trespassers—and he definitely doesn't hold them in the most secure cells in the fort."

"Indeed," Lammar said lightly.

"So then I thought, maybe you were one of his rivals," Porcini continued slowly. "But if that were the case, you wouldn't be in the prison cells. You'd be in the torture hall."

"And we weren't," Lammar said.

"No…so in that case," Porcini said, looking at Lammar carefully, "you're some sort of threat to Deathcap—or someone he needs information from."

"Well, that would be closer to the truth," Lammar said.

"Right, well…what are you doing in the Wandering Wood?"

91

Jarus glanced at Lammar, not sure how much they could tell.

Lammar studied the young Brownae for a moment. "We can tell you," he said, "but then you'll need to be joining us, lad. There's great danger afoot and spies all over the place, and if you knew, you would have to come with us."

Porcini's eyes widened, and he nodded eagerly. "I can do that—I want to come with you. But…where are you going?"

Jarus lowered his voice. "The only way to take down Safacon is to find his three Objects of Power—the Jewel, the Ring, and the Knife—and destroy them."

The Brownae's dark eyes widened even more. "The Objects?" he whispered in a mixture of awe and fear. "But I thought those were just tales."

"They're real enough, unfortunately," Lammar said. "And then there's the Serventiri to deal with. We'll need help to do all this— we'll need to join with the Direns first, so we're hoping to reach Flameton as soon as possible."

Porcini was silent for a moment, taking it all in. "Well, my sister and I can lead you through the Wood—but after that, I don't know the area very well," he said.

"We'll take all the help we can get to get out of the Wood," Jarus said fervently.

They walked in silence until Porcini paused at a corner. "Quiet— there's a couple of guards around this corner."

Two Brownaes and a large man were bickering.

"I don't care how much boss wants us to keep her, I ain't guarding her a minute longer," the man said obstinately. "'Specially not alone. She's a lit fuse—you give her the doubt, she'll take you out."

"Very poetic. Either way, we need someone to stay here," one of the Brownaes said wearily. "Deathcap'll skin us alive if any more prisoners escape—especially if she does. She's our bargaining chip against the Chanterelle."

"What about the prince?"

"The prince disappeared right after the powder exploded," the Brownae replied. Porcini grinned at his two comrades. "We can't lose the princess too."

"Shame for Deathcap," snapped the guard. "I hate every second guarding her—she unscrewed a ceiling beam and dropped it on the head of the last guard here, split his skull in half."

"Well, she's not going to do it again," said the other Brownae. "Come on, Leet—we need you to do this."

The guard scowled. "Fine. But I'll expect a pay raise."

"Yes, of course," the first Brownae said, relieved that the man had relented. The two Brownaes turned away, and for an instant Jarus panicked, sure that the guards would walk right past them. But at the last second, there was a crash from down the hall, and the Brownaes turned away sharply, then jogged off in the other direction to investigate the noise.

Porcini, Lammar, and Jarus edged around the wall—Leet the guard stood alone, clutching his sword nervously as he glanced at the door of the cell.

"Why's he so nervous?" Jarus wondered quietly.

At that moment, there was a low clank from above. The guard leapt back just in time—a steel beam plummeted from the ceiling and crashed to the ground, right where he'd been standing.

"Watch the grating next time," a female voice taunted from above in a sing-song manner.

The guard cursed loudly for several moments before running down the hall, shouting for backup.

Jarus looked up in bewilderment. A moment later, a female Brownae climbed lithely down from the beams above and dropped to the ground. Like Porcini, her fur was a rich brown. Her hair was a shade darker and was cropped short. She wore what had once been a fine dress made of feathers and leather, but it was now tattered and dirty. The earrings she wore were made of turquoise.

"Morel, I found—" Porcini started, stepping forward.

The princess whipped around, pointing a short dagger at them.

"—the group that was imprisoned here," Porcini finished, not even fazed.

"Is that them?" the princess asked, nodding at Jarus and Lammar. "Thought you said there were more."

"They're… waiting outside," Jarus stammered. Something about this Brownae princess took his breath away. She was stocky and well-built, and looked like she had spent most of her life fighting. There was a pride, a wildness to her, and also a toughness that he didn't expect. She reminded him of a wildcat with its hackles up.

"A Cooper and a Siren," Morel said slowly, relaxing as she studied them. Her eyes lingered on Lammar. "Surprising. I thought all the Sirens were on the Mainland by now—you didn't stick around long to help once Safacon rose to power."

The cold tone in her voice rattled Jarus, but Lammar only shrugged. "Ah, well, I'd only just settled in, really. Just redone the flooring in the old place—couldn't leave it. My name is Lammar Skytooth, and this is Jarus Puddlepaw of Mata City."

Morel nodded shortly. "Pleased to meet you."

"We'd better get going," Porcini said. "Those guards are going to come back."

Morel nodded again, shouldered a buckskin pack, and followed as they headed toward the courtyard.

. . . . . .

"What took you?" was the first thing Rygal demanded as he saw Lammar.

"Had to get some help—and we picked up some backup," Lammar said, nodding to the two Brownaes.

Norrin looked at them and raised his eyebrows. "It seems we have a few new additions."

"Morel and Porcini Inmana, the princess and prince of the Chanterelle tribe," Jarus said, hoping Maya would be impressed. She did look surprised, at least.

"Brownaes?" Rygal repeated slowly. He looked at Norrin uncertainly.

95

"Don't know if that counts as backup. We don't have time for this…"

"Oh dear," Lammar muttered, as Morel turned to face him sharply.

"Your quest needs help. Do you really have time to pick and choose?" She eyed him hard.

Rygal, who had a splitting headache from the earlier blow and was in a bad mood from the biting gnats, rose to the challenge. "Well, since you're asking, *princess*, I'm afraid this isn't a stroll in your fine woods. We can't be held up every time we need to rescue you from an angry bumblebee."

"Well, *unlike* the Guardians, who dispersed the minute Safacon showed up, I *don't* plan to run," Morel said with practiced politeness that bordered on sarcasm.

"And so far the Brownaes have done a *wonderful* job at taking him down," Rygal said, not bothering to disguise his sarcasm.

"And neither of us can do anything about those old wrongs," Norrin said crisply, throwing a look at both of them. "We must put aside old wrongs and work together if we are to succeed. Is that clear?"

Rygal looked at Norrin. "She…has to come?" he asked with a forced smile.

"Yes," Norrin said wearily. "We can't leave them here."

"Whatever you're all planning," Morel said, "if it involves taking down Safacon, we're coming with you. Our people were forced out of our lands by first Safacon and then Deathcap—besides, our tribe disappeared north after we were taken, and I haven't the faintest idea where they are. We're coming."

"Very well. But I hope you understand that I am in command," Norrin said, studying her. They stared one another down for a moment—Norrin won. "Now, let's get moving. We must leave before Deathcap's warriors come after us."

Porcini led them out, around the courtyard and into the trees. Jarus felt himself relax as they entered the thick wood again. The muggy air and shadowed light felt almost welcoming after the terror of Deathcap's palace. Norrin urged them on, clutching his staff.

"They're coming," Lammar said in a low voice. "Deathcap's warriors. I can hear them."

Rygal stood stiffly, looking at Norrin. "Do we fight?"

In the instant that he asked the question, a dart whistled through the air, missing his neck by inches. They froze. A pack of Brownaes and ruffians slipped silently through the brush, closing them in a circle, weapons lowered at the little group. Through the ranks strode a dark figure, smirking in triumph.

"What a touching reunion," Deathcap sneered. "And how well you tried to escape me."

9

∽ ∽ ∽ ∽ ∽ ∽ ∽ ∽ ∽

Neely

For a moment the entire party considered fighting, but six of the seven quickly decided against it, well aware that they would be shot swiftly if they tried.

The seventh member was, of course, Morel, who ducked away from the nearest soldier and slashed across his shoulder, then lunged at Deathcap. The other guards had ropes around her in an instant.

"Relax, princess," Deathcap said coolly, while Morel screamed several un-princess-like curses at him. "You're going straight back to your cell—this time, somewhere below ground, with no grating. How would you like that, eh?"

Jarus felt a cold fear gripping him. There would be no escape this time. There were too many soldiers, and Deathcap was there too. He looked at Maya as they were pushed back toward the fortress. "Are you okay?"

Maya looked at him and smiled weakly. "I thought you were dead, Jarus—the guards said—" she swallowed hard. "I'm okay. Are you?"

"Yeah, I'm fine," Jarus said. "They told me you were dead too, and that they'd tortured you."

"I didn't have any information they liked," Maya said, taking a deep breath. "But now…we're going to die, aren't we?"

"We can escape again," Jarus said, even though he knew there was little chance of it. Deathcap wouldn't take chances this time. He'd torture them, get the information he needed, and kill them after. Maya's expression told him she knew this too.

The guards forced them to the ground in the center of the courtyard. Jarus hunched down beside Maya and Rygal as the soldiers stripped them of their weapons a second time that day. Morel had stopped shouting, and now knelt silently, her catlike eyes scanning the situation.

Deathcap's eyes glinted as he studied them. "Well, well. Norrin. I expected you, at least, would have the sense not to come charging into my lands."

"We are not here for you, Deathcap," Norrin told him. His voice was quiet, but Jarus could see the hatred in his eyes.

"Then what other reason have you come?" Deathcap spat.

Norrin said nothing.

Deathcap's eyes narrowed. "Then you will die. All of you. One by one, unless Norrin chooses to explain why you're here."

Jarus knew, dimly, that Norrin wasn't going to give Deathcap the information he wanted, because if Norrin did, then the Brownae prince would still kill them. But if Norrin didn't talk, then Deathcap would probably kill them anyway. They were at an impasse, totally at the will of the maddened Brownaes.

"If you must know," said Norrin suddenly, startling everyone with his calm, measured voice, "we are on an expedition through the Wandering Wood. We are passing through, as I have told you. We are going to Flameton."

"Flameton, is it?" Deathcap hissed. "And what is in Flameton that you so desire?"

Norrin hesitated for a split second, at which point Lammar took up the story. "Why, Deathcap, you don't mean to say you've never tasted sanyae steak? It's positively the most tender, delicious meat you will ever taste. In fact, if you let us go, we'll bring you back some."

"Shut up," Deathcap spat, while his guards tried to figure out what on Orlell was a *sanyae*. "You lie. This is no mere expedition—of that I am sure. And you must be going to Flameton in order to rally the Direns to your cause—to rally them against Safacon. Is that it? And the only reason that would prompt that," here his voice became a low snarl, "is if you had found the Jewel of Power…and so you yourself now plan to conquer Gayrile."

Norrin shook his head. "Deathcap, you honestly fascinate me. Tell me, do you think up foolish things to say when you can't fall asleep at night, or do they just come to you on the spur of the moment?"

The fact that Norrin was able to make jokes here, on the verge of death, was admirable, and it completely threw Deathcap's troops. They stared at the wizard in confusion, then looked at their leader.

"No more words, Norrin," Deathcap barked, nodding to the

guards. "Execute them. Execute them all, right here and now. Let their blood be a testimony to their leader's folly."

Norrin's face hardened. "Kill us, Deathcap, and you'll be none the wiser. You're right, this is no mere expedition."

"Then you will die with that feeble hope," Deathcap snarled. "All of you will. None will challenge the reign of Deathcap, wielder of the Knife of Destruction!"

He drew the knife from his belt. Jarus noticed, for the first time, that this was no ordinary dagger. The blade was long and lean, perfectly made, the hilt intricately carved with ancient runes. But the blade itself drew his attention—it was jet black, shining faintly, like a mirror of black glass. But the reflection within was nothing more than swirling smoke.

"By the power of this Knife," Deathcap hissed, raising the blade, "I shall destroy forever the names of these companions. They shall be as ones who have never existed. All of them, gone forever."

He moved toward Norrin. Jarus struggled against his bonds, but there was no chance now—Deathcap would kill them all, and the mission would be over, just like that.

But in that moment, as Norrin stood before the Knife's black blade, a scream drew everyone's attention. Jarus whipped around in time to see a sudden eruption of flame light up the west side of Deathcap's fortress, burning the dry timbers supporting the stone walls. Two guards had fled from the wall, and now pointed upward, shouting.

"Diren! It's one of those nasty Direns!"

Chaos broke out. Jarus was knocked over; he saw Deathcap jump back, the Knife forgotten, and heard him shouting orders at the startled and confused guards. Lammar had slipped out of his bonds in the same second and freed Norrin and Rygal—the Siren pulled him upright.

"Up, Jarus—we're getting out of here, hang on…"

Jarus stumbled after him, looking back. He saw a blue shape wheeling in the sky, the sun glinting off scales, like a dragon… but the body shape was wrong. The guards fired a hail of crossbow bolts at it, and the Diren dropped quickly down into the trees.

"She's doing well," Lammar said, sounding pleased as he watched. "Dangerous decision, but quite brave… as long as she doesn't get herself killed…"

Jarus finally found his voice. "What—what's going on? Who is that? *What* is that?"

Lammar propelled him toward the woods. "Run, Jarus. I'm going back to help. Neely's bought us all the time she can."

Jarus ran to the edge of the fort, then looked back again. The blue creature in the sky was a Diren, he realized—a Diren with blue scales, sending bolts of liquid fire from its fingertips. Its body looked human enough, but taller, with a long tail and two powerful wings beating at the air.

"Wow!" he panted, in awe of their rescuer despite the current situation.

He turned and bounded into the woods, and crashed into Morel. The princess pushed him back, her eyes narrowed as she looked back toward the fortress. She held a short spear. "Where's the wizard?"

"I—don't know," Jarus stammered. "Have you seen Maya? "

"Who?" Morel asked, confused—Jarus realized they hadn't had time for anyone to introduce themselves. This would just add to the chaos, he realized.

"I'm going back," he said. Morel put her paw between his shoulder blades, stopping him.

"Without a weapon? You'd get yourself killed. Come on—I hear voices over here."

Jarus' nose was swollen from Deathcap's punch during his interrogation, so he couldn't scent any of his companions. He followed Morel as they jogged through the underbrush until they found Norrin. The wizard stood with Maya and Porcini, and looked relieved to see them. "There you are, Jarus—Princess, where's Rygal?"

"I'm here," came Rygal's voice, and he appeared through the trees. He carried two of the packs. "I found some of the gear—I couldn't get all of it. I'm guessing the fire destroyed the rest."

"What in the world just happened?" Porcini asked.

"Are we safe?" asked Maya.

"Why are we all so calm about this?" Morel demanded. "Not all Direns are on the side of King Makana—that one could be a rebel."

"Not that one," Rygal told her.

Morel scowled and started to talk again, but stopped abruptly as a winged figure dropped from the sky and landed in the ferns. The Diren straightened slowly, folding her wings. She stood a little taller than Rygal, but did not yet seem fully grown. Her eyes were a vivid violet, and took in the companions in a moment.

A raven landed on the path, then its shape flickered as it transformed back into Lammar. Norrin smiled and stepped forward.

"Ah, it is very good to see you made it back. And how fares Deathcap now?"

"Not well," Lammar said, chuckling. "That was very well-fought," he said, turning to the scaled figure behind him. The young Diren smiled in recognition to Norrin.

"Hello—sorry I could not arrive sooner." Her voice was soft and shy with youth.

Lammar shrugged. "Can't be helped, and we're all very glad you got here when you did."

Norrin moved forward with a smile. "Indeed we are. How are you, Neely?"

"My skies are wide, thank you," Neely replied in the fashion of her people. She looked at the other companions. "Lammar told me you travel to Flameton."

"Indeed we do," Norrin said. "But perhaps we should discuss this later." He turned to the companions. "Come along, all of you. We must put more distance between us and Deathcap's fortress before we rest for the night."

10

The Warriors on the Ridge

About an hour after nightfall, Norrin deemed they had traveled far enough from Deathcap's fortress. They built a fire, and Norrin examined everyone's injuries. Jarus' head still hurt from Deathcap's interrogation. A cool cloth and a drink of water helped the ache.

"What are we going to do now?" Rygal asked after they had all settled down beside the fire and passed around food. "Norrin… Deathcap still has the Knife. How are we going to get it?"

"So you *were* after the Knife?" Morel asked, raising an eyebrow. "I thought you were going to Flameton."

"We are… we're doing both," Jarus said. He looked at Norrin. The wizard held his staff in his hands, his fingers working over the wood.

Finally he looked up. "First, it's important that all of you understand what we plan to do. This is no simple adventure. It will be incredibly dangerous. Even traveling with us may label you as a threat to Safacon. By continuing, I expect that you plan to endure, no matter how difficult it may get."

There was a pause. Jarus looked at Maya. She looked tired, and her fur was matted and dirty, but there was determination in her eyes. And Jarus felt the same. If there was any hope of rescuing his father, it would lie in the fate of this quest.

Norrin looked at each of them, seeing the interest and determination in the seven faces before him. Then he nodded. "Very well, then. It's time you newer joiners learn what we are up against."

He spoke softly as he told the story again, just as he had back in Bridgeport. He told the full story of Safacon, and of the Jewel of Power. Somehow, in the dense woods with the flickering firelight, the story drew Jarus in all over again. He listened with rapt attention.

"But…this Jewel," Morel said, when he had finished. "It seems… well, wasteful to destroy it. Couldn't something like that be useful? To locate the other Objects, or even defeat Safacon himself?"

"If only it could," Norrin said gravely. "But the Jewel…well, it carries a very dark magic around itself. Magic as ancient as when the High Light first wrought the world, the magic brought upon evil entering it. That magic influences the Jewel—gives it an intelligence of sorts, and it uses that intelligence to influence its user."

Jarus frowned, surprised by this information. "Then Safacon is just being used by the Jewel?" He had thought that the Jewel was no more than a weapon.

"In a way," Norrin said, thinking how to explain it. "Well, imagine it this way. Say you have a sword, a good, sturdy weapon that serves you well in combat. But one day imagine that sword tells you that in order to become the greatest warrior in Orlell, you must do certain things, kill certain people. Safacon is no mere victim to the Jewel's power, but he's no fool, either, and so he sees it as an ally."

"And a valuable ally at that," Lammar said grimly.

"But how can that power be destroyed?" Porcini asked, brow furrowed.

"The Jewel's powers are weakened when it is placed upon the Golden Tablet it was made on," Norrin told him. "Strike it then, and it will be destroyed, as will the Ring and the Knife."

A long moment of silence passed. "But… what can we do?" Neely asked, in her soft, hesitant voice. "We are not experienced warriors. Many of us are not yet grown."

"Indeed," Norrin said, his eyes twinkling. "And I admit that very thought has crossed my mind as well. But in the last twenty-four hours, I've watched Jarus take part in rescuing a princess, Maya resist an interrogation, Porcini bravely free a number of prisoners from Deathcap's grasp, and Neely rescue us all from imminent death. Yes, you four may be the least experienced of our party, but your actions show a bravery that Orlell's finest warrior would wish to have."

Jarus felt a glow of pride at this praise. He looked around, studying his companions. Maya, Lammar, Rygal, Morel, Porcini, Neely, and Norrin. All of them had fear in their eyes, nervousness for what was coming. But there was a determination there too, and even a spark of excitement.

"Now," Norrin said, standing, "let's set up camp and rest for the night. We have a long road ahead of us."

......

The following morning saw the eight travelers on the road, heading steadily northwest through the Wandering Wood. A dense fog filled the forest, and birdsong echoed through the trees. The two Brownaes seemed right at home, weaving their way through the ferns that hung over the path.

Rygal had recovered two packs of gear, which contained most of the food and the bed rolls and blankets. He had also managed to regain their weapons. Jarus gratefully accepted his knife, and slung the strap around his shoulders. He had never fought anyone with his knife—only used it as a tool. On a quest like this, he'd probably end up fighting at some point. He made a mental note to ask Rygal or maybe Morel for pointers.

The terrain, which had been generally flat and steady since Deathcap's fortress, was now far more wild, with the ground sloping down into multiple draws and gullies, and then up again. Upon descending into these gullies, Jarus could look up and see paths crisscrossing the slope of the hill. The Wandering Wood was aptly named—were it not for the two Brownaes, Jarus was quite sure they would have been thoroughly lost.

They had been walking for a good three hours, and the fog was just beginning to lift, when Rygal stooped suddenly, studying something on the ground. "Norrin," he called.

Jarus, who walked right behind Rygal, moved around him to look. On the path was a mark—a footprint. Far too big to be a Brownae's. "Humans?" he asked, suddenly hopeful. "Does that mean we're getting close to civilization?"

He was puzzled and a little worried to see the wariness in Rygal's eyes. Norrin wove his way around the waiting companions to reach him. "What is it?"

Rygal pointed at the tracks. "There aren't any settlements in this part of the Wandering Wood, none that we know of, at any rate."

"Might just be rangers," Morel said, still nettled by her earlier disagreement with Rygal.

Rygal threw her a look, then looked down again. "Can't be. Look at the detail in the print—these are very fine boots, definitely high-end."

"Then it's a ranger with nice shoes," Morel said.

"You think it may be the Serventiri?" Norrin asked.

"Yes, I do," Rygal said, a slight flush creeping into his face as he noticed the doubtful expressions of the Brownaes.

"The Serventiri have never come into the Wood," Porcini said slowly, trying not to offend the young warrior in disagreeing.

"It can't be Serventiri, because we would have scented them," Morel said shortly. "Porcini's right—the Serventiri have no reason to come into the Wood."

"Maybe they heard about our expedition," Rygal challenged.

"Not unless Deathcap or one of his warriors told Safacon. And Deathcap hates Safacon even more than we do, so he wouldn't have done that. Anyway, we would have smelled them," Morel argued back.

"Both of you, stop," Norrin said curtly. He studied the footprint, then looked up at Rygal. "It might be Serventiri, but I doubt it. In all likelihood, it was simply Deathcap's ruffians up to no good in this part of the forest."

Rygal got to his feet, frowning deeply, but didn't say anything more as they started on again. Jarus glanced up at him, a little uneasily. "Do…do you think it could be Serventiri?"

"Well, *clearly* it's not," Rygal said sarcastically. He stopped and sighed. "I'm sorry—didn't mean to snap."

Jarus nodded quickly, and they walked on in silence.

It was twenty minutes before Lammar, who had been scouting up ahead, came bounding back to Norrin. "We've got trouble. I can smell a large group camped up on the next ridge."

"Serventiri?" Norrin asked.

"Can't tell—too far away. I can only scent their numbers."

Uneasy glances were exchanged around the company. "Might just be Brownaes," Maya offered finally, though she sounded doubtful.

"If it's Brownaes then it's Deathcap's group, in which case we're even worse off," Morel told her, setting her jaw. She looked at Norrin.

The wizard looked like he was doing some very quick thinking. "We'll veer west. I don't want to risk it. We can't afford a fight, even if it turns out to be nothing."

Porcini led them down the next path that turned right, and they moved along the ridge. Jarus peered across the gully, trying to see the group Lammar smelled, but he could see nothing. His own Cooper nose still felt stuffy from Deathcap's punch, and he could smell very little. The lack of this critical sense made him uneasy.

They had been moving for five minutes when Jarus felt a breeze ruffle his fur on his left side, and he realized the wind had shifted. In the same moment, Neely, Lammar, and the Brownaes all stopped, sniffing the air.

"I...smell them," Neely said slowly, her brow furrowed and her voice uncertain. "They don't smell...normal."

"It's them—it's the Serventiri," Lammar said, pacing furiously back and forth along the path. "Norrin—how are we going to get around them now?"

"Get down!" Morel shouted before Norrin said anything.

They all dropped to the ground just in time—a noise unlike anything Jarus had ever heard came from the ridge, a deafening, crackling *boom*. In the same moment, a tree below them in the gully splintered and fell forward down the slope.

"*Cannons!*" Rygal sputtered, both shocked and horrified. "Where the *blazes* did they get cannons from?"

"Go!" Norrin ordered, and they leaped up and began running along the ridge, weaving around trees and dropping flat any time they heard a shot. Jarus cared very little where the cannons had come from—in all likelihood, Safacon had managed to steal and smuggle them from the Capital army. He ducked behind a tree, peered around the trunk, and got his first look at the Serventiri.

There were close to forty of them in all, he guessed, their white and gray uniforms blending with the misty woods. As they drew closer, he could make out their forms more clearly. They appeared human enough, wearing helmets that covered the top part of their faces. But they moved with jerking, unnatural motions, as though moved by invisible strings, and their faces were frozen in the same lifeless grin, an army of figurines come to life. Their eyes were hollow, shining deep in their sockets, a cold clear blue. The light made them look like skulls.

"Hurry!" Rygal shoved Jarus forward, just in time, as a blast exploded the tree he'd been hiding behind. They had fallen behind the rest of the group, and now ran to catch up. The Serventiri moved steadily forward, watching through lidless eyes.

Norrin brandished his staff, standing between his companions and the gully, and fired a burst of sparks. It sailed over the heads of the warriors and instead crackled into the barrel of the nearest cannon. There was a dull boom from within the mouth, a puff of jet black smoke, and the cannon jolted back with the force, evidently damaged.

The Serventiri stopped, studied the cannon, and then slowly fell back. They did not seem eager to cross the gully, and retreated slowly.

Jarus and Rygal finally caught up with the rest of the companions, who were huddled fearfully on the ridge. "Where's Norrin?" Lammar demanded.

"He's on his way," Rygal panted. "Everyone all right?" He did a quick head count, and thankfully everyone was accounted for.

"Cannons!" Porcini stammered, in shock from the noise and the close encounter. "How did they… how did they get weapons like those…"

"We might have…been able to…steal their guns," Morel panted, out of breath. "They all carried rifles—we could have fought and taken them."

"After what just happened I don't want to hear a single idea out of you, princess," Rygal snapped, his fear making him cross. "If you'd listened to me when I'd seen that footprint, none of this would have happened."

Morel straightened. "All right, I'm sorry. I didn't know the Serventiri had come this far into the Wood. And I didn't know we wouldn't be able to smell them without the wind."

"Oh yes, lovely confession," Rygal growled, still angry. "And we're *lucky* we're all still alive, because we also didn't know that they had firearms!"

"None of us could have guessed that," Morel spat. "But it's good to know they have firearms now, because if we didn't know, we could have been caught unawares instead, with a far nastier result."

"*Good to know?*" Rygal repeated incredulously—Jarus tried to tell him to lay off, but he was far too wound up now. "Good to know? Oh yes, let's look for the bright side of this situation, just in case next time we have to find it after someone's been killed!"

"Quiet!" Norrin barked. The wizard approached, frowning at Rygal and Morel. "None of us could have predicted this. And none of us are to blame. Rygal, I'm glad you noticed the footprint earlier—we might not have been on guard if you hadn't."

"And we might not have been shot at if you all had listened!" Rygal snorted.

"That's enough!" Norrin told him, his eyes blazing. "I don't want to hear another word about it." He glared at both Rygal and Morel, who dropped their eyes.

Norrin glanced back the way they had come, then took a breath. "Now, then, let's keep going. It seems we have diverted from the main path in our fleeing."

"That's the problem, Norrin," Porcini said hesitantly. "I haven't the faintest idea where we are. I don't know where this path leads. The road we need to take is back there," he gestured toward the opposite ridge, "but I don't want to cross the Serventiri again."

"But this path goes west, doesn't it?" Neely said thoughtfully. "Couldn't we just move in a westward direction, and run into the correct path again?"

Norrin smiled at her. "That is a very good point, Neely. And that's exactly what we have to do. It'll take longer, but it's worth avoiding battle."

Slowly, the group started forward again. Jarus had things he wanted to talk about, but seeing Rygal's face pale and drawn with anger, he decided to keep silent.

11

The Edge of the Wood

Despite the tension flowing through the company after the encounter, they saw no sign of the Serventiri the rest of the day, nor that night. Norrin set up a watch system so that everyone took turns during the night, though no one slept much, jumping nervously at any slight noise.

Morning dawned bright and sunny. Rygal had apologized to Jarus and seemed his usual cheerful self, though he was still giving Morel the cold shoulder. The princess herself ignored Rygal whenever she could, and spoke with cold politeness whenever she had to talk to him.

Lammar had gone hunting early in the morning with Porcini, and the two of them returned with two rabbits and three trout from the stream. They enjoyed the hot meal, then started out again.

Breakfast lifted everyone's spirits. After they had finished, it was decided that they would continue northwest, veering around the hill where they'd seen the Serventiri, until they reached either the main road or the desert itself. Jarus could tell that Norrin wasn't entirely sure where they were supposed to go, and even the Brownaes seemed uncertain. The Wood was so large, and Morel explained that these parts had been long inhabited by Deathcap, and hence unexplored by the Chanterelle tribe. Thankfully, however, they saw no sign of Deathcap, nor any of his allies. Neely scouted ahead, soaring over the trees, and brought back the report.

"Maybe he's letting us go now that we're out of his territory," Jarus suggested to Porcini asked they walked.

The young Brownae frowned slightly. "Maybe…but I don't know. Deathcap will be out for revenge—he's not going to give up that easily."

Jarus was left with that unsettling thought as they walked. He pushed Deathcap out of his mind, and thought instead of his father. It would not take long for Safacon to realize that Carus Puddlepaw was nothing more than an unfortunate witness…but then what? Would he kill him? Let him go? Jarus somehow doubted both of those options, but he didn't feel sure.

He was still thinking about it when they took a break sometime after midday. He ate some of the dried rabbit meat from that morning, and drank some water. The liquid was soothing on his parched throat, and he realized how long it had been since he'd had a good swim. No Cooper enjoys being out of water for more than a few days—the last time he'd swum had been in Mata City, which felt like a very long time ago.

He glanced up as discussion broke out around the company. "We should be nearly there now," Rygal was saying, sounding worried.

"We had to back track quite a bit to avoid the Serventiri," Norrin pointed out, but he shook his head. "But I agree. It may be that we took the wrong path."

"But we've been going due west since we saw the Serventiri," Neely said, her scaled brow furrowed. "We can't be that far off, can we?"

"What's going on?" Maya asked softly, hearing only the end of the conversation.

Norrin looked at her. "By our calculations, we should have reached the desert by this point. There's a chance we missed the right path."

Jarus' heart sank. The path they had been following had been crossed by countless others, winding in all directions—there was no telling which one they were supposed to take.

"We're still going west, though," Lammar said, glancing at Neely. "Sooner or later we're bound to run into it, right?"

"That is true," Norrin said, "and unfortunately that's all we can do right now. We will keep going, and stay on this path."

They shouldered the packs and continued on wearily. Jarus was so tired of seeing the same uniform gray-green of the trees and hearing the incessant chatter of birds that he found himself wishing for the desert. This was ironic, considering that one couldn't get much farther from water than a desert. But perhaps they'd have water to swim in at Flameton.

He fell back a little so that he was next to Neely. The young Diren glanced down as he moved next to her.

"Have you ever been to Flameton?" Jarus asked her.

Neely shook her head. "No. I have heard many things about it, however—about King Makana and his mighty warriors. Flameton is said to be a great city." There was a light in her eyes as she said this—excitement of seeing the city of her people.

"And…they'll let us stay? They'll help us?" Jarus asked.

"I believe so. Mind you, King Makana has no love for Safacon. And he supported the Guardians of Gayrile when they were first established. So I think so."

It was mid-afternoon when they stopped. A breeze blew from the east, carrying a familiar and dreaded scent. The Brownaes stiffened.

"Serventiri," Lammar murmured.

"How many?" Rygal asked, his hand on the hilt of his sword.

"I don't know." Lammar sounded agitated. "I think it's the same group from yesterday."

"Hurry," Norrin said, motioning them forward to the cover of the ridge. He covered their retreat, his hands gripping his staff, eyes scanning the forest.

Every muscle in Jarus' body had tensed at the word *Serventiri*, and now he peered anxiously through the trees, watching for the white armor, the hollow glowing eyes.

Then he heard the sound of pounding feet from the left, and Porcini's voice cried out shrilly ahead. "I see them!"

The companions scattered, panicked by the warriors. Jarus' heart was pounding as he careened wildly through the wood, off the path and down the hill. He tripped over a fern and fell flat, then scrambled to his feet again. He could hear shouting, followed by the clang of steel on steel—they were fighting.

In an instant he was mortified with shame. His companions were prepared to fight to the death, and here he was, fleeing into the wilderness. He whipped out his knife and clutched it between his teeth as he charged back up the hill, all four paws skidding in the loose soil.

By the time he reached the path, the sounds had quieted, and he stood uncertainly, listening.

Something came crashing through the underbrush ahead of him and he froze. Rygal came running down the hill, panting. He held his sword tightly.

"Jarus—there you are. Everyone's been scattered."

"The Serventiri…"

"They've been driven back—Norrin sent a few blasts at them and scared them off, and Neely shot some fire at them." Rygal shook his head in admiration. "They didn't like the sight of Neely's fire at all—thank goodness for her."

They moved down the path, calling as loud as they dared for the remaining companions. They found Porcini first, huddled down nervously in the ferns behind Lammar. The Siren bounded out as he saw Rygal.

"Any sign of the others?" he asked.

"No—I don't know." Rygal sounded worried. "I think Morel's with Norrin—I don't know where Maya went."

Jarus felt weak with fear. "Maya..."

They jogged down the path. There was no sign of movement—the Serventiri had vanished. Had they captured Maya? Had they killed her?

"Morel!"

Porcini's shout snapped Jarus back to reality, and he looked up. Morel stood in the middle of the path, panting and bleeding from a cut on her shoulder. Beside her was Maya, shaking with fear.

"What happened?" Lammar asked.

"Serventiri—they cornered us. Norrin drove them away—he's coming," Morel said, sitting down stiffly.

"She's been hurt," Maya said, looking worried. "She saved me—the Serventiri came at us with their swords."

Despite Jarus' frustration with the arrogant princess, he felt a wave of gratitude toward her for saving Maya.

"We might have been able to defeat them," Rygal breathed, looking down the hill. "If we can drive them back, we can kill them."

This time it was Morel that disagreed. "Definitely not. There's too many of them."

Rygal glanced at her, frowning. "We might have. They didn't have their guns." There was a challenge in his tone—Morel, unfortunately, rose to the bait.

"Right, well, guns or not, we'd waste strength and possibly our lives doing it."

"Not finding the bright side now, are we?"

"Will you two knock it off?" Maya said wearily.

"Stay out of this, Maya," Morel snapped.

"Both of you, quiet!" Norrin appeared from down the path, glaring at Rygal and Morel, who both had the grace to stop talking.

"What happened?" Jarus asked him.

"The Serventiri have numbers but little cleverness," Norrin told him. "They have turned back, for now."

"Where's Neely?" Lammar asked.

"Norrin!" The Diren's voice came from the right, over the rise.

Fearful of some new danger, they rushed through the brush and up the slope. Jarus stumbled over a wiry bush—he stared at it in confusion; the tangled branches were foreign in the forest, echoing an entirely different terrain.

He looked up. The trees thinned out gradually. Sunlight streamed in through the leaves, shining down on Neely, who stood silently.

The companions stopped beside the young Diren to look out at the terrain ahead. The greens and grays of the forest faded away here, into a vast expanse of silver-white ground and red rock.

The Wandering Wood was left behind. Before them, stretching on as far as the eye could see, sprawled the great desert.

PART 2

The Ring and the River

12

Across the Desert

The sound of water dripping on wet stone woke the Cooper, laying huddled in the darkness. His jaw ached from the blow that his captors had dealt him upon his witnessing their deeds. Slowly, his mind began to remember what had happened. His neighbors had been robbed…no, not robbed. They'd been taken. He'd seen them dragged onto the human ship in the harbor.

His son…was he dead?

"Glad you're awake."

The sneering voice made him jolt awake. One of the humans who had captured him, with squinting, leering eyes, peered in at him through the barred window. "You're lucky to be alive. Now, I suggest you prepare yourself. You're about to meet our great lord."

"Where are the others? What have you done to them?" Carus demanded.

The man disappeared, and Carus was left in silence, fearful and unsure.

Then the door opened suddenly, and he shrank back. A man stood there, his face wreathed in shadow, his robes glistening silver-gray. The face beneath the hood was lean, chiseled, calculating. His eyes were black, emotionless, without a scrap of pity or kindness.

Those eyes studied the prisoner for a moment without a word. Carus realized in the same breath that this was the leader his captors had spoken of with such reverence.

"Tell me, Cooper," the leader said softly, his voice like ice creeping over a pond in the dead of winter. "Tell me…what do you know of the Jewel?"

· · · · · ·

The sun peaked over the western horizon, painting the sky orange and pink. Jarus stood and stretched. Grains of sand worked their way through his thick brown fur, and he groomed it out as best as he could. He figured he'd have to get used to that—they were, after all, about to cross the desert.

Lammar was keeping guard, his sharp eyes scanning the terrain. Jarus felt a sudden stab of worry. He and Maya were both Coopers, and after days without swimming, their webbed paws had become cracked and painful. But Lammar—he was a Siren, a creature almost entirely adapted to water. How would he manage in the desert?

"Morning," Lammar said as he noticed Jarus awake. "I was about to wake you all. Figured you'd want your rest."

"Thanks," Jarus said, shaking his head to clear it of sleep. He and Lammar studied the great expanse of flat land before them. "How far do you guess it is to Flameton?" Jarus asked finally.

"Not too far," Lammar replied. "On the edge of that mountain range, way out there." He nodded across the expanse. "Maybe two days of travel, maybe less."

"That seems pretty far," Jarus murmured.

"We'll make it," Lammar said with a slight grin. "Good news is that this desert isn't your typical desert, either, not half as hot as the Lago Desert back on the Mainland. It'll be warm, yes, and dry. But we won't be baked."

Once the others awoke, they all settled around the embers of the fire for breakfast. Jarus ate hungrily. The constant walking, as well as the adrenaline from the last few days, left him surprisingly hungry. He took a drink from a water flask and realized how empty it was. It made sense, though—they had left Lammar's house well supplied for five people. Now there were three more mouths to provide for.

"Before we cross the desert, we must find supplies," Norrin told them all. "Very little grows in the desert, and even less is edible. And we will have to refill the water flasks."

"There's a spring down in the draw, where we saw the Serventiri," Morel said. "But we might have to go back farther to find anything to hunt. Near the desert, there aren't many animals."

Norrin looked uneasy, but nodded slowly. "Yes, I suppose you must. But be very cautious. Lammar, go with the Brownaes and try to find provisions."

The three of them disappeared into the forest as the rest of the companions packed up the remaining supplies. Jarus rolled up the mat and stuffed it into his pack. The blanket was tattered and torn by now, but he was grateful for it. The two Brownaes and Neely didn't have anywhere to sleep at all. Though, Morel and Porcini were comfortable enough in a nest of ferns, and Neely wasn't one to complain.

He looked up at Maya's voice. She walked over to him, wearing one of the backpacks. "Neely and I are going over the ridge. It isn't far, and Neely says she thinks there's a spring there. Want to come?"

"No, that's all right. Be careful," Jarus added, glancing between her and Neely.

Maya smiled and nodded. "We will. It's just down there, so we'll be able to call for help if we need it."

"All right, then," Jarus said as she padded away. He pushed the bedroll over by the second pack as his thoughts strayed to Maya. The fear that had filled him yesterday, when they'd been separated by the Serventiri attack… Maya had been fine, thanks to Morel, but somehow, he had felt something more than just relief.

Over the course of this quest, ever since they had left the safety of Mata City behind, he had felt something change in him. Confidence had replaced his usual awkwardness and nervousness when speaking to people, namely Maya. But the one thing that hadn't changed was the fear at the thought of telling her how he felt for her. Fear of how she would respond, fear of what would happen if she didn't feel the same way, or if their newfound friendship would be ruined…

He couldn't bear the idea of risking their relationship, and shook the thoughts out of his head. No, what mattered now was stopping Safacon and rescuing his father, and Maya's father too. Even Hagar would be rescued. He knew that much. Whatever Jarus might think of Hagar Groundrop, no one deserved to die at the hands of Safacon.

Thinking of Hagar brought a bitter taste of jealousy into his mouth, and he forced the thoughts away.

Maya and Neely returned shortly after with the water flasks filled. It was a little while longer before Lammar and the Brownaes were back. They had found a plentiful supply of roots and berries, and Lammar had caught and cleaned more fish.

"Off we go, then," Porcini said cheerfully, lifting one of the packs.

Rygal shouldered the second pack and, following Norrin, the companions left the Wandering Wood. In a few minutes, they had left all trees behind and moved across the vast expanse of flatland. The desert stretched on before them, a great barren waste of silvery ground with large lumps of red rock and the occasional clump of sagebrush. The ground was hard and parched, with a coating of fine white sand dusting the surface.

Jarus fell into place beside Rygal. Both of them took in the terrain in silence for a little while. "Have you ever been to Flameton, Rygal?" Jarus asked at length.

"No," Rygal said, shaking his head. "Norrin has, a while back, but I was very young. I know King Makana offered refuge to the Guardians of Gayrile after Safacon outlawed them. He created safe houses and hiding places throughout the wilderness near the mountains. So I hope he'll join our cause."

"Makana will be on our side," Lammar said from behind them. "It'll be the Diren councilors we'll have to persuade. They fought hard against Safacon, and they lost many lives. They will be wary to fight him again." He frowned, thinking. "If we had the Jewel as proof, of course, we could persuade them easily. Proving the Objects are real, and not just a legend, would leave the Direns no choice but to join our cause."

"But we don't have the Jewel," Jarus said slowly. "So... what are we going to do instead?"

"I'm not sure," Lammar admitted. "I think we all counted on finding the Jewel in the Wandering Wood somehow. But Deathcap interrupted that plan."

The information weighed Jarus down. The thought of persuading the Direns to join their fight, with nothing other than their word, seemed impossible. But they needed the Direns. The Guardians of Gayrile were in hiding or extinct, and there was no other force that could help them.

A covering of clouds streaked the sky, adding to the overall grayness of the desert, and Jarus walked in silent thought for a while, thinking of Safacon, and of the Jewel, and, occasionally, of Maya. Thinking of Maya filled him with a bittersweet happiness. In Mata City, he would have given anything for a chance to spend five minutes with her. Now here they were, traveling together in a foreign land. It would have been pleasant if the circumstances were different, he thought.

By nightfall, Jarus' legs felt weak and his hindquarters ached. He flopped down on the ground, feeling too tired to set up his bedroll. Rygal offered him a drink of water, and he drank eagerly before handing it to Porcini. They ate a small meal of rabbit meat and herbs before settling down for the night.

Food and water gave Jarus more energy, and he set up his mat and groomed through his fur for a moment before laying down. Every part of him felt hot and sticky. His dark fur, ideal for keeping out the chilly Mata City winds, was totally useless out here.

The desert sounds were so different from the sounds from the wood that it took Jarus a while to get used to them. The piping cries from the wrens and other birds echoed across the expanse. Twice he heard the eerie hooting of a sand-owl from far off in the desert.

Maya settled down beside him, her ears flicking this way and that as she listened to the sounds. "You know… if we weren't on our way to start a war, this wouldn't be very unpleasant."

"It's dry, though," Jarus pointed out with a weak grin. "I could definitely use a nice river to swim in."

"That's true," Maya said, smiling slightly.

The two Brownaes sat down beside them, both of them dusted with white sand. Jarus grinned. "You two look like you've been powdered in sugar."

They looked down at themselves, and Morel grinned and shook

her head. "You should see yourself. The trouble of having dark fur, isn't it?"

Jarus looked down at himself, realizing that white sand covered his paws and fur too. He sighed and nodded.

"Still," Porcini said thoughtfully, "there are some things I could get used to out here. Like that." He pointed upward. Jarus looked up, and the scene took his breath away.

There were stars visible above Mata City, of course, but those often clashed with the city lights, or were covered by clouds. Jarus had seen stars in the Wandering Wood, though he hadn't realized how much the trees had covered them. Now, out here, with nothing conflicting with the sky above, the stars were endless, stretching on forever.

The sight made him suddenly feel very small. "I agree, Porcini," he said softly. "I could get used to that."

. . . . . .

By the time the sun peaked over the horizon, the stars had faded away, and the sky was streaked with red and pink. Jarus was awakened by Rygal, and rolled stiffly to his feet. He took a sip of water, and turned to see Rygal studying the magnificent sunrise with a frown.

"What is it?" he asked.

Rygal nodded at the red. "That vivid red comes from a lot of dust particles in the air—it's the sun's rays reflecting off of them, or something like that. Anyway, it won't just be dust…that's a lot of sand."

"Sand?" Jarus repeated, not understanding why this was a concern. "Is that...bad?"

Rygal smiled grimly. "It is if it's a wall of sand blowing right toward us. The big sandstorms out here could easily have us lost."

Jarus gulped nervously. "You think that's what it is?"

"I don't know—I'll ask Norrin." Rygal moved to wake the other companions.

Maya was still asleep, and Jarus nudged her gently until she opened her eyes. Seeing him, she sat up anxiously. "What is it? Is everything all right?"

"Yes, everything's fine," Jarus said, feeling bad for worrying her. "We're about to get going again."

Norrin agreed with Rygal that the sand in the distance was not an immediate concern, but a valid one, and they veered slightly west. Sand covered Jarus' fur, making him itch. He eventually gave up scratching, knowing he wouldn't be able to get it out until they reached Flameton.

They passed around the water flasks. Lammar's voice was rasping and he was very pale. Jarus could tell both dehydration and the general dryness of the place were taking a toll on him. But the Siren was clearly determined to keep going.

Morel was walking with Maya behind him. He thought about the conversation last night. When Morel wasn't fighting with Rygal, she wasn't half bad, he decided. It was frustrating because he liked both Rygal and Morel, and he didn't want to choose between them.

"How did Deathcap capture you?" he asked Morel, falling back in line to walk with them.

Morel looked at him, then sighed. "Deathcap wanted the Jewel of Power, which has been lost for years. Deathcap demanded that he be allowed to search our encampment. When our father refused, Deathcap attacked, hoping to find the Jewel."

"But did your father have the Jewel?" Maya asked.

Porcini shook his head, joining the conversation. "No. But Deathcap didn't believe him. He—he destroyed our camp, killed many of our people, and captured us both as hostages." He swallowed. "He killed our mother."

There was a moment of silence. "I'm sorry," Jarus said softly. He felt bad for bringing the subject up.

Morel shook her head slightly. "Deathcap thinks he can control the world with the Knife of Destruction, but he can't, not without the Jewel. He forgets that the Jewel is more powerful. And more dangerous."

Jarus looked at her in surprise—it sounded like Morel knew more about the Jewel than he'd first thought. "What do you know about the Objects, Morel?" he asked, interested.

The princess frowned slightly. "Well, not much more than what Norrin told us. I know a bit about the Jewel, and how it is used. My father, the chieftain, searched for it briefly after it was lost, hoping for a weapon to stop Deathcap from taking our lands."

"He never found it," Porcini said somberly.

"Deathcap was too powerful with the Knife—too powerful to challenge," Morel said. "Anyway—I agree with Norrin, that the Jewel might have a kind of intelligence. It's controlled by a series of complex spells, a study called Jewel-lore. The user must master the lore before they can hope to use the Jewel."

"That makes it even more ridiculous for Safacon to take my father," Jarus said, suddenly angry. "As if he could expect a couple of Cooper fishermen to know anything like that."

"He can never be too careful," Morel said grimly. "For all Safacon knows, if someone has the Jewel, they are very good at hiding it."

Porcini looked at the two Coopers. "So—Safacon captured your parents?" he verified.

"Our fathers," Maya corrected. "My—one of our friends betrayed us to them."

The way she said this caught Jarus' attention. He had guessed Maya would break off her engagement after what Hagar had done, but now it was suddenly confirmed… and a long dormant hope had suddenly rekindled in his heart. "Wait… are you able to…?" he started, not sure how to ask the question.

Maya looked at him, raising her chin slightly in defiance. "If Hagar still expects me to have him at the end of this, he's very wrong. And if my father disagrees with my decision, that's his mistake."

Jarus stared at her, impressed and surprised. The certainty in her voice, and the strength with which the words were said, were so unlike the Maya Raintail of Mata City that he was in awe. "Really?" he stammered, trying to hide the wild joy at the news.

The Brownaes both looked confused, but Maya didn't say any more. Porcini asked a few more questions about Mata City, which Maya answered. Jarus walked in silence for awhile, not trusting himself to speak, or to find the right words.

· · · · · ·

Norrin woke them all an hour before dawn. "Up, everyone. We're nearly there. But there's a storm coming our way."

Jarus was wide awake in a moment, and they packed up camp as quickly as they could. The wind had picked up, blowing sand into Jarus' ears and eyes, and tugging on his fur.

"We'll move to the rocks," Norrin said. He was surprisingly calm, though Jarus figured he'd dealt with worse issues than sandstorms.

"What do we do if it comes this way?" Jarus asked Rygal as they headed toward the cliffs. The flat desert land was interrupted by a group of huge plateaus. In front of them was a channel of rock, looking like the hunched wings of some great dragon, standing like a gateway before they reached the plateaus. Then they would have to climb.

Rygal glanced back at the flatlands. "If we were caught out in the desert, it could be dangerous. Sandstorms can get big out here. But we'll be all right in the rocks. And Flameton isn't far ahead of us."

The thought was heartening, and Jarus followed as they entered the channel of cliffs. The heavy shadows made it hard to see far ahead, but he was grateful for the shade. The sun was rising steadily to the east, bright red as it shone through the storm in the distance.

"It missed us," Rygal said, sounding satisfied.

Jarus noticed Neely was looking around, her brow furrowed. "Are we close to Flameton?" he asked her.

"Yes, I believe so," Neely said slowly, frowning, "but there is something else. Something is off. Some scent in the air."

"It's not Direns?" Rygal asked.

"No, not Direns. I… the wind. There are too many scents being blown around." Neely sounded frustrated.

Morel paused a moment, listening. "I hear something. On the ridge above us. I can't catch the scent either."

"Maybe they're Diren scouts," Jarus suggested, not sure what else would be out here. Beyond the desert, the wasteland was desolate and lifeless, miles of red rock.

Porcini's shout made Jarus turn. The young Brownae had climbed up the side of the rock, peering beyond, his face aglow with excitement. "Norrin—I see it—it's so beautiful!"

"What? What is it?" Morel demanded, as they all started forward.

The haze of sand cleared slightly. Jarus craned his neck, trying to see past the edge of the ridge. On one of the plateaus beyond, maybe a half-mile or so away, he could see the spires of a castle, flags snapping in the breeze.

"Flameton!" Porcini cried happily. "It's just over there—past the—"

Then his eyes landed on something ahead, and he screamed. Jarus followed his gaze and felt his heart stop.

Serventiri. Close to twenty of them, advancing gradually on the road at the top of the cliff, cutting them off from the city.

13

Soldiers and Stones

Porcini stood frozen at the top of the ridge, his eyes wide with fear. The Serventiri had stopped in surprise and confusion at the sight of the young Brownae, but now advanced, their hollow eyes shining with wicked triumph.

"Porcini!" Morel cried, and lunged up the rocks towards her brother. Neely took to the air, swooping down at the Serventiri. Jarus saw a flash of flame, heard a shout from one of the warriors—

"Run!" Norrin ordered, and they began to climb. Morel reached Porcini, then disappeared from sight. Jarus could hear shouts and crashes, and knew the battle had begun.

He reached the top of the ridge and looked around, taking in the situation. The canyon they had entered to avoid the sandstorm was only part of a labyrinth of cliffs and slopes that made up the base of the plateaus. The path they were following wound gradually up the cliffs in a series of switchbacks before leveling out, leading them through a second row of towering cliffs that marked the way to Flameton.

Jarus saw Morel reach the road above, brandishing her spear, defending the unarmed Porcini. Neely had swept down beside her and shot a plume of fire from her hands. The Serventiri stepped back in surprise—clearly, they hadn't expected the Diren's attack. But they recovered quickly.

Norrin shot a plume of sparks at them before they reached Morel, causing them to fall back again. "Go! Through the cliffs!" the wizard ordered.

Jarus stumbled to follow Maya up the rocks to the road above, bounding toward the city. He felt so useless—his companions were outnumbered, and all he had was his little knife—and besides, he didn't know how to fight with it!

An odd cracking sound came from above, followed by a rumbling slide of soil and rocks. Jarus looked up. He could see a second group of Serventiri on the ridge high above. They had broken loose a slab of slate from the cliffside, sending it plummeting straight at them.

"Watch out!" Jarus shouted, pulling Maya back. The huge rock plunged into the road and shattered with a magnified sound of breaking pottery.

"Run!" Maya screamed. They ran, dodging the shards of stone in the path. A second grinding crack came from above, and Jarus shoved Maya out of the way, then fell back against the opposite cliffside as the slab crashed down between them. He felt the wind of its fall on his face as it barely missed him, and he collapsed, shaking.

By now they had all reached the upper road, and had begun the treacherous journey through the narrow cliffs. The Serventiri above them continued to hack at the cliffside, sending occasional slides down at them. On the opposite side of the road from Jarus, Lammar and Porcini reached Maya, crouching beside her in the shelter of the cliff. Lammar was weakened and pale from the trek through the desert and dehydration.

Jarus looked back, towards the battle on the ridge below. He saw the spinning, sparking blur of Norrin's staff through the dust, and knew the wizard was still fighting. Neely had joined him, the occasional blasts of fire lighting the rocks alongside the yellow sparks. Rygal was with them. Morel had taken a rifle from a fallen Serventiri, shooting down anyone that tried to follow them.

"Come on," Lammar panted, standing. "We must get help." He and Porcini ran along the road towards the city, keeping to the edges to avoid the falling slate. Maya started to follow, then looked back uncertainly.

"Go—I'll follow," Jarus told her, and she ran after Lammar. He paused, hesitating again as he watched his four companions fighting. But they were drastically outnumbered. Lammar was too weak to fight, Porcini and Maya were unarmed, but Jarus… no, he had no real excuse. Taking a deep breath, he clutched his knife between his teeth and raced to Rygal's side.

Norrin's staff spun in his hands, a glittering pinwheel of sparks that formed a shield as they retreated. Jarus moved into place beside Rygal. The tall young warrior was panting but seemed unhurt. A strange purple-red blood streaked his sword—the Serventiri's blood. The odd artificial scent of the Serventiri, the metallic reek of fresh blood, and the growing stench of death assaulted Jarus' sense of smell.

Jarus had barely reached them when five Serventiri lunged forward, four of them brandishing swords and the fifth bearing a rifle. Rygal rammed his sword through the first warrior's chest, but two others charged past him, straight at Jarus.

The attack came so fast Jarus barely had time to react. He saw the warrior's sword come up, poised to strike him down—he lunged forward, out of the way, and plunged his knife into the warrior's side.

The Serventiri jerked sideways, swinging its arm against Jarus' head in a blow that sent his ears ringing. The warrior, injured and angry, lunged at him again. Jarus slashed through the slits in the Serventiri's armor as the body crashed down on him. He shoved it away, shaking. There was a sharp crack as Morel shot the second warrior, who had lunged at Jarus' turned back, followed by a dull thud as the bodies hit the ground.

The Serventiri lay on the rocks, the blue light in its hollow eyes extinguished, like a candle that had been blown out. Jarus' heart was pounding, his whole body shaking. His stomach heaved from the close encounter, nausea from the attack and from the purple-red blood that covered his paws and pooled on the ground.

Morel grabbed his shoulders—he could hear her speaking something, but all that filled his head was the chilling realization of what he had just done. He had killed. He had killed a living creature, not an animal, but a person…

"Hey—hey, listen to me!" Jarus' vision focused on Morel's face. "Get to the city. Run now."

"I just… I just…" Jarus stammered breathlessly, sickened.

"They're not real, Jarus! Now go!" the princess snapped, turning back to the battle. It was easier for her, she had probably fought and killed many times. Jarus stumbled back. The horror of battle up close chilled him to the core. He'd seen it before, at Deathcap's palace, or during the encounters with the Serventiri in the forest, but that had always been from a distance, where he didn't see or hear or smell the actual killing.

"Hold on, Jarus!" Rygal warned, and Jarus finally snapped out of his daze. They had reached the channel of cliffs. The Serventiri above were already dislodging more slabs to break loose on top of them.

"Heads up!" Morel shouted, and they ran to the edge of the walls as another slab crashed down on the road. Norrin fired sparks at the Serventiri above, causing one to fall, but the others continued hacking at the brittle slates.

Neely dropped to the ground beside them, gasping for breath. "They shoot for my wings—I cannot fly up there."

"Don't worry," Norrin told her gently. "I need you to fly to Flameton, as fast as you can. Help the other three get there. And see if the Direns there will come help us."

Neely nodded shakily and sprang away.

Another shower of huge rocks hit the road. Jarus coughed

through the dust, trembling in fear. He and Norrin edged along the cliff wall, slowly leaving the Serventiri on the ridge behind. For a moment, Jarus was sure they would make it.

But then he saw Morel.

Thinking back, Jarus realized she must have dodged to the opposite wall when the first slate of rock had fallen. Now she was pinned under the ledge, trapped between the cliffside and the huge chunks of stone from the last rock fall. The Serventiri advanced steadily, their eyes filled with triumph.

"Morel!"

Rygal stopped, turned, and saw her in the same moment that Jarus shouted her name. Norrin started to follow, but a hail of gunfire forced him and Jarus back against the cliff wall. Jarus huddled behind the wizard as Norrin spun the staff again, forming a shield.

Through the dust and sparks, Jarus saw Rygal reach Morel and haul the rocks out of the way. He saw him order Morel to run, then turn and engage the first group of Serventiri, all of them slashing viciously at him. One of the Serventiri above them sent a boulder rolling down at Morel—Norrin blasted it to pieces before it hit her.

Rygal retreated slowly, the soldiers pressing in on him. "Come on!" Jarus shouted at him.

"Get out of there, Rygal!" Norrin ordered, his voice tense with fear.

"Hang on—let them come!" Rygal yelled over his shoulder. Jarus heard the cracking slide again, and looked up to see a huge slab beginning to break away from the cliffside—it would crush Rygal the minute he tried to run.

A soldier charged forward, knocking Rygal to the ground, brandishing a knife over him—Morel shot him down before the knife reached Rygal. Rygal kicked the body off him, sprang to his feet, and ran. The Serventiri charged after him.

He wouldn't make it—they would kill him.

"Rygal!" Jarus shouted.

The Serventiri above let the stone fall—Norrin pushed Jarus and Morel back, out of the way.

The huge slab plunged into the road, directly on top of the Serventiri who had followed Rygal into the channel. The impact of the falling stone cracked the road in two. Rygal leapt for the other side of the road, fell to his knees, and disappeared in a cloud of dust and shards of stone.

"Go!" Norrin ordered as he ran back towards the broken road. Jarus stumbled after Morel towards the city, fear for Rygal chilling his core. Rygal had to be all right… he had to be…

"He's alive," Morel panted, looking back. Jarus turned to see Norrin and Rygal emerge from the channel of rocks. Rygal was limping and clutching his leg awkwardly, leaning on Norrin's shoulder for support.

"Are you okay?" Jarus stammered as Rygal dropped to the ground beside him. Blood soaked through Rygal's pant leg above his knee, and he was covered in dust. He scowled and looked back.

"No, I'm not. I lost my sword, darn it."

"We have to keep going," Norrin said, helping Rygal to his feet again. Rygal winced, but didn't say anything. "What were you thinking? You might have been killed," Norrin scolded him as they started down the road.

"I… got them smashed," Rygal panted. He was pale from the shock, but managed a weak grin. "The whole lot of 'em. But it smashed my sword too."

"You are lucky it didn't smash your head," Norrin told him, but he looked relieved and even a little proud of him.

They had nearly left the maze of cliffs behind, with the plateau up and in front of them, when a shot split the air. Jarus turned, feeling his stomach twist. The Serventiri that had been breaking the slabs had now reached the road, and were advancing after them.

Morel stepped forward, raising her spear as she set her jaw, but she never needed to use it.

A garrison of Direns, their scales glittering, fire flashing from their palms, swept down on the road, cutting off the Serventiri. "Yes!" Rygal breathed, hope coming back into his eyes.

The four companions fell back, exhausted, as the defending Diren warriors clashed with the attackers. It was a short fight—at seeing the Direns, the remaining Serventiri turned and fled down the rocks.

One of the Direns landed and moved towards them. His scales were red like the sun in a sandstorm, and he clasped a hand to his armored chest in salute. "Sir. I assume you are the one called Norrin."

"I am," Norrin said, shaking the tall Diren's hand and smiling tiredly. "And I assume you come from Flameton."

The Diren nodded and bowed slightly. "Lieutenant Casper Evenstone, at your service. The rest of your companions reached us a little while ago, with news of Serventiri on the South Step. Forgive us for not coming sooner to your aid."

"We're glad you're here at all," Rygal panted with a weak grin.

"Thank you for your help," Norrin said. "Forgive our hurry, but several of us are injured, and we bring urgent matters to the king."

The Diren soldier nodded. "Of course—come, then." He took Rygal's arm and supported him the rest of the way to the city gates.

14

∽ ∽ ∽ ∽ ∽ ∽ ∽ ∽ ∽

The Palace of the Direns

Jarus followed the tall Diren lieutenant along the road towards the city. His heart was still pounding in shock from the fight with the Serventiri. The horror of battle, the blood, the death… that was something he would never get used to, no matter how many times he experienced it. But he guessed he would experience it again before this journey was over.

The sight of the castle pushed the dark thoughts out of his mind for a moment as they reached the city.

Back in Mata City, Jarus had grown used to the familiar sight of Castle Mata, which overlooked the northern bay. That had been a simple, utilitarian structure, made of gray stones that blended with the overall grayness of the coast.

The castle of Flameton stood in a magnificent peak of gold and red stone. Five towers formed a cluster, the tallest in the center. It was made from the same red rocks as the canyon they had just passed through, with elaborate carvings decorating the stone walls. Jarus had never seen anything like it.

"It's beautiful," he murmured, awestruck.

Lieutenant Casper heard him, and smiled. "It has withstood the attacks of our enemies for centuries. Longer even than Caer Sia has

148

stood. I have no doubt it will continue to do so."

He nodded to the guards as they drew close, and the two burly Direns swung open the heavy gates. Casper turned to one of them, a Diren with yellow scales. "Gaeorn, please escort our guests into the palace. And see that their wounds are tended to."

The guard nodded. "Of course, Lieutenant. Have the Serventiri been defeated?"

"I believe so, but I must be sure before I report to General Hawkblaze. I will return to my soldiers at once."

Gaeorn led them inside the palace as Casper lifted into the air, his powerful wings carrying him back toward the scene of the battle. "You will speak with King Makana?" he asked Norrin, who nodded.

"Yes, as soon as possible. I have important news for him," Norrin said. "But first, my friends need medical attention."

"Of course," the Diren said. "Come, I will escort them to the hospital."

Gaeorn called for the nurses as they walked up a short flight of stairs, down a hall, and into a large room lit with gentle white light. Any wounds Jarus had received in the battle paled in comparison to Rygal's, so he protested at first as a few nurses offered to take him inside. "I'm all right. I'm not hurt."

"This is not the time to be brave, Jarus," Norrin said gently. "The king will see us all after."

Two female Direns took Morel to treat her injuries, while Jarus and Rygal headed into a separate room filled with steam. Lammar stood inside, and looked up as they entered. "What happened?" he asked Rygal immediately, seeing his blood-soaked leg.

"I'll be fine," Rygal said quickly, forcing a smile as the servants examined the injury.

"I didn't ask you that—I asked what happened," Lammar said with a withering look, but he was clearly relieved to see them all alive.

"Maya— " Jarus started, realizing with a jolt that he hadn't seen her.

"She's safe. She's in the girl's side of the hospital," Lammar reassured him. He threw Jarus a curious look, clearly catching Jarus' tone, but thankfully didn't say any more. That was good, since Jarus didn't know how to explain his feelings.

The servants drew water for three basins for a hot bath, each separated by a curtain for privacy. Jarus settled into his with a sigh of relief. The warm sudsy water washed through his fur, working out the particles of sand and grime that had matted it for the last few weeks. "How are you doing?" he called to Lammar as the Siren settled into his own bath. Lammar was still pale from the dryness of the desert, but he looked a little stronger.

"Better, now that you're all here," Lammar said. "And there's to be a feast in a few hours. Honestly, I couldn't be better."

"Except for the Serventiri still on our trail," Rygal grumbled from the other bath. The Diren servants had neatly cleaned, stitched, and bandaged the wound, and then left the room. "How'd they know where to find us? We left them behind in the Wandering Wood. There's no way they can be tracking us this accurately."

"We're a big group," Lammar pointed out. "That many tracks are not easily disguised." He paused thoughtfully. "Still, I agree that it's strange. Norrin and I talked about it yesterday. Perhaps King Makana will know."

"Well, I still lost my sword," Rygal muttered, obviously upset about it.

Lammar grinned at him. "Couldn't have done it in a better place. Diren-made swords are some of the best in the north."

After Jarus finished his bath and dried off, he headed back into the main room of the hospital, where a nurse checked his wounds. He had received a cut along his forearm from the fight, and the soft pads of his front paws were cracked and bruised. The nurse bandaged the cut and rubbed a soothing balm on the dry pads of his paws, which eased the pain. The nurse instructed him to sit still to let the balm soak in, so he lay on a small cot against the wall, allowing his body to relax.

Morel appeared through a door from the other side of the hospital. There was a clean white wrap around her head, and a bandage on her shoulder. "You all right?" she asked him.

"Yeah," Jarus said, sitting up stiffly.

Morel sat on a bench across from him. "Maya asked about you," she said after a few moments.

Jarus looked up. "She did? Is she okay?"

"Yes, she's fine. She only had a few small injuries," Morel told him.

There was a brief silence. "I never thanked you—for saving her from the Serventiri," Jarus said finally, looking up at the Brownae princess. "In the Wandering Wood."

Morel shook her head shortly. "Don't worry about it. In the Chanterelle, that is our way."

"Well, thanks," Jarus persisted. He thought he saw a slight smile cross her face, and knew she was pleased.

A servant entered and bowed slightly to them. "If you please, King Makana has requested your presence." He moved to deliver the message to the others.

Jarus nodded and stood as Rygal and Lammar emerged. Morel slung her battered leather sack around her shoulders again. She hardly ever put it down, Jarus thought absently, though maybe years of constantly moving around the Wood were responsible.

The four of them followed the servant down the hall and away from the hospital. Rygal leaned on a crutch and walked a little slower than the others, so Jarus slowed his pace. "They've welcomed us quick," he commented quietly to Rygal as they walked.

"I'm not too surprised. King Makana is well known for welcoming travelers," Rygal said in the same lowered tone. "No, it'll be persuading the council members to join the fight against Safacon that might prove difficult. Makana must have the support of at least five out of his six councilors before he can help us."

A glorious smell reached Jarus' nose as they entered the king's dining hall. A long table spanned the length of the room. Bronze platters and dishes held rich and fine foods, foods Jarus had never imagined eating.

The other companions were already seated, except for Norrin, who Jarus guessed was still talking with Makana. Maya looked up and saw him.

"Are you all right?" she asked at the same time as Jarus.

"Yes," they both replied together, then stopped awkwardly.

"I didn't mean to leave you," Jarus told her. "The others were outnumbered... I wanted to help."

"I know—I was worried," Maya said as Jarus hopped up into the chair next to her.

"We're here, though," Jarus said, changing the subject. He looked around the room in awe. A chandelier boasting hundreds of twinkling candles lit the room in glowing light. "Have you ever seen anything like this?"

"No," Maya admitted. "It's beautiful."

Conversation paused as a herald entered. "Guests of Flameton, our mighty King Makana." He bowed as a tall Diren entered.

The other companions stood and bowed, and Jarus quickly did the same. He stared at the Diren king in awe. His powerful wings were folded elegantly against his back, framing his tall form. His scales were midnight blue, glittering in the candlelight. His eyes were golden, and studied the companions in turn. There was something in his eyes—a compassion and calm—that somehow put

Jarus at ease.

"Welcome, friends," Makana said. His voice was deep and soft, with the slight purr of the Diren's accent present. "I am very glad to see you all here. But before we discuss your quest," he motioned to the table, smiling slightly, "let us eat, yes?"

There was a ripple of amused agreement, and they all sat down again. King Makana turned to usher in a female Diren with rose-gold scales, who was introduced as Queen Sirsha.

The food, like everything in Flameton, was unlike any Jarus had ever seen, or tasted. There was a roasted lamb, served with spiced flatbread and a salad of greens, olives, and sheep's cheese. Jarus ate hungrily, relishing the taste of the rich food. After days of eating dried meat and bread, it tasted especially good.

He had finished his second plate, so stuffed he could barely breathe, when King Makana stood.

"Norrin has told me of your quest," he said. "I admire each of you for your bravery. What you seek to accomplish will be no easy thing."

"Not without help," Lammar said, glancing at Norrin.

Makana nodded slowly. "Yes. So Norrin has said." He paused. "Safacon has been a threat to our people for decades. He has robbed us of our rightful place and forced us into submission. He must be stopped, and I am ready to lead my army into battle against him."

"Then… you'll help us?" Jarus asked, unable to keep quiet any longer.

The king turned his golden eyes on him. "I am prepared to. But as is the fashion of our people, I cannot order them to fight. They must choose. That is why I need the support of the six councilors, who will come to council tomorrow."

"With all due respect, your highness, what more persuasion do they need?" Morel asked, straightening. "Safacon will kill us all if he isn't stopped soon. My people have lost much of our lands, simply because our allies the Direns have refused to help thus far."

Makana met her angry gaze, his face calm, and Morel dropped her eyes. "I am on your side, princess," he said gently. "You must understand what war with Safacon could cost us. Overthrowing him and his army, possibly stirring up trouble again with the humans. That is a cost that the councilors weigh very heavily. Besides that," he hesitated a moment, "they doubt the power of Safacon."

"If we brought the Jewel, they might listen," Norrin said. He sounded very tired. "Without it, I fear it may be more difficult to persuade them."

"Yes," Makana said. "But I am their king, and they will listen to what I have to say. Beyond that, they will listen to your stories. Especially yours, Norrin. You alone have seen the Jewel in its power."

"I have," Norrin said quietly. "In ways I do not like to remember."

"The council will take place tomorrow morning," Makana said, looking at them all. "Do not distress yourselves with these matters until then. In the meantime, rest well. My servants will lead you to your bedchambers."

Jarus left the table, feeling filled and cheerful for the first time since they had left Lammar's home. Maya smiled a good night to him, which made his mood all the lighter, and he all but skipped up the stairs to the guest quarters. Two rooms had been set up, with the five men in one and the three girls in the other. Beds were prepared for each of them, and Jarus lay down contentedly on his, breathing in the pleasant smell of clean sheets.

"You seem to be in a good mood," Lammar said, curling up in the bed to his right.

"I'm glad we made it here," Jarus said, yawning.

"Mm," Lammar said. "And that Maya is here too?"

Jarus choked on his yawn. "Maya?" he repeated, a little too quickly. "What do you mean?"

"Let him alone, Lammar," Rygal said from the bed to Jarus' left. "He's not ready to talk about that."

"*I* think he is," Lammar said, a slightly mischievous light coming into his eyes. "Come on, you can't pretend you haven't noticed, Rygal."

"Noticed what?" Jarus demanded indignantly.

"Of course I noticed—I didn't think you were going to tease him about it, though," Rygal said, blowing out his candle and rolling over, as if trying to shut out the Siren's grin. But Jarus could hear a definite note of humor in Rygal's voice.

"Noticed what?" he demanded again.

"I think Maya likes you," Porcini said in his soft, matter-of-fact tone.

"No," Jarus said, fighting to keep his voice level, and to hide his own hope that Porcini was right. "She doesn't. She's…engaged. To someone else."

"I don't know," Lammar said, settling down. "She might be having second thoughts."

"She…is?"

"To bed," Norrin called, blowing out the light.

And so Jarus was left in the darkness, knowing, thanks to Lammar, that he wouldn't sleep a wink.

15

A Light in the Library

Jarus was dreaming. His father was trapped between the towering cliffs, as Serventiri rained rocks down on him from above. Jarus screamed for him to run, and then his father became Maya, about to be crushed, crying out his name…

"Jarus! Jarus!"

The hissing whisper snapped him awake. He lay there in confusion for a moment, then realized with a jolt of surprise that Maya was sitting beside him, shaking him awake.

"W-what's going on? Is the council happening?"

"No, it's the middle of the night," Maya said impatiently. She had brought in a candle and set it beside Jarus' pillow. The low snoring from the other side of the room told Jarus that everyone else was still asleep.

"What is it?" Jarus asked her, sitting up and rubbing sleep from his eyes.

"It's Morel. I don't know—something's wrong."

"Is she all right?" Jarus felt a jolt of fear. Had Deathcap infiltrated the castle?

"Yes—I mean, she's not in danger. Jarus, I don't know. She got up a few minutes ago, picked up her bag, and headed out—I don't know where she's gone. But…Jarus, she had something in her bag. I don't know what it was, but it made me feel…bad." She stopped, looking frustrated as she searched for the words.

Jarus looked at her, bewildered, and wondering what in Orlell the Brownae princess was up to. Surely she hadn't run away…

"Well, let's go find her," he said finally, deciding that was probably what Maya wanted to do. She looked a little uneasy but nodded, and taking the candle, they hopped down from the bed and walked through the halls.

The castle was eerily silent. The lanterns still burned along the walls, casting uncertain shadows across the stone walls. Jarus kept his ears pricked up, listening intently. Aside from the soft breathing coming from a few rooms, he heard nothing.

"Where do you think she went?" he asked.

"I saw her go down this way," Maya said, turning down a flight of stairs. She paused, listening, outside a large door. Candlelight flickered from under the door.

Then she froze. "Someone's coming."

They both leapt back, huddling into the shadows, as the sounds of footsteps on the stairs drew nearer. Jarus watched as Porcini, his brow furrowed with worry, reached the door. He set down his lantern and tugged open the heavy door, panting slightly. As the young Brownae slipped inside, the two Coopers rushed forward, through the door and into the room. Jarus pushed Maya toward a large sofa, and they crept under it.

They were in a great library, richly furnished, and smelling pleasantly of old books and pine wood. Shelves and shelves of books stretched out as far as Jarus could see, thick books with strange runes on them.

The area they had entered was a small sitting area—in addition to the sofa, there were two chairs and a desk. Jarus could imagine learned scholars coming here and studying late into the night. Except now there was no one here except the Coopers, and the Brownaes.

"What are you doing?" came Porcini's anxious voice. Jarus saw the young Brownae prince move across the room toward someone curled up in the chair.

"They can't do this, Porcini. They can't." It was Morel's voice. "It's evil, I know it is, Porcini, but—they can't do it."

She was holding something close to her, her paws trembling slightly. A ragged bundle, no bigger than an egg.

"But Norrin's right—it'll consume you, like it did Safacon. You can't control it," Porcini said hesitantly.

"I know," Morel said quietly. "But maybe…if I can learn more of the spells…study some more…then I can bring her back, Porcini."

"But if it can't…its power will consume you. You remember that—all the studying you've done—you know it will destroy you if you try to use it."

"None of us can know that for sure."

Morel cradled the bundle, her eyes glazed and distant. She held the object with both desperation and fear, like a sleeping snake that would bite should she displease it.

An odd feeling filled Jarus, a sickening urge to do something. He suddenly felt as if he could step out and seize the object, hold it close, and it would bend to his will. He would become the most powerful being on Orlell with that object. Memories of the blood and carnage he had witnessed yesterday, with the Serventiri being killed, with Rygal being hurt, flooded through his brain, this time without a fragment of empathy. Death was good. Pain was good. They could all die as long as ultimately, he survived.

He shook his head, suddenly shivering. Where had those thoughts come from? What was Morel holding?

Morel removed one of the wrappings, her face illuminated by a blue glow. "Look at it, Porcini," she whispered. "Isn't it beautiful?"

The blue light flooded through the room, and Jarus felt sick. He did not want to look at the light. He wanted to run and hide, sick with shame by the thoughts that had filled his mind.

Porcini wrapped it again. "Morel—you can't. Safacon can see through it, you know—he'll know where we are."

Morel nodded, clutching the bundle to her chest again. "It needs to be destroyed. I know this. It's a thing of utter evil. But…if it's destroyed…oh, Porcini, don't you miss her at all?"

Jarus didn't know who they were talking about now. But he realized, now, what Morel held. It was the Jewel of Power, created by

Safacon, kept by Morel all this time.

He felt a sudden surge of frustration. How long would she have let them search for it? How many of them would have died before she revealed her secret?

Jarus shook his head, forcing the thoughts away. No—right now, something had to be done.

He moved over to Maya, who was watching wide-eyed in shock. "I'm going to talk to them," he whispered in her ear.

Maya shook her head rapidly. "No—what will you do—they'll fight you."

"I don't think they will," Jarus said. He had heard the note of desperation in the voices of the two Brownaes. They needed something, needed it desperately from the Jewel. That was why Morel had kept it secret.

"Be careful," Maya said softly.

Jarus crept out carefully into the shadows, keeping his eyes on the Brownaes. They both sat with a wretched silence that spoke quite clearly of their desperation. They needed something, something only the Jewel's dark magic could give them.

He took a deep breath, then nudged over a stack of books so that they clattered to the floor. Both Brownaes looked up sharply, Porcini shrinking back like a guilty child, Morel with defiance.

"You," she said slowly.

Jarus didn't take another step. "How long have you had it?"

"Too long," Morel said quietly.

"Why didn't you tell us?"

"What would you have done if I had?"

Jarus hesitated, imagining Norrin's frustration, and Rygal's anger, and the distrust from the others if she had done that. Morel nodded as he hesitated.

Porcini stepped forward slowly. "Jarus…you don't understand. We—she didn't keep it for her own good. It's nothing like that. It… has something we thought it could do."

"And it's worth risking the lives of the entire quest?" Jarus snapped, angry again.

Morel's eyes hardened. "You have such a narrow mind, don't you, Cooper? For you, everything has to be good or bad, right or wrong. Well, sometimes things can be both."

"And sometimes it's very dangerous to blur the lines between right and wrong," Jarus shot back. He took a breath. "I'm not going to fight you. I don't want the Jewel any more than you say you do. I just want to know why."

"We both do," Maya said, emerging from beneath the couch.

Morel hesitated, then lowered her head. "The Jewel…it was found, by a Brownae. That Brownae took it, not understanding what it was. Eventually, she realized that the Jewel was a thing of evil, and had to be destroyed, but she didn't know how. Then came the day that Deathcap attacked."

Morel paused, and Porcini continued the story. "Deathcap threatened to kill us both if our tribe didn't hand over the Jewel. But my father didn't know we had it."

"So the Brownae who had found it—our mother," Morel said, "was killed keeping the Jewel hidden from Deathcap. She gave it to me before she allowed Deathcap's troops to take her. They murdered her. But she wouldn't allow Deathcap to have it."

"Your mother…" Maya breathed in surprise.

"Yes," Porcini said softly. He looked at his sister. "Deathcap seized both me and Morel and planned to hold us hostage until my father handed over the Jewel. What he didn't know was that Morel had it all along, keeping it hidden and disguised as a simple bundle of rags that masked its dark magic, and kept Deathcap from sensing it."

"I couldn't hand it over to Deathcap," Morel said softly. "He would have killed our whole tribe, and our mother would have died for nothing."

Jarus looked at the two Brownaes. He no longer felt angry with them, only a little frustrated that they hadn't said this all before. "And…you didn't tell Norrin…because…?"

"Because I thought that somehow I could make the Jewel bring my mother back," Morel said. She said it calmly without a trace of sorrow, but Jarus felt a stir of pity for her. "It was a childish notion. I didn't know how to use it—I don't even know if that's possible. I just thought that if the Jewel was broken, any hope of seeing her again would die forever." She took a long breath. "But I am sorry I didn't share this sooner."

A long silence. "I forgive you," Maya said finally.

"Me too," Jarus said, startled to realize that he meant it. He looked carefully at the two Brownaes. "You'll tell Norrin now?"

Porcini looked at Morel, who nodded. "Yes, I think we have to," she said. "I can reveal it at the council."

"Sounds like a plan," Jarus said, smiling faintly.

"Now we should all get some sleep," Maya said, straightening. "Morel, make sure you wrap it up tight—I don't want to see any Serventiri peeking through our window."

Morel laughed shortly. "Neither do I. I'll do that."

16

ೋ ೋ ೋ ೋ ೋ ೋ ೋ ೋ ೋ

The Council of Flameton

"Councils are always so inconvenient," Lammar yawned, as Jarus shook him awake. "That's the hardest I've slept since we left my place, and now I've got to get up earlier than I'd care to in normal circumstances."

"Yes, well, this is an important council," Jarus said. He was dying to tell the whole story of the unexpected twist the previous night had taken, but he knew that was Morel's news to share. Porcini looked tense too—Jarus could see him fidgeting with the hem of his oversized tunic.

"Well, time to be up, then," Rygal said, emerging from the lavatory at the far end of the room, his hair in a very slightly less tousled state.

"Jarus needs to brush his fur," Lammar said with another yawn.

"No, I don't," Jarus said, anxious to be off.

"Yes, you might want to. Maya's going to be there."

"Will you lay off on that?" Jarus asked, feeling his face warm beneath his fur. "We're not…"

Norrin opened the door, checking in on them. "Are you four up yet? The council starts in an hour, and you'll need to hurry if you plan on breakfast first."

166

Jarus brushed through his fur briefly, then followed the other three out the door. Porcini looked at him, his furry young face filled with worry. "Jarus…you don't think she'll be…executed…for keeping it secret?" He gulped.

Jarus hesitated. He wasn't sure how the announcement would go over at all today. Did Morel's secret qualify as high treason, because she hadn't revealed it sooner? But surely they wouldn't kill her…

"It'll be all right," he told the Brownae, hoping very much that he was right.

Breakfast had been prepared, and though everything smelled delicious, Jarus could hardly eat anything. The tension in his stomach had driven away his appetite. Morel would reveal the Jewel, explain the story… and then what? Would they punish her? Execute her? Even worse, would they all be under suspicion, since Jarus and Maya knew the secret too?

Morel appeared midway through breakfast, muttered something about sleeping in, and sat down beside Maya. There were dark circles under her eyes, and Jarus guessed she hadn't slept much. He saw her approach Makana and ask him something quietly. The Diren king nodded, and Morel moved to her seat.

The servants cleared away the dishes. In another few minutes, the herald entered and introduced the councilors. There were six of them, all about King Makana's age, although it was hard to guess how old the Direns were. One of them, General Hawkblaze, stood taller than Makana, and the scars scoring his scales told Jarus that he was a seasoned warrior as well as advisor. All these councilors were probably better warriors than any of his companions, in fact. The thought did nothing to ease his nerves.

"Council has now come to order," King Makana announced, rising. "It is now that we will discuss what is to be done about Lord Safacon, and his Objects of Power." His golden eyes rested on Morel. "But first, the princess Morel has something to share."

Morel stood. She looked very small beside the towering forms of the Diren generals. "I have a confession, for all of you present. All this time, as Norrin will tell you, we have been on a quest to defeat Safacon. A quest to find his lost weapons of destruction. The Jewel has been our priority—even before I was rescued from Deathcap, finding the Jewel was our focus. After Porcini and I joined the group, we continued to search for it. We didn't find it while in the Wandering Wood." She took a breath. "But I've known where it is this whole time."

A ripple of surprise and shock passed around the table. Rygal straightened, staring at Morel in disbelief. Norrin looked at her, his face stunned. "You... what?" he asked her slowly.

Morel kept her eyes on Norrin. "The Jewel... the Jewel of Power was found by my mother, in the Wandering Wood, when I was very young. She took it, thinking it was no more than a fine trinket. Eventually, she learned of its great power, and kept it hidden, afraid of Deathcap. When Deathcap attacked our tribe, my mother gave me the Jewel and told me to never let Deathcap have it. She was killed in that attack."

She hesitated for the barest trace of a second. "And then Deathcap captured my brother and I. He never knew I had the Jewel, neither did my father. But I… I have carried it since."

She reached into her bag and withdrew the bundle of rags. A dull blue light leaked from the center, like the blood of the Serventiri.

The silence was stifling. Jarus risked a look around. Two of the Diren councilors looked unsure. Makana said nothing, glancing from Norrin to Morel. Norrin's face was white.

"The Jewel of Power?" Rygal finally repeated blankly. "You're sure…"

Norrin was staring at the bundle on the table, a strange look in his eyes. Jarus realized that the Jewel's magic had affected him too, as it had affected him last night. "Yes. It is certainly the Jewel. If you cannot feel its dark magic, count yourself lucky."

The Diren generals looked absolutely stunned. Even Makana seemed surprised.

Norrin finally looked at Morel. "Why did you not reveal this before?" His voice was calm, but Morel looked down, trying to hide her guilt.

"I…I wanted to try to use it. To bring my mother back. She…I was there when she died. Deathcap's troops murdered her in cold blood, and… I thought that somehow I could bring her back. With the Jewel."

"So I assumed," Norrin murmured. The news had shaken him, but his face was calm now.

"Will she be punished?" one of the Direns demanded. "She has risked the lives of everyone here! Her very possession of the thing is dangerous!"

"And for that I apologize," Morel said quietly. Her face was calm, her tone measured, but Jarus could see her trembling slightly. "I thought as a child thought, unknowing of the risk of what I was doing. And for that I'm sorry."

A tense silence passed. It was Rygal who spoke, unexpectedly.

"We would gain very little by punishing her," he said, slowly and thoughtfully. "It's already done, and she shared the secret before it was too late. And… as much as I would like to see her punished," he threw Morel a crooked grin, "we wouldn't accomplish much by it, except further division and the loss of a half-decent warrior."

"That may have been the wisest thing I have ever heard you say," Norrin said absently, which made the others laugh. The laughter eased the tension in the room, and even Morel relaxed slightly. "You understand the gravity of the situation, princess," Norrin said at length. "And you understand that should something like this happen again, there will be consequences." Morel inhaled nervously and squared her shoulders. "But," Norrin continued, "Rygal is right. Nothing will erase what has been done, and I must admit I am too pleased to see the Jewel out of Deathcap's grasp to be truly angry with you." He looked at Makana. "What do you think, sire?"

"I say the same," the Diren said in his deep voice. He studied Morel. "You must continue to bear it, princess, and not reveal it again. Keep it safe and secret, understood?"

"Yes, sire," Morel said, nodding and taking a shaky breath.

"Then let the council proceed," Makana said. Morel sat down, smiling slightly at the beaming Porcini. Jarus saw her give a short, quick nod to Rygal in gratitude, who nodded back. Whatever animosity had formed between them seemed to have lessened slightly by Rygal's statement of her defense.

King Makana stood, studying those assembled. "Up until recently," he said, smiling wryly at Morel, "the Jewel of Power was lost in the wilderness, gone from Safacon's reach. However, considering all that Safacon has fought for in the past, he will continue to search relentlessly for it, and be ready to fight for it. He can see through it, and his Serventiri can sense its presence, making your having it very dangerous."

They all listened as Makana told the history of the Objects. While Jarus had already heard the story, he listened intently as the king's deep voice spoke of Safacon and his power. A silence followed as he finished.

"Then what do you propose will be done, sire?" one of the generals asked. "They cannot defeat Safacon alone. Many have tried in the past, and none have succeeded."

"And how can we hope to stop such a power at all?" another Diren asked doubtfully.

"Safacon fears us," Makana said. "His army, his might, he knows they are fleeting. We are his last threat, and this is our land. Look at how he hesitates to enter into battle with us. If the Jewel were destroyed, think of what we would regain."

"We can besiege his fortress at the Topstorm," the tall general, Hawkblaze, said thoughtfully. "Safacon does not expect an attack."

"But sire—the dangers," the other Diren stammered. "Now that we know the Jewel indeed exists, we can be sure that all the stories are true as well."

"Indeed," Makana said, thinking. "But Safacon is hated throughout the entire northern hemisphere of Orlell. Allies will gather to our cause. The Direns will be rallied, and prepare to besiege Safacon's fortress as soon as it can be done."

"Then do you believe we should continue our quest to find the Objects?" Norrin asked.

King Makana nodded. "You have done quite well so far. And do not forget that the Ring and the Knife are still to be accounted for."

"But Deathcap's got the Knife still," Rygal said slowly. "How are we going to recover that?"

"Deathcap will follow," Makana said. "His lust for the Jewel drives him. He may reach Safacon before you, but you need not fear his allegiance with Safacon. No, Deathcap will come to you, of that I am fairly sure."

"And the Ring?" Lammar asked.

"I tried to bring the Ring to Flameton several years ago," Norrin said. "I was stopped by Deathcap, who had the same goal, and a few of his followers. They attacked me, we fought, and the Ring was lost in the river."

"It must be found," Makana said. "Our only hope is if the Objects are destroyed, shattered on the Golden Tablet at Topstorm Mountain upon which they were made." He looked over at the councilors. "It will up to be you to decide. Shall Flameton rally to this cause?"

There was a brief discussion among the councilors. In the end, five of the six councilors sided with King Makana. "Very well, then," Makana said, looking satisfied. "I shall have a word with my generals, and send for Lieutenant Casper." He turned to the companions. "Stay in Flameton a little while longer, to rest. Then you must continue your quest to Safacon's palace." He stood. "This council is dismissed."

Jarus let out his breath in relief. Then the reality of what was happening hit him.

The Diren army had joined their cause.

17

ఞ ఞ ఞ ఞ ఞ ఞ ఞ ఞ

Departure

Two days passed, then a week. Jarus knew that the companions would need to leave soon, but none of them truly wanted to. Staying within the protective walls of the city was much more appealing than wandering in the wilderness for days until they reached Safacon's palace. Yet it would have to be done.

He pushed the thoughts out of his head and focused instead on the many sights that Flameton had to offer. Neely was bursting to explore the city of her people, and Jarus often saw her in the company of Lieutenant Casper.

"I think he likes her," Porcini gossiped gleefully. "He's real handsome, y'know, for a Diren."

"Well, as long as Neely still wants to go along with us," Jarus said. He and Porcini were walking back towards the city on the road they had been attacked on when they'd first arrived.

"I bet she won't," Porcini said confidently. "She'll want to stay here."

"I don't think so," came Morel's voice, and they both jumped. The princess had been sitting in the shade of the rocks, watching the hawks reeling in the sky over the desert. Her fur had concealed her perfectly.

"Morel, I was thinking," Jarus said, reminded of something. "If

174

Safacon can see through the Jewel, then maybe we could set a false trail—make him think we're in the mountains or something. Lead him in the total opposite direction." He had been thinking this through last night, and felt quite proud of the idea.

But Morel shook her head. "I thought so too, but Norrin said it doesn't work that way. It's not so much that Safacon can *see* through the Jewel when it's uncovered—he can feel it. He knows where it is. As if he's just following its voice."

"Like it has a… brain," Porcini said, and shuddered. "Creepy. You don't suppose it does, though, do you?" he added worriedly.

"Suppose what?" Maya asked, approaching from the castle with Rygal. The two of them had heard the end of the conversation.

"That the Jewel of Power can…think on its own," Jarus told them slowly, frowning as he thought.

"And it can communicate to Safacon. Which we know it can, somehow, because it obeys his orders," Morel added.

Rygal frowned slightly. "It's possible. The Jewel was made from the core of a dying star, or so the story goes."

"A literal Star, or just a burning rock?" Morel asked, raising an eyebrow. "I mean…no one's seen a Star in over a century. No one really knows much about them."

"They're real?" Jarus asked, startled. His mother used to tell him stories about the Star people, guardians of the sky. But he didn't think they were real.

"Real, just like the Aces were," Rygal said, thinking. "But Morel's right…we don't know if it was a real star, or one of the Star people. The stories are rather vague."

"'*Ere the world be told of time, then the Stars walked land and sky,*" Maya quoted. "The song they used to sing in Mari's Pub at the end of the night, Jarus—the one the minstrels always sang."

"They sang of the Stars?" Porcini asked.

"A little about them, yes," Rygal said. "I know that song. Except that was just one line, Maya:

> *"Ere the Ace-Lord in his line,*
> *Ere the world be born of Light,*
> *Ere the world be told of time,*
> *Then the Stars walked land and sky,*
> *They in the Land Immortal dwell."*

"That was the song, at least, the best I remember it," Rygal said ruefully.

"But what does that have to do with the Jewel of Power?" Morel asked, still not understanding.

"Well, a lot, if we think its core came from the Land Immortal," Maya said, as if it was the most obvious thing in the world. "Think it through. If the Jewel of Power was made with the heart of a Star—a literal Star person—then that means it's partly from the Land Immortal—and that means that Safacon could be…"

"Trying to become immortal," Rygal mused. "I wouldn't put it past him. That's been the goal of pretty much every evil wizard in history. They can gain the whole world, but in the end, they'll still be in a grave."

There was a moment of silence. Jarus had only heard songs about the Land Immortal—according to the Coopers' religion in Mata City, it was a place of eternal rest for the faithful. Out of the companions, Norrin stood apart in his faith of the High Light, the Light of the World who was said to be ruler over the Land Immortal. Yet if the High Light and the Land Immortal were real—which Rygal clearly thought they were—then Jarus could assume that there was a similar place where waited the darker side of the supernatural.

This new idea was chilling. Jarus looked up at Rygal uncertainly as they started to walk back toward the castle. "That's why Safacon wants the Jewel so bad—not just to get more power," he realized.

A shadow had fallen over the conversation. Morel changed the subject. "I wonder…if it'd be better to just wait and travel to the fortress with the Diren army," she said thoughtfully. "Then we'd have help taking Safacon down together."

"It might be," Rygal said, "but Safacon would be expecting that, and not—get down!"

He leapt back, pushing the others back against the rocks and into the shadows. Jarus stared at him in alarm, not understanding what was happening. "What…"

Then he saw them. His stomach lurched as he saw the glints of armor among the rocks. The five companions had entered the narrow gully before the castle, and were now trapped on either side by the arching canyon walls. High above them, on the opposite ridge, Jarus could see the Serventiri.

There were twelve or so of them, moving slowly. Two of them were partly down into the draw, and were turning their heads this way and that, their hollow blue eyes peering down at the road at the bottom of the draw, searching for something. Jarus realized, with a jolt, that he and the others had been talking loudly for several minutes—the Serventiri had heard their voices, but they hadn't seen them.

Yet.

"Rygal," Morel started in a quiet voice.

Rygal hushed her, still watching the warriors. The two who were headed down the slope had looked away, and were making their way down the rocks again. "We can make it," Rygal murmured finally. "We can get out and fight past them, and run to the city. They haven't blocked the way yet."

"No, we can't," Morel said in the same quiet tone.

"Yes, we have to," Rygal said, sounding angry with her again. "Don't tell me—"

"We can't," Morel said, "because there are four dragons around this bend."

Rygal looked at her sharply. Jarus smelled something strange now—some sharp, musky smell that he didn't recognize, coming from the bend in the road.

"Dragons?" Porcini asked, his eyes widening.

Morel peered around the rock, then settled back again. "Yes. Four of them."

"Big ones?" Rygal asked.

"Average size," Morel told him, then added, "for a dragon."

Jarus was dumbfounded by their attitudes. "Isn't that…a problem?"

"A very big one," Rygal said, taking a breath, "because we can't go around them. We also can't go back," he nodded to the road behind them. Jarus risked a glance over his shoulder—several of the Serventiri had reached the road, and were milling around absently. They all carried weapons.

Rygal took a deep breath. "All right…here's what we'll do… I don't want anyone to panic, and I definitely don't want to hear any noise. We're going to walk down the road."

"Towards the dragons?" Maya squeaked.

"Towards the dragons," Rygal said in the same measured tone.

Jarus had once had a dream that he had been caught doing something he shouldn't have, and had tried to run—but he hadn't been able to move. He felt quite a bit like that now—every bit of him was screaming for him to flee, yet he knew that any sudden movement would catch the hollow eyes of the Serventiri.

They edged along the canyon wall, keeping to the shadows. As they rounded the bend, the musky scent grew stronger. In another moment, they saw them.

This breed was nothing like the elegant beasts Jarus had seen drawings of back in Mata City. These dragons were large, wiry, looking very much like the spotted lizards Jarus had seen in the desert. Except they were huge—the shoulder of the largest one was almost as tall as Rygal. They stood in a cluster, hissing, forked tongues whipping in and out of their jaws. Their huge wings, bat-like and plated with scales the color of the rocks, were folded on their backs. Their eyes were dark and beady, unintelligent and savage.

"Garilian Rock-Wyrm," Porcini said with the tone of one narrating a nature book. "Feisty ones, those dragons. Very far-sighted, though."

"What?" Jarus hissed to him, as the five of them all froze—one of the Serventiri had looked their way, but seeing nothing, it continued down the slope.

"Very far-sighted," Porcini said, his voice soft and vague with fright. "Can't…see too well up close."

The Serventiri were moving down the road in their direction—the saddles on the backs of the dragons left no doubt that they were used for the soldiers' transport. The dragons clearly wouldn't leave any time soon. The Serventiri would see the five companions huddled here and it would all be over.

In a flash, Jarus knew what to do. "Rygal—Rygal, Porcini says—he says they can't see well—if we go very slow—"

Rygal swallowed and edged out from the shadow of the boulder, moving slowly and quietly. One of the dragons raised its head, sniffing the air, and looked right at Rygal. For an instant, Jarus felt his insides freeze with horror as the dragon's eyes met Rygal's. Then, amazingly, the dragon only turned away and began fighting its companions over a dead goat.

"Go…" Morel whispered fervently, although Rygal was out of hearing, "go now…"

Rygal took several more steps, then ducked into the shadows around the bend. He peeked back around the rocks, looking satisfied but still worried, and motioned for them to follow.

Morel took a breath and started after him, with Maya following her. Maya was stiff with fear; Jarus could see her trembling like a leaf. But in a few tense seconds, they had turned the corner, safe.

Jarus steeled himself and moved out, Porcini right behind him. The young Brownae was staring at the dragons in awe, studying them as they began eating the dead goat. "Look at them, Jarus— they're amazing…"

"Porcini," Jarus whispered in panic—one of the dragons had raised its head at the Brownae's fervent voice, and was moving towards them slowly. Jarus froze, too terrified to move.

The dragon walked right up to them, sniffing. Its large dark eyes, ideal for spotting prey from high in the air, were not as effective up close. It nosed Porcini's head; the young Brownae didn't move, trembling from both delight and terror.

The dragon seemed to find nothing of interest in the scents, and turned back to its companions. Jarus let out a long, slow breath, feeling about ready to faint. He and Porcini stumbled the rest of the way to the others.

"The blazes was that?" Morel snarled at Porcini the moment he reached her, her fear making her angry. "You might have been killed—you stood there and just watched them—"

Porcini pushed away, glancing back at the dragons, and then looked at his sister again and shrugged. "I'm fine. Those ones— they're a lot bigger than the little leaf-dragons we have in the Wood, Morel, and I think these ones are—"

"The blazes they are!" Morel snapped. "Leaf dragons are the size of your finger!" She took a breath. "Forget it—let's go."

"You…like dragons?" Jarus asked him as they moved down the road again.

Porcini looked over his shoulder. In the distance, the four dragons rose into the air, with the Serventiri on their backs, and flew steadily east. "Those ones shouldn't be tamed. They belong out here. They're not meant to be ridden." He looked appalled at the nerve of Safacon for taming and riding such dragons.

"It almost ate you," Jarus said.

"No, she didn't," Porcini said. "It was a female. The females only eat once a month, unless it's nesting season, when they eat pretty much all the time. That's why it wasn't eating the goat with the others."

Jarus stared at him in disbelief, then shook his head, impressed despite himself. "Well…be glad you weren't the once-a-month occasion, then."

. . . . . .

By the time they reached Flameton, Morel's anger had faded at Porcini, and she and Rygal explained the whole ordeal to Norrin and King Makana.

"Serventiri?" Makana repeated gravely.

"Ten or twelve of them," Rygal said, taking a breath. "Norrin, they had dragons. Mounts."

Norrin shook his head, his face serious. "Well, we will have to watch out for that. But I cannot believe the Serventiri will have left the area for good—they'll be back, in greater numbers. They can sense the Jewel's presence."

Makana nodded in agreement. "You must leave. You cannot stay in one place for long—they will know where you are. You must go, and quickly."

The eight companions packed their few supplies as quickly as they could, all of them sad and a little fearful of what lay ahead. The sun was low when they gathered outside the gates, all carrying their packs.

Makana met them for a last word of advice. "Travel due west until you reach the Rummeryn River. Then follow it south to Safacon's fortress. I will ready my forces—the Direns will come and fight against Safacon, I promise you that." He clasped Norrin's hand.

"Thank you, sire," Norrin told him.

Makana inclined his head slightly. "You may also meet an old ally on the road—his name is Larkin. You can trust him." He stepped back. "In the meantime, travel safe, be wary, and have hope. May the High Light guard your steps, Company of the Jewel."

The companions voiced their thanks, then started down the road, heading west. The light from the setting sun shone in their faces as they left Flameton behind and began the second leg of their journey.

18

§ § § § § § § § §

The Prince's Threat

The eight companions headed due southwest, following the Rummeryn river. For several hours, the terrain was barren and desolate. Towering spires of red rock stood like natural castles amid the canyon walls, the blue-green water completing the wild and lonesome scenery. Norrin led them through the wasteland until, around dusk, the dark expanse of a dense wood stood out before them as the desert and wasteland faded away. The road became distinct again, winding along the Rummeryn's banks through the darkening trees.

They made camp that night in the shelter of the trees. The forest, unlike the Wandering Wood, had no name on the map. By morning, the sun barely reached through the moss-covered boughs to light their way. Ivy and brambles trailed across the path, catching Jarus' paws. "This hardly feels like a forest," Rygal remarked dryly when they stopped for a midday meal. "More like we're charging into a hedge." And so Hedgewood they called it from then on.

Jarus followed Rygal, trying to walk where the tall warrior had crushed down the briers with his boots. "I thought it's supposed to get warmer the farther south you go," he said, as a cold breeze rippled through his fur.

"Not here," Rygal said. "The desert is really the only warm part of Gayrile, but that's because the mountain ranges shelter it from the storms. The terrain will only get more rugged as we get close to the Topstorm."

"And then we will have to fight," Morel said from behind them. She and Maya walked together. Jarus was a little surprised to see how Maya enjoyed being around Morel—their personalities were so different. Still, he had noticed how Morel had picked up some of Maya's gentleness, in the same way Maya had picked up some of Morel's tough spirit. Besides, he was grateful to Morel—she could keep Maya safe better than he could if they ran into trouble.

The thought reminded him of something. "Rygal, can you show me how to fight when we stop next? I'd feel more confident with some pointers."

"You did pretty well when we fought the Serventiri," Rygal told him with a crooked grin. He had received a Diren-made sword before leaving Flameton, which now hung at his side.

"I know, but… I froze up." Jarus swallowed, embarrassed for the way he had reacted. The killing of that first soldier had shocked him. The memory of the purple blood, the hollow eyes, still haunted his dreams.

"That's pretty typical," Rygal admitted. "You won't get over that for a long time. Maybe that's a good thing. Once you're hardened to killing, you can't go back." He threw a glance at Morel, but the princess ignored the comment.

"I'd like to know how to fight, too," Maya chimed in hopefully. "In case we're separated again, or if I'm captured by the Serventiri."

"We won't let that happen, Maya," Rygal said kindly. But he nodded. "All right, I'll give you both some pointers when we make camp."

They stopped a little while later, as the sun began to set. Norrin and Lammar were both busy examining the maps and trying to determine how long it would be before they reached Safacon's fortress. Rygal helped gather wood for the fire, then returned to the two Coopers.

"Okay, well, the first thing you'll want to remember is your size. You will, in all likelihood, be at a disadvantage in a fight because your opponent will be bigger than you. The trick is not letting your opponent use that advantage." He handed them both sticks about the length of a dagger.

"How will we do that?" Jarus asked, confused. The fight with the Serventiri had proved Rygal right already—he had almost been trampled by the soldiers.

"You're small. You're also fast. Both of you," Rygal said. "When you attack, get in and get out fast. Like a hornet. Strike for any vital areas you can—the abdomen, the lungs if you can reach them. A blow to the leg might not kill instantly, but it will still put your opponent out of action."

He had the two of them practice charging forward, trying to tap him with the sticks. It was harder than Jarus had expected—he had to hold the dagger in one paw and bound forward using the awkward balance of his other three legs. Besides that, Rygal was a very skilled warrior, and evaded their blows easily.

"We can work on it more tomorrow," Rygal panted, once they had practiced for a while. Jarus was out of breath too. His body felt sore from both the day's walk and from the exercise. "The biggest thing is practice. But you both did good."

Maya set her practice stick aside and arched her back, stretching. "It feels so awkward—fighting. Like I'll trip over my own legs."

"You'll do that a fair amount," Rygal said with a grin.

"Oh, yes," Norrin called from the other side of the camp. "You should have seen Rygal when he first started."

There was a ripple of amusement around the listeners. "You fought Kado, did you not, Rygal?" Neely asked, interested. "Years ago, when Safacon sent the Hazes against Caer Sia?"

"Well, I didn't do much," Rygal admitted. "I was very young, and inexperienced."

"You're not exactly ancient now," Morel said dryly, which made the others laugh again. She looked at Rygal curiously. "The Brownaes only heard rumors of that battle. The Hazes—they were real, then? Were they like the Serventiri?"

"Yes, and no," Rygal said, his face thoughtful. "The Hazes were created from a spell, a spell that came from the Jewel, as Norrin and I guessed later. They were incomplete. They were men, enchanted and changed to look like wraiths. But they were impossible to kill, under Kado's power, that is. The Serventiri have whole forms, and while difficult to kill, they're mortal." His eyes were distant, reliving the memories.

"The Liznees stopped the Hazes, with help," Norrin said. "It will be up to us to stop Safacon."

. . . . . .

The chilly wind dissipated into the night as dawn came. The sun rose, bringing a slight warmth. Jarus decided to be grateful for it.

He moved to the front of the party, partly so he could see where they were going better, and partly because Maya was walking there, talking with Neely.

"...in the winter we do, yes," Maya was saying. "But the canals don't tend to freeze over—salt water doesn't freeze over easily."

"Then the canals—they fill the whole city?" Neely asked, very interested.

"Yes, we have a whole network of them, as it were—that's how Mata City is such a successful trading port," Maya said, with a touch of pride.

"Ingenious," Neely murmured, nodding thoughtfully.

"But hard to maintain," Jarus said from behind them.

Maya noticed him, and nodded to Neely with a grin. "Yes, we hire cleaners to maintain the canals—make sure the sea water doesn't erode the stone to the point of decay."

"Well...and to get any trash out," Jarus said, quite startled. The way Maya described it made it sound like an almost noble task.

"Not like it's a really… fancy…job or anything."

"But it'd be important—sea water can be very erosive," Neely said, her scaly face serious. "So that's an important job, Jarus."

"Well…" Jarus was quite flattered by this. He risked a glance at Maya; she was grinning.

He took a breath and changed the subject. "So…do you guys have any idea who that Larkin person that Makana mentioned could be?"

"No, I've been thinking about it, though," Maya said. "Perhaps he's another Diren."

"I figured all the Direns live in the city," Jarus said.

"Not all of them," Neely said. "My parents and I didn't—and neither do the renegades."

Jarus looked at her, realizing he knew virtually nothing about Neely's past. "The renegades?"

"Rebel Direns—the ones who reject Makana's leadership. They roam all throughout the wilds of Gayrile," Neely said. She paused. "My parents…they were both ambassadors for the king, during a time when he tried to ally them with Flameton. But the renegades refused, and when my parents went to them with an escort, they saw it as an attack, and killed everyone before asking any questions."

Jarus looked at her, his heart aching for the young Diren. Suddenly, he felt very lucky to have his father. "I'm sorry," he said, a little awkwardly.

Neely only shook her head. "I feel it is better now. Lammar has trained me in the ways of my people. But that was the first time I have been to Flameton." She looked back wistfully. Jarus wondered if her thoughts dwelt on the handsome Lieutenant Casper, but he didn't ask her about that.

The thoughts had just crossed his mind when a scream came from the rear of the party, cut off abruptly.

"Morel!" Porcini shouted. They all turned, and froze. Rygal drew his sword in a flash but paused uncertainly. Norrin took a half step forward.

A ragged group of scowling ruffians and Brownaes in tarnished armor had crept soundlessly through the woods behind them. Now a burly man held Morel off the ground, upside-down, by her ankles. Beside him stood a Brownae with dark fur, holding a knife to Morel's back, a cruel and familiar smile on his face.

"Make one more move, Norrin, and I sever her spine," Deathcap hissed. Norrin, who had started forward instantly with his staff raised, paused. Morel, swinging slightly upside down, clawed at the big man's hand—finding no success, she began shouting at Deathcap.

"Shut up," Deathcap snarled at her, jabbing the flat of the blade into her back—Morel froze, her face livid.

"Put her down, Deathcap," Norrin said quietly. "You won't gain anything by holding her hostage."

"I'll be the judge of that," Deathcap snapped. He paused, composing himself. "It seems we are at an impasse, Norrin. Both of us want the Jewel for our own reasons, and neither of us will last if the other has it. However, I know that you need the Knife to destroy the Jewel, which I still possess. Thus, I am willing to bargain."

"I'm listening," Norrin said. His voice was still calm, but Jarus could almost see his mind working rapidly to come up with a plan.

Deathcap smiled. "I give you your princess. You all go your merry way, and you give me the Jewel." His warriors shifted behind him, all grinning in cruel satisfaction, eager to attack.

"Is that it," Norrin murmured. "What do you plan to do with the Jewel, then, Deathcap?"

Jarus realized that Deathcap didn't know that Morel had the Jewel herself at this very moment. He shot a quick look at the princess—upside-down, she seemed to be trying to reach her pocket. What was she thinking? If Deathcap realized he had the Jewel in his grasp even now… but Norrin was stalling him, and Deathcap didn't even notice Morel.

Deathcap laughed in answer to Norrin's question. "I will rule Gayrile, of course, as my people ought to have done for decades. Though…I may not stop at Gayrile…why not the Mainland?" A light had lit in his eyes. "The Liznees of the Mainland—they will fall before me. The Jewel and the Knife…all I need is the Ring…"

"I should have guessed," Norrin interrupted him midway through. "You know I will not agree to that. My very mission is to rid the world of the Jewel, and the Knife, and the Ring."

"Fool," Deathcap spat—Morel squirmed from her upside-down

position, but the guard held her tightly. "In that case I will kill the princess—you are right, she has no further value to me."

Jarus stared in horror, not sure how they could possibly keep Morel alive and keep the Jewel at the same time.

That was when Morel squirmed again—she had been straining to get her hand inside her pocket, now she reached it, pulling the bundle free, ripping off the rags.

"*Escrariae!*" she screamed—there was a flash of blue light, the Jewel glittered white-hot, the man holding Morel shrieked and dropped her, his hand had melted like wax—

The strange feeling of intensity and darkness Jarus had experienced in the library filled him again, this time accompanied with a fear—the fight had erupted. Deathcap was screaming orders, his warriors had charged.

"*Ventara!*" Morel cried, and the Jewel flashed again—a wall of fire erupted at the feet of the warriors.

"Morel, give it to me!" Norrin shouted, and Morel handed him the Jewel, confused for a moment.

"We can fight them with it!"

"Safacon will know!" Norrin told her quickly, wrapping the Jewel again.

The ruffians and Brownaes eyed the firewall as the flames faded. Deathcap's eyes glowed through the flames as he watched them.

"Someone has been studying Jewel-lore, has she?" he asked viciously, staring at Morel. "See what that brings about, little fool, and be grateful it isn't worse."

The warriors lunged—Rygal decapitated one, then stepped back. There were many of them—too many for them to fight.

Jarus stepped into place beside Lammar, his dagger drawn, and slashed at a warrior. He missed, but the attacker jumped back at the sight of the blade. Between the steep embankment and the river, there was no other way for Deathcap's warriors to pursue the companions unless by the trail, so they had to fight.

"Retreat slowly," Norrin told them—he and Rygal stood side by side, Rygal's sword streaked with blood.

Neely sprang through the trees and over the heads of the warriors, her powerful wings beating the air. Fire licked along her fingers as she sent a blast of flame at the feet of the nearest warriors. Deathcap's soldiers staggered back, yelping and swatting at the flames that licked their clothes. The distraction was enough for the companions to retreat—Jarus jogged after Maya and Porcini, then paused, panting for air, uncertain.

The path curved, then joined with the rocks. The river dropped down into a canyon, a channel of gray rock. The shallow water turned into a roiling stream of brown rapids. The path, which had been carved into the cliff side centuries before, lead upward at an alarming angle, slick and crumbling.

"Norrin…" Jarus started uneasily, at a loss of what to do or where to go. They needed to go now, but this path looked dangerous.

He saw Rygal slash at Deathcap, forcing the Brownae prince back, but one of the other warriors cut sharply at Rygal's injured leg. Rygal stumbled, leaning heavily on his sword. Neely swept down between him and the oncoming soldiers, fire flashing in her palms. It was remarkable how such a quiet and gentle person could be so terrifying in battle.

Jarus saw Rygal stumble, and made a decision. "Up the path. I'll be right behind you." Maya and Porcini nodded, both of them looking scared. Jarus bounded back towards the battle, drawing his knife and clutching it in his teeth.

He nearly ran into Rygal, who was limping—the wound from the battle with the Serventiri had reopened, and blood wet his pant leg. "The Knife, Jarus—we need the Knife," Rygal panted.

Jarus turned—Deathcap stood behind the warriors, pacing down the line like a wolf. His fingers rested on the black hilt of the dagger at his belt. "Go help Maya and Porcini," he told Rygal, and bounded forward again.

He had taken only a few steps when several things happened at once. Neely dove at Deathcap's troops, who fired a hail of arrows after her. Neely lurched midair, and crashed into the thick woods of the Hedge. There was a flash of green as Lammar charged at Deathcap's warriors. His shape flickered as he transformed into a huge green snake, hissing and poised to strike.

In the same second, Rygal's shout of alarm cut through the air. "Norrin!"

Jarus whipped around to see what had happened. Rygal pointed across the river, his face white with terror. Jarus followed his gaze and felt his heart stop.

Across the river on the opposite bank, summoned by the Jewel's power, pressing through the trees in ranks, the Serventiri had come.

19

∾ ∾ ∾ ∾ ∾ ∾ ∾ ∾ ∾

Battle on the Banks

Deathcap froze, the Knife of Destruction half drawn in his hand, as he stared in shock at the Serventiri. There were close to fifty of them, staring across the river with their hollow blue eyes. Their gazes were fixed on the bundle in Morel's pocket.

The sight of them sent chills down Jarus' spine. He knew, even in his brief experience, that there were far too many to fight. They were drastically outnumbered.

Norrin, who stood in the shallow water of the river, broke the silence. Blasting a ray of sparks at Deathcap's troops, he turned to Morel. "Go now—up the cliffs," he ordered.

Morel, for once, didn't argue—she stared in shock and horror at the host of Serventiri. Jarus stumbled towards Rygal, who had also started up the path. Then he turned back. "Wait—Neely!"

Morel ran into him, and pushed him forward. "Jarus, go—they're coming—"

"Neely's hurt!" Jarus shouted at her, swatting her paws away.

"I'll help her! You go, now!" Morel yelled at him, turning and jogging into the underbrush. Jarus watched her for a moment, then ran up the path. He risked a glance across the river, some twenty

197

yards away. In silent procession, the Serventiri stepped into the chest-high waters, swaying slightly with the current, but walking steadily towards them.

Jarus reached Maya and Porcini, who had both stopped to stare in awe and terror at the Serventiri, who had by now reached the opposite bank. "Hurry—we've got to run," Jarus stammered.

Maya looked at him, wide-eyed as she remembered something. "Jarus, did we get the Knife? Where's Deathcap?"

Jarus turned. The shore behind them had erupted in chaos. Deathcap was shouting orders to his soldiers, most of whom had turned to flee at the sight of the Serventiri. The Brownae prince had whipped out the Knife and lowered it at the approaching warriors, shouting a spell—

"*Raeortar!*" he barked. The Serventiri stumbled as though hit with an invisible force. The spell didn't stop them for long, and they surged forward again, rising out of the river, dripping and glinting in the sunlight.

Maya and Porcini ran on up the treacherous trail, keeping their backs as close to the cliff wall as possible. Below them, the Rummeryn churned gradually into a brown froth, a good fifteen foot drop into the roiling water. The sight made Jarus dizzy, and he fell back against the rock.

Behind him, he saw Rygal limping up the path, gripping his sword. Behind Rygal, Morel and Neely had appeared. Neely was staggering after Morel—one of her wings trailed on the ground behind her, twisted at an odd angle. Norrin brought up the rear, covering their retreat. There was little need for this—Deathcap's warriors were now engaged in fighting the Serventiri.

If they could slip away from the battle before the Serventiri defeated Deathcap…

The thought had barely crossed Jarus' mind when he saw Deathcap send a second blast at the Serventiri with the Knife, then turn and shout at his warriors to retreat. The ruffians and Brownaes, already panicked and outnumbered by the Serventiri, needed little prompting, and fled back into the dense Hedgewood.

Their path cleared, the Serventiri turned slowly and started after the companions.

Jarus' mouth was dry. The fear and tension filling him made it hard to breathe. He forced himself to take a deep breath—panicking would do little good now. "Okay—Maya, Porcini, keep going up this path—try to find us a hiding place or something. I'm going back to help Neely."

He jogged back down the sloping path, his paws slipping and sliding on the damp stone. The churning river below dizzied him. Norrin had covered their retreat, and the sheer cliffside forced the Serventiri to come up the path one or two at a time. That was good. Outnumbered or no, Norrin could protect them for a while.

A group of Serventiri had reached the path up the cliffs before Norrin had, and now attacked Morel and Neely. The Brownae princess slashed at them, forcing them back, but they swarmed around her and Neely again. Jarus stumbled towards them, not sure how he could fight that many.

He had forgotten Lammar.

He wasn't sure where the Siren had been waiting, half hidden in the fray of battle. He must have come behind Rygal during the retreat. Lammar sprang up the path, pushing through the Serventiri from behind, as his shape flickered again. A silver-green beast, unlike any Jarus had ever seen before, stood in his place. It looked half like a dragon, half like a huge silvery eagle. Its talons slashed at the startled Serventiri, knocking four of them down into the rapids below. Purple-red blood churned in the brown water.

"Up the path!" the beast ordered, though its voice was the voice of Lammar.

Jarus, still in awe, started back up the path, with Morel and Neely following. Neely sobbed hoarsely in pain and stumbled after them. Her balance had evidently been thrown off by her broken wing. They caught up to Rygal, who was bleeding from his leg but seemed otherwise uninjured.

"Are they coming after us?" Rygal asked immediately.

"Yes, but they advance slowly. They can't all come at once," Morel panted. She leaned against the cliff wall, exhausted.

Jarus looked back towards the sounds of battle. Lammar had joined Norrin, and the two of them were effectively pressing the Serventiri back down the cliff path.

"I don't like this," Morel said, straightening again. "Too narrow, not enough room. If they come around the other side of this path we'll be in a vise."

"Then let's go," Rygal said, gripping his sword. He looked at Neely. "Can you keep going all right?"

Neely took a shaking breath. "Yes. I can walk."

They headed slowly up the rock path. Jarus could see nothing of the battle behind them, and could only hear the crackle of Norrin's staff, or the strange snarls made by whatever creature Lammar had transformed into. He had noticed before that the Serventiri made no sound while fighting. It did nothing to make them less terrifying, though.

They had nearly reached the highest peak of the road, and the path had widened slightly, when a scream split the air in front of them. It was a scream Jarus had heard before, a sound that punched any hope right out of him.

"Maya," he choked, his voice rasping, and before he knew what he was doing he bounded forward, leaping up the path. He rounded the bend in the cliffside and froze.

Maya and Porcini had been backed up against the rock wall. In front of them, moving to join the enemy fighting Norrin, a second group of Serventiri pushed forward. Maya had her little knife in her paw and had shrunk back beside Porcini, who held a small stone club. Both of them were completely outnumbered.

Jarus ran forward as the Serventiri slashed at Maya. His heart leapt into his throat as the blade made contact across her shoulder blades—Maya stumbled to the side, then lunged forward, slashing across the warrior's forearm. Porcini charged in the same second, and the warrior, off balance by the sudden attack, toppled off the path and down into the water.

But the Serventiri kept coming. Jarus sprang to the side of his companions, taking in the situation. The worst had happened, and Morel's prediction had been painfully accurate. They were in a vise—Serventiri behind and before, rock and water in between. Effectively trapped.

The nearest warrior swung his sword at Porcini's head—the young Brownae managed to jump back, trapped against the rocks. Jarus lunged forward, feeling the blade of his knife bite deep into the Serventiri's abdomen. The soldier stumbled, wounded—Jarus slashed at him again in the same place, and the warrior dropped to his knees. A blade lashed across his extended forearm before he could draw it back in time, and he flinched at the sharp pain. The Serventiri behind simply surged over their fallen comrade, pressing the Coopers and Porcini back into the rocks. Maya screamed again, a helpless sound of pure terror.

Then a flash of green pushed past Jarus as he stood defending his companions. Lammar dove behind the Serventiri, sinking his teeth into the warrior's leg. The warrior staggered forward, startled. The Siren's shape flickered as he transformed into the huge dragon-bird again, then into a tall figure dressed in black, wielding a curved sword.

"Down!" Lammar shouted at them over his shoulder, cutting

down a warrior who had come too close. "It's our only chance—down to the river!"

"We can't get down there!" Morel shouted at him—she and Rygal had arrived, fending off the lower group of Serventiri with Norrin.

Rygal slashed another warrior, and paused, leaning heavily on his sword. "Rope," he grunted, and shrugged the pack off his back.

The two groups of Serventiri pressed in on them. The jaws of the vise had nearly closed.

Rygal quickly pulled a length of rope from the pack and slipped it around a solid rock outcrop that hung out from the cliffside. He shouted to Maya and Porcini, who rushed to him—Rygal helped them climb carefully down the rope to the narrow bank of the river below.

The Serventiri had stepped away from Norrin's whirling sparks and the tall black warrior that was Lammar, hesitating. Neely made it down the rope—Morel shouted for Jarus to go next—

Jarus had just turned towards Rygal when a group of Serventiri surged past Lammar, charging straight for Morel and Jarus. Morel flung the broken spear at them, then raised her dagger. Jarus shrank back, unable to move in terror as he watched the hollow, pitiless eyes fill with triumphant light—

Then the black-cloaked figure swept between the Serventiri and Jarus. The warrior-form Lammar swung his sword, hewing off the arm of the closest warrior. "Go!" Lammar shouted again—a Serventiri sword caught him across the back, knocking him forward.

It happened so fast Jarus barely saw it, but it burned into his mind forever. Lammar straightened in the same second that the Serventiri ran the sword through him. The dark warrior vanished, and Jarus only saw the Siren, his teeth bared in pain and battle rage, before the Serventiri flung him from the cliffs, down into the roiling water of the Rummeryn.

Jarus heard himself scream—his voice was unrecognizable with shock and grief. Norrin turned, blasting the Serventiri with sparks, and shouted at Morel to go. She still stood in her place, fending the warriors off with her dagger. Rygal was shouting something—Jarus heard him say Lammar's name.

"Jarus, come on!" Rygal yelled at him. Jarus staggered forward, finally able to find his voice.

"Lammar!" he choked.

"Neely has him!" Rygal said. "Neely has him—he fell in the river—let's go!"

Morel and Norrin stood back to back—Rygal ordered her to run. "Not yet!" Jarus heard her yell. "You go first—I'll be right behind you!"

Jarus dropped down the rope, paw over paw until he reached the wet rock below. Rygal slid down behind him, landing heavily on his injured leg. They both looked up, barely able to see the battle above.

Norrin sent a pinwheel of sparks in a spinning arc that sent the nearest Serventiri up in flames. In the same moment, Morel pulled the Jewel from her pocket and shouted a spell. As if made of wax on a hot day, the nearest ranks of Serventiri melted into the ground, their hollow eyes showing their surprise and confusion as they fell. Their comrades, unable to compete with the Jewel's power, fled.

Jarus jogged beside Rygal along the edge of the river, following the current downstream. The brown water, flecked with white foam, churned past them, as though leading the way. The wet footprints of the other companions showed on the stone—Jarus saw drops of blood scattered among them, and felt sick.

"Lammar," he murmured again, and this time his voice was dull and heavy as a stone.

They left the canyon behind, and entered the Hedgewood again. Jarus saw the other four companions huddled on the bank, in a grove of trees. A still form lay in the middle of them. He looked much smaller lying there. Neely crouched over her mentor, helpless tears filling her eyes.

Norrin rushed forward, giving orders. "Porcini, the medicine bags. Fast. Rygal, I'll need your cloak—we need to stop the bleeding…"

Jarus peeked around him. The Siren lay in the dirt, blood streaking his wet green scales. There was a gaping wound under Lammar's collarbone, and he seemed to be having trouble breathing. Norrin pressed Rygal's cloak to it and turned to Porcini, who had brought over the pack with the medicine kit.

Lammar coughed, his eyes flickering over the companions. "Norrin… the others…" he started weakly, then coughed again.

"Stay still," Norrin told him gently.

"The others," Lammar began again, his voice a little stronger, "they all made it down?"

"Yes. We are all here. Now lay still…" Norrin dug through the pack. The clinking of glass shards from inside told Jarus that nearly everything had been broken.

"Our supplies," Rygal said, gasping for breath and shaking from the terror of the encounter. "Norrin… all our packs, our supplies… I had to leave them behind…"

"Someone's coming," Morel said suddenly, standing and raising her dagger.

Norrin straightened abruptly. Jarus smelled something—a vaguely human scent. He didn't recognize it, and felt a chill go up his spine.

From the shadowed woods Jarus could see a figure moving slowly towards them. The light caught a face with light brown skin and two piercing blue eyes.

"Stop!" Norrin ordered, standing and raising his staff. "I am a member of the Guardians of Gayrile, and I order you to stop. Who are you and what is your business here?"

But the voice that replied was quiet and calm. "I know who you are, Norrin, though it has been years since we have met. I come to help you. My name is Larkin."

Jarus' head swam with adrenaline and shock from the last few minutes, and his vision blurred. He saw the shadowy form of a slightly built stranger moving from the woods towards them just before the shock took over, and he sank into blackness.

20

❧ ❧ ❧ ❧ ❧ ❧ ❧ ❧ ❧

In the House of Larkin

Jarus opened his eyes. For a moment, he could remember nothing, and thought he was back in Flameton, in a soft bed, and the Serventiri had gone to…

The Serventiri!

In a flash everything came back to him. Yesterday's events had been so horrific that it all felt confusing and blurred. They had fought the Serventiri—Lammar had been hurt, badly—then they had run, fleeing into the forest. Their supplies had been lost, Lammar was going to die without the medicine bag, and then…

He sat up slowly. The stranger who had rescued them was called Larkin, he remembered, and had come from the forest just before Jarus blacked out. He felt his face warm as he remembered that. Fainting. That was a very noble look, he thought bitterly. And in front of Maya too.

His thoughts returned to the stranger who had saved them. The name Larkin was vaguely familiar, but he couldn't place it. He looked around. He lay in a soft bed in a small room, with a slanted ceiling. Faint green light poured through the curtains to his right. Books and knick-knacks inhabited the tall shelf beside the window. More objects were strewn across the floor, adding to the general

207

clutter. But it wasn't messy. The room had a homely and cozy feel.

There were two other beds in the room. Porcini lay asleep in one, murmuring something in a fearful dream. The other bed was empty, but judging by the rumpled state of the blankets, it had been recently inhabited.

Jarus got up stiffly. His legs and back ached as he did so. The grueling run up the cliffs, followed by the battle with the Serventiri, left his muscles quite sore. He noticed that the cut on his forearm had been cleaned and bandaged. Curious and still a little fearful, he jumped down from the bed and padded to the door.

It opened on a short carpeted hallway. Three other doors opened out on the hall, but they were closed. It reminded Jarus of a small and rustic inn. A muffled conversation came from his left—he recognized Norrin's voice, talking to someone else.

"We hate to trespass for long," Norrin was saying. "Thank you for all you have done. Makana mentioned we might find you—but I admit, I didn't know you were still here."

"I have been forced into secrecy and hiding, along with the other Guardians, following Safacon's rise to power," the other speaker said. His voice was soft and rich, carrying the hint of an accent. "If all I can offer is a refuge for those resisting him, I am glad to do so. Stay as long as you wish."

Jarus stepped out hesitantly. He saw Norrin, standing on the stair top, talking to the second speaker. The stranger was small and stocky—he would have stood barely taller than the Brownaes. His skin was olive brown, and his hair was dark, cut short. His beard was dark too, neatly trimmed on the chin, and he also had a long mustache. His ears pointed slightly at the tips.

Norrin noticed Jarus, and his tired face broke into a smile. "Ah, Jarus. Come over here. I am very glad to see you awake."

Jarus walked towards them, eyes still on the stranger. The short man smiled at him too. His eyes were very dark blue, as though the night sky had lent him its color. "Welcome, Cooper," he said, bowing slightly. "I hope your arm is not in pain."

"No, it feels better," Jarus said, looking up at Norrin.

"Jarus, meet Larkin, of the Dwarve people of Daffodalion," Norrin said. "He was one of the first allies of the Guardians of Gayrile, though I have not seen him in years."

"Many years, old friend," Larkin said, chuckling.

Jarus nodded respectfully to the Dwarve, then looked up at Norrin. "What… what happened? Where's everyone else?" He felt a sudden stab of fear. Neely had been hurt. Maya had been bleeding from a cut on her shoulder blades. Rygal had been injured too. And Lammar…

"Safe. Everyone is safe, Jarus," Larkin said gently. "The ladies are all still asleep. I have treated their injuries and bound the Diren's broken wing. I have also re-stitched your friend Rygal's wound. You might want to tell him to rest a bit before he starts on another adventure," he added to Norrin. "Stitches take a little while to heal."

"I'll try," Norrin said with a wry smile.

"Lammar…" Jarus asked, his heart sinking. The image of the Siren, hanging from the Serventiri's sword, entered his mind, and he felt sick with fear.

"He is alive," Larkin said. "I have cleaned and stitched the wound. It did not damage any vital organs—he is very lucky for that. It is a painful injury, yes, but not a fatal one."

"He's alive?" Jarus repeated, feeling weak with relief.

The Dwarve healer nodded. "Yes. He is resting now, but I think I can promise he will live." He smiled at Jarus' relieved and joyous expression. "So, you are the young Cooper who started this whole venture? Who pried old Norrin into challenging Safacon again?"

Norrin chuckled, and Jarus looked away, embarrassed. "I guess—not on purpose, though. I mean, Maya and I didn't—we didn't know we had to—well—" he paused, not sure what to say.

Larkin shook his head with a smile. "I am only teasing you. I must say, I am quite impressed with what Norrin tells me. You are, all of you, quite brave to embark on such a quest. The others will be interested to hear," he added, looking at Norrin.

Norrin looked at him inquiringly. "The others? Who all is here?"

"All who still remain free and alive," Larkin said. "Come, they will be waiting downstairs."

Jarus looked at the Dwarve curiously, not understanding what was going on. From the look on Norrin's face, this was important. He had never seen the wizard in such earnest.

He followed them down the flight of stairs at the end of the hall, and down to the ground floor of the great house. At the foot of the stairs, he paused, in awe as he took it all in. The rooms above had reminded Jarus of an inn—this room reminded him of the council room in Flameton. Several round tables, with chairs set around them, furnished the room. A large fire blazed in the hearth at the center of the room. More chairs were set around it. A door led off to the left, where Jarus could smell food cooking. Another flight of stairs went up to the right, towards another hall of rooms.

There were close to twenty people assembled in the room, all of different species. Humans and Direns, a few Elves, and Jarus saw two tall, silver-skinned Liznees standing by the fire. They were a rugged group—most of them wore tattered clothes and travel-stained cloaks and boots. All of them carried a weapon of some kind.

Jarus didn't recognize any of them, naturally. But Norrin did. The conversation ceased as they reached the bottom of the stairs. Norrin had stopped, looking around the room, disbelief and joy written on his face.

"They've been hiding here," Larkin said. "Word got out that you had come last night, and so they all gathered this morning."

Norrin said nothing, stepping forward toward the group, who had moved towards him. Each of their faces bore the same joy. They clasped hands, talked, laughed, and nearly all embraced him, any formality forgotten. Tears shone on Norrin's cheeks, tears of joy and relief.

"We thought you might never come," one of the warriors, a tall, burly man, chuckled.

"How long… how long have you been here?" Norrin asked him, looking around the group, still overwhelmed.

"Too long," a Diren with violet scales murmured, shaking his head. "Now that Safacon's cracked down on any resistance efforts, most of us were forced here, in hiding."

"We heard a group was plotting to take down Safacon—word reached us from Flamcton a few days ago," another man said. "And we thought, who could it be but old Norrin?"

Affectionate laughter rippled around the group. Norrin shook his head, his eyes shining with tears as he looked at them all.

Jarus looked at Larkin, who watched the happy scene with a smile. "They… they're all…" he started slowly.

"Guardians of Gayrile, yes," Larkin said. "Or what is left of them. The others have all either been killed, or imprisoned in Safacon's dungeons for decades. All the people you see here used to fight under Norrin's command. He thought them all dead for years. Gathering together was too risky—Safacon would kill us all if he sensed another uprising."

Jarus looked at him, catching the pronoun *us*. "You were a Guardian?" he asked.

The Dwarven healer nodded. "Served with them, yes. I assisted as the main healer of the group. In this line of work, that is an appreciated service, believe me." He shook his head wryly. "All these warriors—after the Guardians were disbanded, they have tried to aid the resistance efforts. Now, Safacon has taken control of nearly all the main cities, and captured or killed any insurgents he can. So they have come here, hidden in the surrounding forest."

Jarus remembered the soldiers in Bridgeport, and nodded thoughtfully. He felt a surge of happiness for Norrin—the relief and joy on the old wizard's face as he spoke with his old comrades seemed to be contagious.

It was some time before the rest of the companions, minus Lammar, woke up and headed downstairs too. Norrin introduced them all to the twenty Guardians assembled in the room. Jarus only remembered a few names. His main attention was drawn to Maya, who had come downstairs with a bandage on her left shoulder blade.

"Are you okay?" he asked her.

Maya nodded. "Yes, I'm fine. Larkin said it will heal up pretty soon—it didn't need stitches, thankfully." She managed a shaky smile. "I'm glad you're all right. I wasn't sure if you passed out from an injury or something."

Jarus felt his face warm with humiliation. "No... I'm fine. I... didn't realize you saw." *Of course she saw*, he berated himself. He had fainted in front of the entire company right after Larkin had arrived.

Morel caught the end of the conversation. "Happens to everyone," she said lightly, shrugging. "Battle is a fearsome thing. If you weren't scared, I would think you stupid."

"Who's stupid?" Rygal asked, coming over to them. He still limped slightly, but there was a neat brace wrapped around his knee.

"You are, with the way you killed that last Serventiri on the cliffs. You even *posed* after you stabbed him," Morel said critically.

"I don't pose," Rygal said loftily.

"Yes, you do. You swung your head back so your hair flew over your shoulder while you raise your sword," Morel told him, imitating the pose. Rygal grinned at that.

"Hmm, maybe I should do that after we break the Jewel. Maybe Safacon has taken a lot of damsels in distress prisoner. Maybe they'd be impressed."

Jarus shook his head, smiling. It was good to hear Rygal and Morel's friendly bickering. It had been a long time since they had argued the way they had done when they'd first met.

Larkin disappeared into the kitchen for a moment, then reappeared, announcing that breakfast was ready. Everyone filed into the kitchen to fill their plates. Jarus took a double helping of eggs, potatoes, and sausage, and returned to get a mug of tea. He sat with Maya, Rygal, and Neely. Neely's injured wing had been wrapped and bound protectively against her back for it to heal. She looked tired, but the pain was obviously less.

Jarus devoured his food so fast that his stomach hurt a little after. He drank his tea, letting the food settle, which was when Larkin reappeared from the stairs.

With him was Lammar.

The companions all stopped eating, staring joyfully at the Siren.

There was a large bandage on Lammar's chest, and he looked very tired. But he grinned slightly.

"Hello."

His companions swarmed him in an instant, all talking at once. The room filled with a hubbub of noise as they did so. Lammar only grinned and nodded as he listened, delighted to see them all.

"We are in your debt, Larkin," Norrin told the healer, who only smiled.

"Not at all, old friend. It would not be the first time I have saved his life, particularly. Fourth, if I remember correctly."

"Third," Lammar told him wryly. "That business with the dragon… that doesn't count." He looked up. "Now, it smells delightful in here. I'm starving."

"That has always been the first sign of your recovery," Larkin said, which made the others laugh. He had the Siren sit down and brought him a plate of breakfast. Several of the Guardians crowded around Lammar to greet him and to ask how he was feeling. Lammar seemed to know most of them, and answered their questions patiently.

"Nothing exciting, Rupert," he replied to the burly warrior who had first greeted Norrin. "Climbed up a cliff and got stabbed by a Serventiri. Nothing you haven't heard before—or experienced, for that matter."

"What shapes did you take?" one of the other warriors, a younger man, asked eagerly.

Lammar thought for a moment. "The snake, the wyvern, the big tall warrior. Didn't have time to do much else," he added, sounding disappointed.

There was an appreciative murmur from his audience as they agreed those were their favorite shapes. "What *can* you turn into, Lammar?" Porcini asked him curiously

"Anything really," Lammar said. "I have to see it first. Then I can take its form. The only two drawbacks are that powers don't transfer over—unfortunately, I can't breathe fire in a dragon form. And the other downside is that the shapes of everything else stays the same after I've turned back. For example," he said, holding up a bit of egg, "if this were a Serventiri, and I were a dragon and wanted to eat him, I'd have quite a belly ache when I turn back."

There was more laughter. The atmosphere of the room was light, cheerful even. The soft hum of conversation, the smell of the food and the log fire, the gentle morning light entering the windows was peaceful, calm, comfortable.

Most of the Guardians left after breakfast to tend to their homes. While Larkin's house was a central place of meeting, the Dwarve explained that it was dangerous for them all to gather there too often. So, the remaining outlaws lived in the thick woods beyond, in cabins or huts, within five miles or so of Larkin's house. "Safacon has little reason to search these woods, so we are safe here," Larkin said. "In fact, I was surprised yesterday to see the Serventiri. I guess they only came because of the Jewel."

"What will we do about the Jewel, Norrin?" Morel asked slowly.

"Yesterday, with the Serventiri… if they can track the Jewel, they know we have it. They'll keep coming."

The realization sent a shiver down Jarus' spine. They hadn't beaten the Serventiri yesterday. Yes, they'd killed a number of them, but more would come, following the Jewel like wolves catching a scent. He thought of how much damage had been done in that one battle—so many injuries, and Lammar had nearly been killed. And that battle wouldn't be the last.

All eyes turned to Norrin. The wizard rubbed his chin thoughtfully. "The Jewel must be destroyed on the Golden Tablet, which only makes our need to find the other Objects more urgent. As for the Serventiri, the best we can do to keep them off our trail is to keep the Jewel covered and hidden. They won't be able to sense it as keenly then."

"Then you believe the Serventiri can sense the Jewel's presence?" Larkin asked.

Norrin nodded. "I believe it—I've seen it happen. You would not believe how quickly they arrived yesterday, after we used it to fight Deathcap. No—we can no longer use the Jewel in that way. The risk is far too great. Besides, it is a thing of darkness. Its magic comes from another time, another place, and from another shadow."

"What 'other shadow'?" Maya asked.

Norrin smiled at her. "Well, that is a conversation for another time. What we can gather, at least for now, is that the Serventiri can track the Jewel—and thus, they can track us as well. So we will have to be ready for them."

Neely looked up slowly. "Norrin… what is to be done about the other Objects? The Ring and the Knife—we cannot hope to destroy the Jewel unless we have all three."

"Deathcap still carries the Knife, then?" Larkin asked, looking at Norrin. When the wizard nodded, he frowned deeply. "That is indeed a grave threat."

"Deathcap is driven by lust for power—he will do anything to get the Jewel," Norrin said. "No, what Makana said in Flameton is true. Deathcap will come to us—and when he does, we will have to fight."

"What about the Ring?" Jarus asked curiously. It seemed to be the Object he knew the least about. "What does the Ring do again?"

"The Ring of Light controls light and darkness, day and night, and so, in a way, it controls time itself," Norrin said. "As for its whereabouts, it was lost years ago in the very river we are now following. Whether or not it was carried by the current, or sank into the muddy bottom, I am unsure. But I searched for it for years and never found it."

"It may be still in the river," Larkin said. "At any rate, no travelers have found it, as far as we know."

Jarus felt overwhelmed at the prospect. Finding a tiny ring in a vast expanse of water and mud and sand seemed impossible. Unless someone else had found it first?

Rygal seemed to share his thoughts. "Norrin… how are we going to find it?" he asked doubtfully. "It could be anywhere. The river bottom could have shifted and buried it forever. Or someone could have found it and be hiding it—the Brownaes had the Jewel for years, and no one knew."

"I know," Norrin said heavily, "but the most we can do is start looking now. But we have a decent chance to find it. The other Objects are attracted to the Jewel. If the Jewel is near them, they will emit the same magic and energy. With any luck, we will feel the Ring's pull if we pass it by."

"So we'll be able to…*feel* the Ring's magic?" Porcini asked slowly, his face crinkled in thought.

Larkin nodded to him. "Its power is enhanced by the Jewel's proximity. I believe the best chance you have is to search the river thoroughly as you travel," he added to Norrin. "I know the Guardians here are willing to help you, too, if you wish for them to join your quest."

Norrin shook his head almost before Larkin had finished. "No. I want them to stay here. I have no idea what we will be facing when we reach the Topstorm, and Safacon may have some sorcery set up that will warn him of our arrival. You know how he seems to know every time the Guardians have tried to gather."

"Yes," Larkin said, looking unconvinced. "But they are ready to fight for you. All they need is a leader."

Norrin shook his head again. "It is too risky. Safacon knows their names and their faces. He would see us coming a mile away. No…I have a plan for them to fight Safacon, but I am still working on it, and storming the gates will probably not work best. I will speak with you and them later."

Larkin nodded slowly. "All right. If you think it is best. At least let them help you search the river near the house today."

"Of course," Norrin said. "We'll search that stretch of river today, and then move on in a few days once Lammar is recovered." He threw a slight smile at the two Coopers. "I seem to recall that some of us like to swim?"

. . . . . .

Norrin guessed the Ring had sunk to the bottom of the river, and either lodged among the rocks, or sunk into the mud. He hoped it to be the former. The odds of finding it seemed very small to Jarus, but it was better than doing nothing at all, and so he, Maya, the Brownaes, and a few of the Guardians headed out to the river with Norrin and Larkin.

It had been so long since Jarus had swum, he had almost forgotten the thrill and joy of it. The way the cold water rushed through his fur, washing away the grime from the last few days on the trail, the way his webbed paws pulled him through the water. The churning mud from the rapids beyond had settled at this stretch of river, and the cold, clear water refreshed and rejuvenated him. He could feel some of his fear and worry fading away, and let himself relax.

The rocks along the bottom were multi-colored orange, browns, and blues, quite different than the gray of Mata City's canals. He skimmed along the river bed, enjoying the chill of the water, looking for anything small and gold.

He surfaced to take a breath, feeling a huge smile cross his face. For the first time in a long time, he allowed himself to hope that he would, indeed, return to Mata City. To hope that they would succeed in the quest. He would gladly take back the life of a canal cleaner, the hard work he did to support his father—all of it. It was a safe and peaceful life, at least.

He looked at Maya, who had jumped up onto the rocks along the bank and was shivering slightly at the chill. "N-no luck," she reported through chattering teeth.

Jarus grinned at her. "It's not *that* cold…"

"It's cold enough," Maya said, scowling playfully.

"That's because you're in the shade—come sit in one of the sunny patches."

Maya moved to a different rock in full sun and stopped shivering.

"Better?" Jarus asked, grinning.

"Maybe," Maya admitted. She was smiling, the sunlight catching the glittering droplets in her fur, and her eyes twinkling happily in the afternoon light. Jarus felt his own cheerfulness increase as he studied her. Maybe when they returned to Mata City…

Then his happiness dissolved. When they returned to Mata City, he knew exactly what would happen. He would go back to his life as a canal cleaner, and she would return to a life of luxury, of garden parties, of rich suitors. Just because she had decided against marrying Hagar didn't mean Jarus had any more of a chance.

His expression must have changed, because she looked at him curiously. "What's wrong? I'm teasing you, Jarus—the sun feels great out here."

"It does," Jarus agreed absently, and dove under the water again, watching as the rocks sped past, and wishing the water could wash away every barrier that stood between them.

21

The Division of the Company

It rained that night, drumming on the windows and dripping down from the eaves. Jarus heard it all night, and thought wistfully of his pleasant swim yesterday. Well, there would be no swimming today, although he guessed they would still spend the day looking for the Ring in the river.

He still had a little more time to sleep, he thought, and snuggled back into the blankets.

"Jarus!"

Jarus jumped as Porcini whispered right into his ear. The young Brownae stood above him, his eyes wide.

"What is it?" Jarus asked.

"Well, it's nothing, not really, but—Norrin and Rygal got up a bit ago, and they're talking with Larkin out in the hall. It sounds like something's wrong."

Jarus got up and followed Porcini to the door. Together, they listened intently.

"...how they managed to catch up to us this fast," Rygal was saying.

"We never truly outran them, they would have crossed the river, and beside that, they can sense the Jewel's presence," Norrin said quietly.

"They are not far off," Larkin said in a lowered tone. "I am loathe to wake your companions, but… better safe than sorry, as the saying goes."

"How far are they, anyway?" That was Rygal.

"Maybe an hour, maybe two—depends on which report you believe." There was a pause, then Norrin sighed. "Larkin is right. Wake the others. I'll go tell the girls…"

Norrin's footsteps retreated down the hallway, and Jarus and Porcini stepped back just in time as Rygal opened the door. He looked surprised.

"What are you doing up so early?"

"We heard you talking—what's going on?" Jarus asked.

Rygal took a breath. "Well…it might be nothing. But a message came from one of Larkin's scouts in the north that a large group of Serventiri are coming this way. It was delivered by a Dwarve who told the same report. We're not exactly sure how far away they are, but we can't lead them here." He moved to wake Lammar, who was still asleep.

Jarus stuffed his few possessions into his bag and followed Porcini into the hall. Morel and Maya both stood there, their fur disheveled. Neely was helping Norrin gather the gear.

"Good morning," Jarus told them. Maya mumbled something and yawned—Morel looked barely awake and about ready to stab whoever had woken her.

The companions met downstairs—by that time, Rygal and Norrin had explained the situation to everyone. Jarus felt a stir of fear. If the Serventiri caught them in the same way they had last time…if someone was hurt bad again…

"Let's go—we don't have much time," Rygal said, shouldering his pack.

Norrin clasped Larkin's hand. "Thank you for your hospitality. We are in your debt."

"Think nothing of it," Larkin said with a slight bow. "The best way you can repay it is by continuing your mission, and stopping Safacon."

"Then we will attempt to do so," Norrin said. He paused. "The others—tell them I am sorry I didn't have much news. Remind them that Gayrile has always had a better alternative to any Jewel— the Guardians will rise again. Mind the plan."

"And they are ready to follow you, if the sooner you send word," Larkin said with a mysterious smile. "But you must hurry."

Norrin looked at him, remembering something. "We cannot leave you here unprotected…"

"No matter—the Serventiri seek the Jewel, not this house—and even then, there is magic set up around these parts that will protect us," Larkin told him. "Now go."

The eight companions slipped out the door and into the chill morning air. Dawn was coming, and it was spitting rain. Jarus shivered at the chill breeze and sniffed the air. No sign of Serventiri… but their scent was carried faintly on the wind.

Norrin led them down the path along the river, staying just within the trees. Another set of rocky cliffs rose up before them again in great rows of stone. Jarus gulped. There were far too many places for Serventiri to hide in those rocks.

They moved quickly from shadow to shadow, pausing every now and then to listen. But there were no sounds, no sign. The Serventiri seemed far away.

Perhaps it wasn't Serventiri, Jarus wondered suddenly. Maybe they'd just mistaken it in the early light. But…he trusted the report, at any rate.

After several miles, with the sun rising steadily, there was still no sign.

Maya looked at him, frowning slightly. "Maybe…it's nothing?"

The words were just out of her mouth when Neely screamed, "Get down!"

Jarus crouched and looked up—up ahead, Norrin had ducked just in time. A scaled gray dragon had dove from the rocks, clawing at him, a Serventiri on its back—Norrin straightened and sent a flare of sparks from his staff, knocking the rider into the river.

"Keep to the edge!" the wizard warned. Jarus huddled under a rocky outcrop, watching, every muscle in his body tense. He could smell the odd artificial scent of the Serventiri…they seemed to be up on the rocks above them.

"Could we go in the river?" Rygal panted—he had drawn his sword and was peering up the cliffs.

"No, it's too exposed—we have to stay in the rocks," Norrin said, his eyes scanning the path. "Right, let's move…slowly…"

Following the wizard, the companions began to edge their way down the path, staying as close to the rock walls as possible. Jarus peered up the sheer rock face—he guessed the Serventiri would be up there, somewhere…but the companions could only go forward. The river trapped them to their left, and the rocks were at the right—they had to stay on the path.

He bumped into Porcini, who had stopped to watch as one of the dragons swept low over the river.

"What breed of dragons are these, then?" Jarus asked him impatiently. His fear made his voice harsh.

"Northern Redclaws," Porcini murmured, keeping his eyes on the dragon. "Big ones. Easy to domesticate, but not very smart. You know…the reason they call them Redclaws…it's because their claws are long enough to get—"

Whatever the reason the dragons were called Redclaws, Jarus never found out, because at that moment the Serventiri on the dragon pointed at the companions, and the dragon swept towards them. Trapped against the rock, Jarus shrank back in terror.

Norrin blasted it in the mouth with sparks, and it reeled back with a snarl, dislodging its unfortunate rider, who fell into the swirling river. "Come along," Norrin muttered, moving forward again, "quickly…"

The rocks faded up ahead into the shadowed forest. If they could get into the trees, they might be able to escape.

It was in that instant that another dragon dove, blasting fire from its jaws. Jarus saw the flames, and in a split second, the only thing he could think of was getting away as fast as he could. Instinct took over, and he bolted. The other companions were running too, pushing past each other in panic. Jarus reached the woods, running, terrified and heart pounding, and tripped over a rock and slammed his head into a tree.

Darkness swam in his vision as he lay there, dazed. Then he sat up. The sounds of the dragons were fainter, as was the scent of the Serventiri, but the battle was still happening…

"Norrin!" he shouted, his voice small and scared in the silence.

A hand gripped his shoulder, and he jumped back in panic. "It's me—it's all right," Rygal said quickly.

"Where's—"

"Porcini—have you seen Porcini?" Morel's voice came from behind him, tense with worry.

"He was back at the rocks," Rygal told her, looking back at the cliffs.

Lammar and Neely stood behind Morel—Lammar was pale, and fresh blood stained his bandages.

"Where's Maya?" Jarus asked.

They all looked at each other uncertainly. Jarus felt panic rise in his chest. Maya and Porcini—the smallest and most inexperienced of their company, missing—and where was Norrin?

A sudden cry came from the woods. "Rygal? Rygal?"

"Maya!" Jarus shouted, and the companions jogged towards her voice.

Maya was sitting huddled by a fern, her eyes wide and frightened. "Did…Norrin make it to the woods?" she asked softly, trembling.

"I—no, we haven't seen him yet—why, where is he?" Rygal demanded, sounding worried now.

Jarus' panic doubled as Maya began to sob. "Maya—what happened—where's Norrin?"

"He—told me to run—Porcini had—Porcini was—" Maya choked out.

Morel stepped forward, her voice hoarse. "Porcini? What happened to Porcini?"

Maya took a shaking breath. "He—oh, Morel—he stopped to see the dragons, he loves dragons—and—the one that shot the fire—it picked him up and carried him away!"

"No!" Morel said, leaping upright and starting back towards the cliffs, "no, they can't take him—"

Rygal took her shoulder, his face gray with fear. "And Norrin—what did Norrin do?"

"Shot the dragon with sparks—it dropped Porcini, I think, he fell in the river—one of the dragons breathed fire at Norrin and he jumped in the water too—I don't know what happened—they're gone…" Maya trailed off, her voice hollow and quiet. The horror of it seemed to have frozen any emotion in her.

"They might have made it," Morel said immediately. "The river—it will carry them this way…"

"Norrin wouldn't have let the river carry them, because the Serventiri would have picked them out of the water…he would have got to shore and then followed the one that took Porcini," Rygal said, his voice holding the same lifelessness as Maya's.

"What do we do?" Neely asked, her eyes wide.

There was a long silence. "We wait," Rygal said finally, standing. "Wait for an hour…if they're not here…we have to keep going."

"We can't leave them!" Jarus said.

"Norrin wouldn't want us to wait behind and risk losing the Jewel to the Serventiri," Rygal said quietly. He didn't seem to have the energy to argue with his usual volume. "That's what they're tracking. They'll know that we still have it, and follow us."

"I'm not leaving Porcini," Morel said flatly.

Lammar spoke quietly. "You can do that, princess. Stay here. But you know there's no chance of fighting them. If Norrin and Porcini are alive, they'll rejoin us as soon as they can. But the Jewel is what the Serventiri want and they'll keep coming for it."

"Maybe I'll fight them with it!" Morel challenged, rising. "Maybe I'll stay here with it!"

"If you do that, I'd think you a fool. There are countless Serventiri, too many for you to control them with the Jewel," Lammar said, his voice still level. His eyes were locked on Morel's.

"It's better than just giving up!" Morel shouted at him, her voice shrill.

"Do you think that's what we're doing? Giving up is staying here. Giving up is waiting until the Serventiri come and kill us all, and take the Jewel."

Jarus was bewildered by the scene playing out before him. Not from Morel—he'd seen her fire often enough. But he had never, not once, seen the look in Lammar's eyes. The total lack of fear or doubt somehow told Jarus that the Siren had more idea of command than anyone else here.

Morel looked between the Siren's eyes and the rocky bank behind them. Lammar spoke again, his voice almost gentle.

"If Porcini is alive, Norrin will find him. You can trust me on that. He is more powerful than any of you have seen yet. But I need you, princess. If we're attacked, I have no backup. Neely and Rygal are both injured, and the Coopers don't have your experience. And you know that if you try to fight the Serventiri now, you're already giving up. Giving up on Porcini, on the quest, and on everything you say you stand for."

There was a tense silence. Morel looked back toward the cliffs, as if she could see where the Serventiri had taken her brother. "One hour," she said finally. "We'll give them one hour to get back to us. If nothing, then we keep going."

Lammar nodded to her, then looked to the others. "Rest if you can. I'll wake you when we keep going."

. . . . . .

Porcini lay in a pool of water, dazed, hearing the distant pound of wings and strange roars of the dragons. The Serventiri were searching for him, he guessed distantly.

What had happened?

He sat up, and slowly it all came back to him. He had been telling Jarus about the dragons. Then one of them had dove and breathed fire, and it had been pandemonium. Porcini had tripped as he ran—the dragon had gripped his shoulders and swept him into the sky. The ground had dropped away—he had screamed for Morel, but Morel didn't hear him.

But Norrin had. The wizard had turned just in time and blasted the dragon in the wing, making it lurch in its flight. It had dropped Porcini, who had toppled into the frigid water. Porcini surfaced just in time to see another dragon breathe a plume of fire at Norrin. Flames licked along the ground at the wizard, catching his beard and clothes, and Norrin had dove into the river. Porcini had shouted in alarm at the sight of the flames, and the dragon had turned and lifted him again, carrying him up river towards the cliffs. Gasping, panicked at the thought of falling, Porcini could do nothing but hold on tight and scream, hoping someone would hear him.

Then there came a second blast of sparks, the dragon dropped him, and he plunged into the river again. Dazed, he had allowed himself to float downstream, wondering briefly if he'd float far enough for the others to find him…he doubted it. The dragon had carried him very far upstream.

He lay down again, head pounding, the world spinning slightly.

Had he been injured in the fall? He hoped not…it would make finding and rejoining his companions a lot harder… His shoulders hurt too—he felt four small gashes in each one made by the dragon's claws.

Then, vaguely, he heard a voice—wonderfully familiar. "There you are, boy…don't be afraid, we'll be all right…"

Strong arms lifted him, and he recognized the voice as Norrin's. Wearily, he raised his head and looked at the wizard. There were a few burns on Norrin's face, and his beard was badly singed. But he smiled at Porcini as he sat him down a little ways from the river.

"Norrin?" Porcini asked groggily, sitting up. His head throbbed, and he laid down again. "What… where are we?"

Norrin stacked a few dry branches together, then touched his staff to it, starting a small fire. The warmth was comforting. "As best as I can make out, Porcini, we're about fifteen miles upriver."

"Fifteen!" Porcini said in shock, sitting up again abruptly. He wished he hadn't—his vision blurred and he had to lay down. "Fifteen miles…Norrin, what will we…the others…"

Norrin tossed a few more branches on the fire and pulled off his wet cloak, hanging it to dry. "This isn't your fault, Porcini. The good news is that we do have a plan in place—one that Lammar and I, along with King Makana, worked out a while back. Rygal and Lammar are to lead the companions to Safacon's palace, and you and I will rejoin them."

"How?" Porcini asked, eyes wide.

"Well, we will follow the river. We're on the opposite shoreline, and I think I can promise you we'll have no more run-ins with Deathcap, at least."

"What about the Serventiri?"

"Ah yes, well, they are a different matter." Norrin rubbed his brow tiredly. "The Serventiri are following the Jewel, which means they may pass us by entirely. Or they may not. We'll have to be very cautious."

Porcini took a breath. Night was falling. It was strange, being out for a whole day… at least Norrin had found him. "My head hurts," he confessed at last.

"I would imagine so—you have suffered quite a concussion," Norrin told him with a faint smile. "The medicine I carried in my pack is wet, but no less effective—I will give you some of it in the morning. For now, rest, and try not to worry."

Porcini settled back against the ferns, shivering slightly, and then scooted closer to the fire. He was soaking wet, and the breeze chilled him to the bone. In the distance came the wild sounds of the forest animals, and, far off now, the cries of the dragons, still seeking the Jewel.

It would be a long night.

22

⌇ ⌇ ⌇ ⌇ ⌇ ⌇ ⌇ ⌇

Journey to the Falls

By the time the hour had passed, it had already been established that Norrin and Porcini would not be rejoining them here. Morel did not argue this time—she seemed to have accepted the fact. The Serventiri still soared the sky on their dragons, and going back to the river would lead to nothing good.

Rygal and Lammar held a brief discussion, then they began walking down the path, following the Rummeryn as it flowed southwest. It was not until the sun had begun its descent that the cries of the dragons faded, and Lammar deemed they had left the Serventiri behind…for now.

Serventiri or no, they had to stop and rest, and so they did. Lammar's wound had reopened in the panicked flight at the cliffs, and Rygal re-stitched it while Maya searched through the packs for an evening meal.

Morel sat silently on the bank of the river, watching the water go by in silence. Jarus glanced at her occasionally, a little worried. Finally he looked at Maya. "Do you think…we should maybe…?"

Maya looked over at the princess and sighed. "I don't know. Let her be alone for now. Nothing we can say can make her feel better."

Jarus nodded, knowing she was right. Oddly enough, he didn't

235

feel grief—only afraid. There was no telling if Norrin and Porcini had made it. Even if they had, the rest of them were without their leader, and the wisest person in the group. He remembered snapping at Porcini right before the dragon had dove, and felt a stir of guilt.

Maya cut a few slices of bread, then put the loaf back with uncharacteristic silence. Jarus looked at her carefully. "Maya…it wasn't your fault. You know that."

Maya smiled faintly. "Yeah…I know. I just wish…there was something I could have done. To help. All I could do was run."

Jarus looked at her curiously. "But even Rygal couldn't have done anything, and he's the best warrior I've ever met." He paused. "Well, after Norrin, probably. Or maybe Lammar."

Maya nodded, and hesitated. "Yes…I…I suppose I just wish I could do something useful. I don't know how to fight. I'm barely keeping up with everyone as is."

"I think you're doing great," Jarus said, with a bit of conviction. Maya looked up at him with a quizzical expression, and he blushed. "I mean—this quest isn't all fighting. You've been brave and strong and you're keeping up with a lot of others who have done this sort of thing before."

"So are you," Maya pointed out immediately.

Jarus shook his head. "No, but we're talking about you."

Maya finally smiled. "Well…thanks for that." She dug in the bag until she produced several strips of meat. "Here—guess this is dinner." She got up to pass everyone else's food around.

Jarus watched her as he ate, wishing there was some way he could tell her how much he admired her—and not just in the way she carried on with this quest. He shook the thoughts out of his head. No, without Norrin and Porcini, there'd be a lot more to do, and there was no place for love in that.

······

A restful night's sleep followed by dawn watch seemed to refresh Rygal, who woke them early in the morning. "Been thinking— Norrin and Porcini might be able to find the Ring on their way back to us," he pointed out as Maya passed out breakfast.

Jarus brightened a little at this. As far as they knew, the Ring was north of Larkin's house, which was where the dragon had dropped Porcini—maybe Norrin would find it.

They packed up their camp and then started walking. They had left the rocky hills behind them, and now the path wound through the scrubby woods. The road never strayed far from the river. Jarus watched the water stream by them.

"Maybe we could build some rafts—then we could float down to Safacon's palace. It'd be a lot faster than walking," he suggested to Lammar.

The Siren studied the river a moment, then frowned. "It would, but I'm not sure we want to come sailing into Safacon's fortress. Our goal is to enter secretly."

Jarus nodded, a little disappointed. "How far do you suppose we are from the mountain—the—the whatever it's named?"

"The Topstorm?" Rygal asked, and Jarus nodded. Rygal thought for a moment. "I'm not quite sure. Norrin and I reviewed the maps at Larkin's, but I don't remember it too well." He paused. "We're getting close to the falls, and after that, I think it was only around twenty miles to the Topstorm. Safacon's fortress is said to be right at its base."

This news was encouraging. They were getting close. "And the Golden Tablet?"

"I'm not sure. No one is, really. No one has been to Safacon's fortress in years—who knows what he's got in there. Norrin said he thinks the Tablet is on the slope directly above Safacon's fortress."

They walked in silence for a while. Jarus thought of his father, likely held captive in Safacon's palace. He found himself also thinking, unexpectedly, of his mother, wherever she was. He wondered if she knew or cared what was happening. Maybe she did…

He paused as a new thought hit him.

What if…what if his mother *hadn't* run off—what if she'd been taken—captured—by *Safacon*?

Suddenly, his heart was pounding. Ada Puddlepaw had disappeared without a trace. She hadn't been having a secret affair, as far as Jarus knew, but either way he highly doubted it. His father had pursued the matter as far as he could afford—they weren't able to pay for a professional investigator.

But maybe…maybe she had been kidnapped. Taken in the same way Carus had been.

Maybe she was still alive.

Jarus couldn't shake this idea, and told Maya about it the minute they stopped for afternoon meal. "Maya—I need to talk to you."

Maya looked a little puzzled, and followed him a little ways away from the others. Jarus immediately told her his whole theory. He watched her face carefully as he finished, and was greatly disappointed to see some doubt there. "Well…it's possible, I guess, Jarus…I don't know."

"Why not? What else could have happened?" Jarus demanded.

"Well, she might have—"

"She *didn't* run off," Jarus interrupted indignantly.

Maya shook her head patiently. "No, I'm not saying she did—but Jarus, she didn't really…I mean, your family…well… Safacon wouldn't have had any reason to capture her, would he?"

Jarus paused. He hadn't considered that. "But… why not? I mean, Safacon is out of his mind—he wants the Jewel so badly that he's been kidnapping people left and right that he thinks could have it."

"Yes… *wealthy* people," Maya said uncomfortably.

The word punched Jarus in the stomach, and in a flash his excitement was gone. "Oh," was all he said, his voice dull.

Maya looked at him unhappily. "I—I'm sorry—you might be right, I just thought we'd better look at the facts—for what might have motivated Safacon to do that…" She trailed off.

"No…you're right," Jarus replied quietly. "For that matter, we've never had anything of value that Safacon or anyone else would want."

"Well, I don't know," Maya said suddenly, looking at him. "It's better than arranged marriages and dinner parties and never feeling like anything more than… more than a lot of money and a pretty face."

She looked down, quiet. Jarus looked at her in surprise. "I…I thought you enjoyed that kind of thing. I mean… that's the way your family has always been."

"I know," Maya said. She hesitated. "To tell you the truth… that's not the way I want things to stay, if we make it back. Not after seeing how King Makana and the Direns have used their wealth to help people—not just kept it for themselves. The way they share with everyone, especially the less fortunate. And to think that I've lived without questioning any parts of my life for so long…" she trailed off, then began again. "I don't think I'll ever go back to that life again. Not if we survive this quest. There are so many other things I want to do, so many things I want to learn, and I know they won't fit in that life."

Jarus was startled. The conviction and passion in her voice were a completely different Maya. No longer did she sound like the quiet, fragile girl he had known in Mata City, the girl who followed the restrictions of her class without question, the girl who never thought for herself. This Maya stood before him, bruised and battered, a wound across her shoulders from a Serventiri's sword, fur covered in dirt and grime. There was a light in her eyes that was entirely new.

"I thought you said you couldn't change that," he said finally. "In Mata City, when you first told me about you and Hagar being engaged. You said that you couldn't do anything about it… because that's how things work in the upper class."

Maya glanced at him and shrugged slightly. "Well, that *was* true. But that doesn't mean I can't make my own decisions." She looked up at the trees, the breeze blowing her fur gently. "Being out here, on this quest—I feel stronger now, Jarus. Strong enough to tell my father what I really want."

Jarus stared at her, not sure what to say, suddenly filled with wild hope.

They continued on the rest of the afternoon, passing the thundering waterfall that marked twenty miles from the Topstorm. The roar of the falls could be heard from the camp as the companions settled down for the night. Jarus sat awake on first watch, thinking through his and Maya's conversation.

Perhaps his mother was out there, still alive.

And perhaps Maya would be there with him to find her.

23

❧ ❧ ❧ ❧ ❧ ❧ ❧ ❧ ❧

What Porcini Found

"Time to get moving," Norrin said.

Porcini stretched and stood carefully. His head hurt much less, which was good, and while his body was still sore from the slap of the water, it was nothing compared to yesterday's ache. He had slept through the night, and Norrin woke him at dawn. It was cold and windy again, and Porcini shivered.

"You will warm up as we walk," Norrin told him with a slight smile.

Porcini nodded, looking around. "Norrin—will we go back to Larkin's?" Warm beds and large meals sounded especially appealing right now.

"Not today," Norrin said. "If we can make it there tomorrow, then yes, we will. It is on the other side of the river, however, and we won't cross unless we have to."

They headed down the path, moving steadily southeast and following the river. The path on the west bank was wilder than the other road, a crumbling dirt road overgrown by briers. The woods reminded Porcini very much of the Wandering Wood, which was comforting to him. The desert and the rocky cliffs had been so different from the tall trees he was used to.

He looked up at the wizard, who strode resolutely ahead. There was a calm resolve in Norrin's face that impressed Porcini—even with this sudden change of plan, he still seemed completely in control.

"Norrin…" he began uncertainly, not sure if he should ask the question. Norrin glanced at him, and he continued. "Norrin—who were the Guardians of Gayrile? I heard you mention them when Larkin first came."

Norrin was silent, then nodded slowly. "I can tell you as we walk. The Guardians of Gayrile were established shortly after the fall of the cruel queen Kircadash, many years ago. Safacon was not yet a threat, and a time of peace had filled the northern part of Orlell."

"Peace?" Porcini repeated, surprised. "Then Safacon hadn't created the Objects yet?"

"We think not—if he had, he had not yet used them to take control," Norrin said. "The Guardians of Gayrile were founded, as I said, shortly after the fall of Kircadash. The Liznee people of Coonsia helped organize them as a measure of security to protect the Northern Isles. I was one of its founders, in fact, along with several others. For many years we continued in our mission of protecting the commonwealth and maintaining peace in Gayrile."

Porcini listened, very interested. "Then…what happened to them?" He had a guess, and he already knew it was nothing pleasant.

Norrin sighed heavily. "When Safacon rose to power, he did it very carefully and methodically. Many people were fooled that he was nothing more than an especially eccentric politician, and followed him without thought. Safacon had the Jewel, and with it he made the Serventiri. They forced the people into submission, forced them to obey his every order. The Guardians resisted and tried to fight, and he killed…many of them." A shadow crossed Norrin's face, and he paused before continuing.

"The surviving Guardians were forced to go into hiding and wait to bring down Safacon's regime in secret. Some were right on the front lines, forming secret militias and such, like Rygal's father did. Others, like Larkin, remained in hiding, standing as a safe house for the insurgents."

"But what about the Direns?" Porcini asked. "Couldn't they have stopped Safacon? They have control of Gayrile, don't they?"

"Well, they do, in a way," Norrin said. "Garilian politics are a bit complicated, Porcini. All of us answer to the High King of Coonsia, because Gayrile is a Coonsian territory. But by the time people realized Safacon was indeed a threat, it was too late—he had already taken control and sent his deputy Kado to the mainland, along with an army of immortal warriors."

"Immortal?"

"To a point—those warriors were called the Hazes. They were… well, incomplete, as it were. Safacon was still perfecting the enchantment. He never managed to complete that project, for the Jewel was stolen from him before he could do more."

Porcini thought this through. The story of Kado and the Hazes was not entirely unknown to him—Rygal had told him about that battle on the journey. He looked up at Norrin again. "Then once we beat Safacon, do you suppose the Guardians will return?"

"I hope so," Norrin said with a half-smile. "Rygal has been recruiting loyal and fierce warriors almost as soon as he returned from the battle with Kado. Once Safacon is gone, the Guardians can be re-established, and we can begin helping the commonwealth again."

"And my father's tribe can help," Porcini said. "The Chanterelle tribe—they can help the Guardians too." He wasn't entirely sure how all the politics worked—and he knew that the Brownae tribes had fought against the humans over territory for years. But now, with Safacon as a common enemy, they were allies.

Norrin stopped abruptly, his brow furrowed. Porcini looked at him in confusion. "What is it?"

The wizard's face was puzzled—and a little worried. "It's here—it's close—how did we miss it?" he was murmuring to himself.

"What?" Porcini asked, a little concerned now, and wondering if Norrin was starting to go crazy.

Norrin turned slowly, looking at the river. "It's very close…yes, this is the place…the place where Deathcap fought for it, and it fell in the river…" He turned sharply, gripping Porcini's shoulders, his face suddenly elated.

"What—" Porcini started again, alarmed.

"It's very near, Porcini!" Norrin said in a hushed tone, his face showing great excitement. "How on Orlell did I not notice it before— no matter, this is the place, I am sure of it, and I can feel it…"

"You can feel what?" Porcini asked.

"The Ring, of course, the Ring of Light! I can sense it—when Deathcap last fought for it, this was the place where we fought—and the Ring fell into the river!" Norrin turned towards the swirling water, eyes alight and scanning the banks.

"But where is it?" Porcini asked excitedly.

"I am not sure—still in the river, most likely—we may have to wade…"

Porcini's heart sank a little at that. It was a chilly morning, and the idea of being wet was not appealing. But Norrin was so excited that he hated to let him down. "All right—what should I do?"

They moved towards the water. Norrin was pacing up and down the bank, like a dog catching a scent on multiple breezes of wind. "Close…closer…" he muttered to himself, pausing every now and then. Finally he stopped, looking straight out in the water. With the rain a few days before, the river was deep and full, churning brown. "It is in this stretch of river—whether it is close to the banks or in the center, I am not sure."

"What if it's in the middle?" Porcini asked worriedly. Neither of them would be able to swim out there and dive for something as small as a ring. The water would be too murky to see anything.

"We'll start with the shallows. We might have time to—" Norrin stopped abruptly, looking upstream. His face had suddenly gone pale.

Porcini followed his gaze, and felt his heart sink. Four shapes reeled in the air, getting closer to them.

"The Serventiri," he whispered, hearing the eerie cries of the dragons.

"Get back," Norrin warned, and they huddled back in the shadows of the trees. Porcini watched as the group flew closer. He realized, suddenly, that the Serventiri would be able to sense the Ring's reawakened magic too—and the dragons could dive for it.

Norrin stood, clutching his staff, looking like he was thinking hard. "We cannot let them get it… we need to stop them."

"How?" Porcini whispered.

The dragons swept low over the river, hovering over the water— Porcini could see the Serventiri peering into the murky river, excitement in their hollow blue eyes.

Norrin stepped forward. "I will distract them. You must watch the water. If the Ring is washed close to shore, it will be up to you to grab it and flee."

Porcini looked at him in shock. "Washed to me? But what do I do with it? What about you?"

"You'll be all right—keep to the trees…" Norrin moved forward onto the shoreline. The Serventiri seemed to be trying to convince the dragons to dive into the frigid water. The dragons, clearly not interested in this option, hovered uncertainly above the surface.

Norrin stood on the shore, the river lapping at his boots, and waited. The Serventiri saw him first—Porcini watched them straighten, then point at the wizard. They reined the dragons up sharply, then charged.

Norrin sent a ray of crackling yellow light from the end of his staff, creating a line between himself and the Serventiri. The warriors stopped, the dragons reeling over the river, snarling.

Porcini watched, not sure what to do. Norrin stood erect, as if he could feel some powerful force rising from wherever the Ring was. Then he lowered his staff again, and struck the water directly by the shoreline just as the dragons lunged forward.

A cloud of steam shot up as the staff touched the water—in an instant, Norrin and the warriors vanished from view into the cloud. Porcini could see flashes of dragon fire, met here and there by sparks.

"Norrin!" he called fearfully. The wizard couldn't possibly beat them all on his own—but he wouldn't leave until he had the Ring safely away from the Serventiri.

Porcini steeled himself, forgetting his fear, and stepped toward the river edge. The cold water lapped at his toes—he took a deep breath and then dove.

The cold took his breath away as the water closed around his body. He surfaced, gasping and sputtering, then dove again. The fog and murky water made it almost impossible to see anything— Porcini swam down until he touched the rocky bottom, and began crawling his way along, feeling for anything.

There was a muffled crash up above, then a mighty splash—Porcini surfaced, taking a deep breath, and stared in shock and awe. One of the dragons, its great hide burned and slashed, floated a few feet away from him. Its rider rose up out of the water inches from Porcini's face, the skull-like eyes boring into his own.

Porcini shouted and leapt back, heart pounding. The Serventiri looked around, then dove into the water.

It could sense the Ring—it would get to it before he did.

"No!" Porcini yelled, and plunged into the water again. The glowing blue eyes of the Serventiri lit the murky water as it clawed through the rocks into the mud. Porcini gripped its wrist in his paw and pulled it back—it struck at him, knocking him back up to the surface. Porcini took a huge gulp of air and then plunged back into the freezing water.

The Serventiri's face bore a look of excited triumph—the Ring was close at hand. Porcini struck at it as hard as he could through the water, knocking it back, and clutched at the mud for something to use as a weapon. His hand found only a fistful of soft mud—in a moment, the Serventiri returned, flinging Porcini out of the water with its artificial strength.

Porcini crashed into the muddy water by the bank, coughing and shivering. The steam had cleared—he could see other Serventiri in the water, thrashing like monsters in a feeding frenzy, seeking the Ring.

"No!" Porcini shouted. He still clutched his handful of mud, and now knelt to wash it away.

Then he froze. In his hand, covered in mud and silt, was a small round object, an unmistakable shape. Heart pounding, he washed away the mud, and stared.

In his hand he held a ring of gold, small and simple, with a pure black stone set in it. The stone held a darkness deeper than its color—a power that Porcini had only seen glimpses of.

He knew, without a doubt, that this was the Ring of Light.

For a moment he stood there, totally at a loss of what to do. The Serventiri were still seeking furiously in the water, but in a few moments they'd realize that he had it, and then they'd be after him. "Norrin," he mumbled fearfully, then called as loudly as he dared, "Norrin!"

The Serventiri stopped, and looked up slowly, their eyes training on him. Porcini stood unmoving, too terrified to move as they started forward, the three remaining dragons following with ominous growls.

"Norrin!" Porcini shouted again, this time in true fear.

The Serventiri had nearly reached him when the wizard leapt between the two, sparks shooting from the ends of his staff as he fought back the warriors. Two of them were killed instantly—the others shrank back, then lunged.

24

§ § § § § § § § §

The Parlay of the Serventiri

It was just after they passed the falls that the Serventiri caught up to the six companions.

Lammar had been leading them steadily along the east bank of the river, as it wound its way closer to the Topstorm. Yesterday had been so foggy that Jarus could see hardly anything, but by afternoon the mist had lifted, and they had seen the mountains. They rose above the trees, craggy black peaks, the tallest of which was wreathed in clouds. That, Lammar said, was the Topstorm.

Lammar had wisely decided to cross the river last night to throw any pursuers off their trail. After that, they had seen nothing of the Serventiri that morning, and had continued down the path.

They were walking in single file, moving quickly and quietly. The same bland gray-brown of the shabby trees filled the terrain, and the slight breeze carried a damp, mildewed smell to Jarus' nose. While the domain of Safacon was said to be a place of wealth, here on the doorstep, the land was wasted with rot and decay, the life drained out of it by the Jewel's power. Conversation was limited, and Jarus was so tired he barely had the energy to talk at all.

Morel and Rygal were talking in lowered tones up ahead, and Jarus could hear bits and pieces of their conversation. "Maybe they

251

found the Ring," Rygal was saying.

"Maybe," Morel said, glancing up the river. "The Serventiri could sense that though, right? So then they'd attack them?"

"I'm not sure," Rygal murmured. He shook his head. "I would hope that Norrin would try to avoid battle, but I'm not sure he'd have much of an option if the Serventiri are searching for the Ring too."

"Norrin could fight them," Jarus spoke up from behind.

"He could," Lammar said, "but it might not end well."

There was a moment of silence. Jarus wondered suddenly if they would ever see Norrin or Porcini again. He hoped so, but if the Serventiri caught them, did they have a chance?

He swallowed and pushed the thoughts away.

Rygal stopped suddenly, looking up. "Dragons—there are some dragons. The Serventiri are back."

He had barely spoke the words when Jarus saw the dragons land on the opposite side of the river. Twelve of them, each carrying two or three Serventiri warriors. One of the dragons landed on their side of the river, and the Serventiri on its back dismounted. The warrior spoke, his voice oddly echoing, slow and careful. Jarus hadn't realized they were capable of speaking—though he guessed that Safacon could speak through them, to a point.

"Company of the Jewel!" the Serventiri called. "We come to parlay."

Jarus looked at Lammar doubtfully. "Parlay? Is this a trap?"

"Might be—but it might be easier to hear them out than try to outrun them," the Siren murmured. He looked at Rygal. "Go answer them—see what they want. We'll wait here."

Rygal moved out of the forest to the shoreline, his hand resting on the hilt of his sword. "Right, then—what's your parlay?"

The Serventiri studied him a long moment, then continued speaking. "Lord Safacon does not care about your travels through his land. All he wants is the Jewel. Give it to us, and we will allow you to continue on."

Jarus realized the Serventiri had no idea what their quest actually was, which was why they thought this was a good bargain. But the very essence of this journey was to destroy the Jewel—which made giving the Jewel away unthinkable.

Rygal clearly knew this too, and looked uncertain now. "Well… my companions and I will have to talk this over."

The Serventiri leader stared at him with empty blue eyes, then nodded. "Very well. We will be back in an hour."

He mounted the dragon and flew across the river.

The companions stepped out onto the riverbank, looking at Rygal. "We can't give them the Jewel," Neely said slowly.

"We need the Jewel," Morel said.

"Norrin told us to keep it safe," Maya said.

"I know!" Rygal said shortly. He took a breath. "We can't give the Jewel away—but if we refuse, they'll kill us all in an instant."

"Maybe we could run?" Jarus suggested, although he knew that wasn't a good option. They had been running so long, they couldn't keep doing this.

"We'll fight," Lammar said quietly. He stood, green skin battered and bruised, looking at Rygal. "We'll fight them back and then run for all we're worth to the Topstorm. That's the only chance we have."

Rygal took a deep breath. "All right. That's what we'll do." He looked at Lammar. "Do you have a plan for attack?"

"Yes, but I'd like to hear yours first. You've done this sort of thing more recently than I have," the Siren said with a crooked grin.

Rygal seemed to analyze the situation. Jarus could almost see the gears turning in his head. "Can you shape-shift?" he asked Lammar.

"I'll do my best—still a bit sore," Lammar said.

"Try to scare them back a bit—do something really big," Rygal said.

Lammar grinned wider and nodded. "Naturally. But that means the Serventiri will come after you once they realize I'm the diversion. The dragons could burn you to a crisp if we're not careful."

"Right," Rygal said, looking uncertain. "What would you have us do, then?"

Lammar looked at Neely. "How's your wing?"

"I can fight, but I cannot fly. Not for a little while longer," Neely said.

"That's fine. That's good. Try to lure the dragons down to you. Your fire will draw their attention—dragons hate any creature that can use fire in the same way they can," Lammar told her.

"What do I do?" Morel asked.

"You and Rygal, you'll be here, covering the retreat. Kill whoever comes after us," Lammar said.

Jarus felt his heart sink a little. Once again, he had been left out of the battle plans. "Wait—I can fight. You'll need all the help you can get."

Lammar looked at him for a moment, then nodded. "All right then—stay with Rygal." He looked at Rygal. "Wait the full hour. Let them think you'll surrender. Wait until their leader comes back, and our attack will be unexpected."

He slipped into the water and swam soundlessly toward the group of Serventiri. The hour passed slowly. Jarus' mouth was dry. He sat between Rygal and Morel, which made him feel a little safer. His eyes rested on Maya, who sat across from them beside Neely. She was silent, but Jarus could see the worry in her eyes.

"They're back," Morel said quietly, a few moments later.

The dragon touched down on the beach, and the warrior dismounted as Rygal walked out. "What say you, travelers?" the Serventiri asked.

Rygal took a breath. "Our mission is to be rid of your master and his Objects of Power. That is why we cannot give you the Jewel. That is why we are on this journey."

The Serventiri said nothing. It seemed to hesitate, as though registering the answer. Then, in a blur of motion, it drew its sword and hacked at Rygal.

Rygal parried the attack and ran the warrior through. In the same second, there was a snarling hiss from the opposite bank as Lammar began his attack.

Jarus stared. He had seen Lammar transform into a snake before—

now what he saw was twice that size. The huge green reptile reeled over the Serventiri, its hood furled out, forked tongue lashing out from between its mighty fangs.

"That's our signal!" Morel said as they turned to run.

The huge Lammar-snake had sent the Serventiri into a panic—a few of them were scrambling for their guns, but the snake's coils crushed the weapons in a moment. But the warriors were not taken off guard for long— in a few moments the dragons had taken to the air.

Jarus watched in awe as Neely climbed to the top of one of the trees—injured or no, she was still a formidable fighter. She fired a blast of flame from her palms at the dragons as they flew above her. That got their attention—snarling, they rounded on her. Neely shot fire once more, then dropped to the ground just in time—one of the dragons had lunged, its huge claws slashing at the tree.

Neely crashed to the ground, shielding her head from the shower of branches, then leapt to her feet. She winced a little as her injured wing was jostled from the drop, but didn't say anything of it. "I think that did it, Rygal—they are angry now. "

The words were barely out of her mouth when the dragons dove, their claws raking at the trees, belching fire down on them. A wave of heat ruffled Jarus' fur, and he stumbled back, bumping into Maya. The fire licked along the damp boughs of the trees, hissing and crackling. Acrid white smoke filled the air, making Jarus gasp. Throat burning, he grabbed Maya's arm and pulled her back along the river bank.

"Stay low!" he heard Rygal shout. More fire came from above. The trees were too wet to ignite immediately, but the smoke filling the air made it difficult to see or breathe.

Through the haze and the blur of tears, Jarus saw the shapes of the dragons dive at them again. Gunfire crackled as the Serventiri fired down at them, trapping them between fire and bullets. Neely raised her hands and shot flames back up at them, which caused them to swerve away. But there was no chance the companions could get a clear shot at the Serventiri.

Morel held the Jewel—the rags had fallen off partly, and blue light shone brightly from her hands. It was as if the Jewel was letting the Serventiri know where exactly to shoot—and now gunfire rained down on them again. For being experimental weaponry, Jarus thought, those guns were formidable weapons.

Morel raised the Jewel and shouted a spell. The Serventiri seemed to lurch slightly on their dragons, but barely reacted. Either Morel had used the wrong spell, or the Jewel had chosen not to obey. Jarus somehow suspected both.

Rygal and Morel were pinned down ten feet away, smoke swirling around them, both of them doubled over and coughing. Neely huddled behind them, the bandage around her injured wing hanging loosely, gasping at the pain. There was no sign of Lammar... he was likely still across the river... had they killed him?

The dragons dove again, lighting the trees directly above them. Sparks, branches, and embers rained down on the companions. Smoke filled Jarus' nose and eyes, and he gasped for fresh air. Maya huddled next to him. Her fur was singed in parts, and her breathing was weak from the smoke.

"It's okay," Jarus panted to her, shaking her slightly. She straightened weakly, coughing, barely conscious. Jarus' mind was foggy from lack of oxygen. He pulled Maya down beside him, listening to the crackling flames and the coughs from his other companions.

This was it. This would be the end. There was no escape.

"It's okay," he croaked again, voice hoarse. Maya's eyes opened, fixing on his face at the sound of his voice. The light from the fire reflected on the river water, shining back on her face, turning her blue eyes into sparkling pools. He didn't feel afraid, suddenly. They were going to die anyway. "Maya… I need you to know… I—"

A crash cut him off—there was a snarl from above, and a dragon, rider and all, crashed through the trees and lay dead, between them and the others. Jarus stared at it in shock, squinting through the smoke. The dragon's body was scored with slashes, made by curved and sharp swords—

He looked up. Through the haze of smoke and heat he saw a group of winged, scaled warriors attacking in clean formation, swords flashing, fire glinting in their palms.

"It's the Direns!" Morel cried, hope coming back into her eyes.

Jarus saw a raven circling above them, a familiar voice coming from it—Lammar was there, alerting the Direns to their predicament. He saw the Direns charge, meeting the Serventiri and their dragons head-on. The rigid discipline and the training of the Diren army outweighed the Serventiri easily, and Jarus could see them fighting calmly, while the Serventiri looked panicked.

He got to his feet—the smoke was clearing, and a breath of fresh air reached his lungs. Gasping, he half-carried, half-dragged Maya's still form to the river bank. A breeze blew down the river, filling his lungs with clean, cool air. He lay there, coughing, too weak to do anything else.

The raven landed next to them—its shape flickered, resuming the shape of Lammar. "Are you all right? Where are the others?"

"Trees—the fire," Jarus managed to choke, nodding toward the cloud of smoke. He saw Neely stumble onto the shore, dropping to her knees on the river bank. Lammar transformed into the tall, dark warrior and moved to help Rygal and Morel.

Maya still lay unmoving—a sudden terror filled Jarus. They had been breathing in smoke for several minutes. "Maya," he gasped, shaking her slightly.

Maya's eyes flickered open and she coughed weakly, inhaling a rasping breath of clean air. She coughed again, gasping. Jarus held her tightly, too relieved to think twice. He let go awkwardly as Rygal and Morel stumbled out of the trees, with Lammar.

The Diren warriors descended from the sky, landing in a semi-circle around the companions. King Makana stepped forward. His blue scales were streaked with ash and muck from the battle, but he seemed unhurt. The companions all bowed.

"King Makana—you have our thanks," Lammar said.

"That is no greeting for friends," Makana told him with a smile, kneeling to clasp the Siren's paw. "It is good to see you all alive. We left Flameton a day ago, and hoped we would find you on the way."

"The Serventiri—they've been tracking us for days," Rygal said in between coughs.

"Then we are very glad to have got here in time," Makana said. He frowned slightly and glanced around. "Where is Norrin?"

"We had a… change of plans," Lammar said slowly. He quickly explained what had happened after they had left Larkin's house.

"Sire, did you see either of them on your way here?" Morel asked anxiously.

"We did not," Makana said, "though we also flew high above the river, and it could have been easy to miss them." But his face was concerned. Jarus felt a familiar prickle of fear for Norrin and Porcini. Makana noticed their worry, and added gently, "Do not despair. My guess is Norrin will find the Ring on his way back to you, and will meet us at the Topstorm."

"Then you march to battle?" Lammar asked him.

Makana nodded, looking back in pride at the large group of warriors behind him. There were nearly seventy of them, Jarus guessed, quite a force to be reckoned with. "We are the advance force. We will provide a diversion for you all to slip into Safacon's palace and destroy the Objects. Then the rest of the army will join us." He looked at Morel unexpectedly. "I also have a task for you, princess. The Chanterelle have gathered in the mountain passes near Topstorm Mountain. I think they mean to attack Safacon, but you must persuade them to wait to join us. Together, we will be stronger."

Hope had lit in Morel's eyes, and she nodded and bowed. "Sire, it would be my honor."

The tall Diren smiled at her, then his face became serious. "Unfortunately, there is one other piece of news which I carry for you all. Deathcap has pursued you. Our sources report that he has amassed his allies near the mountain pass as well."

The mention of the Brownae prince made Jarus' mouth dry with fear. But he also realized, in the same moment, that they needed the Knife of Destruction from Deathcap. If they were going to fight and take the Knife, it would have to be now.

He looked at his companions. Lammar straightened and nodded shortly. "Right, then. We'll be ready for him." He looked at King Makana. "Sire… I assume you have a plan of attack?"

"Attack?" Rygal repeated, looking at him in surprise. "Attack Deathcap?"

"In my experience, it's usually best to strike first," Lammar said with a shrug, and looked back at the king.

"Well said," Makana said, and nodded. "Let us set up camp and I shall tell you our strategy."

25

The Captives

Porcini stepped back and tripped over a tree root as the Serventiri attacked. Norrin struck at the closest one, but gave ground as the Serventiri advanced, eyes on Porcini. Porcini held the Ring close, his heart pounding.

"Norrin—I found it," he stammered as they retreated, eyes on the Serventiri.

Norrin looked at him in surprise, and Porcini held it up. The wizard's face was a mix of joy that Porcini had found the Ring, and of fear that the Serventiri were here to see it. "Here—hand it to me—"

The Serventiri surged forward at the sight of the Ring—Norrin put it on, made a fist, and lowered the Ring at the Serventiri. *"Dorroe!"* Norrin shouted, and a ray of energy flared from the stone in the core of the Ring. There was no blast, nothing shot from it— but the Serventiri froze, completely still except for their faces, which showed utter fury.

"That will hold them for a while," Norrin muttered, taking Porcini's arm as they jogged away.

"But, Norrin—I thought they can track us easier when we use the Objects—won't they know?" Porcini panted as they ran. He was shivering violently from his dip in the river, and from fear.

"They already know where we are—at any rate, there are too many for me to fight alone," Norrin told him. He still wore the Ring, but held his other hand protectively over it, covering it.

"What did you do to them?" Porcini asked, a little in awe of what had happened, and glancing back at the Serventiri.

"The Serventiri are controlled by Safacon, but ultimately they answer to the Objects, because the Jewel is what created them," Norrin said. "The Ring controls time, so I could stop them—freeze them in place—for now."

The sounds of the dragons came from the sky—more Serventiri were coming. Norrin turned, raising his staff.

The dragon dove, dodging the blast. It didn't attack—instead, it reached out with its claws, seizing Norrin by the shoulders and carrying him into the air.

"Norrin!" Porcini cried in alarm, but then his cry turned to terror—another dragon had gripped him too, lifting him into the sky.

Porcini squirmed uselessly in the dragon's claws. He could hear Norrin's voice, and wondered if the wizard could use the Ring to make the Serventiri leave them alone. The river fell away below him, disappearing in the trees. The Serventiri were going southeast— away from Larkin's.

Taking them to Safacon.

"No!" Porcini cried, then gripped frantically to the dragon's claws as they unexpectedly lurched in the sky. They were going down, slowly—maybe Norrin had used the Ring's powers to control them again—

But the moment of hope was short-lived. The Serventiri landed, shoving Porcini roughly to the ground, where they swiftly tied his arms behind his back. They took both Norrin's staff and the Ring—Norrin's eyes were filled with fury, but there was little he could do; the soldiers kept their weapons trained on him.

They would not die like this, Porcini thought, and a reckless determination mingled with his fear as he struggled to his feet and lunged at the Serventiri who guarded him. The soldier flung him aside with relative ease; Porcini started to get up again when the soldier brought the pommel of his sword down hard on his head.

The world swam into blackness…he heard Norrin call his name, then his vision faded away.

. . . . . .

When Porcini's eyes opened, he thought he had been struck blind. He lay on a cold, hard surface, shivering slightly.

As his eyes adjusted, he remembered what had happened at the riverbank. The Serventiri had taken the Ring…they had taken him and Norrin. Porcini's heart sank with fear. What would they do now? Where was he?

He looked around. He was in a cell, the walls and floor made of sturdy gray stone. Thick cobwebs hung in the corners, their pale color reflecting the weak light that leaked through a small, rectangular window above the door. Lantern light, Porcini guessed. It was the only light that managed to enter the cell—other than that, it was completely dark.

Porcini took a shaking breath, willing himself to be calm, though he couldn't possibly imagine how they would escape, or get the Ring back. What would happen to him, then? And where was Norrin?

"Norrin?" he called faintly. His voice echoed in the cell.

There was no reply. He was alone.

Porcini huddled against the wall, fighting the despair that filled him. They were captives of Safacon. He had no idea where Norrin was, and—as far as he knew—Safacon would kill them both. Tears swam in his vision, and he buried his face in his paws, trembling with cold and sorrow.

A sound roused him. Porcini looked up sharply at a soft, grating sound coming from the corner. He felt a surge of fear as he saw a hole in the corner. Something was moving toward him.

"Hey!" he shouted, hoping to scare the creature away.

"Hey," came a soft voice, making him jump. It was quiet and tired, and the accent was slightly familiar—it took Porcini a moment to place it—it was the accent of someone from Mata City, the same accent Jarus and Maya had…

The speaker crawled out of the hole. It was a Cooper, still young, with handsome dark fur that was now matted and patchy from weeks without proper nourishment or care. His eyes were blue, and fixed with interest on Porcini.

"I've been in here for weeks—haven't seen anyone else in this cell. These tunnels—they run from cell to cell. I don't think Safacon knows about them." He moved closer, and Porcini saw he was holding a small bundle of wood and a flint and steel. "It's freezing in here— let's get you warmed up."

In a few moments the strange Cooper had a small fire going. Warmth filled the cell, and Porcini huddled closer to the blaze. "Thank you," he said, looking up at the Cooper. "I'm Porcini Inmana, of the Chanterelle tribe."

The Cooper bowed slightly. "Pleased to meet you. My name is Hagar Groundrop."

In Porcini's weary state, he barely registered the name, and only nodded. Then, out of nowhere, recognition dawned as he remembered the story Jarus had told him, and he stared in wonder at the Cooper.

26

≈ ≈ ≈ ≈ ≈ ≈ ≈ ≈ ≈ ≈

The Parlay of Deathcap

Jarus knew something was wrong the moment he saw Rygal's face the following morning. He sat with Morel and Maya by the crackling fire in the center of camp. Diren soldiers milled around them, all busy, but the companions enjoyed the moment of rest. Now, Jarus could see that the quiet would not last much longer.

"What is it?" he asked.

Rygal looked at him grimly. "Deathcap. He's camped over the other side of the ridge. And he brought company."

Morel seemed to understand, and her face fell with worry. "He hasn't allied with the rebel Direns...?"

"He has indeed, as much as we can make out," Rygal said wearily.

Jarus wasn't entirely sure what this implied, but Morel was hardly ever worried by anything, which made him worry too. "What are we going to do? Are we outnumbered?"

"Not quite," Rygal said, then admitted, "but it'll definitely be a close fight. Lieutenant Casper brought back the report—he estimates around forty rebel Diren warriors. Add that to Deathcap's gang of ruffians, and you have a decent army."

"And the rebels are better fighters than Deathcap's ruffians," Morel said, shaking her head. "The Chanterelle fought them for years—

267

they are deadly in battle."

Rygal looked at her. "That reminds me—Makana wants to talk to you. We think the Chanterelle are in this area too, but they won't show themselves—they can't tell which Direns to trust, obviously. If you go with Casper and his warriors to find them, we may have them on our side too."

Morel nodded and stood, slinging the satchel with the Jewel around her shoulders and sliding her knife into its sheath. "Good. I'll go speak to the king."

"Makana is meeting with his generals," Rygal told her as she started off. "Casper can fill you in on the rest."

"All right, then. Don't start the fight without me," Morel added over her shoulder as she walked towards the center of camp. "I don't like it when people do that."

Maya looked up at Rygal. "So we should get ready to head out?"

"Lammar wanted me to ask you two about that. We technically have enough warriors—you can sit this one out if you like." Rygal studied them both carefully.

"All right, then," Maya said, looking relieved. The cut across her shoulders was still fresh, along with the horror of the last few days. Jarus was just as tired, but at the same time, he felt the need to fight beside his companions. It was preferable compared to sitting and waiting in the camp, unsure of who was alive and who was dead.

"I'll fight," he said.

Rygal nodded shortly. "Get ready, then. Makana is going to explain our plan in a few minutes."

Jarus slipped his knife around his shoulders, then turned to meet Maya's eyes. "We'll be all right," he said, noticing the worry on her face.

She nodded quickly. "Okay. Stay safe. I'll be here." She turned away, moving back toward the tents. Jarus stood awkwardly for a few moments, wanting to call after her. He was going into battle. He might never have the chance to tell her how he felt for her.

But he couldn't bring himself to say anything, and after a frustrated pause, he turned to follow Rygal.

King Makana and two of his generals stood beside a second fire, speaking in lowered tones. Lammar was there also, the Direns dwarfing his small form. He looked over as Rygal and Jarus approached, and went to meet them.

"You're both ready to fight, then? Good." He looked over at the Direns. "To fill you in, we know Deathcap and his allies are on the other end of the valley, on the other side of the ridge. Makana wants to lure them down from their hiding places, to even the playing field. Then his warriors will attack the rebel Direns who have joined with Deathcap."

"What about the rest of Deathcap's warriors?" Rygal asked.

"Yes, well, we're hoping the Chanterelle will join us to fight them," Lammar said. "If not, Makana's warriors will split into two groups— some in the air, some on the ground to help fight the ruffians."

If that happened, both groups would be outnumbered, Jarus

realized. The thought made his mouth dry. They were counting on the Brownaes, counting on Morel to be successful.

"We'll just have to hold our own until then," Rygal said.

"Yes," Lammar said, "but remember, our main target is to get the Knife. We can't do anything further without it."

The three of them moved to join the Direns. Makana nodded in approval as he saw them. "We will be glad for your assistance, friends. Meet you General Hawkblaze and General Warnwing." The two Diren warriors nodded respectfully. Makana looked at the three of them again. "General Hawkblaze will lead the group on the ground. Follow his command. Lammar, I will speak with you for a moment."

Jarus trotted behind Rygal as they followed the burly Diren general toward a group of soldiers. "We will attack only after the king's signal," Hawkblaze explained to them as they walked. "Makana hopes to negotiate and possibly avoid confrontation. Knowing Deathcap, that will not be easy." He bared his teeth in a fierce grin. "At which point, we will have to fight."

"Any news from the Chanterelle?" Rygal asked him.

"Lieutenant Casper's garrison, along with Princess Morel, went to make contact. We do not know much more," Hawkblaze said. He frowned thoughtfully. "The Chanterelle will be wary to fight. Deathcap's power is well-known throughout the Wandering Wood—they already fear him."

"They'll come," Jarus said, wishing he felt more confident. "If Morel has anything to say about it, anyway," he added.

Hawkblaze assembled his warriors. There were thirty of them, all experienced soldiers, but Jarus could see the uncertainty in their eyes. No matter how skilled they were, the Knife of Destruction was a looming threat, and one that weighed heavily on all their minds.

General Hawkblaze quickly explained their strategy. The Direns would walk down into the gully and call Deathcap's forces down to them—bringing the battle down to level ground. Makana would give the signal only after he deemed it necessary. Jarus wondered if Deathcap would call off the attack after seeing the Diren forces… but he doubted it. Lust for the Jewel had driven the Brownae prince mad.

After Makana's signal, they were to fan out, engaging the Brownaes and ruffians in Deathcap's force. General Warnwing would lead the second group of warriors into the air to combat the rebel Direns.

It would be a risky attack, but Jarus knew that if they didn't confront Deathcap now, the Brownae would keep pursuing them, with the Knife of Destruction. And any hope of stopping Safacon lay with the Knife. His mouth was dry as they started moving over the ridge.

The path crested the hill, then descended abruptly. Jarus felt tense with anticipation. In the swirl of winds channeling through the gorge, he could smell only a mix of scents, and had no idea where they were coming from.

A dark figure dropped down to the path before them, standing in their way. Deathcap stood upright, twenty feet from them. The Direns tensed. Deathcap watched them carefully, then his eyes settled on Makana, who stepped forward in front of General Hawkblaze. The Brownae prince eyed him with a fixed stare, then smiled slowly.

"King Makana. A pleasure to see you." He bowed mockingly.

Makana did not move, staring at the Brownae prince. "Why come you here, Deathcap?"

Deathcap straightened. "The Jewel, of course. You know as well as I that this foolish group cannot hope to succeed in their errand. I am surprised you have not taken it from them already, and given it to one more…worthy."

"Someone like you?" Makana asked, raising an eyebrow. "And what would you do with the Jewel, Deathcap? You think you could undo the wrongs done to your people—the Jewel would only control you, as it does Safacon."

Deathcap laughed. "Foolish statements, Makana. Now, I have come to bargain, and I advise you to listen. I have no quarrel with your people. Give me the Jewel, and your race will be spared when I conquer Gayrile."

Makana looked at the Brownae for a long time, then slowly shook his head. "You misunderstand, Deathcap. You misunderstand that the Jewel is a thing of evil. Leave it in the hands of any, and it will twist them and consume them. It must be destroyed, along with its maker."

Deathcap's smile vanished. "Very well. Then you have chosen to die." He turned and shouted an order in the Brownae tongue.

Warriors sprang from behind their hiding places, streaming down into the gorge like ants. Brute-faced ruffians and armored Brownaes charged down towards the group below. There was a flash of fire, and Jarus turned to his right—a second force of enemies had lifted into the air. Rebel Direns, their eyes wild with hate, their wings tattered, their scales covered in mud and grime, dove like eagles toward their enemies. Jarus fell back, terrified by the sight of them.

Makana raised a fist, and in perfect unison, General Warnwing's garrison leapt from the opposite cliffside, spreading their wings and meeting the rebel Diren forces midair. Swords glittering, fire flashing from their hands, the Direns tackled each other in the air. Jarus saw the rebels snarling like wild beasts, clawing and tearing at the wings and faces of Warnwing's warriors. Blood dripped down from the fight above like rain.

He looked back just in time to see Deathcap join his forces and lunge at the group on the ground. Hawkblaze drew his sword, killing two Brownaes at once, and as several more lunged at him, he sprang from the ground, opening his wings unexpectedly and knocking them all back.

Jarus found himself face-to-face with a wild-eyed Brownae carrying a spear. He ducked just in time, then lunged forward, slashing at the Brownae's face. He missed his intended target, but the blade cut down the length of the Brownae's arm. His attacker let out a cry of pain and fell back, into the path of the Diren warriors, who finished him off.

A blow caught Jarus across the back of the head, and he stumbled forward. Dazed, he turned to face another Brownae wielding a club. This time, he parried the blow, then plunged his knife blade into the Brownae's chest. He whipped the blade out again, turning to meet another attacker. There were so many of them, pressing in on the outnumbered Direns. The scent of blood filled his nose.

He back-pedaled into Rygal, who stood surrounded by Brownae bodies. The tall young warrior held his sword loosely, panting for breath. "You all right?" he asked Jarus.

"Yeah…" Jarus managed to wheeze. That last blow across his head had hurt badly, but he tried to ignore it. He and Rygal stood beside the semi-circle of Direns, who fended off attacks from Deathcap's warriors. Makana's forces had killed many of the attackers in the first few minutes, but Diren bodies littered the ground too. It was impossible to tell whose side the fallen Direns had been on.

The ruffians had closed around the circle of Diren warriors. Jarus felt his mouth go dry. They were surrounded and gradually more and more outnumbered. Above them, Warnwing's forces still battled the rebel Direns—they wouldn't be able to come help.

"This is bad," Rygal grunted, slashing at a pig-faced brute who came too close.

Deathcap's voice rang out over the scene. "Give up, Makana. You have no hope of winning this fight. Surrender, and I will make your deaths less painful."

For answer, Makana gave a signal to the Direns on the ground. In unison, they rose up into the air a few feet before diving down again, fire licking across the ground at the ruffians' feet. The attackers screeched in pain and fear as flames seared their feet and clothes. The circle broken, Rygal and Jarus charged forward, straight at Deathcap.

The Brownae prince whipped around to face them—Rygal barreled into him, knocking the prince sprawling on his back. Deathcap grunted in pain, then began to laugh. "Oh, so *you're* Maran's little boy. Funny. I thought you would fight better than that… not that he was ever the greatest warrior either."

"Rygal, don't—!" Jarus yelled, but the taunt about his father had goaded Rygal into rage. Furious, he charged forward at Deathcap again. Deathcap whipped out the glittering black Knife, pointed it at Rygal, and shouted a spell. Rygal lurched as though he had run into an invisible wall, and crashed to the ground. He tried to get up, but his limbs were limp and lifeless, as if his muscles had been vaporized.

"Rygal!" Jarus shouted again in desperation. Deathcap rounded on him and lowered the Knife again. Jarus sprang behind a rock just in time, and the blast missed him. The Knife—they needed to get the Knife. But how?

Jarus heard Deathcap laughing softly, and charged out at the Brownae. The prince looked startled, but recovered quickly, and slammed the pommel of the blade against Jarus' head. Jarus fell beside Rygal, stars swimming in his vision. Through tears of pain his saw Deathcap approach them, his eyes glittering in triumph.

"Not so brave now, are you, fools?" he hissed, lowering the Knife at them.

"No…" Jarus cried desperately, staggering to his feet.

Deathcap smiled and lowered the Knife at Rygal's face. *"Devrando!"* he shouted, the word making Jarus' heart stop—there was death in that word, death for Rygal and soon him.

There was a blast from the Knife—Rygal flinched back, but in the same moment a second spell was shouted from above.

"Revrandar!"

The voice came from the rocks above them—there was a mighty flash of blue, and Jarus watched in awe as a wave of blue light engulfed the curse from the Knife, then pulled it back in the other direction—

Into the core of the Jewel that Morel held out in a shaking hand.

Jarus looked at her in amazement, hope filling him again. The princess was out of breath, but her eyes held a fire as she looked down at the battle-strewn valley. Behind her, filing in ranks, an army of leather-clad Brownae warriors stood. "Let's go!" she shouted, and the Brownaes charged down at Deathcap's startled forces, their strange and eerie war cries filling the air.

Morel jumped down the rocks, landing behind the evil Brownae prince. "Put down the Knife, Deathcap," she ordered, her voice low. "Now."

Deathcap stared at her as the Chanterelle Brownaes clashed with his own allies behind him. His gaze was livid. "You'll turn into quite a little witch with all your Jewel-lore and spells if you're not careful, princess," he spat, turning away from Rygal. "In truth, we are very much alike. Both of us keeping the power for our own reasons."

"That's where you're wrong," Morel told him as they circled each other. "We're going to destroy the Objects—like Norrin said." She stole a glance at Rygal, and Jarus realized how important this was for her. She was willing to give up on her hope of bringing her mother back in order to save Orlell.

Deathcap lunged at her, shouting a curse—Morel let the Jewel engulf the Knife's blast again, then slashed at Deathcap with her dagger. Deathcap parried the blow—Morel's blade shattered, the Knife's power overwhelming it, and the evil prince struck at her again. Morel stepped back, aiming the Jewel at him. "Last chance, Deathcap," she said, moving slowly towards him. "Surrender."

"*Relarg!*" Deathcap barked, and the blast shot from the Knife. Morel allowed the Jewel to engulf it—and at the same second, Deathcap lunged in, pointing the Knife at Morel's face.

"*Devrando!*" he shouted—there was a flash, and Morel was flung back against the rocks, landing still on the ground.

"No!" Jarus screamed, jumping up. Deathcap rounded on him, the curse still on his lips, and lowered the Knife at him.

He had forgotten Rygal.

The young warrior leapt to his feet and plunged his sword into

Deathcap's chest. The Brownae froze, staring in shock at the sword for a moment. Then his eyes glazed over, and he crumpled to the ground.

Rygal turned away from Deathcap's body and ran over to Morel. Jarus bounded after him, his heart pounding in fear. Morel lay on her back in the soft grass, her eyes closed, unmoving.

"Morel—come on—come on…" Rygal murmured, shaking her lightly.

For an instant Jarus' heart plummeted with grief. Then the princess' eyes fluttered open. Jarus let out a gasp of relief, then noticed the Jewel glittering slightly with the curse it had absorbed—a split second before the curse had hit Morel. Morel blinked dazedly, her gaze focusing on the two worried yet relieved faces looking down at her.

"Please tell me neither of you just kissed me."

Rygal and Jarus, both too relieved to say anything, could only laugh.

Morel stood shakily, rubbing her head. The force of the Knife had flung her back and knocked her out, even though the killing curse had been absorbed. Her eyes landed on Deathcap's unmoving body, and she looked at Rygal. "I'm sorry I missed that. I guess you…" she hesitated, the words an effort.

"Yes?" Rygal prompted.

Morel's mouth tightened in a line, then her expression softened, and she smiled faintly. "You… you did good," she admitted.

Rygal's eyes lit up, and he grinned widely. "Hold on, what was that? Jarus, write that down, so we can show Norrin as proof. She actually gave me a compliment."

"Don't overdo it," Morel said dryly, but she was smiling too.

"I won't, considering I technically started whatever quarrel we've had all this time," Rygal admitted.

"Well, you've saved my life a few times since then, plus that business at the council. So I'll consider us even." She extended a paw, and Rygal clasped it in agreement.

"Finally," Jarus said, beaming at them. "Although the bickering was entertaining," he added.

"Who said we would stop doing that?" Morel muttered.

27

The Cooper's Story

Hagar Groundrop.

The name carried a memory of walking through the Wandering Wood with Jarus, who was telling him about how he and Maya had come here…how Maya's father had been betrayed by Maya's fiancé…whose name was Hagar Groundrop.

"*You're* Hagar Groundrop?" Porcini exclaimed, his voice echoing in the little room.

The Cooper looked at him, absolutely confused. "You've…heard of me?"

"Yes—sort of—Maya told me—well, Jarus told me, technically, and he said you—"

"Maya?" Hagar repeated, straightening and staring at the Brownae. "You know Maya? Is she all right?"

"Yes, I know her—I don't know where she is—our group got separated," Porcini said. He stared at the Cooper. "You betrayed them—you betrayed them both to Safacon." Being cold and wet and tired made him suddenly angry. This was the Cooper who had got them into this whole mess.

Hagar looked down. "I…yes. And I regret it every day."

"Why?" Porcini demanded. "Why did you do it?"

Hagar looked up at him and took a breath, his blue eyes lit by the dim firelight. "Being here…things have changed me. I regret everything I've done, who I was in Mata City." He looked up at Porcini. "What did Jarus tell you about me?"

"He…" Porcini hesitated. Most of the things Jarus had told him about Hagar weren't the…nicest… things. Nothing he'd like to repeat.

Hagar seemed to sense this and shook his head with a weak grin. "I'm guessing they weren't all good stories. And I suppose I rather deserved it." He hesitated. "Porcini…my life back in Mata City was one of surfaces. Money and people and possessions were all that mattered—no true friends, no real life. When Sariv—he's one of Safacon's henchmen—came to Mata City and offered me a large sum if I pointed out the richest people to him, I didn't think twice. I was confused why he asked for it, of course, but I didn't really consider why he wanted that information. But I knew that they would come for the Raintails—and I thought that if Maya was at the house when they came to capture her father, I could fight them off. I could impress her father, and Maya would finally care for me."

"And…it didn't work?" Porcini guessed.

Hagar took a deep breath and shook his head. "No. They had more warriors than I expected. They took Mr. Raintail and myself—Maya escaped. I didn't think they would hurt him—I didn't think they would hurt either of us. But…they did." He paused, and Porcini saw a shadow of the terrible memory cross his face.

"They captured him because they thought he had the Jewel," he said quietly.

Hagar glanced up at him. "Yes—they mentioned something about a Jewel. Something about searching the houses of the rich until the thing was found. When we were brought here, we faced him—Safacon. When he found out that we didn't know anything about a Jewel, I think his henchmen were planning to kill us." A puzzled look crossed Hagar's face. "He didn't though—he mentioned something about using us as bait, and then imprisoned us."

"Bait?" Porcini echoed.

"Yes—he said someone named Norrin was trying to rally the…the Guardians of Gayrile. Said this Norrin was trying to take Safacon's empire down, and he would come to rescue us." Hagar looked at him in confusion. "I don't know anyone named Norrin—I definitely don't know why he'd want to rescue us."

Porcini looked at him, not sure what he should reveal. "Norrin is a wizard—one of the best of this time. And Jarus and Maya have convinced him to help them find you and Maya's father, and Jarus' father too."

"They did *what*?" Hagar repeated in disbelief.

Porcini hesitated only a moment, and then told Hagar the whole story of the quest. The Cooper listened with rapt attention the whole time. "Anyway," Porcini said as he finished, "we've got the Jewel, and Norrin's got the Ring. Except I think the Serventiri took it when we were captured, in which case Safacon has it. Deathcap the Brownae prince still has the Knife, as far as I know—we don't know how we'll get that back."

"But Jarus and Maya—Norrin—the Direns—they're coming?" Hagar asked in awe.

"Yes—as far as I know," Porcini said slowly. "King Makana was rallying his army."

A spark of hope had come back into Hagar's weary eyes. "Help is coming," he repeated softly, a slow smile crossing his face.

Porcini looked at him. "I'm sorry I don't know much else," he said. "Not about Maya. You must be awful worried for her. Jarus said you're her fiancé." He watched Hagar's face carefully as he said this, and was startled to see Hagar shake his head.

"No. I—I might have thought once that we would be happy together, but she has never cared for me in that way. I understand now." He looked up. "I never meant for this—for any of this—to happen. Please forgive me."

"I'm not sure it's my place to forgive you," Porcini said uncertainly. "But I know you owe Mr. Raintail an apology—Maya too, if she gets here." He looked around the room, focusing on the problem at hand again. "Right—that tunnel—where does it go?"

Hagar looked at the hole. "It runs through the walls, between the wood and the stone of the castle. You can crawl through like a termite."

"You can get to the other cells?" Porcini asked.

"Yes—sort of. You can get into some of the others, the places where the wood is more rotted," Hagar said. "But the wood is so weak we could probably break through it and widen the hole if we needed to get everyone together." He looked carefully at the young Brownae. "What are you planning?"

"I'm not sure yet," Porcini said uncertainly. "Did you see anyone else come in, about the same time I showed up?"

"There was an old man," Hagar said. "He smelled like dragon. When they put him in his cell, I heard him yelling at the guards. He called himself Norrin and demanded to speak to Safacon."

Porcini's heart leapt in hope. "And?"

"He didn't stay there very long. The guards took him away right before you woke up," Hagar said. He looked worried. "If that's the leader of your group, I'm a little concerned about the rest of you."

"The rest of us aren't here," Porcini said. He thought a moment. The news that Norrin had been taken had made his heart sink, but he told himself that it wasn't necessarily bad news. Maybe Norrin could negotiate with Safacon, get him to surrender. He looked at Hagar. "How many others are here?"

"Many," Hagar said slowly. "They're not all in good shape. There was another Cooper who showed me these tunnels—a female Cooper, older. She nursed me back to health when I was first brought here, and I promised I would get her out if I ever tried to escape." Hagar paused, frowning. "I don't know where they're holding Mr. Raintail or Mr. Puddlepaw."

Porcini thought for a moment. Then he nodded slowly. "If we can get word to the other prisoners, there might be a way to break out of here."

"Break out?" Hagar repeated.

"Yes... now tell me about those tunnels. We need to come up with a plan."

28

ઉ ઉ ઉ ઉ ઉ ઉ ઉ ઉ ઉ ઉ

The Topstorm

"We're getting close," Lammar said.

It had been a full day since the defeat of Deathcap and his forces. After Deathcap had been killed, and the Knife recovered, the rest of the attackers had surrendered. Chief Cedar, Morel's father and the leader of the Chanterelle, had agreed to meet with King Makana and discuss their next strategy. While there were decades of unrest and hostility between the two species, they eventually agreed to travel together into war against Safacon, united against a common enemy.

They had moved on through the mountain pass. Snow was falling by the time they set up camp that night, and by morning a fresh powder coated the trail. Jarus followed behind Lammar, his teeth chattering from the chilly breeze. The Direns, used to the warm desert, looked cold too, while the furry Brownae warriors were right at home, moving lithely among the rocky cliffs as they marched upward.

Finally, the trail leveled out, then dropped steeply down into a valley. Jarus paused, looking down. The world dropped away below his feet. Directly across from them, the second set of arching mountains rose up, encircling the valley and leaving the fortress below in shadow. To their right, the craggy head of Topstorm Mountain rose above them, the tallest of the range. Below it, built into the rocky shoulders of the mountains, was Safacon's fortress, an elegant castle wrought of black iron.

It was a fortress unlike any Jarus had yet seen on this journey. There was a strange sort of beauty in its make, but also a darkness that chilled him more than the wind and snow. They had finally made it here—soon, it would come time to do what they had come to do.

Makana studied the valley in silence, his keen eyes watching the warriors patrolling around the palace in the valley below. "My forces will take to the sky," he told the companions. "Once we engage the enemy, go into the palace. Beware of Safacon—even without the Objects, he is a powerful sorcerer." He turned to the stocky figure of Chief Cedar, who waited behind him. "Lead your warriors through the main gate. There will be Serventiri there, so be very cautious, but try to keep the fighting contained in the courtyard. My warriors will join you as soon as we can."

"Of course, sire," Chief Cedar said briefly, nodding his head. He gave a swift order to his waiting warriors, and the Brownaes turned left, moving slowly down through the rocks. Their dark fur disguised them perfectly, an army of half-visible creatures come for revenge. Makana watched for a moment, then gave a signal to the Direns, and they lifted into the air.

"Here we go, then," Lammar muttered, and followed as they

descended into the valley. The path dropped steeply, forcing them to move slowly, taking careful steps. When they finally reached the valley, clouds had covered the sun, and it was spitting rain.

The companions stood a quarter mile or so from the palace gates, on a crumbling gravel walkway. Jarus kept his eyes on the palace, tense with anticipation. He waited for a shout from the watch tower, a cry of alarm. But there was no sign, no sound. The valley was dead silent.

Lammar scented the air for a moment before deciding it was safe, then led them off the path into the draw beside the road. The towers stood above them like hulking watchmen. They moved on, trudging through the stagnant water that had gathered in the ditch. At least down here, they were out of view of any guards in the towers.

The ditch led to a stone tunnel about four feet high. Rygal and Neely had to stoop, bent almost double as they moved up the channel. For once Jarus was grateful for his small size. "What's this tunnel for?" he asked Lammar.

"Drainage," the Siren told him. "Being in a valley like this comes with its drawbacks during the rainy season—this makes sure that the water won't flood the courtyard and ground floor."

Jarus kept his eyes ahead as they moved under the palace. They had to be directly under it now, and he could see the light from the courtyard up ahead.

Maya seemed remarkably calm. "This isn't too bad. No worse than the culverts back home."

Jarus nodded—in times of flooding, large steel pipes acted as drainage for the overflowing canals in Mata City. "Do you remember that one spring—when we got that late rain?" he asked her. "And the canals overflowed into the culverts?"

Maya grinned and nodded. "I was seven—all the kids thought they were fun to play in."

"I swam through the culverts," Jarus said. "I thought it'd be scary—but it was fun."

"I swam through too," Maya said, shaking her head. "My mother yelled at me about it when I got home. She said it was dangerous."

"Which it was," Jarus said, chuckling despite himself.

"No more than this," Maya said softly, taking a breath.

There was a silence. The other companions walked on ahead of them. Jarus realized, with a jolt, that in a matter of minutes, all of them could be dead. He looked at Maya, thinking of a hundred things he should have said before it came to this. "It'll be all right," he said, though the words were futile.

Maya smiled. "I hope so. As long as we can save our families, once we break the Jewel." She looked at him with a slight frown. "By the way—what were you going to say to me? The day by the river?"

Jarus looked at her in confusion. "When?"

"By the river. When the Serventiri had us trapped with the fire, right before the Direns saved us. You started to say something to me."

Jarus felt his face warm as he remembered that. "Oh…I…I guess I was just worried… about the battle…" was all he mumbled.

Maya looked confused and a little hurt. "Oh… I thought… never mind."

Jarus looked at her, suddenly feeling hopeful. "What…what did you *think* I had to say?"

But at that moment, there was a mighty crash from above, followed by a shout. Jarus heard the sounds of many feet running along the walls, followed by crackle of gunfire. A flash of fire came from the courtyard. The Direns had launched their attack.

"Go!" Rygal shouted.

The companions ran the rest of the way into the courtyard and froze. Battle had erupted around them. Jarus stared, stunned and dazed by the swirl of fighting and the deafening noise. "Where do we go?" he cried, overwhelmed by the sheer masses of Serventiri.

He saw Lammar and Neely charge forward into the fray, saw Rygal slashing at the throngs of soldiers and realized they were all going to be separated if they weren't careful.

That was when someone knocked him back against a stone, and the world went dark.

PART 3

∽ ∽ ∽ ∽ ∽ ∽ ∽ ∽ ∽

The Sorcerer's Mountain

∽ ∽ ∽ ∽ ∽ ∽ ∽ ∽ ∽

29

Porcini's Plan

The two wizards stood soundlessly in the room, studying each other for a long moment. One stood stiffly, shorter than the other. His hair and beard were singed by fire, and the scent of smoke still clung to his clothes. His dark eyes stared hard into the eyes of the other. The other man stood tall, wreathed in white garments. His face was clean-shaven, no hair on his head, his skin shockingly pale in contrast to his eyes. They were black, so dark the pupil seemed to blend into the iris. The mouth was thin and wore a mocking smile.

"Is this what it has come to, Norrin?" he asked softly. "You stand, a prisoner in my fortress, and I speak first?"

"Those who speak first are often not the wisest," Norrin told him. "But you have kept me imprisoned for nearly two days, without a single word from you. So I assume you have brought me here for a reason."

"Well said," Safacon said calmly. He fingered the Ring of Light in his palm. "Curious, curious. I never expected you to have it still, after all these years. It really makes no difference. The Ring has no further use to me, nor the Knife, for that matter." He tossed the Ring back to Norrin, who caught it.

Norrin masked his confusion and growing concern at that statement, and slipped the Ring back into his pocket. He looked up, meeting Safacon's cold black eyes. "So what is your newest interest then, Safacon?"

Safacon smiled. "My interest lies in the Jewel alone. The Jewel was made from a substance, a power if you will, that our world has never seen, not even in the ancient times. I did not create the Jewel, you understand. It was already a force long before any of us, I think, have breathed. A thing of beauty, of power, of immortality." He paused. "Such a force cannot be… contained. A doorway cannot be contained, can it?"

The two wizards studied each other in silence. Norrin finally spoke slowly. "A doorway?"

Safacon smiled again, but the smile could not hide the small light of fear in his eyes. A fear of the truth he spoke of. "Indeed. It is not what any of us thought it to be. You have known this for some time, I think. I can see it in your eyes. Known of what lies beyond the Jewel."

That was when the first sounds of battle reached them.

· · · · · ·

By the time Porcini and Hagar had made their way through the tunnels between the cell walls, Porcini could hear the faint sounds of commotion from above. "What's going on?" he wondered out loud.

They had spent the entirety of the last day and a half planning their strategy. Porcini had been ready to attack as soon as possible, but his head still ached, and besides, rushing blindly into a fight probably wouldn't end well. Hagar had brought him food and water and visited him when he could, also bringing him snatches of news. Norrin had been returned to his cell—he was being held in the upper level of cells, it seemed. But this morning, Hagar had brought news that the guards had taken the wizard away. At this message, Porcini knew they had to act now.

Hagar looked up, hearing the sounds of many feet running, and a distant crash. "I'm not sure. They might be doing another drill—they do those often. Or maybe some sort of raid."

Porcini nodded, trying not to get his hopes up. There was no way Norrin could have taken on the entire Serventiri army alone. Unless, of course, his other companions had arrived...

Suddenly, his heart was pounding with anticipation.

They crawled through the tight walls of the tunnel between cells, cobwebs clinging to their fur, the light growing fainter. For a moment, panic at the dark and close walls overwhelmed Porcini, and he froze, panting for breath. But then a faint light reached his eyes from ahead. Light streamed through a hole in the wood, leading into the cell.

"This is the bigger cell—it's where Safacon keeps a hundred or so of them," Hagar said.

"A hundred?" Porcini whispered back, hearing the muffled sounds of many voices out in that room. "How many..."

Hagar and Porcini crawled through the hole into the room, and

Porcini stared in shock.

A crowd of people stood in the room. There were a few cots lining the walls, and mats on the floor, but clearly not enough bedding for everyone. The others lay stretched out on the floor, sleeping on scattered straw. There was an alcove in the far corner, blocked by a tattered curtain, that served as a privy. The whole room reeked of unwashed bodies and human waste.

No one seemed to notice as Hagar and Porcini entered. "We're the only ones able to fit through the tunnel," Hagar explained.

Porcini was overwhelmed for a moment by the sight. "Where did they all come from?"

"This is the resistance," Hagar said. "These are the rebels who tried to fight against Safacon's reign. Safacon imprisoned them and their whole families."

"Are any of them…were any of them with the Guardians of Gayrile?" Porcini asked, an idea suddenly coming to him.

Hagar frowned, not understanding. "The what?"

"The Guardians—the ones who fought at the start…" Porcini stepped forward, studying the crowd. There were many of them—men, women, and children. They were weary and had the same hopelessness that Porcini had seen in Hagar's eyes when the Cooper had first come to him. "Hagar, if we could get them weapons…"

Hagar raised his eyebrows as Porcini's meaning dawned on him. "They could help us fight?"

Porcini considered the idea. He and Hagar planned to visit the cells, inform all the prisoners, and gather them together. Then they could slip out through the drains and unlock the doors… there was a small army waiting here, and if they had any chance of stopping Safacon, they would need as much help as possible.

"They can help," he told Hagar. It was crazy, he thought, leading an army of half-starved prisoners to fight the greatest sorcerer of their time. But if it worked…it could buy them time until the Diren army arrived.

He jumped up on a cot and raised his voice. "Hey—hey, everyone, listen!"

Conversation slowly faded, and all eyes turned to him. Porcini took a deep breath.

"All right. You are all imprisoned for resisting against Safacon's reign, right? Imprisoned for standing up for what you believed—for standing up for your freedom?"

There was a growl of assent from the waiting crowd. Porcini had their attention now. He paused, and continued. "Well, that's why I'm here too. But I'm just one of a quest of companions that believe the same as you do. And they're on their way—with assistance of King Makana's army of Direns."

He was drowned out by shocked and excited exclamations from the crowd. All of them had heard of the Direns.

"Listen!" Hagar yelled, and they fell silent again.

"Safacon wants to regain his Objects of Power," Porcini said. "My friends are going to destroy those Objects, and in doing so defeat Safacon. But they need help. That's why we're going to break out of here and fight."

A few cheers, but Porcini noticed that many of them looked uneasy.

"Do you have any idea how many have died trying to do that?" an older man asked warily.

"Even the Guardians of Gayrile were no match for Safacon!" a woman protested.

"I know," Porcini said. "But this time is different. We found the Jewel of Power, and we're going to stop Safacon. Our leader believes we can—I agree with him, and you should too. He's Norrin, one of the leaders of the Guardians of Gayrile."

That got their attention—the name was familiar to them. More exclamations, and everyone began talking to their neighbor.

"Quiet!" Hagar cautioned, and they all fell silent just in time—a guard had walked down the hall. Porcini waited until the guard had gone, then threw the crowd a glare.

"We have to be smart. We can't just storm out there—they'd kill us all. Hagar and I are going to the other cells and let the others know." He paused, then selected a tall man from the crowd. "You, sir—can you be in charge and help decide who is well enough to fight?"

The man nodded in agreement, and Hagar and Porcini started back toward the hole. "We'll be back soon—we'll let you all out if this works," Porcini said. His chest was tight with anticipation.

"You think this will work?" Hagar asked him as they started down the tunnel again.

"I think so," Porcini murmured, wishing he felt more sure.

They reached another hole, and crept into the cell. This room was smaller, with fewer people. There were humans, some Brownaes, and Porcini saw a few Coopers.

They all started as Porcini and Hagar pushed their way through the hole, and Porcini quickly repeated the plan to them. This group was calmer, quieter, but no less excited.

"How many are there of us?" a very young girl asked.

"I'm not sure yet exactly—but enough to give Safacon some trouble," Porcini said. He paused, looking around the room. His eyes rested on an older Cooper standing in a corner, listening with rapt attention. His shaggy fur was peppered with gray. There was something familiar in his dark eyes.

"You say the Guardians of Gayrile are fighting for us?" the Cooper asked, studying Porcini carefully.

"I suppose we're rallying them now," Porcini said. "Can you help organize this group?"

The Cooper nodded, then his eyes fixed on Hagar. "Is he fighting?"

"I will, Mr. Puddlepaw…and I'll find the others," Hagar said.

Porcini looked at the Cooper, realizing in a moment who he was. "You're…Mr. Puddlepaw? Jarus' father?"

The Cooper looked at him, startled. "My son—how do you know

my son?"

"He's one of my friends—he's on his way here even now," Porcini said with a grin.

Joy lit in the old Cooper's eyes as he smiled widely. "I knew he would—brave lad," he said, grinning in fierce pride. Then he frowned. "But they'll need help. This Safacon has many warriors." He turned to the other prisoners and got their attention as he began giving orders.

"Let's go, Porcini," Hagar said, and they continued on down the tunnel.

"Maya's father—do you know where he would be kept?" Porcini asked him.

"I'm not sure—but there's an upper level of cells I haven't been to yet," Hagar replied.

"Why?" Porcini asked, a little impatiently. Hagar threw him a pained look.

"I've only been here for a month or so, remember? Besides, I spent the first week or so unable to walk around at all… after they let me out of the interrogation hall." His expression became haunted, reliving the horrific memories that Porcini knew he couldn't even imagine.

"Sorry," he said. "Where are we going right now? I don't hear any voices this way—these cells sound empty." Their surroundings were eerily quiet. Porcini lowered his voice, worried that the guards might hear them and ruin the plan entirely.

"The Cooper I told you about. She's the one who helped me at the start. She's tried to escape before, and I promised to help her escape too, in case we ever attempted it," Hagar said. He paused by a large hole blocked by a tattered cloth, which concealed the passageway from any guards who glanced into the cell.

"She's in here?" Porcini asked, not sure why he had stopped.

Hagar nodded. "I don't know much about her. Only that she's been here for a long time. She never even told me her surname." Silently, they slipped into the cell.

A female Cooper sat on a cot by the door, listening to the sounds outside. Her fur was sprinkled with gray of age, but not enough of it to conceal the beautiful auburn of her pelt. She turned towards them and smiled as she saw Hagar, her blue eyes twinkling.

Blue eyes… that looked uncannily like Jarus'.

Porcini stared at her, hardly daring to believe it. Jarus had never said much about his mother—he had told Porcini that she had disappeared years ago, that she had been kind and loving and brave…

And Porcini suddenly connected the pieces as he looked at the female Cooper, who looked at him in curiosity.

"Who are you?" he blurted before thinking.

Hagar looked at Porcini, startled by his intensity. "Her name is Ada, Porcini—and she saved my life when I was brought here. She tended my wounds, and—"

"Ada…what?" Porcini prompted.

Hagar looked baffled—he had no idea. The other Cooper was still studying Porcini in silence, and finally spoke softly, her voice slightly rasping from disuse.

"My name is Ada Puddlepaw. And from the look in your eyes, child, there is more to your coming here than a simple meeting."

30

Morel's Spell

Jarus' head ached. His eyes flickered open weakly, and the darkness faded gradually. He could hear shouts, cries, clashing of steel on steel…the battle was happening beyond. He appeared to be in the courtyard, huddled behind some sort of berm.

"Am I dead?" he muttered to no one in particular.

A familiar voice answered. "No, you're not dead—pretty banged up though."

Jarus looked up. Morel crouched beside him. She carried a stolen rifle, and peered over the edge of the berm of piled rubble. Maya was beside her, looking at Jarus in relief. "You're okay…I wasn't sure. Morel and I dragged you out of the fight—some Serventiri knocked you down pretty hard. You've been out for maybe ten minutes."

"I'm all right," Jarus said groggily. "Where's everyone else?"

"I don't know. Lammar and Neely headed towards the palace, I think," Morel said. "I lost sight of Rygal. I think he headed up the mountain."

"And Norrin's here," Maya said, smiling widely.

"What?" Jarus said in shock, sitting up.

"Norrin's here," Morel said. "I don't know how, but he's here.

The Direns attacked the west tower first, and there was a flash of sparks—then we saw Norrin going up the mountain."

Jarus felt a surge of hope. Norrin was here, which meant…

"We've got to get the Jewel up to him," he said. "Who has the Knife?"

"Rygal did," Maya said, looking uncertain. "I think he made it up the mountain with it, towards Norrin—but about a hundred Serventiri went after him."

"What about the Ring?"

"I don't know. Hopefully Norrin has it," Morel said, but she looked uncertain.

Jarus looked between the two of them, thinking. Morel had her rifle and several spare bullets, and he had his knife. Still, storming across the battlefield probably wouldn't be their best tactic.

"We could cut through the palace," Morel said, seeming to guess Jarus' thoughts. "Almost all the guards are out here fighting—we could slip in and go out the back way, up the mountain."

Jarus considered this option. Morel was right—most of the guards seemed to be focused on the fight. But if they were captured…

Maya looked uneasy too. "The Serventiri will be able to sense the Jewel the minute we get in there… won't they?"

"Not if we keep it covered—and anyway, I don't see any other option," Morel said shortly. "We've got to hurry—if we don't get moving, we'll be captured anyway."

Jarus finally nodded. "All right. Let's go. Be careful."

The three of them moved out from behind the pile of rubble they crouched behind and onto the outskirts of the battlefield. The Direns had landed in the courtyard, and were battling the throngs of Serventiri. Bodies lay everywhere, some battered beyond recognition. Blood streaked the damp stones and stained the snow. The stench of death hung in the air.

A set of double doors were directly ahead of them, the main gates leading into the palace. Morel made them wait as a group of soldiers exited, hollow blue eyes glowing with anticipation of the battle beyond. None of them noticed the Brownae and the two Coopers huddled by the wall.

After the Serventiri passed them by, they entered the palace. Jarus looked around, taking in their surroundings. The palace was made almost entirely of gray stone, the same substance that made up the mountain towering above it. Their paws made no sound on the stone tiled floor as they moved cautiously down the halls. A set of roughly hewn stairs led up to their left, to the upper story of the palace. Jarus glanced up them. "Up or down?"

"Down," Morel said, her voice echoing slightly in the sudden quiet. "We'll move along the ground floor until we're away from the courtyard, then take the first door out and up to the mountain."

"And what if Safacon's here?" Maya asked quietly.

Morel debated the question. "Well… we'll deal with him if we have to. I'll bet he's gone after Norrin, though."

Jarus hoped she was right, but all the same, he didn't like being in the palace one bit. The chilly air, carrying the dull, dry scent of the mountain rocks, filled his nose, not quite masking the ever-present artificial smell of the Serventiri. He wondered uncomfortably if they were being watched.

The hall slanted down slightly, curving its way around the expanse of the courtyard. It was cold inside, and dark, the only light coming from a few torches along the walls. In these winter evenings, the sun would set early, and night would come fast. Jarus hoped they would break the Jewel before nightfall—he wasn't keen on fighting an army of angry Serventiri in the dark.

"Where do you think they keep the prisoners?" Maya asked in a low voice.

Jarus realized, with a jolt, that he hadn't worried about his father for the past few days. The urgency of destroying the Objects had made him forget about their original mission for coming here. "I'm not sure—but they're in here somewhere. Maybe in another section of the palace."

As he said it, he realized with a sinking feeling that he had no idea where the prisoners could be. The palace was one big labyrinth of stone, with who knew how many passages and levels. He figured they wouldn't keep prisoners in the towers—those would be reserved for Safacon and his generals, probably. So that meant they would be down here, or maybe below them, in another level…

Morel suddenly stopped and motioned for them to be silent. "Shhh…there's a group of soldiers up ahead."

They moved against the wall, huddling in the shadows. A garrison of soldiers moved past them, talking in lowered tones. Jarus noticed with a jolt that these were not Serventiri—their eyes did not glow blue, and their conversation was quiet and natural.

They were humans—real, living humans.

For a moment he was so surprised he nearly slipped out of their hiding place to talk to them, but stopped as he saw the emblems of Safacon branded on their shoulder guards.

The soldiers passed them by, and Jarus looked at Morel, dumbfounded. "Those weren't Serventiri—those were real people!"

Morel nodded wearily. "Yes, Safacon has many warriors—not all of them are Serventiri."

Jarus was stunned. Somehow, it felt different to be fighting mindless Serventiri rather than fighting a real person. "But…why are they with Safacon?"

"Press-ganged, bribed, bewitched—who knows," Morel said, as they moved forward again. "That's where part of the tension between the Brownaes and the humans comes in, you know. Many people respected Safacon in his early years of power, respected him as a skilled leader. He fooled a lot of people."

Jarus turned to Maya as they walked, remembering the earlier conversation. "Maybe we should find our fathers first—if Safacon escapes after we break the Jewel, he might go after the prisoners."

Maya considered this. "Maybe…but we don't even know where they are."

The halls twisted and turned like a great snake as they walked through the palace. Jarus fought to keep his sense of direction. The monotonous gray stone and winding corridors would make it very easy to get lost in here.

They had just entered another hall, moving deeper into the palace, when a sudden shout made them all turn. A second group of human soldiers stood behind them, yelling and pointing.

"Run!" Morel shouted, and they ran down the twisting hall. Behind them, the soldiers gave chase, their swords glinting in the faint light.

Jarus risked a glance over his shoulder. The soldiers were almost on them, and several of them had guns—the three companions ducked into a narrow, dark passage, running down the shadowed hall.

"Dead end," Maya whispered in the silence suddenly.

Jarus looked up—the hall they had entered was blocked by a locked door. The soldiers had passed them by, but it wouldn't be long before they realized the companions had doubled back. And then they would be trapped…

Morel looked at the door, tugged on the knob for a moment, then bit her lip. "Over here… we'll be all right…"

She drew out the Jewel and touched it to the lock. *"Allora,"* she whispered. There was a soft glow of blue light, a series of clicks in the lock, and then the door swung open.

"Morel, they'll know!" Jarus said in alarm as the blue light faded.

"Go—I can buy you time," Morel said quietly. She had turned, holding her rifle at the ready as she walked slowly down the hall and towards the distant sounds of the soldiers.

"No, don't…" Maya started.

Morel turned to them, jerking her head at the now opened door. "Go. Go now, before they come."

The soldiers had come—Jarus heard them shouting as they saw the Brownae princess. Morel held up the Jewel. *"Ventara!"* she shouted, and fire shot from the Jewel's core—Jarus heard the startled guards cry out—

"Here!" Morel yelled, shoving the Jewel in her bag and sliding it across the floor towards the two Coopers. "Go now—get it to Norrin!"

"Morel—" Maya started fearfully.

Jarus picked up the bag, staring once more at Morel. "We'll come back—we'll save you—"

"Go!" Morel ordered again—the soldiers had got past the fire, and Morel fired into their ranks.

The two Coopers slipped out the door and up a flight of stairs, fading into the safety beyond.

Morel fired until she had no more bullets, then stepped back, pointing her knife at the guards. Her hand shook slightly—this would be the end, she was sure. "Come on, then," she snapped, taking a half step back.

It was a cold, clear voice that replied from behind the guards. "Ah, princess, you impress me. I did not expect you would master the

Jewel in such a way."

The soldiers fell back. From out of the ranks strode a tall man clad in swirling robes, his eyes dark and pitiless, a slow smile crossing his pale face. Safacon.

Morel had frozen, terrified for an instant. Safacon smiled at her. "But, ultimately, no matter how much Jewel-lore you study, you will not be able to bring your mother back. That's what you wanted it for, wasn't it? Well, I am afraid to disappoint you, but you were sadly mistaken. The Jewel is a great weapon, but not that great. It will, however, be the weapon I need to bring justice back to Gayrile."

"You're wrong," Morel spat at him. "The Jewel will be destroyed, and you will too."

"Perhaps," Safacon chuckled. "But you are in no position to threaten me, little one." He nodded to the warriors. "Bind her and take her with us."

31

∽ ∽ ∽ ∽ ∽ ∽ ∽ ∽ ∽

The Fallen Servants

Jarus and Maya crept up the stairway. Behind them, the sounds of gunshots had faded. Morel would have been killed, Jarus realized, startled to realize how much the thought hurt. Even with her gruff manner and crisp words, the princess had been one of his companions, and the fact that she had sacrificed herself to save them made his heart ache.

"I don't think they killed her," Maya said softly beside him.

Jarus looked at her. "You don't?"

"No—I mean, think of how often Safacon and the Serventiri have tried to capture us this whole journey. That dragon could have just killed Porcini and Norrin, but it didn't. Safacon hasn't killed us, he wants us alive for some reason—that's why I think he took Morel prisoner."

"Maybe…" Jarus murmured, heartened to hear this. But he knew Morel's situation was little better captured than killed. "What will he do to her?"

"I don't know," Maya said, looking worried. Morel had become her friend and protector over the last few weeks, like a big sister— losing her hurt.

311

Jarus thought for a moment. "I'll bet you're right though," he said. "Safacon won't kill her. He wants his Objects back. Norrin has the Ring, Rygal has the Knife, and we have the Jewel. So he'll probably try to use Morel as a bargaining chip to get them all back."

"And if Norrin doesn't agree…?" Maya asked uncertainly.

Jarus wasn't sure. He knew Norrin wouldn't just hand over the Objects…but he wouldn't let Morel be killed either. Besides that, he also realized they had no idea whether or not Norrin had the Ring. He'd only assumed that at the start of the assault of the Topstorm.

They reached the top of the stairs and looked around. They had entered another hall, this one long and much nicer. Torches lit the room in pleasant light. Tapestries hung along the walls. The floor had been swept and the sounds of battle were fainter. This was where luxury lay for Safacon and his supporters.

Jarus and Maya moved down the hall, their eyes taking in the surroundings. Even the great library of Flameton could not surpass the sheer amount of wealth that had been poured into this area of the palace. The rich colors and beautiful furniture felt foreign compared to the plain gray stone of the lower levels.

They stopped suddenly as the sounds of footsteps came from down the hall behind them. Jarus listened for a long moment. They were long strides, heavy ones—a man moving towards them.

"Quick," he hissed, and he and Maya ducked behind one of the curtains by the window. Jarus peeked out from their hiding place, watching as a burly figure moved down the passage, carrying a torch in one hand and a sword in the other. His eyes scanned the hall carefully, and the light caught his face. Jarus' heart sank as he recognized Barret, one of the two men who had taken Mr. Raintail and Hagar.

They watched as he slunk down the hall, watching every shadow. It was only when he disappeared around the corner that the two Coopers slipped out from behind the curtain.

Jarus waited in silence, thinking. They couldn't fight him…but if anyone knew where the prisoners were kept, it would be Barret. He was sure of it. Once they freed their fathers, they could run up the mountain and bring the Jewel to Norrin. If they managed it…

He thought for a moment. "Okay, if we can catch Barret, we can maybe force him to tell us where our fathers are."

Maya raised her eyebrows. "All right, I think two Coopers can do that. All we need to do is make sure he doesn't sound the alarm and kill us both, but that shouldn't be a problem. Jarus…" she said, making a placating gesture that said *see what I mean?*"

Jarus thought about that. "Right…well, do you have any other ideas?"

He knew she was right about the idea of fighting Barret—it would be incredibly difficult to do so without being killed themselves. But they needed to find the prisoners soon…and if they weren't careful, they wouldn't have the chance.

"We'll go quietly," he said. "And…well, if worse comes to worse, we have the Jewel." He hoped very much that worse did *not* come to worse, because he knew the Serventiri would be able to sense the Jewel the minute they used it. And besides, he hadn't spent years studying Jewel-lore like Morel had—he didn't remember any of the spells, and he doubted he'd actually be able to use it.

"Look out!" Maya shouted suddenly, shoving him out of the way.

They had rounded the corner, and Barret had been waiting for them. He slashed viciously at Jarus—Maya's reaction saved him just in time. The two Coopers leapt out of the way, staring at the tall man.

Barret grinned widely, his teeth yellow. "Ah, there you are at last," he sneered. "Two little Coopers off exploring Safacon's lovely palace? Well…I'm afraid I'll have to detain you!" He lunged forward.

Jarus drew his knife from the sheath on his shoulder and parried as he ducked out of the way. Barret looked at the Cooper holding the little knife and laughed. He slashed again—Jarus blocked, but the force of Barret's blow knocked the knife out of his paw. It clattered on the floor a few feet away.

Barret chuckled darkly. "Don't worry, little one. It won't hurt one bit, not really." He raised the sword again—Jarus shrank against the wall, trapped.

Then Barret gave a screech of pain. Maya had come from behind, sinking a mouthful of needle sharp teeth into his calf. Barret rounded on her with a bellow of rage—Maya recovered Jarus' knife and slashed Barret's leg as she leapt clear of his sword blow.

"Where is my father?" Maya demanded. Her voice trembled

slightly with fear, but there was a fire in her eyes.

Barret straightened and smirked. "So that's it, is it? You've come all this way…to free your father?"

"Where is he?" Maya demanded again, moving forward.

Barret laughed, Maya's reaction answering his question. "Ah, I see you did. Well, your father is in a safe place…a better place, really."

Maya's face went white with fear. "No…he's not…"

Barret slashed at her—Maya, caught off guard, stumbled out of the way, but Barret lifted her with his other hand, gripping her throat. Maya gave a cry and squirmed desperately as Barret's grip tightened.

"No!" Jarus shouted, leaping forward. He didn't have his knife, he didn't have anything to fight with, but a rage had filled him and he leapt onto Barret's back, his claws raking the man's skin.

Barret gave a shout of surprise and pain, dropped Maya, and clutched blindly for Jarus, who held on, fighting like an angry cat. Barret stumbled, then reeled backwards, crushing Jarus between his body and the wall.

Jarus dropped to the floor, stunned, his left shoulder aching— Barret rounded on him, raising his sword.

Then a blue scaled shape lunged between them, seizing Barret and pinning him against the wall. Jarus blinked, his vision blurred with pain, and saw Neely, gripping Barret's shirt front as the man struggled.

"You all right?" Lammar's voice came from far away. Jarus looked up, his vision swimming back into focus. Lammar and Maya both knelt over him.

"Let me go! I don't know anything!" Barret howled, squirming in Neely's grip.

"Where are their fathers?" Neely demanded, pressing him against the wall harder.

"I—I don't know—I don't—"

"Start talking," Lammar said in a calm, conversational tone, "or I will take Neely's place, and I promise I'm a lot less patient than she is. I'm cold and hungry—and not especially picky either." He eyed Barret up and down.

Barret's eyes went wide as he looked between the Siren and Neely, who held him tightly against the wall. "They're—they're in the prison cells. Down this hall, down two flights of stairs, and to the right."

"Excellent," Lammar said. "Let him go, Neely."

Barret stepped back and seemed to consider fleeing. But in damaged pride, he whipped around again and raised the vicious knife, slashing at Neely's turned back. Jarus shouted a warning— Lammar moved faster. His shape flickered as he transformed into the huge green snake—Barret slashed at him too late, and the snake's fangs closed on his throat.

It all happened in a matter of seconds.

Jarus turned away, trembling, as Lammar returned to his original form. "Never turn your back on them," Lammar told Neely, who looked shaken. "He was a thief and an assassin. Not the most trustworthy type."

Neely nodded, her eyes wide. "Thanks," she managed to pant.

Lammar moved over to the two Coopers, studying them both for signs of injury. "Are you both all right? What were you thinking, taking on a fully armed man like that?"

Neither of them replied for a moment, still shaken. "We… were going to find our fathers," Jarus finally panted, unable to come up with a better reply.

"Understood. But next time, you must have more of a plan than that," Lammar said firmly. His face softened, and he shook his head. "Well, let's get going. We don't have long to find the prisoners before the Direns fight their way into the palace, and then it will be total chaos."

"You think Safacon would have them killed?" Maya asked anxiously, her eyes wide as they started down the hall.

"It's hard to guess what Safacon would or won't do," Lammar said. "I don't think he'd kill the prisoners, at least not yet. But if he realizes what you plan to do, he might hold them hostage."

"Until we give him the Jewel," Jarus murmured, shouldering Morel's pack again. Lammar noticed it, and his eyes widened.

"You have the Jewel? Where's Morel?"

"I don't know… we were attacked in the lower levels. She told us to run with it," Jarus said wretchedly.

"Then Safacon must have captured her," Neely said worriedly. "Or killed her."

Lammar thought quietly for a few seconds, clearly startled by the news. Then he nodded slowly. "Most likely she was captured. Safacon can use her. Either way, we need to get the Jewel up to the Tablet as soon as we free the prisoners."

He started off at a jog down the hall, and the others followed.

• • • • • •

Rygal sprinted up the hill for several minutes before Sariv saw him.

The thin, snake-like servant of Safacon had barely noticed him when Rygal had first emerged from the courtyard after the Direns launched their attack. Fire rained from above, and the war-frenzied Brownaes had swarmed into the castle, causing total confusion. Rygal had lost view of the other companions and he had stood in uncertainty for several tense moments.

That was when he saw Norrin's fire.

The familiar crackle of yellow sparks drew his attention—in the tower directly above him, the one closest to the Topstorm, a blast had shot through the walls, sending bricks raining down. A tall figure emerged from the hole, leaping to the rocks just above him with a speed and agility that betrayed his appearance. Rygal saw a group of Serventiri fire at him from the opening in the wall—the cloaked figure spun his staff in a wide circle, blocking the shots midair almost casually, then fired a second blast that sent the Serventiri reeling back.

There was only one person Rygal knew who could have pulled

318

something like that off.

Hope filled him again. Norrin was here, which meant that maybe—just maybe—Norrin had the Ring. And that meant they needed to get to the Golden Tablet up on the mountain.

He ran through the castle gates and began the steep ascent up the mountain's sides. His eyes were fixed on the outcrop above to his left—a small structure stood there. Norrin was rushing toward it, and Rygal guessed that must be where the Tablet was. That was why Norrin didn't see the shadowy, slender shape of Sariv as the assassin began to pursue him. Rygal saw him, though, and now he ran even faster, his sword gripped in his hand. The Knife of Destruction thumped against his leg as he ran.

Norrin reached the outcrop first. Built into the mountainside, weathered by wind and rain, was a large covered structure made of solid stone. Columns held the crumbling roof up, though Rygal could tell they were badly eroded and looked about ready to fall. He slipped past them quickly, eyes on Sariv.

Norrin moved to the far side of the structure and turned, his eyes fixing on Sariv as he set his staff before him. "That's far enough."

Sariv paused, then smiled slowly. "Norrin… how nice to see you again. It's been a little while, hasn't it? The last time I saw you, you were leading a bunch of vagabond warriors, the last of your pitiful Guardians of Gayrile, when my master began his rise to power."

"It has been awhile," Norrin said calmly. He noticed Rygal coming—Rygal saw relief cross his face, then he looked back to Sariv. Rygal continued advancing slowly and quietly from behind.

"Well, this little rebellion will end, like all the others," Sariv spat. "You and your companions will be killed, and Gayrile will be safe from your kind forever."

"Safe?" Norrin repeated, his face darkening. "Safe from your master's tyranny? Safe from the Objects he holds so dear? No, Sariv, you know as well as I that Gayrile is not safe as long as Safacon reigns. And your trust in your master will be your downfall."

Sariv laughed, sneering. "You lie, wizard," he spat. "I do not see the Jewel before you on the Golden Tablet now, do I?"

Rygal noticed the Tablet for the first time, directly behind Norrin. It looked like an anvil, the top of it made of gold. The rest of it was made of heavy steel, and it glinted slightly in the fading sunlight.

"The Jewel is here," Norrin said. "By morning, it will be destroyed along with Safacon's power and empire."

Sariv hesitated, and Rygal lunged forward, hoping to capture him then and there. But as he moved, his sword caught on a loose stone, generating a dull clang.

Sariv whipped around, his eyes narrowing. Rygal cursed his own clumsiness, but forgot about it in another instant as he attacked.

In the years following his adventures during Kado's war, Rygal had trained for hours on end with his sword. Now the motions felt comfortable and fluid as he parried Sariv's blow, then slashed in again. He saw Norrin turn back to the Tablet, setting the Ring upon it. There was an odd cracking hiss, and a film of golden light shimmered over the surface as the reversing of the spell began.

Sariv saw the spell begin too, and glared fiercely at Rygal. "You won't win this," he sneered. "You'll all be killed—my master will come and end this."

"You just keep thinking that," Rygal spat back, lunging forward again. Sariv stood between him and Norrin, and there was no way Rygal could get past him to get the Knife on the Tablet…

He slashed twice at Sariv, then drew out the Knife, ready to toss it in Norrin's direction. But in that instant, Sariv lunged forward, driving his shoulder into Rygal's chest and heaving the younger man back. The Knife slipped from Rygal's fingers as he fell, and it clattered behind him, down the path.

Rygal leapt to his feet, but Sariv had reached it first, diving down upon the Knife. He raised it, his eyes glinting with a sudden idea. "Perhaps you are right…perhaps Safacon will fall," he said, gazing into the Knife's strange blade. "But…why should there not be a new empire?" He looked up, grinning madly. "Sariv the Great, wielder of the Knife of Destruction—yes, I will be greater and more powerful than even Safacon!"

Rygal stood slowly, glaring at him. "Put it down…now."

Sariv laughed. "And why would I do that?" He was backing down the path. Rygal could see a group of Serventiri approaching from behind, led by a tall figure in silver robes.

"Greater than I, Sariv?" the leader asked softly, his voice low and with a touch of dark humor.

Sariv whipped around—his face went white, but Rygal's eyes fixed on the tall man moving towards them. His eyes were so dark they seemed almost black, standing out strikingly on his pale face, an unpleasant smile touching the corners of his thin mouth.

"Norrin…" Rygal started, a touch of fear chilling his heart as he stared at the sorcerer before him.

Safacon stared at Sariv, who was shaking. "Master—I—no—forgive me—"

"Give it to me," Safacon said shortly, holding out a hand. Sariv, trembling, held out the Knife.

"Master…please…"

"Is this not mine?"

Sariv relaxed. "Yes, master—it is yours, it was always yours…"

Safacon smiled coldly. "So it is." He plunged the blade into Sariv's chest before the man could move, speaking the killing curse of the Knife in the same moment. *"Devrando!"*

Rygal jumped back as Sariv's body jerked, then went limp, the life extinguished. Safacon flung the body down the mountain—there was a dull crash from below as it landed amid the rocks.

The sorcerer turned slowly to face them. His black eyes glinted as he held the Knife. "Well… companions of the Jewel," he said in disdain, "I have come to bargain."

He nodded to the guards, who stepped forward. Between them, bound and gagged, struggling furiously, was Morel.

32

Into the Maze

After the incident with Barret on the upper levels of the palace, Lammar suggested they return to the ground floor. While this was closer to the battlefield, there was less chance of running into any patrols, and Lammar guessed that the only soldiers down there would be the prison guards.

They headed in the direction Barret had told them to go to find the prisoners, pausing every now and then to listen. The lower levels seemed to be deserted, and the halls were silent. Aside from a lantern on the walls every now and then, and maybe an open door letting in light from the courtyard, it was mostly dark.

After moving down the stairs, they entered a series of winding halls moving gradually in the same direction. There they paused, looking around uncertainly. "Where to now?" Maya asked softly, her voice echoing in the deserted halls.

Lammar thought a moment, looking around. "I'm not sure… let's keep going. Keep an eye out for any guards."

They started down the maze of halls. Jarus noticed the barred doors blocking each opening, and realized they had reached the prison levels. But the cells were empty. "Do you smell anyone?" he whispered to Lammar.

The Siren scented the air. "Yes…faintly. I can't tell if they were here recently or not—impossible to tell in all this stone."

"Perhaps the prisoners escaped when the battle started," Neely suggested softly.

Jarus thought about that. There was a chance, of course…but he wasn't sure.

"Either way, we need to get to Norrin as soon as we can," Maya said. "The Serventiri will be able to sense the Jewel."

"Or we could use it against them," Jarus said, although he figured that would only make things worse. They would only further alert the Serventiri of their presence. The thought made his spine prickle with uneasiness. It was incredibly difficult to see or hear anyone in the dimly lit halls, and the winding corridors transformed the prison cells into a confusing labyrinth.

He was jolted out of his thoughts as Lammar suddenly stopped. Neely took a pace forward and paused, her head cocked to one side.

"I can hear nothing," she whispered hesitantly.

"They're there," Lammar assured her grimly. "I can smell them."

At the far end of the hall, a group of Serventiri appeared, their hollow blue eyes glowing in the darkness. They stopped as they saw the four companions.

For a second both groups stared at each other. Then one of the Serventiri gave a signal, and they charged forward.

"Great, here we go again," Lammar growled, his shape flickering as he transformed into the huge green snake. Neely had lunged forward too, prepared to fight tooth and claw—quite literally. Jarus and Maya jogged behind them. Jarus wasn't sure what they planned to do—but retreat was not an option anymore. Not now, this close to finding their fathers.

Three Serventiri had fallen—the rest of the group hesitated for a moment, then retreated, running back down the hall.

"After them—they'll sound the alarm," Lammar panted, resuming his regular shape and running forward. The four of them raced down the hall and turned down another corridor. The sounds of the Serventiri had faded, but Jarus knew they would come back soon, with greater numbers.

The sounds of clinking armor came from somewhere in the dimly lit maze—the four companions froze, panting, tense with fright.

"Where are the prisoners?" Jarus breathed, sniffing desperately for some scent of life. His father had to be down here—yet he could smell nothing but stone, and the gradually approaching Serventiri.

They started down the hall again, not sure where they were going, even less sure if they were going towards or away from the Serventiri. Jarus' heart was pounding—the terror of not knowing where the danger was coming from was overwhelming. Maya's face was drawn with the same frightened determination. Both of them could practically hear the time ticking away.

"We'll find them," Jarus told her. "They're here—I'm sure of it."

Maya nodded but didn't say anything.

A sharp crack from a rifle silenced his thoughts—Neely screamed from ahead, yelling for them to get back. The two Coopers turned, retreating back down the hall as the sounds of battle erupted behind them. Jarus saw flashes of yellow fire reflecting on the stone—Neely was fighting. The fire cast strange, elongated shadows up the walls, as if the darkness had taken form to battle alongside the Serventiri.

Neither of them saw the wall at the end of the corridor until they ran into it. Stunned, Jarus stumbled back, groping along the smooth stone for a door or gap, anything for them to slip through. Nothing. They had missed the way to escape and had been forced into a dead end.

"Quick—back out," Maya said, and they sprinted for the distant light at the end of the tunnel.

A tall figure blocked the way, and they skidded to a halt—Maya crashed into the figure with a scream, raising her little knife in defense. "It's me—it's me!" came Neely's shaking voice, just in time, and Maya lowered her blade.

The three of them backed against the wall. "What's happened? Where are they?" Jarus panted.

"Behind me—Lammar's holding them off, he is covering our retreat. Where is the door out?" Neely looked past them down the hall, and Jarus saw her face fall as she realized they were trapped.

"We'll have to fight our way out," Jarus said, peering past her. It was pitch black in the hall beyond. With no windows to let in light, and the torches extinguished by the Serventiri, he could see nothing. He had noticed before that the Serventiri seemed to be able to see just fine in the dark.

"This is bad," he muttered, unnecessarily.

Light flickered dimly at the end of the hall—Lammar's shape was dimly outlined as he re-lit one of the torches on the walls, then ran the rest of the way to them.

"What's going on?"

"This is a dead end," Jarus told him. Lammar peered past him, seeing the end of the corridor, then looked out into the main hall again. From the way he had come came the soft clicking of armor. One by one, pairs of glowing blue eyes appeared in the darkness.

Slowly, relentlessly, the Serventiri approached the trapped companions.

Jarus realized, in a flash, that if they didn't get out, it would all be over. The Serventiri would get the Jewel, and take it to Safacon—he debated using a spell, but he didn't know how to do that, not like Morel had—

"Maya, take the Jewel," Lammar said, his voice quiet. "Go down this hall, back up into the main levels, and run. Don't stop running until you get to Norrin."

Jarus expected Maya to argue—she said nothing, only slipped the bag off of Jarus' shoulders and slung it on her back. Her paws were cold, trembling slightly. The dull finality of what was happening hit him in the chest.

"Make them pay for this," he whispered to her as she took the Jewel. In the dim light, he could see tears shining in her eyes. "Please—get the Jewel to Norrin and finish this. And please try to find my father."

"I will," Maya said softly. Her voice was quiet, but steady.

"We'll cover you," Lammar said. His shape flickered as he transformed into the tall, black-cloaked warrior. He seemed to melt into the darkness, with only the faint glint of his yellow-green eyes visible. Neely moved to stand beside him, fire glowing softly in her hands. Maya studied them, then carefully edged out into the hall.

There were no words. No time to tell her anything. For the first time, Jarus felt brave enough to speak. Facing oncoming death made him lose some of his fear, in a strange way. He moved past her as he started towards Lammar, finally managing the words.

"Maya—you should know—I wanted to tell you that I…" The glowing eyes of the Serventiri drew closer. So many of them. The hopelessness of what was happening overwhelmed him.

But Maya looked at him, smiling faintly. "I know… so do I."

Jarus looked at her. In the faint light, he saw her beautiful eyes glittering with tears. Then she slipped past him and turned down the hall beyond. The wild joy that filled him with her response drove away his fear.

He stepped into place beside Lammar, and they watched as the Serventiri approached.

And then they heard something else.

A sound rose from the hall from behind the group of Serventiri, making them pause. It was the sound of many voices roaring in defiance and fury, a battle cry echoing through the halls. Behind the Serventiri, Jarus could see an army of torches making their way at great speed toward them.

A mob of raggedly dressed, half-starved people burst into the corridor, brandishing rusted swords and scavenged weapons as they attacked the Serventiri. Jarus stared in shock and awe. There must have been close to three hundred of them, all fighting viciously. Torchlight flooded the hall again, illuminating the battle.

The Serventiri, taken off guard, rounded on the ferocious charge. Surprised and attacked from behind, they reacted too slow. The ragged army attacked with great speed, in a coordinated, well-planned charge.

"Circle around them!" came an order. The voice that shouted it was young, familiar—Jarus peered through the throng in disbelief. A small Brownae with brown fur yelled orders to the rag-tag warriors as they encircled the Serventiri. The Serventiri seemed to hesitate for a moment, their simple minds unable to understand what had happened to them. Then they attacked, charging out at the gradually forming circle.

"Let's go!" Lammar shouted, and the three companions joined the battle. Jarus slashed at a Serventiri warrior, then bumped into the Brownae—

"Porcini?" he managed to stammer, stunned.

Porcini blocked a blow from another warrior, then grinned at Jarus. "Oh hey, glad you guys made it."

"Porcini… what…?" The sounds of battle cut off Jarus' baffled questions. He focused on the fight, though he could barely make sense of it. Porcini was here, leading an army of ragged and surprisingly skilled warriors—where had they come from?

"Push them back!" came Lammar's voice. He and another warrior had forced open one of the cell doors. Porcini's warriors pressed forward, forcing the Serventiri to retreat back into the cell. A few of them tried to fight, but the strange newcomers were stronger—Jarus saw them striking skillfully at any Serventiri who resisted.

In another moment, the Serventiri had been forced into the open cell, pressed together like fish in a net. Lammar and Neely slammed the door closed, locking it securely. The Serventiri clawed at the locked door, reaching out through the barred window, trying to touch the lock. But they were trapped. The cells had been built to hold creatures more powerful than they were.

There was a brief, relieved silence. Then the newcomers began speaking, congratulating one another, tending to the wounds of the injured. Jarus saw the look of surprise and joy on Lammar's face— he could hear many of the strange warriors greeting the Siren by name.

Porcini moved over to him, beaming. "You all right? Why are you down here?"

"Porcini…" Jarus said, barely able to form words. "How—who are all these people?" He gestured briefly at the ragged army.

Porcini grinned. "Behold the Guardians of Gayrile—the survivors, anyway. They've been locked up down here for years, along with many others who were willing to fight. Hagar and I got them out—some of them fought with Norrin, and now they're ready to fight again."

"Wait, wait," Jarus said. "Hagar? Hagar's—"

Porcini turned—a Cooper with dark fur approached slowly. He was very thin, and his once sleek fur was matted and patched from weeks of malnourishment. But Jarus would have recognized him anywhere.

Hagar looked at him, his gaze sliding away. "I admit I'm glad to see you here, Puddlepaw," he said at last, voice low.

"I… I wish I could say the same," Jarus said finally, startled to feel the hatred burning in his chest. His resolve to forgive Hagar, so easily decided before, was a completely different issue when Hagar was standing here before him. And worse, Hagar seemed to have changed.

Porcini looked at Jarus. "Is Maya here too?"

"No… she's taking the Jewel to Norrin." Saying those words made his grudge with Hagar seem so irrelevant. There were bigger problems happening now.

Lammar and Neely both approached through the crowd. After greeting Porcini warmly, Lammar turned back to business. "How many here?"

"Maybe two hundred who can fight. Maybe more," Porcini said, studying the waiting warriors. Jarus was impressed to see the set in his stance. There was a commanding aura that belied his usual quiet personality. "I'll check with the wounded. Most likely they'll all want to fight, no matter their injuries."

"Good. That's good," Lammar said, nodding in approval, "because we'll probably have to fight several groups of Serventiri to get up the mountain."

"The mountain?" Hagar echoed, looking uncertain. "What's up the mountain?"

"It's the only way to end this. Norrin, with any luck, should be up there now. Rygal went after him, carrying the Knife, and hopefully Maya will get the Jewel there too," Lammar said.

"Let me check with my warriors," Porcini said, straightening as he turned toward the waiting group. Jarus watched him, still startled. The term 'my warriors' wasn't an exaggeration—the ragged former Guardians followed the young Brownae's command without question. He had to smile to himself.

"There's something you need to see," Hagar said quietly.

Jarus looked at him. He had almost forgotten he was there. "What?"

Hagar nodded toward the group. "Over here. They're both waiting." He hesitated as they moved through the ranks of warriors, started to speak, but stopped.

The crowd parted slightly. Standing before them were two Coopers.

They sat beside each other, both of their fur sprinkled with signs of age—the male, a grizzled gray; the female an elegant silver. Jarus' gaze was drawn to the female Cooper as she looked at him, smiling, tears shining in her eyes.

The world seemed to melt around him. He could hear nothing, his heart pounding in his ears, his vision fixed on the Cooper. Finally, he managed to croak one word, his throat tight with emotion.

"Mom?"

33

Reunion

Rygal took a half step back as Safacon moved closer. He glanced back at Norrin, looking for some direction, some idea of what to do. Morel, held by the two Serventiri, squirmed fiercely, but the two soldiers barely reacted. Safacon ran a delicate finger down the blade of the Knife, removing a spot of Sariv's blood, and cast a patronizing gaze at Norrin.

"Ah, Norrin, I understand we are both men of action. So I shall keep it brief. Give me the Ring, and your princess will go free."

"Don't listen to him!" Morel screamed. One of the Serventiri kicked her in the stomach so hard she doubled over, gasping.

Norrin stepped forward, hands raised slightly, spread in a placating gesture. "Wait. Wait. She holds no value to you, and if you hurt her, any deal is off."

"No value?" Safacon repeated thoughtfully. "That's a rather hurtful thing to tell her. No, she actually has great value to me. She is a fascinating creature. As I have heard, she has mastered several spells of the Jewel quite well." He cupped Morel's chin in his hand, turning her head upward. Morel snapped at his fingers, and he withdrew his hand.

"What do you want with the Ring, then?" Norrin asked. "If what you said earlier is true, the Ring has no value to you either."

Rygal looked at him in surprise, then back at Safacon. Safacon shook his head. "No value, but still some *use*, if you understand my meaning."

"I don't," Norrin said. "Now let her go, and we will talk. Or take me prisoner in her place until we come to an agreement."

Safacon thought for a moment, then nodded. "That seems satisfactory." He nodded to the guards, who dropped Morel to the ground, then surged forward to bind Norrin. Rygal stepped between them, raising his sword. His heart was pounding, the blood roaring in his ears.

"Not yet, Rygal," Norrin ordered sharply. He laid a hand on his shoulder, gently pushing past him. "Wait. We will talk first." Calmly, he held out his hands to the guards, who bound his wrists tightly and shoved him over to Safacon.

Safacon looked over at the Golden Tablet, seeming to notice, for the first time, the glittering, sparking Ring resting on its surface. "Ah, I see you've already started the process. Interesting. I find it odd you still refuse to utilize the Objects' powers—I always took you to be smarter than that."

"Perhaps," Norrin said. His voice was remarkably calm. Rygal studied his face, searching for some sign, some clue as to what he was supposed to do. He could see the same confusion on Morel's face too. Norrin was still speaking. "I suppose I never thought to use the Jewel, Safacon. Not for myself, not for Gayrile. I knew Gayrile, at least, always had a better alternative."

"Oh?" Safacon asked, raising an eyebrow. Something clicked in Rygal's mind, a memory stirring from a discussion days ago, at Larkin's, when Norrin had said that before… and suddenly, adrenaline was rushing through his veins. Safacon frowned, not comprehending. "And what alternative was that, Norrin?"

Norrin smiled. "The Guardians."

. . . . . .

"I never told you—either of you," Ada Puddlepaw whispered into Jarus' ear. She held him close, wrapped in one of those tight hugs that Jarus never realized how much he missed.

She was here. In Safacon's palace. After six years and who cared how many days, she was here.

"How…" he managed to choke. His voice seemed to have faded away.

Ada pulled back, looking him up and down. Her eyes shone with bittersweet tears. "I'm sorry for never telling you the truth of who I was, or what I did. It was too dangerous for you to know. Of course, you ended up getting wrapped up in it all either way." She shook her head wryly.

Jarus looked her up and down, still in shock. She really was here. He was overwhelmed with joy, but needed an answer. A long one. "Where *were* you?"

Ada exchanged a look with Carus, then turned back to her son. "It seems you already know of the Guardians of Gayrile. Well, they had other allies too, allies on the Mainland."

Jarus' head began to spin again. "Allies—wait—you were a—"

"I never fought with them," Ada interrupted him before he asked the question. "But I was an informant. One of the only set of eyes and ears for them in Mata City, actually." She smiled faintly at the disbelief on his face. "When Safacon rose to power, I helped relocate many of our allies. Get them away, safe from Safacon. After the Guardians were outlawed, I worked against Safacon—we worked especially hard to stop his weapons smugglers, which definitely angered him. Then I settled down with you and your father. I hoped, if I remained inconspicuous, that Safacon wouldn't find me." She shook her head. "I was wrong."

"Safacon captured her that night, so long ago," Carus put in, unable to keep quiet anymore. He sat beside Ada, putting an arm around her as if to keep her near forever. "Seems he was looking for any remaining spies."

"I wanted to help the Guardians, especially once they were outlawed," Ada said softly. "I don't regret that—my only regret is not telling either of you." She hugged both of them close again.

"People talked… people all said… you ran off," Jarus mumbled through the hug.

Ada laughed, a sound Jarus had missed more than anything. "Well, I'm sure my reputation will be tarnished past repair when we return home. Though maybe that's for the best. No one could know the truth of it—if they did, all of Mata City would have been in danger."

Jarus remembered what the kidnappers had told Maya the night they had taken her father—the threat to kill. He understood it now. "We would have helped," he said. "Pop and I—we could have all done it together."

Ada shook her head slowly. "We might have. I was too worried to put any of you in danger. But now," she looked at Jarus with pride in her eyes, "now, I know we will do it together."

Jarus hugged her again, if only to make sure she was really there. It was so surreal, all of it—yet the pieces fit together. "Then—you were here all this time? Captured?"

"Yes," Ada said, taking a breath. "I tried to escape—to make it back to you. I tried many times. It never worked." The shadow of a dark memory clouded her face for a moment, but she shook it away. "I found the tunnel first—the one that Porcini and Hagar used to get us all out. That tunnel allowed me to enter some of the cells. When Hagar came, he had been beaten, nearly to death."

"Your mother saved me, Jarus," Hagar said softly from behind.

Jarus had forgotten he was there, and turned to face him. Hagar met his eyes steadily. There was no trace of the smirking, sneering Hagar that Jarus had always hated. He was humbled now, and the change was startling. It didn't make Jarus like him any more, though.

Lammar approached suddenly, which reminded them all of the situation at hand. "There's trouble up above," he said. "One of Porcini's scouts just came downstairs with news that Safacon has reached the Golden Tablet, up on the mountain. We think Norrin's up there too, but no one's quite sure."

"Maya has the Jewel," Jarus said, feeling his heart sink. "Lammar—Maya took the Jewel—she'll run straight into Safacon if we don't warn her."

"Then we'll go after Safacon too," Porcini said. He stood behind them, looking at the Guardians he had recently freed. "That's the only way, right?" he added, turning to Lammar. "All three Objects have to be on the Golden Tablet if we're going to break them. The Jewel will *have* to be taken where Safacon is."

"Yes," Lammar said, nodding slowly. Jarus knew this had to be done—but the idea of taking the Jewel straight past Safacon made his blood run cold. There was no telling what sort of dark magic the sorcerer would use to regain his lost weapon.

Lammar turned to the waiting group, his tone of command demanding everyone's attention. "No time to waste, then." He selected one of the former Guardians from the crowd. "Robert, lead half of this group up the mountain now. Try to draw the battle away from the Tablet. I'll lead the second half to join you in a few minutes, after we tend to the wounded." The man named Robert nodded and began selecting warriors to join him.

"What about me?" Porcini asked.

Lammar looked between him and Jarus. "You two are going to free Morel. In all likelihood, Safacon has captured her and could be using her to bargain with Norrin as we speak."

"Maya—" Jarus and Hagar both started at once.

"She'll be up there too, with any luck," Lammar interrupted. "Either way we don't have time to go look for her. Look at what is happening. If Maya isn't up on the Topstorm, I give you my word that I will find her myself after Safacon is stopped. But Norrin and Rygal are outnumbered up there right now, and Morel is in danger."

Jarus knew he was right. Maya was smart. She would run and take the Jewel straight to Norrin, who would break the Objects. Still, not knowing where she was, or if she was in danger, chilled him to the core. He could see Hagar felt the same, which didn't make him feel any better.

"I'm going with them," Hagar said shortly.

Lammar didn't argue with him. "Good. You three, go now."

Porcini led them up two flights of stairs, up to the ground floor of the castle. Light greeted them, light from the lanterns and windows, and Jarus squinted at the brightness for a moment. Then his eyes adjusted and he jogged after Porcini, with Hagar trailing. "Do you know where we're going?" he asked. The looming bulk of Topstorm Mountain leered down at them. There was no telling where on the mountain the Tablet was.

Porcini hesitated, and Hagar spoke. "It's on the southeast side—directly above us, behind that rise. There's some sort of temple housing it. I heard the guards talking about it," he added, as they both looked surprised.

"Good," Porcini said. He pushed through the door, peeked out cautiously, and then stepped out. They stood outside the walls of the palace. "No one here—I guess they all headed up to fight."

"Look!" Hagar said, pointing.

Jarus looked up. Swooping down towards the rise Hagar had described was an army of Direns, descending with fire and steel upon the host of Serventiri that had gathered there. "The Diren army!" he said, feeling a surge of hope. The second group from Flameton joined with the weary first charge and charged down, just as Makana had described to them days ago.

"Those aren't the rebels?" Hagar asked as they ran upward towards the distant battle.

"No—they're on our side. And the Brownaes should be here soon too," Jarus said. Hagar nodded but said nothing. It was so strange, Jarus realized, how difficult it was for him to forgive this Cooper. He could forgive Morel, who had hidden the Jewel from them. He could forgive his mother for lying to them all those years about who she was and what she had been doing. He could even feel a stir of pity for Safacon, who at this point was controlled entirely by the Jewel's dark magic. But Hagar Groundrop? That felt like something else entirely.

"So… Maya told you what happened that night they captured us?" Hagar asked finally.

"I was there," Jarus said. "I watched." Another silence. They moved up the hill steadily, weaving around hulking boulders and patches of shrubbery. "How many Coopers did you turn over to them?" he asked finally.

Hagar looked at him. "I didn't know about your mother, Jarus. This deal—I only started helping them a few months before we were captured."

"Nice wedding gift to Maya."

"I didn't want her to be hurt. I wanted to impress her… to fight the men off when they came for her father," Hagar said haltingly.

"Oh, and impress your father-in-law while you're at it, too. Creative." The words were sarcastic and sneering. Jarus wished that he could take them back. But years of enduring Hagar's rudeness and snobbery seemed to have morphed into these snappy insults.

Hagar said nothing for a moment. "I've apologized for my treachery, but I know the part that really gets you is Maya, Puddlepaw," he said finally, his voice crisp. "I've seen how you look at her, after all these years. I saw the jealousy in your eyes that day by the canal, the day before Safacon captured her father. Ultimately, you know it will be Mr. Raintail's decision."

"No," Jarus said, as he realized the truth suddenly. "It'll be Maya's. It will be her choice alone, as it ought to be." He paused. The fact was painful, searing his heart, but he knew it was the truth. "And if… if she chooses you, now that you've changed… I respect that decision. And… I wish happiness to you both."

There. He had said it. The very idea brought burning tears to his eyes, but he knew that was the truth, and the purest way to prove his love for her.

Hagar looked a little startled. "I… well, thank you." An awkward pause.

Porcini spoke quietly from up ahead. He had reached the ridge, and huddled behind a large rock. "Get down, and look at this."

The two Coopers quickly dropped down beside him. Jarus peeked over the ridge.

The ground dropped away slightly, forming a shallow valley. Twenty yards to their left stood a crumbling ruin of a temple. Beneath it sat an anvil-like shape, made of steel and glittering gold. He saw Rygal and Morel standing just in front of it. Behind them stood several Diren warriors. King Makana stood a little ways in front of them.

To their right, directly below Jarus' vantage point, stood Safacon. Serventiri had encircled the valley, hemming them in with a wall of armored forces. Norrin was beside him, his wrists bound, his staff lying out of reach at his feet.

Safacon stood smiling, confident, unworried. His fingers played over the mirror-like blade of the Knife of Destruction.

34

The Return of the Forgotten

Jarus watched silently from the ridge, huddled between Porcini and Hagar. None of them moved. The voice of Safacon, cold and curt, carried up the rocks to them as he spoke to Makana.

"King Makana. I wondered how long it would be before you paid me a visit. Sympathizing with the weaklings as usual, I see."

Makana's wings fluttered slightly in the breeze. He towered over Safacon, with General Hawkblaze and General Warnwing standing just behind him at the ready. "In the name of the High King of Coonsia," Makana said steadily, his deep voice filling the valley, "your reign ends today. You have terrorized Gayrile's people for long enough, bleeding your civilians dry with taxes, tormenting their streets with your soldiers. You have failed Gayrile in a time when her people most needed you, and for that alone we demand your immediate surrender."

"Surrender?" Safacon laughed. It was a high, clear laugh, tainted with a madness that chilled Jarus to the core. "Surrender now? When you are surrounded by my forces? Ah, Makana. Have you noticed that I have *not* killed you all yet, when I could do so with the Knife? But I have not done so... because I need you alive.

Consider yourself lucky—you are both still of some use to me."

"Put the Knife down, Safacon," Norrin said. "Every time you use it, or the Ring, or the Jewel—every time, they drain away more of your humanity, more of your sanity."

"Sanity?" Safacon laughed again. "Our view of sanity is very limited, Norrin. The Jewel takes the mortal mind somewhere else entirely, to a place of power you can only dream of."

"At what cost?" Norrin asked. "Safacon, stop this before any more lives are lost. We will talk—you, Makana, and I. And I think after hearing our council you will decide not to continue entertaining this mad power that has seduced you."

Porcini looked at his two companions and whispered. "Morel's safe with Rygal. The Direns are all here—what should we do?"

Jarus had no idea. Everyone in that valley was in danger as long as Safacon held the Knife. He waved it every now and then at Makana as he spoke, but the Diren king didn't flinch. Safacon smiled at him. "Brave, aren't you, sire? I will test that bravery, and that of your soldiers', if you refuse to leave my domain in peace. Leave now, before this pointless rebellion gets further out of hand."

Makana did not answer, only nodded to his warriors, who took a few steps forward, their weapons at the ready. Jarus saw the circle of Serventiri tighten around the valley, moving to meet the Diren army. Safacon raised the Knife in the same moment. "*Devrando!*" he said, almost casually. Jarus only saw a flicker of shadow spit from the tip of the blade before it hit the Diren lieutenant to the right of

Hawkblaze. The Direns froze as the lieutenant's limp body fell to the rocks.

"I still have purpose for you, Makana," Safacon hissed. "I have none for your friends. I will kill them, all of them, if you insist on fighting me."

He raised a hand and shouted a strange command. Jarus noticed that none of the Serventiri reacted, only turned expectantly, looking up at the hulking mountain above them. The command had not been for them—then who or what…

From above them came a rumble as heavy doors were opened. The noise was followed by a second sound, a horrible noise somewhere between a growl and a scream. It was vaguely familiar, but no dragon Jarus had yet seen had made a sound like that.

Then, creeping out of its den above, the beast emerged and began crawling slowly down the mountain to join its master. Jarus wanted to speak, but stopped, unable to turn his gaze away. The creature was huge, close to forty feet long, he guessed, dwarfing every dragon he had yet seen. Its scales were iridescent white, like a pearl, seeming to cast many colors around it. Its face was gaunt, the muzzle long, filled with sharp fangs. But its eyes were hollow and glowed blue.

"What—what sort of dragon is that, Porcini?" Jarus stammered.

"No—no, that's not a dragon—I don't even know what that is." Porcini's voice trembled with horror as the beast crept the remaining distance down to the waiting armies, its chest rumbling with another horrible high-pitched snarl.

Safacon smiled. "Fight if you will, Makana. My warriors come aplenty—and I shall have you know that they are eager for your demise."

The battle began before Jarus noticed—there was no command, no noise from either side to give warning, not like he had pictured battles. Half of the Diren army, led by King Makana, rose gracefully into the air, then dove at the giant dragon like crows attacking an eagle. The massive beast snarled its hatred and rose onto its hind legs, clawing at its attackers. Its talons shredded the wings of a warrior, and the helpless Diren plummeted into the rocks.

Fighting had also begun on the ground—Jarus saw Rygal and Morel fighting alongside General Hawkblaze, striking at the Serventiri who had approached. He searched the throng frantically—Norrin and Safacon stood where they had, Norrin's hands still bound, seemingly helpless as he watched the fight.

"Come on!" Porcini said, and the three of them ran down the rocks. Jarus' paws skidded on the loose gravel, but he kept his eyes on the bloody battle unfolding before them. Bodies already littered the ground, bright red blood mixing with the strange purple of the Serventiri's blood. Every now and then he heard Safacon shout the killing curse, picking Direns out of the sky as if he were hunting waterfowl.

"We have to get the Knife!" he yelled to Porcini, but his voice was lost in the battle. He crashed into a Serventiri, leapt out of the way just in time, and ended up side by side with Morel.

"Where's the Jewel?" the princess shouted over her shoulder to him.

"Maya has it—she's coming," Jarus yelled back. Again, he felt the cold fear clutch his stomach. Where was Maya? She should be here by now… what if she had been captured? Or worse—

He was unable to finish the thought. General Hawkblaze's deep voice reached his ears. "Serventiri! Coming from behind!"

Jarus turned. A second host of Serventiri reached the battle, clashing with the Direns from behind. There were so many of them—they outnumbered the Direns five to one. *If we lose this fight…* The unwelcome thought crossed his mind, and he forced it away. He saw glimpses of fur amid the Diren's scales—so the Brownaes were here now too.

The Knife flashed again, and another Diren lieutenant dropped dead from the sky. Safacon laughed, looking into the Knife's black blade. "Give it up, Makana," he called in a sing-song tone.

Jarus looked up—he saw Makana gather his troops in the air, trying to come up with a plan. The Serventiri-dragon let out another bellowing screech and clawed at them. The howls of pain and death from their allies echoed in Jarus' ears—cries from the Brownaes and Diren soldiers, cries from the few Guardians fighting beside them.

They would all be killed. And Safacon would take the Jewel back.

"No," he panted hoarsely. Safacon blasted down another Diren lieutenant with the Knife—blinded by rage and desperation, Jarus lunged forward, his little knife clutched between his teeth. Safacon saw him coming, smiled, and lowered the black blade at him—Jarus froze, the world slowing around him as Safacon opened his mouth to order his death.

"Wait!"

Norrin's voice froze everyone in place. Safacon whipped around to look at him. "What do you want?" he snarled. "What are you going to do, great and powerful Norrin, who gives up on battles before they start? Try to talk your way out of this—this battle has already begun. I will kill them all, and let you watch their bodies pile upon each other. What say you to that?"

Norrin smiled. "I wanted to tell you," he said, "that you have left your back door unguarded."

Safacon turned sharply, looking back down the road. The hillside blocked Jarus' vision—he could see nothing, but could hear the fall of many boots. "What is it?" he demanded to no one in particular.

An army of warriors in tarnished silver armor clashed with the Serventiri blocking the road. Jarus could only see glimpses through the Serventiri's white armor—the Serventiri swarmed around the road, slashing frantically at the unexpected arrivals. And still they were pushed back—Safacon's soldiers fell, giving ground to the warriors.

"Who *are* they?" Hagar stammered.

Jarus stared. In clean, ordered ranks, the warriors pressed though the Serventiri's circle, moving onward. Some carried swords, but others wielded staffs, spinning them in glittering arcs as they blocked the Serventiri's gunfire. Flashes of red and blue fire sparked from the ends of the staffs, lighting the shallow valley in multicolored glory.

And Safacon stood frozen, as if the shadows of long past had come back to haunt.

Leading them strode Lammar, in the guise of the tall black warrior with the sword. Beside him was a familiar burly warrior—Jarus realized it was one of the warriors they had met at Larkin's. Behind them, shoulder to shoulder, walked many others, a sea of faces that were vaguely familiar to Jarus. More warriors from Larkin's house, raggedly dressed former prisoners—

Yet to Norrin, the faces were far from vague. Norrin brought his bound hands up above his head, then down sharply. Sparks shot from his fingertips, burning away the ropes that held him. Safacon jumped back, his face drawn and white with fear and rage. Norrin seized his staff, then moved past Safacon to stand before the ranks of warriors.

"It's not possible," Safacon panted, his eyes wide and wild with hate.

"Tell that to our rage," Norrin said, his deep voice filled with a power and authority that Jarus had only seen glimpses of. No longer was this the Norrin who hesitated to confront Safacon, who hid in the shadows, whose fear for safety overruled his passion for freedom. No longer did the wizard wear the guise of a fisherman.

Norrin spun his staff—sparks flickered from the ends, then

billowed into golden liquid fire that ran up and down the length of the staff, running over the wizard's hands and illuminating the light of battle lit afresh in his eyes. Across the glade, Rygal stared with his mouth open.

The Guardians of Gayrile stood at the ready behind Norrin, their weapons drawn, fear long gone from their hearts, vengeance glowing in their eyes.

35

The Broken Spell

The Serventiri turned, leaving the Brownae and Diren soldiers behind, and rushed to meet the host of warriors wielding the terrible multi-colored flames. Safacon's face was blank with shock. The Guardians of Gayrile were a thing of the past, a thing he had long dismissed as extinct. He had never even imagined the possibility that they were still here—they had been so soundly defeated last time.

Yet here they were.

Safacon raised the Knife of Destruction, shouting orders at the Serventiri as they met with the onslaught of warriors. Red, yellow, blue, and green fires leapt from the staffs of the Guardians, searing the armor of the Serventiri. Norrin stood at their front, giving orders. The tall dark warrior who was Lammar stood next to him, fending off warriors with his mighty sword.

Jarus got to his feet shakily. There were close to two hundred Guardians, now engaged in battle with the Serventiri. But they were still outnumbered. More and more of Safacon's soldiers seemed to arrive every minute, clashing with the exhausted Direns and Brownaes. Makana descended to the ground, organizing a counter attack. The huge Serventiri-dragon seemed to have tired of fighting the Direns, but now it turned towards the ranks of Guardians, bellowing a challenge.

A paw gripped his shoulder, and he looked up into Hagar's eyes. The Cooper was bleeding from a cut across his cheekbone, but was otherwise unhurt. "You all right?"

"Yeah—I'm fine," Jarus said, standing and looking around. He and Hagar stood between the two separate battles—to their left were King Makana's Direns and the Brownaes, fighting the second group of Serventiri, and to their right was the flashing, flaming battle between more Serventiri and the Guardians. Through the haze of smoke, illuminated by rainbow lights, Jarus saw Safacon, watching the fighting with a twisted smile.

"The Knife," he panted. "We have to get the Knife, Hagar. It's the only way…" The two of them crept forward, across the smooth stone toward the tall figure in billowing silver robes. In the uncertain light, he appeared as a wraith, a shadow of darkness in the flickering smoke.

Safacon saw them approach, and smiled at Jarus. "Ah, the Cooper. So you are back again to challenge me. I admire your courage, I must say."

"Hand over the Knife, Safacon," Jarus said, wishing his voice were stronger and deeper, like Norrin's voice. His words were small and nearly lost in the swirl of battle around them.

"Oh, young one, you know naught of what is happening here,"

Safacon chided him, shaking his head. "You were swept into this conflict like a leaf into a torrent. Your home is far away from here. You have just united with your parents, have you not? And even… found the one you love?" He winked meaningfully, making Jarus flush. "Why destroy such a wonderful ending to your story? Return to your home, with your family, with your beloved—far away from Gayrile, far from the Jewel. Safe forever. I will not hurt you—my mission is here and here alone."

Jarus' heart pounded as he considered Safacon's words. The sorcerer knew exactly how to get to him. He knew what Jarus wanted, and he was ready to deliver on his promise if Jarus left now.

"Don't listen to him," Hagar said quietly, looking at Jarus. "That's the same sort of thing he told me. That if I obeyed him, I could live a peaceful, safe life. It doesn't work like that."

Safacon chuckled. "Ah, so you are young Mr. Groundrop. I suppose I remember you now. I remember the pleasant conversations we had in the interrogation rooms. So many interesting things you told me. So many lives ruined by your treachery. And now you fight side by side with *him*?" He looked at Jarus and laughed. "My my, what an interesting twist. Do you know he would have traded you all away for the reward I offered?"

"And I was wrong," Hagar said, his voice stronger. "Wrong to follow your orders, Safacon. Wrong to believe you were the right cause to fight for. And that is why you will lose. You've lied so many times, you've forgotten the truth."

"And what truth is that?" Safacon asked, his voice cold.

Hagar smiled. "Your own mortality. That's why you wanted the Jewel all along, isn't it? You think some dark magic can keep you from the clutches of Death itself?"

Safacon's face was pale with rage. Then he spoke, eerily calm. "You are smarter than I thought, Mr. Groundrop. But not as wise as I." He looked at Jarus and lowered the Knife. "As for you, I have no use of you. A shame you chose such an ending to your story. Now, you die." The Knife's black blade flashed as Safacon shouted the killing curse.

Jarus felt something crash into him, with more force than he had ever felt, punching the breath from his lungs. He fell back onto the hard stone—he heard Porcini shout, "No!" and saw Safacon smile in satisfaction—

And then he sat up abruptly, realizing that he was still alive. Three paces beyond, thrown back by the force of the Knife, was Hagar.

"No," he whispered hoarsely, feeling a stir of panic, followed by a stab of grief that seemed to cut through his very heart—he reached for Hagar's unmoving form as his heart plummeted in despair. Then he rounded on Safacon. "You—how—"

Safacon laughed again. "Interesting decision for him. Even though you have always hated him, it seems he was willing to die for you."

He turned and began to walk toward the Golden Tablet, where the Ring lay unprotected. Jarus tried to lift Hagar's body, despair throbbing through the muscles of his limbs, draining him entirely of strength. There was a bellowing snarl from above, and he looked up to see the eyes of the huge Serventiri-dragon fix on him. He barely moved—there was no way he would escape in time.

The great beast bowed its head, screeching in triumph as it opened its jaws.

"Ventara!"

The word was screamed from behind Jarus—he thought it was Morel's voice for a moment, but then realized Morel was standing across the valley from him, watching in wide-eyed shock.

A bolt of fire shot over his head, into the open mouth of the massive dragon. The beast screamed in rage and fury, reeling back. Jarus whirled around.

Covered in dust, her fur streaked with blood, holding the Jewel in a shaking paw, was Maya.

Jarus had no idea where she had come from. Thinking back later, he realized she must have come with the group of Guardians with Lammar. But there she stood.

"Maya…" he choked through the smoke and dust.

Maya rushed to him, then stopped abruptly as she saw Hagar. Her face dissolved in grief. "Hagar… no…"

Porcini ran to them, interrupting the moment. "The Jewel—we have to get the Jewel over there now. Hurry."

Maya tore her eyes away and ran after Porcini. Jarus followed, the smooth stone cold under his paws. The world around them seemed to slow as they ran. Jarus heard nothing—the roar and shouts of the battle mixed and blended into a blur. Ahead of them, visible only by the glittering blue light shimmering over its surface, was the Golden Tablet. Safacon had nearly reached it, striding over the narrow step and under the sheltered area.

This was it. He no longer felt afraid. This whole time, the thought of death had terrified him. Now, he accepted the fact. If he died, he would do so fighting Safacon. Fighting alongside his friends, his family, and those he loved. The fearful Jarus of Mata City was gone, changed, just as Hagar had changed, even in the last moments. And he felt braver.

The three of them were joined by Rygal and Neely as they stepped up into the covered structure. Safacon was silent, watching them. His face was strikingly pale in the glowing blue light. His black eyes fixed immediately on the Jewel that Maya held.

"You can't stop it," he whispered. His voice was cold and rasping. "The Jewel's power is nearly complete. Can you not see it? Its power grows every time it is used, gathering energy from that which it destroys, fed by the Ring and the Knife."

"Move away," Rygal said shortly, stepping forward, pointing his sword at the sorcerer. "I won't ask again."

Safacon laughed as he stepped to the side. "Ah, son of Maran, are you so bent on your mission that you forget to whom you speak? I have seen worlds, places, powers that your mortal mind can only dream of. The Jewel is the gateway to allow it to enter this world." His eyes glittered feverishly. "To reach such power, I am prepared to do anything."

He raised both arms above his head, speaking in a language Jarus didn't understand, yet the words made chills run down his spine. Black ribbons of smoke swirled around Safacon's hands, and the ground shuddered beneath Jarus' paws. The Jewel suddenly glowed white-hot in Maya's paws; she cried out and dropped it.

Then a beam of sparks struck the gathering blast in Safacon's hands, sending him staggering. Norrin stepped forward, his staff a swirl of bright orange flame. "Now!" he called to them as he struck at Safacon again.

The Jewel had rolled back towards the step, white hot—Jarus snatched it up. It singed his paws, burning the soft skin, and he winced in pain, but stumbled forward on his hind legs and placed it on the Tablet.

There was a crackle of blue light, a shower of white sparks, and the Jewel lay beside the Ring, covered by a film of blue.

The Knife would be last.

Safacon held it in his right hand, occasionally using it to parry Norrin's rapid blows. There was a madness in his eyes as he battled his old teacher. The Serventiri gathered around the covered structure as if they had forgotten the fight around them, completely drawn to the Objects. The Guardians were pressed back, defending the steps.

Black fog filled the temple as Safacon spoke the dire words again, striking again and again at Norrin. Porcini and the two Coopers jumped up, running to aid their leader—there was a blast that threw them all back. A flare of pain shot through Jarus' shoulder as he was flung back into the stone columns. Gasping, he sat up. Porcini lay unconscious several feet away—beside him, Maya straightened painfully.

"You still think you have power here?" Safacon's mocking voice hissed inside Jarus' mind. He reeled back, startled. Maya cried out and shrank to the ground, clutching her head.

Norrin shouted something—Jarus heard nothing, his conscious completely occupied by that cold, hissing whisper. He felt himself moving forward, unconsciously, toward the Jewel. Safacon's voice deepened into another, unfamiliar. A penetrating voice that seemed to echo in his thoughts.

"My power is far greater than yours, foolish mortal. My allies have seen that. You have lost your chance to surrender. Now, you shall die, and I shall grow more powerful through your death."

Jarus fell against the Tablet, gasping. The world swirled around him, his vision blurred. Then, quite suddenly, he saw Maya, across the Tablet from him. Her blue eyes were filled with fear, but in the moment he saw them, he felt his own strength return to him, forcing the horrible snarling voice out of his head.

"Maya… you need to trust me," he managed to pant. "Stay there… be ready for my signal."

She nodded shortly. Jarus turned, leaning on the Tablet for support. His eyes were fixed on the Knife in the swirl of black shadows that cloaked Safacon's tall form. Norrin and the Guardians had been pushed back. The Serventiri had encircled them, trapping them back against the structure.

Jarus lunged.

The muscles of his back and hind legs, strengthened from the long journey and years of cleaning canals, propelled him forward. He sprang, his shoulder driving into the back of the sorcerer's legs. Safacon reeled into the wall, startled. The black shield surrounding him faded for a moment, and Norrin pushed forward again.

Jarus reached up, seizing the Knife of Destruction by the crosspiece. Safacon was just as fast—he knew what Jarus wanted, and he was prepared for it. Jarus' paws closed around the hilt at the same time that Safacon shouted the killing curse.

"Devrando!"

It happened in a split second, but in that moment, Safacon realized what he had never once expected had just happened. He had been outwitted. Jarus pulled the Knife from Safacon's hands, but instead of holding onto it as Safacon had expected, he flung it across the floor in the same moment that Safacon screamed the curse. The Knife, useless unless in a wielder's hands, slid harmlessly across the floor—straight to Maya, who crouched beside the Tablet waiting.

Maya lifted the Knife and slammed it down upon the Golden Tablet beside the Jewel and the Ring.

Safacon's blow hit Jarus right behind the ribs, sending him flying into the wall by the Tablet. "No—no—what have you done? What—have—you—done?"

Jarus saw Safacon approach through dazed eyes—he felt someone lift him, dragging him out of the way, and heard Maya's voice vaguely from above—

"Stop, Safacon." Norrin's deep voice made Safacon whirl around. "He has defeated you. You have lost." He raised his staff over his head, then brought it down in a crackle of golden light upon the Tablet.

There was an explosion of blue, a magnified sound of shattering glass that echoed in Jarus' ears for days to come. Blue fire erupted from the core of the Jewel, searing up into the sky, and down, into the ground as though to burn into the very heart of the world. Blue light ran along the lengths of the wall of Safacon's great fortress, and the stone melted like wax.

Safacon was screaming, staggering forward as though drunk. He fell against the Tablet, his fingers clawing along the surfaces, despite the white fire that licked along his clothes, burning the skin. He reeled back as his maddened mind finally registered the pain, the white flames engulfing his body as he fell, until the horrible screams finally stopped.

The ranks of Serventiri froze, then the light in their eyes went out and they seemed to melt into the ground, dissolving with the Jewel's power. Jarus shrank back against the wall. Through the blinding light he saw glimpses of the Jewel's power as it faded—then, finally, the power of all three Objects as they broke upon the gold. Below them, veins of blue ran up the walls of the palace as the great fortress dissolved into the valley floor. The Serventiri had disappeared.

A hand gripped his shoulder, hauling him back—the crumbling columns that held up the covered area were about to give way. He fell outside, rolling down the step, and stumbled toward the group of warriors. There was a groaning crack as the Tablet split in two, the sheer force of the Jewel's power finally overcoming it.

But the Jewel had already vanished. There was a tremendous rush of blue, a rumble as the mountains themselves shuddered at the force, and then, suddenly, all was still. The valley was silent in early dawn, quiet, chill, and expectant with the coming snow.

36

§ § § § § § § § §

Sunset

News of Safacon's downfall had reached Bridgeport by the time the companions arrived. The little fishing town buzzed with activity—though Jarus guessed that in the three days following the battle, the story would have circulated throughout all of Gayrile. He overheard excited conversations as they moved through the city.

"I haven't heard much about it—only know he's gone," an eager young sailor told his friends.

"How'd he go?" one of them asked critically.

"No one knows—'cept it seems the Direns had somethin' to do with it," the first speaker said.

"I heard rumor of the Brownaes, too," another man piped up. "A whole army of them, storming the gates."

"That's not what I heard," the first speaker snorted. "From what I know, it were the Liznees, a mighty army of 'em that finally done it."

"That can't be right…"

Jarus frowned slightly as they entered the inn, and Norrin paid for rooms. "Norrin…shouldn't we tell them the real story?"

Norrin glanced at the speakers and smiled. "Ah well, these are just rumors. They'll float through town for a couple weeks, and then the real story will get out."

It had been three days since the battle on the Topstorm, though Jarus figured it would be a very long time before the freshness and the terror of it had faded. Safacon had been defeated, the Objects destroyed. The companions rejoined the Diren army and the Guardians of Gayrile in the aftermath, to both rejoice with what had come and to assess what had been lost.

King Makana had been killed in the last moments of the battle, diving down upon a host of Serventiri to save a group of Brownaes that had been cornered. The loss hit Jarus harder than he had expected. He had only known the Diren king for a few weeks. Yet he had admired and respected him more than he had realized. Along with King Makana, General Warnwing had also fallen in battle with the massive dragon just before Maya arrived with the Jewel.

And then there was Hagar. Jarus had no words to describe the grief that had, suddenly, filled him as he thought about it. Hagar Groundrop, who had always tormented and mocked him. Hagar Groundrop, who had betrayed them without a thought into the hands of Safacon. Hagar Groundrop… who at the very last, had chosen to fight on their side. Who had reunited Jarus with his parents. Who had leapt between Jarus and the Knife and taken the killing blow.

If anything, all Jarus could think of to describe it was his own foolishness and unforgiveness, even after Hagar had changed. His death had hit Maya hard—she had been mostly silent on the journey back to Bridgeport, only speaking occasionally with Morel or Neely.

The Direns had left them the day after Safacon's defeat, traveling back to Flameton with the fallen king's body. King Makana's death would bring about many changes, all of which would need to be addressed quickly. The Chanterelle Brownaes had headed back to the Wandering Wood, where they would reclaim the lands stolen by Deathcap. Morel and Porcini had chosen to accompany their companions back to Bridgeport before rejoining their people.

They had traveled to a port a mile or so from Safacon's fortress, then sailed the short trip back to Bridgeport. The eight companions were accompanied by several others who had lived in Bridgeport or even Mata City before they had been captured by Safacon. The Puddlepaw family and old Mr. Raintail joined the group heading south.

"But what about Safacon's followers?" Rygal had asked Norrin the night before, as they all sat in the cabin of the ship.

"Yes, well, thankfully, most of them will be dealt with by the Coonsian Capital," Norrin explained with a wry smile. "Now that Safacon has been exposed as a sorcerer, and as the tyrant we all knew he was, his followers and generals will be taken in for questioning. Most of them will be imprisoned. With Safacon out of the way, the Liznees can finally interfere, legally that is."

Jarus didn't fully understand all this, but he was glad to hear it. "What about the Jewel, Norrin?" he asked in the silence that followed. He felt the other eyes of his companions rest on him.

"What Safacon said… about it being a doorway… and that voice we heard…"

He had told Norrin about the horrible snarling voice that had filled his consciousness just before they had destroyed the Objects. A voice that had seemed to come from the Jewel itself, a voice that still haunted his nightmares.

"The Jewel is destroyed," Norrin told him gently. "You need no longer fear its power. As for the place it came from, that is a darkness that we must still defeat, and one that I will have to explain later. Not now. For now, we have peace."

Jarus slept fitfully that night in the inn at Bridgeport, in a room with Porcini, Lammar, and Rygal. Across the hall, his parents slept in their room. Reunited. His family finally brought back together. Thinking of it filled him with a calm that drove the lingering horror of battle away.

They were going home.

. . . .

Jarus awoke to a soft clinking sound, and voices.

"I think I got more," came Porcini's voice, sounding delighted. *Clink clink.*

"No chance," Lammar snorted. "And besides, remember what Norrin said… it's not the reward that matters."

"Yes, I know—but Lammar, it's more than I've ever had!" *Clink clink.*

Jarus sat up, looking in confusion at the two of them. They were seated on Porcini's bed. Several bags sat beside them—Porcini had one open in his lap and had spread its contents on the blankets. Jarus was startled to see a large amount of gold coins.

"What's all that?" he asked.

They looked up—Porcini beamed. "We've been given thank-you gifts, Jarus—each of us. Here, this is yours." He tossed one of the sacks to Jarus—it landed on his bed with a clinking thud.

Jarus opened it and stared. There was more money in there than he had ever had—at least a year's worth of income that he and his father had barely provided. Except now…

"Where did this come from?" he said, touching the gold in awe.

Lammar smiled. "Seems word of our heroics finally got out, Jarus. A lot of people are very happy now. The gold is from the Direns— King Casper thought it right."

"King?" Jarus repeated, remembering the red-scaled Diren lieutenant. "You mean he's…"

"Yes, the Direns have elected him as their ruler. Makana had no heir, after all—and it seems he wanted Casper to succeed him." Lammar looked satisfied. "He's a good man—he'll make a fine king."

Jarus closed his sack of gold, looking around. "Where's everyone else?"

"Downstairs…if you can make it down," Lammar said, shaking his head.

Jarus looked at him in confusion as he started out the door—in a few more moments, he understood. A crowd of people had gathered in the parlor downstairs, all talking in excited voices. As Jarus moved towards the stairs, the room suddenly fell dead silent as everyone stared up at him. Jarus met their eyes, not understanding.

Then someone started clapping.

In moments, the entire room was filled with people applauding, cheering for him. Jarus looked at them in confusion, his face warming with both embarrassment and pride.

He headed the rest of the way downstairs as the crowd parted, moving quickly to a table where Norrin and Rygal sat. The two of them smiled at Jarus.

"Good morning," Norrin said over the din of voices—conversation had resumed.

"Morning," Jarus said, looking around. "All these people…where did they come from?"

"Well, news that the Company of the Jewel are staying here got out," Norrin said, "and now it seems this is the most popular inn in town. The innkeeper is so delighted, he's offered to prepare us all a breakfast feast before we depart."

"Well, that sounds delicious," Jarus said, realizing how hungry he was.

Morel and Maya entered a few minutes later. Morel looked disdainfully at the crowds. "Too many people—all here to see us," she muttered as she sat down.

"Oh, come on Morel, we deserve a little publicity," Rygal said, grinning.

Morel shook her head at him, hiding a smile. "Well, maybe a little…but this is too much."

In a few more minutes, the innkeeper ordered the crowds out—most people were there simply to see the companions—and served breakfast.

Jarus ate so much his stomach felt tight by the time he finished. Lammar, on the other hand, seemed a bottomless pit. The Siren seemed quite satisfied at the quantity of food now available to him, and Jarus watched, first impressed and then slightly concerned.

"Light above!" he said finally as Lammar finished another bowl of butternut soup and started on a roll. "Lammar, isn't that your fifth bowl of soup?"

"Yep," Lammar said through a mouthful.

Ada, who sat by Jarus, looked at the Siren, then back at her son. "Did he eat this much on the quest?" she asked, in disbelief.

"There wasn't anything to eat on the quest," Lammar told her, taking another roll. "I nearly died of starvation."

"You did not," Morel said indignantly. "You ate everything we gave you and looked around for more."

"Well, as Rygal said," Lammar said, swallowing, "we deserve a little publicity. In my case, a little luxury."

Rygal snorted laughter into his cup of juice, and Morel threw him an exasperated look.

Jarus finished his bowl, then headed outside, into the chill coastal breeze. Droplets of rain wet his fur, carrying the scent of the sea. He and his father had checked on the boat last night, and were pleased to find it right where Jarus had left it. Tomorrow, they were going home.

"It's cold out here," came Maya's voice from behind him, and he turned. She stood by the rocks overlooking the short cliff down to the ocean, watching the morning sunlight glitter on the water.

"It feels like home," Jarus said with a smile as he moved to stand by her. The familiar briny scent and the cold wind brought back the memories of Mata City. They were safe smells, reminiscent of times long past. He did the math in his head. It had been nearly a month. In a strange way, it felt like longer. The mundane activities and lifestyle of Mata City felt like they had been lived by another person, another Jarus. In a way, they had.

The two Coopers sat side by side for a long silence, but it was a companionable sort of silence. Jarus spoke finally. "I'm… I'm sorry about Hagar."

Maya looked down, smiling sadly. "I am too." She paused. "I heard… Morel told me he saved you. She told me he had changed."

"He did," Jarus told her. "He said…that he was sorry. And that he still loved you." The words tore at his heart, but he knew they were the right thing to say. Maya deserved to know.

She looked up at him, meeting his eyes. There were tears in her eyes, but Jarus was startled to see something else there too. A look that Maya Raintail had never before given him, not even in Mata City, a look that sent his heart into a strange flutter.

"I talked with my father," she said finally. "Last night. I told him about the journey, about everything we did. And about the times you saved my life." She smiled as Jarus started to protest. "You did— probably more times than I saved yours. And I finally told him what I really want to do with my life, which is something I didn't think I'd ever be brave enough to do."

"And?" Jarus prompted.

"He said it wasn't the path he would have chosen for me, but he said he would support me whatever I did. And he said he never would have forced me to marry anyone—he was glad I told him how I felt, but wished I had told him sooner."

"That's good. That's great," Jarus told her, smiling. He paused. "So… what do you want to do?"

Maya looked out across the water. "I want to build boats. Ships. More ships like the ones the Coopers have, but make them available to everyone, not just the rich."

"Neat," Jarus said, nodding. "You'd be good at that," he added. Maya laughed and shook her head. "You would," Jarus insisted, grinning. "As long as you let me test-sail them before you sell any."

"Well, let's plan on that, then," Maya said. She leaned against him. The sweet smell of her blonde fur filled Jarus' mind, and he sat very still, enjoying the feel of her fur pressed against his. "We're going home tomorrow," Maya murmured, half to herself. "It's just the start of the winter holidays. I wonder what people will say when we get back."

"Probably all sorts of crazy rumors," Jarus said, and she laughed again. He liked making her laugh. It gave him some sort of bravery to say his next words. "Maya—I know it took me a long time to tell you this. I was actually going to tell you a few times on the quest, but I—" He cut off his rambling as she looked up at him. "I love you. I always have."

"I love you, too," Maya said, settling back against him. They watched as the waves lapped along the harbor mouth. Jarus rested his head on top of hers as they sat, feeling a lightness in his heart that competed with the accomplishment of their successful quest. A quiet peaceful sort of joy filled him, different than the wild fluttery feeling he had experienced before. A mature and gentle love, threatening to spill over and overflow his heart.

. . . .

"Wait—you're going to get married?" Porcini squawked.

Jarus took a deep breath, about to continue talking, but was cut off as the six other companions all roared their congratulations. Rygal clapped him on the back of the shoulders, nearly knocking him flat, Morel and Neely both embraced Maya with big smiles, and Porcini stumbled over to him, looking happy but completely baffled.

"It won't be—a huge thing—haven't planned much," Jarus mumbled, sensing anything he would say would be lost in the thunder of happy conversation.

Lammar nodded in satisfaction to Norrin. "I knew it. Knew it before they did, actually."

Maya rolled her eyes at the Siren, grinning. "Don't ever change, Lammar."

"He won't," Norrin murmured with some feeling. He smiled at the two Coopers. "I am very happy for the both of you. You will do well together, of that I am quite sure."

"We're invited to the wedding, right?" Porcini demanded in another breath.

Maya laughed. "Of course—you all are. My father says we'll have it at Raintail Manor—expect an invitation in the next few weeks."

Porcini looked at Jarus critically. "Hang on—I think I might remember guessing that Maya liked you back in Flameton. Didn't I?"

"You might have," Jarus said, shaking his head with a grin.

"I still called it first," Lammar said loftily, stretching.

They had gathered in the girls' room of the inn, where Jarus and Maya had announced the news. Jarus grinned as he looked at his companions. Each of them so different, but all friends by this point.

By morning, they would all leave the inn, returning to their separate homes. Morel and Porcini traveled west, towards the Wandering Wood. Lammar would accompany them halfway, at least to the swamps. Neely had said she would return to Flameton, where the new King Casper had offered her a position among his couriers. It would suit her well, Jarus thought. Norrin and Rygal would remain in Bridgeport, with much to be done among the Guardians of Gayrile and the newly reformed government.

He would miss them. Each and every one of them. They had all endured so much, and that sort of companionship tends to last forever.

Yet as he boarded the ship the following morning, with his parents and Maya and her father, he felt a deep peace. As Gayrile faded into the distance, along with the harbor where his companions had waved their goodbyes, he understood where it had come from. Hope filled his heart again, after the long years of missing his mother, of yearning for Maya, and all that time feeling purposeless.

No, as Norrin had told them before, now was a time of peace. Whatever dark things lay ahead, Jarus felt ready to face them.

Epilogue
Three weeks later…

"We weren't sure how we were going to do it," Rygal concluded the story. He was unaware of the small audience that had gathered around him in the tavern. "After all, even Norrin wasn't sure about challenging Safacon again. And by that point, his power had grown so great. Especially through the Jewel. I'll send you a report on that later, like you asked—I forgot to do it earlier, sorry." He took a sip of his drink, smiling in appreciation. "This is really good cider, by the way…"

His audience made a slight, frustrated sound—the one Rygal was actually telling the story to said nothing, only smiled at the young warrior. Rygal continued quickly. "So Safacon has fallen, and the Jewel. Norrin says he thinks the Jewel is only part of the picture though—whatever place it came from, whatever darkness it was formed from, that darkness hasn't been beaten. And it'll be back. Norrin says he thinks it'll be back soon."

The thought made him falter for a moment. Rygal had fought Kado. He had just fought Safacon, too. But somehow, after what Jarus had told him about the rasping voice from the world beyond the Jewel, and seeing the Jewel's power for himself, he feared it more than any man he had yet confronted.

A few of his listeners—mostly farmers, who had only come to hear the strange young Garilian's story—had faded away, returning to their meals and drinks. The one sitting across the table from him still listened with rapt attention, his face half shadowed by his hood. His voice was quiet as he leaned forward, elbows on the table, the softest hint of his accent present in the words.

"You agree with Norrin, then?" Dandio Ki asked. The firelight played over the left side of his face, keeping the scar on the right side in shadow.

"Yes," Rygal said, then added slowly, "do you?"

"I do," Dandio murmured, nodding. "That sort of power always has a source, a purpose. I fear it may be quite a while before we learn of it, however."

Rygal nodded slowly. He stood. "Well, I'm glad I could ask your advice on it. I have to get back to the harbor to catch my ship west—I'm in Mata City for the next few weeks—got a wedding to go to."

"Ah, yes, that's right," Dandio said, smiling. "Well, send my best to Norrin. And try to stay out of trouble for a while at least—we don't want to ruin the Puddlepaws' wedding. Keep them out of harm's way for as long as we can."

Rygal nodded again, then left the tavern, striding down Caer Sia's streets in the last lights of day.

Dandio remained at the table, finishing his wine while he thought. The news of Safacon's downfall was a relief. But there were new issues to address, new questions raised by the destruction of the Objects. There always were, he thought wryly.

And so he sat, thinking of the story Rygal had told, and leaving his mind to wander and puzzle over the mystery of the sorcerer's Jewel.

To Be Continued...

Glossary/Pronunciation Guide

Ada Puddlepaw
Jarus' mother; a secret informant and ally to the Guardians of Gayrile

Barret (BARE-et)
one of Safacon's henchmen

Brownae (BROWN-ee)
race of 4-feet tall, furry forest dwellers

Caer Sia (care-SEE-uh)
the capital city of Coonsia

Carus Puddlepaw (CARE-us)
Jarus' father

Casper Evenstone
a Diren lieutenant

Coonsia (COON-see-uh)
a country in the northern Mainland of Orlell

Dandio Ki (dan-DYE-oh KEE)
commander of Caer Sian army, brother of the High King

Gayrile
Northern island; a territory of Coonsia

Hagar Groundrop (HAG-er)
wealthy Cooper

Jarus Puddlepaw (JARE-us)
young Cooper of Mata City

Lammar (lah-MAR)
quick-witted Siren; informant to the Guardians of Gayrile

Larkin Sitka (LARK-in)
Dwarve healer

Makana (mah-KAHN-ah)
King of the Direns

Mata City
northern Coonsian city inhabited by the Coopers

Maya Raintail (MY-ah)
daughter of a wealthy Cooper merchant

Morel Inmana (more-ELL in-MAHN-ah)
fiery Brownae princess

Neely (NEE-lee)
young Diren

Norrin (NOR-in)
exiled wizard; Rygal's guardian

Orlell (or-LELL)
world of fantasy and adventure

Porcini Inmana (por-SEE-nee)
race of Netrocrians who remained loyal to the Light in the Dividing War

Rummeryn (RUE-mer-in)
Gayrile's largest river

Rygal (RYE-gull)
young warrior and member of the Guardians of Gayrile

Safacon (SAF-ah-con)
cruel, conniving sorcerer

Sariv (sah-REEV)
Safacon's second henchman

Serventiri (ser-ven-TEER-ee)
Safacon's artificial soldiers

Sirsha (SEER-sha)
King Makana's wife

Wandering Wood
a vast expanse of tangled forest

Acknowledgements

Thank you to my mother Leslie, for your painstaking editing and your help to fix the little plot errors in draft after draft of JoP. Also, to my dad, for your insights into developing the characters early on in the writing.

Thank you to the many, many readers who asked, pushed, and nagged about book 2. You are my motivation, my reason to continue writing this series. I hope you enjoy the story.

I want to thank my writing students from class of 2021-22. You guys are such an incredible support. Keep writing and reading and learning. I am honored to be your teacher.

Once again, thank you to my husband Levi. You are my rock, my steady ground in the uncertain stages of editing and rewriting. Thank you for your patience, your advice, and your love for this crazy writer wife.

All praise be to the Lord!